The War in
HEAVEN

One Soldier's Journey Beyond

The War in
HEAVEN

One Soldier's Journey Beyond

AUSTIN J. HEPWORTH

gatekeeper press

Columbus, Ohio

The War In Heaven: One Soldier's Journey Beyond

Published by Faith. Family. Freedom.

ISBN: 9781619848733
eISBN: 9781619848740

Printed in the United States of America

Contents

Introduction

THE BOOK OF REVELATION IN the Bible and the Church of Jesus Christ of Latter-Day Saints teach about a War in Heaven, a war that took place prior to this earth's existence. This War was waged by Lucifer against God, and has already included many spiritual casualties in its wake, including many who chose to follow Lucifer instead of God. Little is actually known about the details of this War, making the story in this book surrounding the events of the War fictional.

However, the War in Heaven, I believe, was not a typical war. Guns were not fired, swords were not used, and people did not die like they do on the earth. In other words, this book is not an action story, and is not meant to offer an easy, entertaining read. Rather, it attempts to dive into the heart of the conflicts present in the War, to show the War through the issues that were at stake.

This book follows a weapon used, in my opinion, in the War in Heaven—the weapon of speech. There were certainly other weapons used, but speech was necessary as the War was over the hearts of the children of God. Speech is the tool to convey knowledge, and knowledge was necessary to change hearts. This book mainly includes conversations between individuals, individuals tasked with a role and place in the War, a place to reach the heart of one who has suffered too much to believe in God any longer.

For reading this book to be worthwhile, it will take mental effort, and will likely take a decent understanding of the Gospel of Christ, as taught by the Church of Jesus Christ of Latter-Day Saints. The material in this book dives in depth into the Gospel of Christ, as the individual to be reached in the story has questions and concerns that permeate deep into the fabric of life itself.

Hopefully, this book inspires thoughts, questions, and ultimately, the ability to see the importance of faith. Too many in today's world lose their faith over unanswered questions, and too many in today's world seek entertainment rather than truth, knowledge, or learning. If this were simply another entertaining story, it would come and go as quickly as a TV can be turned on and off. This story, therefore, is different than other stories, and should be read understanding that it is intended to stretch, rather than entertain, the mind.

Ultimately, this story offers an explanation of the importance of faith, religion, and God, and offers an explanation as to why millions of people believe God lives, why they believe they are his children, and why they believe he has a perfect plan prepared to enable us to escape the darkness of this world to enjoy the riches of eternity. Truth is found through effort, through understanding the entire picture, and through the things God has revealed to us. In other words, we have to have the determination to exercise our mind, heart, and faith to find answers to some of our deepest questions life brings to us.

It is my sincere hope that, while this story is fictional, it will provide a springboard to further you along in your search for truth, in your search to understand the things and ways of God. I know God lives, and I know he has answers to the deepest questions and issues inside of us. While things may seem complicated in this life, a more thorough understanding of faith, opposition, sacrifice, and similar principles will aid in cutting through the complexities to better appreciate and recognize the truths of life.

As your read, please remember a few simple things. God lives. Satan lives. Both want to give you everything they have to offer, and it is essential to be fully aware of the fruits of choices and actions made on this earth, as the final choices are truly eternal. Ultimately, remember too that the War in Heaven is a battle over the most important and prized of God's creations—*you*.

Chapter 1

"RANIER!" A WOMAN SCREAMED AS the walls shook and strained to remain standing. Ranier's eyes shot open as he gasped with pain. He couldn't fully grasp his surroundings, especially through the noise and commotion around him. His mind seemed foggy and everything far away, but the woman's scream awoke a part of him to full consciousness. "That voice," he thought, "what, what do you want?"

As his mind whirled, fear gripped his heart and began encircling him. For some reason, he didn't fear what was going on outside, but certainly feared what the voice had awoken inside him. For as long as he could remember, he would hear the same woman scream his name nearly every time he started to fall asleep. This time though, he wasn't falling asleep, but seemed to be slipping into a different kind of unconsciousness, an unconsciousness which was only bringing the certainty of the woman's voice to a more poignant reality. Moaning from the pain he suddenly felt again, he started to more fully grasp that the walls continued to shake and rattle as he heard exploding sounds all around.

Breathing deeply to try and not scream from the pain and fear he felt, he tried to move and stand up. "Run" he thought desperately, "just run." He didn't know why and didn't know where to run to, but everything inside him screamed for him to get away before she arrived. Despite repeated efforts, his body refused to respond. Each attempt to move shot additional pain through his body. As he assessed his situation, he realized he also felt cold, extremely cold. The world at this moment seemed to be so different than he had ever before experienced, but yet it felt as if he had been here before. With his mind racing, he tried to figure out where he was and what was happening. He had to do whatever it took to get away from her.

However, his outside world was not safe, nor was his world internally. He felt trapped, with nowhere to run to, especially since his body was racked with pain. He knew he had been hurt, badly hurt, but was still surprised he didn't fear the outside world too much. Something inside of him seemed to welcome the almost sure death, but something inside of him fought desperately to stay alive, to run for another day from that woman's voice. Somehow, he knew that death and the woman were connected.

Straining his mind as adrenaline pumped through his body, memories of his past began surfacing and images started flashing through his mind. He cringed at the sound of shattering glass, at the chaos that followed, at hearing the woman's voice, and at the darkness, so much darkness. "What are these memories?" he wondered as he struggled to breath, as the memories seemed out of place and not associated with any of his memories of his life. Unable to place the memories or understand them, he kept searching his mind for answers. As he did so, memories surfaced of what felt like home, the place he always longed to be. He remembered the garden, his favorite toys as a child, and the people who lived around him. While focusing on the pleasant memories, he suddenly felt as if a knife of ice sliced him through the center.

Tears began running down his cheeks as the memories became clearer. Ranier was not one to ever cry, but he knew no one was around, and the pain from the outside in and the inside out was breaking him down. "My home" he thought, "my home that never existed." He began to realize that the hollowness he carried during his life was due to his longing to return to a home he never had, to a home which simply never existed other than in the depths of the desires of his heart.

"Why?!" he yelled in frustration, "why has nothing good ever been a part of my life?!" Tears began falling readily as he thought of the numerous times he had asked this question, especially at the memories of the times he had asked God and received no answer. Pain was all he had ever known, and the pain he had experienced had all but eradicated any belief he might have had in a god or being that loved. Love was just a fairy tale, and life was meant to be suffered through. As the tears continued, he found himself letting go of the desire to live any longer. "I have suffered enough," he thought, "and the only way to escape the suffering is to stop living."

His eyes were growing heavier as the emotional and physical pain continued to intensify. The noise and commotion outside continued on, but he grew less aware of it. His mind returned to focus now on the woman's voice as he tried to figure out why he heard her voice and why the voice brought such fear with it. "What do you want?" he thought again even though he had asked this question many times before, "and who are you?" Realizing that the darkness was gathering and his breathing had stopped, he pressed deep into his heart to understand before it was too late. Suddenly, intense emotion washed over him, a face flashed into his mind, a face from long ago. "No!" he screamed as everything fell completely dark, "No!"

Chapter 2

"DO YOU THINK WE SHOULD wake him yet?" Ruby asked as she finished applying the healing oils to Ranier's temples.

"No," James said with heaviness in his voice, "he has a long road ahead of him and will need all the strength possible. But," James continued, "our work here is done for the time and we must go on." Offering Ruby his hand, James helped her stand and the two made their way towards the door. Placing his hand on the doorknob, James looked at Ruby for reassurance. Ruby nodded hesitantly, and James opened the door.

Immediately, the crowd outside began asking questions. "How is he?" "When can I see him?" "Why are you leaving so soon?"

Putting his hand up to silence the group, James replied "You must wait to see him. Only Elleana is allowed in the room right now." Elleana quickly stepped forward as James looked her squarely in the eyes. "Promise me you will stay by his side. You need to be there when he wakes. We have done all we can right now, but there will still be a long road ahead before he fully recovers. As his mother, you are the main one available now who will be able to help him in his journey to recovery."

Elleana nodded while trying to hold back the tears. "I promise" she was able to weakly mutter.

"And remember," James continued, "you have to prepare him for what lies ahead. This is part of God fulfilling his promise to you. Honesty is the only way for him to fully recover."

"How will I know when he's ready though?" Elleana asked between the tears, tears which fell in fear that she might fail and lose him forever, "and how will I have strength to tell him?"

James looked away. "Pray for strength" he replied, "and tell him when he remembers enough to ask, or once you know the answer, whichever comes later. It's possible too he learns before you even have to tell him."

Elleana could no longer hold back the tears. She looked at Ranier, at his dark hair peppered with silvery grey streaks, his rigid face, and strong body. She thought of the piercing blue of his eyes and of the pain she could see in them. She had been with him daily, and was always saddened to see the depth of the pain his eyes carried. While she was happy to see him again, the reunion also brought pain for her. She didn't handle pain well, nothing like he was able to. She felt the pain of the reunion was too great for her, and there were still so many things she didn't understand that she felt it was much too soon.

James guided Elleana to the chair by Ranier's side. "I have to go now, but remember, hold on to the promises. God promised healing, and healing includes understanding. Forever hold onto that hope. The darkness and the pain will not last forever." Elleana nodded again through her tears, and James and Ruby departed out the back to avoid the crowd in front.

Coming to, Ranier tried to look around. Everything seemed different. The noise, shaking, and other commotion he had just been experiencing had ceased. His body no longer hurt like it did before, and the darkness seemed far away, though he still shook as he thought of those memories. He could sense people talking and could understand their words, although it seemed they were speaking directly to his mind.

"Ranier!" he sensed his mother say with excitement. "You're here! You're here!"

"How is this possible?" he thought, "I haven't been with my mother for years." Ranier's bewilderment was fueled by the number of friends and family who he could somehow sense were likewise excited to see him. All he could remember was feeling so far from them before.

"How did I get here?" he asked out loud even though he couldn't see anyone yet.

Laughing at his lack of understanding, his mother replied "We brought you here."

"But how?" Ranier asked.

"We carried you from the battle," his mother replied, "all of us were there to bring you here. James and Ruby worked for some time to help you, and I have been by your side for quite a while now waiting for you to come back to consciousness."

"James and Ruby?" Ranier thought, confused, "who are James and Ruby?"

He sensed Elleana reply, with a trace of a smile in her voice, "You will remember soon. No need to rush things right now. I'm just so happy to be able to be with you again Ranier."

Of course, Ranier was full of questions, but there did not seem to be time to ask any. His eyes still were not working, and so many people wanted to visit him. Friends and family from long ago all crowded in to welcome him. As each person visited, he remembered more and more of his past, but doing so only made him more confused. Finally, he asked his mother "Am I able to take a break from the visits and have time with you?"

Smiling, Elleana replied "They have waited a long time to be with you again Ranier. All of our time is short and there is a lot left to do. Finish seeing them all and then we'll have a little time together." Reluctantly and confused, Ranier agreed to continue the visits.

Finally, the hundreds of people had all had an opportunity to visit with Ranier, and they had left to continue on with their "work" as they called it. Ranier was confused by the constant references to their "work," but he grabbed his mother's hand as he felt it brush his and asked "Mother, what is this place? It's so different than anything I remember."

Taking a deep breath, Elleana asked "What do you remember Ranier?"

"I have memories of a home" was his immediate reply, "I remember a home."

Puzzled, Elleana said quietly "We never had a home Ranier."

"Yes we did!" Ranier said emphatically, "I remember being with you in a room, a room . . ." He paused for a minute trying to explain his memory of the room. "A room," he said again, "a room where everything . . ." He was at a loss for words, and struggled to explain what he was remembering. "A room where . . . everything . . . felt safe . . . , and I remember . . ."

Elleana was surprised by his choice of words. Cutting him off Elleana asked "a room where everything felt safe?"

"Yes," Ranier replied, "I remember feeling safe in that room with you."

"Oh," Elleana said softly, "you're already remembering back to before . . ." Elleana's voice trailed off as she breathed a heavy sigh.

"Back to before what?" Ranier demanded to know. "Mom, I don't understand what any of this is about!"

Breathing deeply again and fighting back the tears, Elleana looked out the window. "Ranier, there is a lot I am supposed to tell you and a lot I am working to understand. If you can be patient with me I will work through it all, and you will understand."

Ranier, perplexed at the emotions of his mother, laid his head back down and said "I can be patient. Let me know when you are ready to talk." Elleana nodded and wiped a tear away.

After both Ranier and Elleana had sat in silence for a while, Elleana finally spoke. "Ranier, what do you remember about Earth?"

"Earth?" Ranier asked.

"Yes, Earth" Elleana replied. "I need to know what you remember so that I know where to start." Sensing the confusion on his face, Elleana continued with a serious look in her eye "Ranier," she said, breathing deeply again, "you died. You are now in the portion of the Spirit World called Yuli."

"I died?" he asked. "I couldn't have died, since I'm talking to you right now."

"Your physical body died, at least for the time being" Elleana replied, "but your spirit lives on. I, along with the others, helped bring your spirit here while your physical body isn't working."

Ranier rolled his eyes and said "Mom, you've always known I don't believe in this religious stuff. Please, just tell me the truth about things."

"I am telling you the truth" Elleana replied, and it's not true that you've never believed or been interested in religious stuff. There was a time when you were very committed."

Ranier could feel his frustration building, as there was no way he was going to admit he believed in anything religious. Attempting to avoid the religious discussion, and acting on the growing frustration inside, he angrily said "Mom, I need you to talk straight with me. I can't handle all of this nonsense!"

"Before I can explain anything more, you have to at least accept the fact that you're dead." Elleana said as she tried to deflect Ranier's frustration. "If you can't even believe that, you won't believe anything else I have to tell you."

Ranier clenched his jaw. There was just no way he was going to believe in spirits. He had always mocked those who did.

Elleana put her hand on his shoulder. "Ranier, think about the people who came to see you. My grandfather came to see you, and he died before you were ever born. James and Ruby also came and helped administer to you, and they lived on Earth hundreds of years before you were born. I understand that you didn't believe in spirits or in life after death while you were on Earth, but it's time to now. You can't see yet, but if you could, you would see that I am actually younger than you as a spirit."

"That's nonsense!" Ranier exclaimed, "there's no way my mother could be younger than me!"

"Physically speaking that's true" Elleana said in agreement, "but spiritually speaking you are one of the oldest Intelligences, and I am far younger. It's just that I was born before you on Earth and was blessed to be able to be your mother there. The home you remember, the one where you felt safe," she continued, "is the home you lived in before you came to Earth, after the darkness came." Choking back the tears again, Elleana continued "I was never able to give you a home on Earth. Your father left me after he found out I was pregnant, and I spent my days begging for food. You are my only good memory of Earth, as you were all that I had and all that I loved."

Ranier paused as the memories started to return. He was remembering watching his mother working desperately to find food. He remembered crying from the pains of hunger, and he remembered the cold, the incessant cold from the lack of clothes. "Mom" he exclaimed as he shuddered from the memories, "stop! Let's focus on something else for the moment. We're here with each other, and we don't need to dwell on the negative."

Smiling, Elleana replied "that's why I love you Ranier. You always worked to change my focus to the good things in life, even when things were so bad."

Still not entirely sure of what to believe, Ranier asked "So, if I'm supposedly dead, then you must be too. How long have you been here in Yuli?"

"Too long" Elleana said with a sigh, "too long. I died when you were seven years old. I couldn't find enough food for us both, and so I gave whatever I could find to you. That makes for fifty earth years here as you died at the age of fifty-seven."

"Fifty years?" Ranier asked.

"Yes, but I wasn't alone, luckily. Other family members have been here to help me, such as my grandpa."

"What have you done during all this time?" Ranier asked.

"I've learned," Elleana replied, "I've learned all I can about God and his ways."

"God?" Ranier said with a hint of mocking in his voice, "I thought we both agreed, even though I was young, that God didn't exist. If he did, we wouldn't have had to suffer so much."

Elleana looked Ranier in the eyes, even though Ranier could not see. "Yes," she replied, ignoring the mocking tone, "it definitely seemed that way to me. But, as a young child, you firmly believed in God and you prayed daily for him to save us from our troubles and bring peace to our lives." Smiling weakly she continued, "your prayers gave me the hope and strength to keep working, to keep hoping that something would change. But," she said as her voice lowered, "after a few years of that, we both gave up hope that God lived as nothing ever changed for us.

"Even though I—we, I guess—gave up hope then, I've been learning and learning since I died, and have decided to work to believe there is a God. I'm hoping to be healed from the years of pain and heartache" she said as her voice trailed off and the tears built up again. "God has promised to wipe all tears away from our eyes and to heal all wrongs" she whispered through her tears. "Dying brought me no relief from my suffering as my spirit was in just as bad a shape as my body was in. My poor condition in life was due to the condition my spirit was in, and that carried through to Yuli as the condition our spirit leaves Earth in remains with us. I'm still working to be healed, and I'm slowly accepting that God is my only hope to be healed."

Ranier wasn't sure what to say. He was angry at God for all of the hard times he had been through and especially for allowing his precious mother to suffer. Ranier had no desire to believe in God and had decided long ago to make it on his own. But, seeing the resolve of his mother to try and believe made him unsure of how to handle the situation.

After thinking for a little while, Ranier asked "So, does God show himself to spirits? Why do you have to work to believe?"

Elleana looked at Ranier again. "Ranier, if we talk about these things, you have to promise to give me the opportunity to fully explain all that accompanies these things. A simple yes or no does not suffice, and it will take some time."

"Fine," Ranier said in frustration, "I'll listen. But first, tell me where you learned all of these things."

"James and Ruby taught me, they are a married couple serving as missionaries from Paradise, the other part of this Spirit World."

"Missionaries?" Ranier asked incredulously. "Why in the world are there missionaries for the dead people?"

"Ranier," Elleana responded firmly, "you have to let me start at the beginning, or else none of this will make sense to you."

"Fine, fine" Ranier replied putting his hands up in the air in frustration, "I'll listen while you talk."

Nodding, Elleana breathed deeply again. "Ranier, I believe that what I am about to say to you is true. However, I still don't fully understand everything, so be patient with me as I'm sure you will want to know more than I currently know. Save those questions for James and Ruby though, and they will be able to teach you more when they return."

Ranier lowered his eyes, "I have no reason to trust or listen to James and Ruby" he said. "Of course not," Elleana said patiently, "but I do. They saved me from a lot of my problems and are helping me to fully recover. And, you wouldn't be talking to me right now if it weren't for them."

"They don't seem very good at what they do" Ranier countered back, "you still seem to carry a lot of pain and I still can't see."

"That's true Ranier, but you can't tell how much they've done for you already and how much they have done for me. Their greatest gifts are in the messages they share, and they've asked that I be the one to share these messages with you right now."

Frustrated still, Ranier folded his arms tightly. He didn't like any of this and certainly didn't like seeing his mother believing in spirits. But, since he had no other way to explain this situation, he didn't know what to say. He was rarely at a loss for words, but this experience was too far outside his realm to even begin to know what to say.

Touching his arm softly, Elleana said "Ranier, I absolutely love you for your strength of character and your fierce independence, and I'm not trying to take that away from you. Please just let me share what I have learned as I'm certain it will help a lot."

Not knowing how else to respond, Ranier gave his mother a stiff nod but kept his arms tightly folded.

"Ranier, the overall principle I will try to communicate is truth, truth and progression. Truth is the foundation of our existence. Truth has always existed. It was not created or made, neither indeed can it be. Truth has always produced and existed of, and will always produce and exist of, Intelligence, and Intelligence always moves in a stream as it can never remain still. In other words, Intelligence seeks progression, and our existence began in the great Intelligence Stream."

Upon hearing this, Ranier couldn't help but roll his eyes. Elleana frowned, "Ranier, you promised to listen."

"I know Mom, but you sound so strange talking about this silliness."

"Bear with me," she replied, "I may not be the most eloquent story teller, but I am your mother, and this is a necessary part of understanding what is going on right now."

"Okay" Ranier said as he threw his hands up again, "okay."

Elleana, sensing his frustration, suggested they go for a walk. Ranier wasn't too excited about this since he couldn't see, but Elleana reassured him that he would be fine. As they began to wander outside the house, Elleana tried to begin again. "Ranier, at one time, there were no trees, flowers, planets, stars, or beings as we know them. Rather, the only thing in existence was the great Intelligence Stream. This was so as all truth was combined into one.

"The great Intelligence Stream produced by truth was made up of many parts, some large and some very small, some advanced and some not advanced. Each part had the ability to think on its own, although each part was connected to every other part. Even though each part could think, the parts varied significantly in their ability to think and act, although all of the parts were connected to each other. While there were individually distinct parts, each part was connected as part of the whole. As all of the parts were connected, each part could work to achieve a greater ability to think and understand through exploring the connections with the other parts of truth, and various parts chose to put efforts towards progressing in this manner."

Shaking his head, Ranier asked rather incredulously "Mom, have you been reading some type of strange story? I don't get what you are trying to tell me."

Trying to remain calm, Elleana said "Ranier, I'm trying to tell you your history—our history—the history of the Universe, both old and new. You have to understand it to be able to understand why all of the bad things have happened in your life, and it is only in understanding the bad that we can come to understand God."

"But I don't want to understand God" Ranier said firmly. "He was never there for me and I don't plan on seeking after someone or something that doesn't care about me."

"Trust me, I understand your pain and frustration," Elleana said, "that's why I want to share this with you. You carry a heavy burden, one of loneliness, pain, frustration, anger, and most of all, you don't know who you are."

"That's not true!" Ranier shot back, "that's not true!"

"What is true then?" Elleana asked.

Clenching his teeth together and breathing angrily, Ranier tried to think of something to say, but nothing came to his mind.

"You don't know what is true," she continued, "which makes it so that you can't even understand the feelings inside yourself."

"Fine" Ranier said through his clenched teeth, "go ahead, tell me who I am and what's true."

"I'm trying" Elleana responded softly, "I'm trying, so please bear with me."

Despite her best efforts, Elleana's fears were rising inside of her. She had always doubted her ability to tell Ranier anything of this nature, and she simply could not understand why she had been asked to talk to him. "I can't give up yet" she thought to herself, "I have to keep trying."

After breathing deeply for a few minutes to regain composure and calm her fears, she continued, "Going back to the Intelligence Stream, there were two parts of the stream, two very special parts. These two parts had worked the hardest and were the most advanced of all the parts in the Intelligence Stream, and they worked together to learn and progress. Each had unique attributes, and so they used their individual attributes to aid the other, and through working together they progressed far more rapidly than all of the others in the Intelligence Stream. After some time, the two parts realized they could work together to access all of the connections in the Intelligence Stream. Doing so, they were able to gain access to all truth, even though they could not fully comprehend it all at the time. The two parts were named Elirah and Charity.

"These two parts, while seeking to comprehend the truth they were surrounded by, gained access to a new level of understanding. In other words, they begin to feel, or at least sense that it was possible to feel. Their knowledge they had gained told them there was far more to existence than knowledge alone. Something was pushing them to seek to move to a higher plane, a higher state of existence than in the Intelligence Stream itself. Despite their best efforts, however, they couldn't find a way to move beyond the Intelligence Stream. Of course, they never found any outer boundaries to the Intelligence Stream as it seemed to continue on perpetually."

At this point, Rainer interrupted Elleana "Do you mean to tell me that you believe I used to float around in an Intelligence Stream?"

"Float probably isn't the right word" Elleana said, "but yes, you were part of the Intelligence Stream, and I was too."

Shaking his head in disbelief, Ranier said "Okay, don't expect me to believe any of this stuff, but continue."

"Eventually," Elleana said as she fixed her eyes on Ranier, fighting her emotions and fear inside of her, "Elirah and Charity realized the knowledge they had gained was not enough to tell them how to move beyond the Intelligence Stream. Their knowledge and ability to understand was limited to things of the Intelligence Stream itself, but their knowledge pointed to other possibilities, including a possibility to experience a higher state of existence through feeling. As they worked to feel and experience this new state of existence, they eventually connected enough knowledge to understand that in order to move to a new level beyond the Intelligence Stream, they would have to create something that didn't exist before.

"Everything they tried to create was immediately negated though. The law of opposition is a foundational truth, and as Newton described it, 'For every action there is an equal and opposite reaction.' Because of this, any attempt to create was immediately destroyed. They learned that all parts in the Intelligence Stream had a counterpart, and that the interaction between part and counterpart prevented anything from ever being built. As they searched for something to create, the only thing they had to work with was more Intelligence. After trying numerous ways to create something, and having each attempt met with no success, they finally realized that, at a minimum, they may be able to create a new Intelligence, one that had never before existed.

"Since Intelligence is not matter, they had nothing to work with but their own Intelligence. In order to create, they began to realize, rather than build something which is immediately destroyed by the opposition, they would likely have to change something that already existed. After some time, Elirah came to feel there should be a way to create a new Intelligence by dividing himself in half. He knew though that a part could not live, or continue to exist as it should, as just a half, and he knew this would require another Intelligence working with him. If he divided in half, and another Intelligence divided in half, then their halves could be joined together to create a new Intelligence, and the remaining halves could be joined together in an eternal relationship as well where they would help bring life to each other. Thus, in order for a higher state to exist, Elirah came to understand it would be impossible to get there without two Intelligences sacrificing their identity, or selves. He discussed the concept with Charity, and Charity agreed with the idea.

"As Elirah and Charity had worked together for so long and had worked to experience the ability to feel, they realized they were gaining something for each other, something they didn't have words for at the time, but something we would refer to as a trust and appreciation for each other. Even though Elirah and Charity didn't have words for everything yet, they understood the principles behind everything, but they had to believe that many of the principles could actually be realized as they had no way to touch, see, hear, or otherwise experience the grandeurs that existed as part of these principles.

"Elirah and Charity knew that if they divided in half, and joined a half together to create a new Intelligence, they could only continue existing if they remained true to each other. Therefore, it was necessary for them to covenant and eternally promise to remain together. They could sense this was a sacred and holy matter, as their existence depended on remaining true, and so, prior to undertaking to create a new Intelligence, they covenanted with each other they would remain together and always stay true to each other. They also laid out a plan for how to structure a Universe and provide for the well-being of every person and life who would be created, as they knew that there was great responsibility associated with creation.

"After covenanting with each other, they linked together, divided half of each other—as no Intelligence could divide itself—and joined their halves together. They continued their existence as the remaining halves, and drew power from each other and the covenant they had made to remain together. So long as their two Intelligent halves remained together, they would both be able to continue existing eternally.

"When they joined their two halves that would not continue as them together into one new Intelligence, Saytah was created, and the entire Universe changed forever in a flash of a moment. A 'Big Bang' if you will."

"Why would the creation of Saytah change the Universe forever?" Ranier asked trying to throw his mother off, as he was not believing anything his mother was saying, and did not like hearing his mother talk this way.

"Well," Elleana said, trying not to let any of her emotions escape, "the Intelligence Stream existed with all truth contained in the Stream itself, meaning that all light and darkness, good and evil, virtue and vice, was contained in the Stream. In other words, everything in the Intelligence Stream had a counterpart. However, when Elirah and Charity divided in half and joined their halves together to create Saytah, the dark counterparts that existed did not do the same, which meant that Saytah is the only being and thing to exist without a counterpart.

"Once something existed without a counterpart, that something could have the power to create, to change things, to divide the Intelligence Stream into its respective counterparts as the law of opposition would not have effect on something with no counterpart, and so Saytah's work and efforts would not be negated but could last forever. Elirah and Charity had learned that through sacrifice, the law of opposition could be overcome. Sacrifice thus became the foundational law for all of existence, as it was the only way to create and defeat the law of opposition.

"Ultimately, Saytah's existence caused the Intelligence Stream to divide upon contact with his Intelligence. Usually, each part of the Intelligence Stream was bound to the Intelligence Stream by its counterpart, but when Saytah came into existence without a counterpart, he wasn't bound to the Stream, and he quickly learned that under his direction, he could use his one-of-a-kind nature to divide other parts from their counterparts, and the Universe was born."

Elleana could sense this was a lot for Ranier to take in, so she stopped and waited for him to respond.

After being in thought for a short time, Ranier, still trying to get his mother to stop, changed tactics for a moment and asked "Why didn't the dark counterparts divide and form a new Intelligence, to destroy the uniqueness of Saytah? From what I know of evil and darkness, evil is always trying to destroy that which is good." Ranier hoped his mother would realize he was smart enough to see through any of the story, and simply give up trying.

Smiling at the depth of the question, Elleana said "Yes, darkness always tries to destroy that which is good as by nature, the counterparts are drawn together. However, good and evil can only be good and evil if they operate under a certain set of laws, or principles. Good is good and can cause one to progress because it is unselfish, evil is evil because it is selfish. To divide one's Intelligence in half is an unselfish act, one that evil, by nature, is incapable of doing as selfishness entails, among other things, holding on to everything obtained. Thus, when Elirah and Charity acted unselfishly and divided themselves in half, they were acting in a manner that evil was incapable, by nature, of replicating as good is willing to let go, but evil always holds on to what it has."

Elleana had been watching Ranier closely, knowing full well of his intentions. It wasn't easy for her to handle the antagonism she felt, but she could sense that something little had flickered for a moment inside him.

"Should I know Elirah, Charity, and Saytah?" Ranier asked. "I don't have any memories of these names or who or what they are."

Grateful for a question she could easily answer, Elleana replied, "Yes, you do know Elirah and Saytah. On Earth Elirah was known as God the Father, and Saytah was known as his Son, Jesus Christ."

Thinking about this, Ranier asked "And Charity?"

"Yes," Elleana said, "you wouldn't know Charity from Earth. She is known affectionately as Heavenly Mother though."

"Why wouldn't I know her from Earth?" Ranier asked. "If she is the mother of Jesus, wouldn't I know her as Mary?"

"No, you wouldn't. Mary and Charity are not the same. Mary was Jesus' mother on Earth, but Charity was his Heavenly Mother, and he was her Only Begotten Son, as he was the only Intelligence ever created by dividing two other Intelligences in half."

Elleana could sense that this answer frustrated Ranier. "Mom, I don't know what type of things these people are telling you, but if you're trying to match up Earth's religions with this silliness it isn't working. I don't know of any religion that discusses ever having a Heavenly Mother."

"Yes, Earth knows very little of Heavenly Mother" Elleana said, "but there is a reason for that."

"What is it?" Ranier asked with some shortness in his voice.

"Let me continue the history" Elleana replied gently, trying to avoid a confrontation. "Jumping ahead right now will only cause more confusion than good, but I promise you will understand Charity's story before too long. For now though, let's take a break and let me introduce you to some people who mean a lot to me."

Chapter 3

EVEN THOUGH RANIER COULDN'T SEE, he could sense that other people were around. He wasn't very happy that his mother had led him to visit others right now as he wasn't in the mood to visit with other people.

Sensing his feelings, his mother replied "It's important for you to meet others Ranier. And be carefully about your thoughts and feelings, they are readily transparent here."

"What do you mean?" Ranier asked immediately.

"Communication is different as spirits, as there is no need to actually talk. We have been talking to make it feel more natural for you, but spirits that are used to communicating simply communicate through thoughts mind to mind."

"What?!? Can others read my mind?"

"Yes," Elleana replied, "spirits communicate heart to heart, mind to mind. They have no need to actually speak."

If there was anything Ranier hated more than his current situation and his inability to explain what was taking place, it was the thought he was an open book. However, there was no time to assess the matter or figure out how to deal with it as he felt other spirits draw close to him and his mother.

"Elleana! It's so good to see you! How are things coming at your station?"

"I'm not sure," Ranier heard Elleana reply, "others are filling in for me right now." Perceiving the question before it was asked, Elleana continued "my son has joined me, and I have been given authorization to be with him until he is told all that he needs to know."

"Well well well, you should introduce us."

"Yes," Elleana said, "I definitely had planned to." Still not sure if he truly was an open book or not, and still unable to see, Ranier found himself not enjoying this situation one bit, but he fought to have any negative thoughts or feelings escape.

"Ranier," Elleana said while ignoring Ranier's uneasiness, "this is Seth. Seth lived in the 14th century on Earth. Seth is in charge of our neighboring unit and is always willing to help whenever we need anything. Seth has a lot of wisdom and has helped me through a lot of my struggles while here."

"She's too kind" Ranier heard Seth say, "but I am always willing to help, if you ever need anything."

Ranier wasn't sure what to say. He sensed that Seth was a larger, gruffer man and wondered why his mother would be associating with such a man. Suddenly, he heard Seth laughing. Slightly horrified, Ranier realized he had forgotten he was an open book and was disappointed with himself. He felt Seth give him a good-natured slap on the back.

"Yes," Seth said good naturedly, "I often wonder too why people associate with me. I don't know what I really have to offer, but I try to do what I've been asked to do."

Trying to move on from this awkward moment, Ranier quickly asked, "and what have you been asked to do?"

Elleana quickly interjected "Seth, he doesn't know anything yet."

Ranier could feel himself getting angry again as he hated being so in the dark and hated how much this entire situation was so confusing.

"Well well well," he heard Seth say again, "you're still learning about all of this huh?"

Ranier didn't reply as he didn't know whether he could trust this man or not.

Seth ignored the intense distrust radiating from Ranier and continued, "You asked what I have been asked to do. I lead a small group—I guess you may know it as a battalion—in the war."

"The war?" Ranier asked incredulously. "My mother tells me I just died in the war, and now you're claiming to somehow be a part of that?"

Seth laughed as Ranier grew more frustrated. "The war on Earth that you died in is only a small battle compared to the war we're a part of."

"A small battle?" Ranier immediately shot back, "it involves many countries and has been dragging on for years!"

"Yes, yes," Seth replied, "it a lengthy war. However, that war is still just a small part of this war."

"And what is this war?" Ranier asked.

Glancing at Elleana and realizing that Ranier really didn't know, Seth said "why, it's the War in Heaven. It's been going on ever since the Mirror was broken."

*　*　*

After speaking with Seth for some time, Elleana and Ranier returned back to the place they had been. While there, Ranier's mind was racing through everything Seth had told him. Elleana had been called out for the moment, and so Ranier was letting his thoughts and emotions run uninhibited as he didn't fear being an open book since no one was around to read him. Elleana really hadn't let Seth say too much yet, but everything was so strange. Seth's mentioning of the Mirror being broken resonated deeply inside Ranier as he had dark memories associated with the sights and sounds of breaking glass. And the woman's scream always seemed to accompany broken glass. Additionally, the claim that there was a War in Heaven taking place troubled Ranier, especially as it related to his understanding of God, or Elirah as his mother called him.

Ranier had always struggled with the concept of God. He did remember praying and pleading as a child that God would change his life, that some miracle would occur to relieve the suffering of him and his mother. He remembered his dismay, his anger, and his hatred that grew and grew as nothing changed. Even though he was young at the time, he remembered the decision he made to give up on God. He realized now it was how he decided to deal with the pain in his life at the time.

From the time he was small until now, he could never understand how so much bad could exist if God existed, and how a supposed 'loving' God would not intervene in his life to stop all of the pain. He also didn't understand how there could possibly be a War in Heaven with the concept of God as he knew him from Earth, but with the fact he was speaking to his mother, he was also realizing there was a lot he didn't know.

He certainly couldn't explain this situation he was in. People really could read his mind and heart, and he was with his mother, even though she had been dead for 50 years. It did not all add up with how he had decided to view his existence. When he decided to deny that God existed, he also decided to deny most of what was included in religion. Spirits, afterlife, commandments—he had given up on them all. Now though, his mother—the only person he ever loved—was asking him to listen so that he could understand the why associated with all of these things. It was a troubling proposition for him, but either way things were troubling since he had no way to explain his current situation.

He had already considered the possibility he was dreaming, but somehow, he knew he wasn't. Everything was just too real to be a dream. The only way to sort through it all, he decided, was to listen to what his mother had to say. Even though he didn't have a desire to believe in God, he at least wanted to be able to figure out his current situation so he could know what he should think. "I hope Elleana returns soon" he thought as he lay on the bed, still unable to see.

* * *

Ranier came to with a start. He realized he wasn't on the bed anymore, and everything smelled differently. He sensed a heavy strain in the air and could feel that something was not right. He still could not see though. Trying to contain his frustration, he attempted to move, but pain shot through him like a lightning bolt. He gasped at the pain and gasped at the intensity of the cold wrapping around him like ice. "Ranier!" he heard the woman scream again. This time, Ranier recognized something in the voice, something he had not recognized before. However, he could not find the words to describe what he recognized.

He was realizing the voice came from . . . from the deep . . . from the deepest feelings in his heart. Ranier couldn't quite place it still as he had always tried to stay away from these feelings. They felt as if they were pure darkness, and attempting to understand them or even feel them would cause him to be enveloped in darkness. His whole life he had worked to avoid this part of himself, but the woman's voice penetrated through the deep and up to his consciousness.

"What do you want?!" he yelled. At that moment, he somehow knew he had been on the run from the woman, that every decision he made in his life was subconsciously based on trying to avoid her and trying to avoid a repeat of the past. As the word 'repeat' crossed his mind, he was shaken by the realization that everything was set to repeat, and no matter how hard he tried, he couldn't avoid that fact. He couldn't comprehend what this really meant, but the realization that everything was set to repeat was now seared across his soul.

"Hurry with the stretcher!" Ranier heard a voice yell. "This man is dying!" Ranier finally came to enough to realize his chest was being compressed by a strong man as a few other individuals were trying to bandage his legs and arms. "He needs blood! And we've got to get his bleeding stopped" snapped another man. "Quickly, quickly! I can only keep his heart pumping for so long" said the man compressing Ranier's chest.

Slipping in and out of consciousness, Ranier struggled to maintain his bearings. He would come to and be aware for a few minutes of a new room, of new faces, of intense pain, of monitors sounding their alarms, but he couldn't sense his mother anywhere. Somehow, he knew he was back on Earth, and he was not happy with the situation. But, there was nothing he could do and was at the mercy of those trying so desperately to save his life.

When he was conscious for more than a few minutes, he would reflect on everything he had learned from his mother and Seth. As he reflected on these matters, the thoughts plagued him greatly as they stirred emotions he had long tried to bury—emotions deep within the dark depths of his soul. He hated how the darkness always seemed present with him. While he had given up on God a long time ago, he hadn't given up on trying to escape the darkness he felt within. No matter how hard he tried on his own though, the darkness persisted, and it always caused deep pain, fear, and discouragement.

While thinking about the darkness, Ranier also thought about his life. He was always lauded for his courage and bravery and was part of the military's elite forces. People viewed him as being strong, but he was realizing that his perceived strength did not come from the willingness to face his true fears. Rather, it came from his intense motivation to run from his true fears, and his courage, strength, and bravery in life were manifestations of his commitment to run from the darkness inside.

As these emotions continued to stir, and as the painful days wore on, Ranier felt, first faintly, and then stronger and stronger, that he was being placed on a course taking him to the heart of his fears, to the heart of his darkness, and this time, there would be no running away. In other words, he was being taken back to his past as his life was fully on course to repeat every portion of the darkness he knew so well. Crying due to fear for the first time since he was a child, he wept silently as he fought the urge to cry out "God, if you really exist, please help. O please help me." He refused to ask for the help he wanted as he was still upset at God for allowing such darkness, despair, and pain to be a part of his life.

Sadly for Ranier, his body seemed to be getting better slowly, even though he felt things were getting worse internally. He could hold conversations with the doctors and nurses, and the pain seemed to be subsiding some. He didn't want to be on Earth anymore and he longed to be with his mother. He also sought desperately for more information about the War in Heaven and about who he was. He remembered being angry when his mother told him that he didn't know who he was, but he was realizing she was right. He didn't know who he was because he had always run when he got close to discovering that. Now, he had no idea how to get close to who he really was without his mother's help.

After a few more days, a group of doctors came in to Ranier's room. "Ranier" one of them said, "you are still in a really bad way. You have a number of organs that keep shutting down. We need to do an intense surgery in hopes of enabling your organs to work again. The surgery will probably last about 20 hours or so." The doctors watched Ranier's face for any sign of expression and were surprised to see Ranier just shrug.

"Whatever" he said without any hint of emotion in his voice. "It makes no difference to me."

As the nurses prepared him for the surgery, Ranier hoped things wouldn't go well so that he could just be with his mother again. He realized he now accepted the fact he would see his mother again, and he waited anxiously for that time. Something told him though that the surgery would work, almost as if he had been through this before. However, he still hoped he could see his mother and get through a lot more of his questions.

"Are you ready?" a nurse asked Ranier.

"Ready as I'll ever be" he muttered to her. He didn't look forward to more pain, and didn't look forward to the recovery time after the surgery. "Why the pain?" he thought angrily. "Why must there be so much pain in life?" For as long as he could remember, he faced pain of some form or another on a daily basis. His darkest memories, though, revolved around the loss of his mother when he was a child. He remembered seeing her body lying motionless in the street, of screaming for help. He shuddered at the memories.

She was all he had ever had and all that had ever meant anything to him, yet he lost her at the tender age of seven. He fought back the tears as he reflected on his feelings. For years he had refused to cry, trying in vain to show God and others he was strong enough to be on his own, that he didn't need anything good in his life. But, those years had only left him with a hollow nothingness, and he found himself longing to see his mother again, longing to have a place to call home, a place away from the darkness inside.

As the haunted memories of his dead mother crept through his mind, other dark moments from his life surfaced as well. He remembered the beatings from various people assigned to take care of him. As a child, and still to this day, he didn't know what he did wrong or did to anger them. They just beat him, and he seemed to be an outlet for their frustrations. As a child with no parents, he had nowhere to turn, and could only run from them.

The street gangs took him in, of course, but life was brutal on the streets with all of the fighting and violence between gangs. As a child barely twelve, he had been sexually assaulted on the streets and left for dead. The physical and emotional pain he felt at that time eclipsed most anything else he had ever felt. All he wanted was a father, and his precious mother, yet God had taken both away.

After spending some time recovering in a hospital, he was again placed with a family. This family didn't physically beat him, but the verbal assaults were intense and their language constantly degrading. He knew as a young teenager he was of no worth, and that there was no one who would ever love him. His heart hardened through this time to become nearly impervious to things said or what others thought of him.

He fell in love, once, but still hated himself for making that mistake, and blamed it on his youth. She had played his emotions well, took everything he had, and then left him, leaving him with another layer of rejection to deal with. The only way for him to deal with these things was to become more hardened inside, and he joined the military, both as an escape from life and as a way to completely turn his heart off from the people of his past.

In the military, he had fought in a number of wars and had always been significantly injured, but somehow survived. The pain from each injury still remained with him though, as his body never entirely healed from any of the major issues. This time around seemed to be no different, with his body seeming to heal even though he wanted to die and be done with existence. To handle the pain, he turned to drugs, but these only provided temporary relief from the depth of the pain he felt inside.

Despite the depth and pain associated with these feelings, he could sense there was something deeper and darker, something he could not remember but something that had been with him every day of his life. It was from this that he ran, that he placed all barriers possible to his heart. He was truly terrified of one day having to meet this fear face to face, and as the nurse was applying the antiseptic to his arm, he found himself cringing—not from the nurse's actions, but from the certainty setting in that he was on a path to face the darkness inside. As the anesthesia entered his body, he quickly slipped into a deep sleep, but not quickly enough to avoid the shock of fear as he heard the woman scream "Ranier!"

Chapter 4

"RANIER! RANIER! HURRY UP! We don't have much time!" Ranier's eyes flew open, but he still couldn't see anything. His pain was gone at the moment. He could sense alarms sounding and a flurry of activity taking place, but he could also tell that his mother had been speaking to him. "Mom?" he replied.

"Yes! Ranier, the doctors are going to get your heart and other organs going again, so you only have a limited time during this surgery and we have a lot to discuss."

Ranier smiled an awkward smile as he still had no idea what to think of his situation and had no idea if he should feel happy or not about it. Right now though, he wouldn't worry about figuring it out. He just wanted to savor the time with his mother.

"I'm honored you're excited to see me Rainer" she said kindly, causing Ranier to remember he was an open book again. "I'm excited to be with you too" she continued, "but again, we haven't much time. There is a lot you need to understand."

"Yes," Ranier replied in agreement, "there is a lot. But tell me, what am I afraid of?" Ranier could sense the question caught Elleana off guard, but he waited for her response. He could also sense she was working to keep her thoughts and feelings away from him.

Finally, after much effort, Elleana replied quietly, "you fear the truth. In particular, you fear knowing the truth about who you are."

Upon hearing this, Ranier's eyes narrowed and his face muscles tightened. Ranier didn't like being in the dark, he didn't like the answers from his mother, and he didn't like that his mother believed he was afraid of some knowledge. "Mother," he responded with a hint of anger, "there is something deep and dark inside of me—something from my past that I will have to face again. I need to know what it is."

Even though he could not see, he could sense the pain and tears silently falling from Elleana.

"Ranier, your fear and darkness inside is the same fear and darkness inside me, which is the same fear and darkness as that faced at the deepest levels by the whole of humanity. The fear, the fear . . ." she trailed off for a minute, "relates to understanding who we really are. We are all afraid of the truth, because we have built our existence on many lies, and the truth causes us to have to let go of the things we built to define ourselves and our existence. However," she continued as her head dropped, "I don't know if I have enough faith or strength yet to communicate the answer to you to explain the truth of who you really are."

Ranier was perplexed as he could not understand what could be so dark. However, he was also perplexed as he certainly could feel that something was so dark, and it troubled him that his mind could not understand what he felt in his heart.

Elleana, sensing his feelings, said "Ranier, the mind is limited in its ability to understand by the assumptions it bases its understandings on. For example, many people assume they only came into existence when they were born. Accepting this assumption causes limits to be placed on what your mind can comprehend or see as true. To fully be able to understand God, we have to let go of our own knowledge as our knowledge is almost always based on some incorrect assumptions. However, our hearts are more able to feel things as they are, and so we can often have a serious disconnect between our mind and heart, as our mind is almost always limited in understanding what is in our heart."

After thinking for a few moments, Ranier asked quietly "What assumptions do I accept that are false?" Elleana smiled at the sheer breadth of the question, to which Ranier, upon sensing Elleana's smile, narrowed his question by asking "What assumption is at the root of my inability to understand the darkness in my heart?" Elleana did not reply. "Mother, please answer me."

"Not yet," Elleana replied as her voice slowed, "not yet."

"And why not yet?" Ranier asked with frustration in his voice.

"Because I'm waiting to be strong enough for James and Ruby to tell me, and until they tell me, I don't know what to tell you" Elleana responded.

Ranier felt the sharp pain emanating from his mother, and he recognized the pain as he had felt it many times before. "Why do they keep secrets?" Ranier asked through a muffled frustration.

"Line upon line, precept upon precept" Elleana responded. "They only teach me what I'm strong enough to handle. They don't want to give me a large trial of my faith before my faith is sufficient to handle such a trial. I'm not strong like you Ranier, and I can't handle things all at once. The things you will learn here in this time you are in surgery were taught to me slowly, based on my strength and faith."

Sensing he wouldn't be getting the answer he wanted to know, Ranier changed the subject and asked "Why is faith necessary? Why do religions always preach about faith?" Ranier never missed an opportunity to drive straight to the heart of his questions.

"The short answer" Elleana replied after thinking for a moment, "is that is how God gained his power and position, and since we went to Earth to become like God, we have to go through the same process of learning through faith." Understanding that this answer wasn't sufficient, Elleana continued "let me explain more by returning to explaining life in the Universe after Saytah was created."

"Very well," Ranier replied as he knew he wouldn't get anything more until he knew the history of the Universe, "tell me about that."

Elleana nodded, even though Ranier could not see, and said "Saytah was not bound to the Intelligence Stream since he had no counterpart. Since he was literally half of Elirah and half of Charity, he knew everything they knew, and he understood that wherever he touched the Intelligence Stream, he could cause the light to divide from the darkness.

"He touched the Intelligence Stream where Elirah and Charity were located, causing Elirah and Charity to be divided from their counterparts in the Intelligence Stream. Light and dark continued to separate as Saytah touched the Intelligence Stream, and individual Intelligences suddenly found themselves with the ability to act and move separate from the Intelligence Stream and separate from their counterparts.

"The light and dark split into two separate spheres, with the light traveling to the right of Saytah's touch and the dark traveling to the left in a thunderous roll, similar to when lightning flashes with the thunder to follow. The worlds of light and dark were spherical as they ultimately were attracted back to each other. Remember this point as it forms the basis of all we face in life—light and darkness, due to their nature, are attracted to each other, and even though the light was split from the darkness, the light and darkness eventually came under a pull drawing it back towards its point of origin.

"The pull back to each counterpart produced a figure eight shape to the Universe, with the eight lying on its side. I believe you would recognize the shape of the Universe as being the same shape as the infinity sign. This shape, of the two circles next to each other, became the sign of the extent of existence as it represented the extent of all creation at the time. The Intelligence Stream ran through the middle of this infinity shape where the sides of the circles of light and dark would touch.

"However, this state of existence was unstable due to the attraction of the counterparts back to each other. When the counterparts came back together, they would annihilate each other. Once annihilated, there would be no trace of them as individuals, and they would return to the substance comprising the Intelligence Stream." Elleana stopped as she surveyed the emotion evident in Ranier's face. "What's wrong?" she asked Ranier.

Ranier quickly shook his head while saying "I don't know. Something you were discussing... something... just isn't... I'm not sure honestly. I just can't seem to grasp what is taking place."

"I understand" Elleana said as she took his hand as a mother takes a small child's hand. "I am sorry you have to learn so quickly. However, we have to hurry. Our window of opportunity is quickly closing as the doctors continue to work on you."

Ranier knew she was right, but he hated thinking about going back. While he didn't understand what was taking place, he did know he had no desire to return to his body, to the pain, to the misery, to the loneliness. He yearned for home, for a place where he could feel safe and rest, just like so long ago.

Elleana squeezed his hand tighter as tears came to her eyes as well. "We'll make it home Ranier" she said, "we'll make it home. Together."

"But our home was destroyed!" Ranier yelled out as the pain of hopelessness shot through him. The long years of pain on the earth were all coming out, and were finding expression in anger.

"Yes, yes, it was" Elleana said softly, "but we aren't without a home. We have a home, we just haven't been there yet. Our journey on Earth is a journey to our new home, a home that we can only obtain as we exercise faith."

"Faith?" Ranier asked incredulously, "faith in what? The world is falling to pieces, God, if he does live, has forsaken me, and you are dead! Why do you even bring up such a ridiculous thing?" Sensing the pain Elleana felt at his statement made Ranier say softly "I'm sorry mother, I just don't understand faith, why we even talk about it, or what good it has ever done anybody. It seems to only serve to wound as you watch your hopes and dreams be crushed time and time again as life continues its merciless course."

Elleana took a few moments as she tried to control her emotions. She knew it wasn't easy for Ranier and that his life had been exceptionally hard. She knew too of the pain it caused her to watch him bear so much pain. But she also knew it was her job to help him understand, as she was the only person who had a chance of reaching the small flicker she had seen inside of him earlier.

"Faith," Elleana said directly, "is opening your mind and heart to accept a principle that, even though not understood, is true. Everything currently in existence was made through faith, and if we are to achieve the true ability to create and to progress, we too must learn how to live and work through faith. This is how Saytah progressed to where he currently is, and it is how we too must progress. Truth simply cannot be understood prior to opening one's mind and heart to the possibility it exists, and it cannot be seen prior to taking action on the belief that it exists."

"The only thing I can trust is my mind" Ranier said slowly through clenched teeth. "Everything else has turned on me. The only truth I know is that of pain, misery, and loneliness."

"That's not true" Elleana said firmly. "I haven't turned on you, and you know the beauty of love as it was something you lost when I died. The pain you experienced then was the loss of something good, something beautiful, and something true. Our pain is our greatest avenue to discover what is true as our pain is evidence of something lost, something not right, or something damaging. That's how it was for Saytah, and that's how it also is for the rest of us."

Ranier was quiet for a minute as he thought about her words. In some ways he marveled at the intelligence of his mother. Of course, as a child, he thought she was the wisest person on Earth, but he had never truly known his mother, as he only knew of her desperate search for food each day to keep him fed. He thought about how horrible it must have been as she went on day after day in so hopeless a cause. "What made you go on, when we were starving on Earth?" he asked as the memories raced through his mind.

"I believed," she said through tears surfacing as she thought of those times and the accompanying pain, "that a better world existed somewhere. My heart refused to accept that the sum total of my existence was to starve to death. I was a mother, and had you to take care of. Something deep inside kept me going, against all odds, as it refused to believe that happiness could not be found. When I first laid eyes on you as a baby, I felt a love so deep and so out of place in our world that I knew it came from another world, another place where the darkness could not go, and so I tried and gave my all in search of it."

"Have you found it?" Ranier asked gently.

"I believe I have" Elleana said quietly, "and even though I have not seen it yet, I believe I have."

* * *

Ranier suddenly wanted to scream. Elleana was gone and it took everything he possessed to not shout obscenities as the doctors and nurses continued to work on him. He did not want to be here, trapped in his body, and he did not appreciate what they were doing. "Let me go!" he tried to scream, but nothing came out. The tubes in his throat prevented him from saying or screaming anything. He was stuck, like a prisoner in a jail, and could only watch helplessly as the doctors fought to keep him on the earth.

After a few days, a doctor came to speak with Ranier. After removing Ranier's breathing tube for a short time, the doctor said matter-of-factly "Your tests are looking positive. Your body is healing, and you should be able to return to battle soon."

"Return to battle?" Ranier asked in great surprise, "why don't I get to go home?"

"The war is not going well," the doctor replied, "your home, your town, your state, is gone. The only thing left to do is to fight."

"Fight for what?" Ranier shot back in anger as he had no desire to return to the war, "if everything is gone, then what am I fighting for, and how am I supposed to fight if I can't see?"

"Your vision will return soon enough" the doctor replied calmly, "and as to what you are fighting for, it is the same thing you have fought for your entire life—the right to exist."

"And how do you know what I have fought for my entire life, and just who do you think you are saying such things?" Ranier asked with narrowed eyes in a slow, steady breath laced with a threatening tone.

"I am James" the doctor replied matter-of-factly, "and I have been with you your entire life."

The shock that rocked Ranier was hard to describe. His world was spinning as his heart knew this was the James who was with his mother, but his head could not accept that fact. "What?" he yelled at the doctor, but the doctor was gone.

A nurse walking by his room heard him yell and poked her head in. "Can I help you?" she asked.

"Where did that doctor go?" Ranier demanded to know.

"What doctor?" she asked in confusion, "all of the doctors are busy right now."

"James!" Ranier shouted angrily "where is James?"

The nurse still confused, replied, "there is no doctor named James. I think it is best for you to sleep right now. You still have a long road to recovery."

Ranier was frustrated with himself and felt he couldn't trust anything he experienced. He had been talking to his dead mother. A man from her world had just appeared in his. His injuries must be worse than he realized he thought, and he thought he must be going crazy. Yet, he knew this wasn't true. His heart knew he really had talked with his mother, and that James, the same James of which his mother had spoken, had visited him. He felt as if his world were crumbling around him as he could no longer explain his existence or anything that happened to him. Reeling in frustration, Ranier closed his eyes to try and escape his feelings.

Memories and thoughts danced through his mind, in no particular fashion or order, but all were laced with darkness. The darkness seemed to grow deeper and darker as his eyes grew heavier, and soon Ranier was fast asleep.

*　*　*

Ranier awoke with a start to the warmth of light beating on his face. He glanced around and noticed stunning beauty as light danced over everything he saw. "I can see!" he thought in wonder as he soaked in the beauty of his surroundings. Something about this place seemed so familiar, yet so far away. As he strained to remember, he suddenly recognized that he was home, in the place he remembered as his home. Memories came flooding back as he surveyed his room, his garden, and all of his surroundings. The beauty of it all filled his heart with wonder. His heart yearned to be there again, to stay, and never leave. Ranier's thoughts were suddenly interrupted by a man and woman standing by him.

"Come with us" the man said.

As Ranier followed them, he recognized the man as James. "That must be Ruby" he thought to himself. The woman turned with a smile and nodded as Ranier felt his face flush as he remembered he was an open book to spirits. Ranier tried not to think, but it was too hard not to as he followed the two.

"We're going to show you your history" James said as he sensed Ranier's questions. "And no, Elleana will not be here as it is too hard for her to watch. She is still healing, and it has been a lot for her to try and teach you. She did at least get you to a point where you were receptive to learning, even though" he said to affirm his understanding of Ranier's feelings, "you still refuse to believe any of it." Without turning, James continued "Yes, your history is not a pleasant one, just as the history of the rest of the universe is not always pleasant."

Ranier's reaction to hearing this was to immediately think this was another proof that a god doesn't exist.

"God didn't make your past miserable" James said firmly, "God is the only reason the past didn't destroy you and the only reason there is anything worth living for left in this Universe. And God will," he continued, "give you a home free from all of the troubles of your past, if you are willing to accept him." Ranier wasn't sure what to say or think in response, and so he continued on in silence as he tried hard to control his thoughts.

Eventually, James and Ruby stopped. Ranier realized that he had been traveling for a while and did not recognize any of the surroundings. "This" Ruby said as she spread her arms, "this is where you can watch the history of the Universe, where you can see the beginning of the war, the War in Heaven. You will get to see the history through the eyes of an important figure in your history of the Universe."

Ranier was quite interested. He had joined the military at a young age, as young as he was able. He had always been fascinated with the stories of bravery and courage and battles, and had fought for years and years trying to live up to his childhood views of a soldier at war. Ranier remembered what Seth had talked about, and had a curiosity growing inside him to better understand this so-called War in Heaven.

James looked at him intently. "Pay attention Ranier. There is a lot to see and understand. And don't, for any reason, stop paying attention. You will never get this opportunity again unless you make it to the Celestial Kingdom."

Ranier was confused by the reference to the Celestial Kingdom, but still nodded his head in agreement. Suddenly, Ranier couldn't see James and Ruby anymore. As he looked around, he stood in amazement as he caught sight of a great stream moving. He recognized it as the Intelligence Stream his mother spoke of. He saw Saytah rise out of the Intelligence Stream, not bound by any counterpart therein, and he realized he was witnessing the moment right after Elirah and Charity had joined together and divided in half.

He watched as Saytah reached and touched the Intelligence Stream, dividing it, and he saw the light and darkness shoot forth at great speeds, eventually circling back, forever attracted to its counterpart. He saw that the highest levels of the Intelligence Stream, when divided, could move and act on their own. They were now individuals, with the ability to think and act, and they worked actively to avoid getting close to the dark side of the Universe. In other words, he watched them work to fight against the natural pull inside them back to the darkness.

Suddenly, Ranier focused on an Intelligence who had just divided off of the Intelligence Stream. He realized his perspective was shifting rapidly as his view changed from an outsider's perspective to the perspective of the Intelligence he had just seen divide from the Intelligence Stream. Ranier watched in fascination as the creation process continued with light being divided from the darkness. As individual Intelligences gained their freedom, they would rejoice in the ability to be an individual. However, their joy would soon turn to fear once they realized they were being pulled back towards their counterparts. As Ranier watched, he could feel the horror of seeing light and dark meet. Something about the annihilation process was truly sickening. Ranier could understand the fear arising in the Intelligences of meeting their counterpart and being annihilated.

There was so much Ranier wanted to see, but he was limited to the perspective of the Intelligence that he had seen in greater detail than the others. Ranier watched as this Intelligence traveled around, visiting with other Intelligences. Occasionally, he caught glimpses of Saytah dividing all types of matter and levels of Intelligence from the stream. Ranier could sense that all of it had always existed, but that it was Saytah who gave it form, who gave it life, who gave it individualism, who gave it freedom.

The Intelligences, once divided from the Intelligence Stream, quickly joined together and worked to create a barrier between the light and the dark as they pushed non-thinking matter in hopes of stopping their dark counterparts from crossing over and annihilating them. However, the barriers they created were quickly eaten away as the non-thinking matter met its counterparts on the dark side, and so the race to keep the barrier firmed up remained constant and unending.

Ranier suddenly noticed a bright Intelligence working hard to keep the barriers firmed up. He recognized it as Elleana. She worked closely under the direction of Charity, and seemed to share a special relationship with her as she always stayed close to her side. He looked to find himself, but was unable to do so. After some time, it appeared that the Intelligences were growing weary with all of their work on the barriers, especially since the barriers would be destroyed so quickly, and he watched as the Intelligences demanded that Saytah, Elirah and Charity do something about it. The Intelligences wanted their existence to be made sure. Ranier wondered who the Intelligence was that gave him his perspective of these events. He didn't feel he was seeing this through his eyes as none of this seemed familiar to him.

After trying to remember something—anything—that might help him sort through everything he was seeing, Ranier noticed that the Intelligence had been watching Elirah, Charity, and Saytah counseling together for some time. Eventually, Saytah spoke to the Intelligences about creating a new state of matter, a higher state that was not subject to annihilation. The Intelligences were all excited about the prospect of a higher state of matter, and Ranier saw as the Intelligences gathered and excitedly watched Saytah touch the Intelligence Stream again. This time there was a strong explosion and a massive rush as spiritual matter was created by dividing a particular type of energy in the Intelligence Stream.

The spiritual matter was the opposite of the Intelligence matter, as the positive version of spiritual matter was repelled from the negative, or dark, version of spiritual matter and the two types of matter separated to the opposite ends of the Universe. Somehow Ranier understood quickly that due to its nature of repulsion, spiritual matter could never be destroyed as it could never come back together again to annihilate itself. Ranier continued to watch as Saytah, Elirah and Charity worked to form a spiritual body to house the Intelligence portion of them in. Ranier did not see how the spiritual bodies were eventually created, but he saw how wondrous the bodies appeared to the Intelligences, especially as Elirah and Charity took their place in the first spirit bodies. While he did not see the entire process, he knew Saytah had created the bodies in a way for Elirah and Charity to enter them.

Elirah took his place as the first to enter a spirit body. The body had been created with a special type of tool from Saytah, similar to a portal, that allowed an Intelligence to be pulled from the dimension it existed in into the spirit dimension. Ranier could see that this tool resided near where the heart exists in his physical body, and that it resembled the shape of a rib. Once Elirah was in his body, Elirah took the tool and placed it in the body created for Charity so that her Intelligence could be pulled into the spiritual dimension and be enabled to stay in the spirit body. Once Charity and Elirah were in their bodies, the rest of the Intelligences also desired to have the opportunity to inherit a spiritual body as the body gave them the ability to progress, learn, and better their lives.

Elirah and Charity began creating spiritual bodies for the rest of the Intelligences. They created a body first for Saytah. Ranier could see that Elirah possessed the ability to provide the specific energy necessary to make the tool work that brings Intelligences to the spirit dimension, and could see that Charity possessed the tool. In this way, the tool was functional when Elirah and Charity worked together to join their hearts as one.

As Elirah and Charity worked to create spirit bodies for the rest of the Intelligences, their hearts worked together in perfect unity. Ranier saw that the tool was not passed on from Charity to other spirits who were created, and that Charity and Elirah were the only means an Intelligence had to gain a spirit body. Having a spirit body enabled the Intelligences to have far more power and ability to fight against the incessant encroachment of the darkness, and enabled them to be even more free and individual than before as they possessed a form.

Elirah and Charity quickly became known as the Father and Mother of the spirits in the heavens. Saytah was known as the Father of the Heavens because he was the Creator of all of the matter and Intelligences, and had created the spirit material and means necessary for Elirah and Charity to take on spirit bodies and to allow others to take on spirit bodies. Saytah, though, was also a son of Elirah and Charity, the firstborn as a spirit and their Only Begotten as an Intelligence. Thus, Saytah gained the affectionate title of the Father and the Son.

As Ranier watched in wonder, he saw how all of the Intelligences on the light side of the Universe gained a spirit body. However, they still had to fight against the darkness as the darkness could penetrate the spirit body and still annihilate the Intelligence inside. Thus, despite the magnificence and wonder of the spirit realm and the spirit bodies created, the Intelligences continued to demand that their existence be made sure.

After another series of long councils, Ranier saw that a proposal was quickly gaining popularity among the spirits. The proposal seemed to be something about a Mirror being created. Saytah had always known he could create spiritual material that would reflect light, and that its spiritual counterpart would reflect darkness. In this way, a Mirror could force light to remain on one side of it and darkness to remain on the other side. However, the two materials would have to come and be held very close to each other, a feat that would require strict order to reign in the Universe so as not to upset the two counterparts which were, by nature, repulsed away from each other. Ranier noticed that Saytah, Elirah, and Charity were not the ones pushing the plan, but that the spirits kept pushing for the Mirror to be created.

Saytah, Elirah, and Charity spoke of the consequences of creating the Mirror, of entirely blocking out half of the Universe. Saytah counseled that existence could only be made sure through seeking an understanding of light and dark, and that an existence with the Mirror would remove the opportunity to progress and improve. The spirits though did not believe this, as they viewed their spiritual dimension, with the worlds and other things that had been created, as being the pinnacle of progression. They were happy, they claimed, and wanted safety and security to become a set part of their existence. Saytah plainly taught that happiness is not found in just being safe or in the possession of goods, it is found in progression, since progression is the root of our existence, as manifested by the movement of the Intelligence Stream, always seeking a forward and upward path.

Despite the counsel of Elirah, Charity, and Saytah, the spirits overwhelming sought to have the Mirror created and demanded that it be done. After some time, Elirah, Charity, and Saytah decided that the only way for the Intelligences to learn was by their own experience, and that the creation of the Mirror would be a necessary step in helping the Intelligences to learn, trust, and understand enough to progress. Saytah was chosen to create the Mirror as he was the only one who didn't have a true counterpart and thus who would not be annihilated. The Mirror had to be established where the light and dark came together—in the middle of the Intelligence Stream, or in the meridian of infinity.

Chapter 5

THE CREATION OF THE MIRROR produced great celebrations across the lit Universe, and Ranier could feel the excitement and anticipation growing as the moment set apart to create the Mirror approached. There were some who did not support the Mirror because of the counsel of Saytah, Elirah, and Charity, but most of the Intelligences felt that the Mirror would forever make their existence sure.

Saytah, Elirah, Charity and others had rehearsed the creation of the Mirror many times. Charity wanted to be certain that creating the Mirror would be safe for Saytah. After extensive evaluation, she felt it would be safe so long as Saytah remained on the lit side of the center of the Intelligence Stream. Saytah, however, knew that if he remained on the lit side of the Intelligence Stream, he would be forever unable to progress and to help the rest of the Intelligences progress.

While Saytah had knowledge of everything, he also knew he did not fully understand everything as there were many things he had not yet experienced, and he knew that experience was an important part of true understanding. He had the gift of foresight, due to his knowledge, and could see that he would not understand, truly understand, everything until he ventured into the darkness. Charity sensed that Saytah had thoughts contrary to her desire for him to remain with her. Due to this, Charity had Saytah promise that he would always return to her. Charity made the same promise to Saytah, and Charity finally agreed to let Saytah create the Mirror as she relied on his promise that he would always return to her.

In the blink of an eye, Ranier realized he was now witnessing the creation of the Mirror. He realized he was intently focused on Saytah and that all of the others in the lit Universe were as well. Ranier caught a glimpse of Charity, who watched as Saytah set forth into the Intelligence Stream. Ranier saw sudden worry spring into Charity's face, and turned to see the cause of the worry. Ranier saw that Saytah appeared surprised at the depth and intensity of the flow of the Intelligence Stream. Saytah was known for his foresight and ability to see and understand the future, and his surprise upon entering the Intelligence Stream made Charity immediately worry that he hadn't been able to see something, even with all of their simulations.

The lit Universe fell silent as the Intelligences watched Saytah with fascination. In all of his simulations with Elirah and Charity, Saytah had always performed the simulation on the lit side of the Intelligence Stream. However, as Saytah neared the center of the Stream, he sensed something he had never sensed before, something he had not been able to see, even with his gifts of foresight. Even though he had never felt this sensation before, he had always believed that something like it existed, although he had not been able to imagine how glorious of feelings it produced inside of him.

As he paused in the Stream to understand what he was sensing, he could see a Universe forever bound to a state of safety and maintaining the status quo. However, he could also see that the other side of the Intelligence Stream, the dark side, held the key to a Universe of glorious splendor, far beyond anything he could comprehend. As he paused and evaluated what he felt while trying to gauge what he could see of the future, he understood it was not in the darkness that the glorious Universe existed, but that in understanding the darkness he would find the key to unlock that Universe.

Saytah's entire being longed for what he sensed, and he could not bring himself to consign him and the rest of the Universe to a state frozen and devoid of progression. He knew he must discover this Universe he sensed and provide a way to take everyone there, as he found himself longing to take everyone there with him. He looked back at the lit Universe, and he immediately saw the worry and strain in Charity's face.

Saytah could see he would have to act quickly as he knew Charity would never let him do anything that might cause himself harm. He knew the pursuit of the wonders he felt would be a dark, fearsome, and lonely journey, but he also knew that the splendorous wonders and the state of the Universe he could sense would make every dark moment worthwhile. At that moment, Saytah knew he was the only being capable of passing through the darkness, as he could not be annihilated, and that the eternal fate of the Universe hung on his decision at this moment.

Having faith in what he felt, trusting that he could one day still fulfill his promise and return to Charity, and acting without full knowledge of where the key to the Universe he felt lay, he suddenly moved to the other side of the Intelligence Stream, the side where the darkness lay.

"Saytah!" Charity immediately screamed. Charity's scream shook Ranier to the core. "Saytah" she screamed again as she raced as quickly as she could towards him, "Saytah!" But it was too late. Without hesitating a moment, Saytah had made the Mirror, and no light from Heaven's side could travel through it. Charity arrived moments after it was created. She stood at the Mirror sobbing and heartbroken as Saytah was nowhere to be seen. Her Only Begotten was gone.

Ranier's heart skipped a few beats at the sight. It was more than he could bear to watch the sorrow that racked Charity. Other Intelligences were struggling in shock as well, and Ranier heard some of them begin to ask "Saytah?" "Saytah!?", and as their voices continued to escalate with fear and shock, "Saytah!?!?" Ranier tried to look away but he was not in control of the view that he had. As Ranier continued to try and not see the sadness and shock before him, he realized that the Intelligence whose eyes he was witnessing this through was growing increasingly upset and was about to scream.

Suddenly, Ranier felt as if he were torn in two as he heard the Intelligence whose eyes gave him his current perspective scream "Saytah!" along with the others. Even though the scene was more than he could bear, it wasn't the fact that the Intelligence screamed "Saytah" that made him feel as if he were torn in half. It was the fact that he recognized and knew the voice so well.

The Intelligence whose eyes he was seeing through at the moment had the same voice as the woman who screamed his name whenever he would fall asleep. In fact, the scream he heard every night had the exact same urgency, tones, and piercings of the scream he heard for Saytah, except that the scream he heard was for his own name. Ranier tried desperately to see the Intelligence whose eyes he was seeing out of, but this was the only Intelligence he could not see. The entire situation was too much for Ranier, and he found himself blacking out as his emotions were more than he could bear. However, he did not slip fast enough into unconsciousness as he heard the same woman pierce his spirit with her scream of "Ranier!"

Chapter 6

RANIER MOANED. HE FELT UTTERLY exhausted and too tired to move as he lay in pain. While his body still hurt from its injuries, he felt great emotional and spiritual pain from the sights he had seen. The intensity of the emotions surprised him. What surprised him more was realizing the pain was so intense because he actually believed what he had seen. Ranier did not want to believe what he had seen, but his dizzying emotions at witnessing it all let him know that something inside him knew this had happened before.

For some reason, witnessing Saytah, the Creator of the Intelligences, disappearing into the darkness produced both horror and great hope inside of him. However, he had little time to sort through his emotions in regards to Saytah due to the sheer terror he felt when he realized he was seeing the situation with Saytah and the Mirror through the eyes of the woman who always screamed his name as he was falling asleep. Something about her struck at the depths of his spirit, and the thought of her sent dark shudders throughout his body.

Ranier realized he was passing in and out of consciousness, but was entirely unaware of how much time had passed. The pain and confusion he carried was simply too much to deal with, and it would overcome his body. He hated the pain and wanted so badly to escape it, yet the pain was also how he defined himself. He only knew pain in his life, and being free of it would be like leaving an identifying piece of him behind. However, since it was a piece of his identity he did not like at all, he found himself in a constant circling struggle of trying to move past the pain but holding on to his identity, holding on to who he thought he was. He realized these feelings he had were like the light and darkness, wanting to be free of each other yet constantly attracted back to each other.

After some time, Ranier sensed the presence of another individual. His eyes flew open, but he could not see anything again. "Who are you?" Ranier asked quickly.

"I am James" came the simple reply.

"Where am I?" Ranier immediately demanded to know since he still felt so much pain.

"On Earth" James replied simply.

"Then how are you here?" Ranier asked with sharpness.

"The Spirit World is on Earth" James replied calmly, "it just exists in a dimension you cannot see."

"What I mean," Ranier replied with a hint of anger in his voice, "is why do I only sense you and not others, such as my mother?"

"You don't have the spiritual gifts necessary to sense their presence. Elleana accompanies you as often as possible, but you have never known it." Sensing Ranier's next question, James continued "I have the ability to come to you as I am on an errand from God. He gives us the power necessary for you to sense we are here. And, Elleana will be allowed to join me shortly. You will be learning things she doesn't yet know or that are hard for her though, and so she cannot come until after we have discussed those items."

Ranier was not very happy with this answer, especially because Ranier did not like James. As he tried to pin down the reason, James continued "You don't like me because I was the one who taught your mother, and you don't like that I appear to you without warning. You also don't like the fact that I am confident in the things I have taught your mother. And, you are upset with me because you still cannot see."

Ranier did not know what to say or think, as he struggled to make heads or tails of each situation. He did not know what he could believe anymore. Trying to change the focus of the subject some, Ranier asked tersely "Why is it that I cannot see?"

James replied "God wants you to learn to use some of your senses you blocked long ago. You are blind so you can learn to see and understand the truth. You see," he continued, "you have always been a very strong, independent person, but that strength comes through the confidence you get from seeing and taking in everything around you. Unfortunately, you have come to accept that there is nothing more to life than that which you are able to see. God wants you to understand though that there is much more to life than what you are able to see, and the only way for you to learn that lesson in a timely manner is through being blind for the time being."

"And you expect me to believe God loves me?" Ranier quickly shot back. "Why does God use such horrific ways to try and teach me? Why does he inflict blindness on me rather than just teaching me what he wants me to know? I can't believe in your God, as his ways are not ways of love. If I ever believed in a God, it would be one that doesn't use such cruel ways and allow such bad things to happen."

Ranier smiled when James was silent. He liked the thought that James didn't have an answer for what he had just said. "That will teach him" he thought.

He was disappointed though when he heard James say in his same steady voice as always "Ranier, God did not 'make' you blind. You were the one who asked to be blind."

"What?" Ranier said in a voice dripping with a threat, "I asked to be blind?" he asked slowly, with each word punctuated with anger.

"Yes," James said, "you did." James waited patiently for Ranier to get his anger a little more under control before proceeding with any further explanation.

"How dare you suggest this is my fault" Ranier said in a low, sharp tone of voice.

"Ranier," James replied calmly, "I can explain your blindness, but to understand it, you will have to understand the rest of the general history of the Universe, as well as your personal history. There is little pleasant in any of it, and it will not be easy to deal with all of the ramifications. However, you need to know so that you can accomplish your mission. There is still a great battle to be fought, Ranier, and you need to be ready."

This was all so frustrating to Ranier. He had no desire to fight any battle, he had no desire to live on Earth any longer, and about all he wanted was just to be with Elleana, the only person he had ever truly loved in a lasting way. He knew though there was no way for him to escape this situation. His body was stuck in a hospital slowly recovering, while he did not get to choose who his visitors were. The thing he hated the most though was that the purpose of all of this seemed to be geared towards getting him to believe in God, and that was just something he had no desire to do. His life had been much too hard to believe in God, and the pain of his past just wouldn't allow him to even want to believe in God.

James let Ranier think for some time. James was sympathetic towards Ranier's struggles, as it was not easy to understand the why of suffering without understanding the entire picture of the history of the Universe. Man was so quick to blame God, James thought, rather than recognize everything God was doing to rid the Universe of suffering. He will understand though, James thought, he will understand.

When James could sense Ranier had calmed down some, he asked Ranier "Why do you think there is suffering Ranier?"

Ranier realized he had been pondering this question, but hadn't quite put words to it. "I don't know" he said stiffly, "I don't know."

"A simple answer to that question" James said, "is that the Mirror didn't last forever."

"What is that supposed to mean?" Ranier asked with some frustration.

"It means, simply, that the light and dark halves of the Universe came back together. They were separated for a long time, and the spirits enjoyed a Utopia like state for a while, but, eventually, it was destroyed when the Mirror broke."

"And how did that happen?" Ranier asked. "I thought strict laws were put in place to ensure that the Mirror was never broken."

"That is true," James replied, "the laws were certainly strict. However, strict as the laws were, they did not stop the law of love, and Charity for that matter, from having their say. You see," James continued, "Charity was entirely heartbroken over losing Saytah. Elirah and Charity believed Saytah must still be alive, as the Universe stayed lit, and Saytah was the ultimate source of all light. While they were sure that things would not remain lit without Saytah, his absence made her question her own understanding.

"As she tried to reconcile what she knew with what had happened and what was happening, her light dimmed significantly. Charity and Elirah retreated to the spiritual dimension to be alone for a time while they worked to deal with their loss. 'Why?' Charity wondered, 'Why did Saytah step to the Other Side of the Intelligence Stream? He knew it was not part of the simulation.'

"'Yes,' Elirah would say, 'But Saytah could see more than all of us. He had to have sensed something that we did not.'

"'What more could we have given him?' Charity responded, 'Why wasn't our association and affection enough for him? What could exist that is better than what we had to offer? I gave everything I could to make him happy, and he left because he sensed something we didn't?'

"This was a troubling point for both," James continued, "and their conversations always seemed to spiral down to this point. 'What could be better? Why would he leave? Why?' After many rounds of the same conversation, Elirah and Charity eventually realized their light was dimming and the happiness they once enjoyed was nearly gone. Finally, Elirah suggested that they come up with a new way to look at the situation, especially since the level of light enjoyed was directly proportional to the truth embraced, and since their light was dimming, it seemed to indicate they weren't receiving the truth related to Saytah."

James could sense these points really struck at Ranier as Ranier was listening attentively. James, however did not want to pause and break the current mood, so he continued to explain about Elirah and Charity's struggle.

"'What if,' Elirah suggested, 'Saytah saw that we didn't understand the Other Side, or he saw knowledge he could bring back to us, or he saw the Mirror would only work if made on the Other Side of the Intelligence Stream? What if he saw that more good would come from it?'

"'I can't imagine what that 'more good' would be' Charity responded sadly.

"'But,' Elirah said gently, 'Has Saytah ever been wrong before? Did he ever do anything with only his interests in mind?'

"'No, he always was concerned about others, and he always saw more than anyone else.'

"'Then why would it be any different now?' Elirah questioned back. 'Why have we lost faith in him simply because he did something we did not understand? He was selected for the mission precisely because he was considered the most intelligent and the least likely to ever be annihilated.' For the first time since the Mirror was created, Elirah saw Charity begin to show signs of increasing life.

"'He's still alive, isn't he?' she thought out loud. 'And if we believe he had a good reason to do what he did, even if we don't know what that is, then we should be able to discover what that reason was and how to connect with him.' After thinking awhile, she continued 'And he did promise me he would never leave me. That promise has been what makes this time so hard, because my perception has been that he left me, but maybe, just maybe, I need to believe that he keeps his promises. He never broke a promise before, and while I don't see how, he may still be able to keep this one.'

"Little did they know," James said with a trace of excitement in his voice, "that Saytah had also decided to exercise faith that they would work to find a way to reach him. He had realized after some time it would be impossible for him to return on his own or to reach the key to the Universe that he had felt on his own. He also was exercising faith and believing that they would not give up on him.

"Thus, at that moment when Elirah and Charity decided to exercise faith in Saytah, two individuals on the Heaven side of the Mirror and one individual on the Other Side of the Mirror were exercising faith in each other, and it was at that moment that true faith was born in the Universe. Neither side knew for certain about the things they believed in, but they all chose to believe and act on that belief. Thus was born the beginning of the greatest power to exist in the Universe, and thus began the Gods to work through faith to achieve."

Ranier had been quiet for some time, but he suddenly asked "Where do I fit into all of this? You are giving me an extensive history, but I want to know about me, not Elirah, Charity, or Saytah."

James smiled, even though Ranier could not see it. "Ranier," he replied, "it is only through understanding Elirah, Charity and Saytah that you can come to understand yourself. I will tell you about yourself, but not until the other pieces are in place. Once those are in place, I can give you the one critical piece of information about yourself that you don't know, and your entire life will become clear to you."

Ranier's eyes narrowed reflexively. "One piece of information?" he questioned.

"Yes," James replied, "one piece of information, one word actually. Of course, you have to understand all of these other matters for the piece to make sense, but it is one simple piece, and it speaks volumes about who you are and why evil, suffering and pain exist in this Universe."

Ranier's eyes remained narrowed as he thought about what James had said, even though he still could not see anything. James was certainly confident in what he had to offer, and Ranier could find no way to discredit any of it yet as he was still too unfamiliar with it all.

James, sensing that Ranier was open to hearing additional information, continued explaining about Saytah. "When Saytah created the Mirror, he was surprised to be rocked by an explosive force as the Mirror was set. He was knocked some ways from the Mirror, and it took him some time to come to his senses again. When he did, he discovered everything was dark, and none of his gifts worked like he was used to. He also could not see, and for the first time in his existence, he felt truly alone. He missed Charity and Elirah, and all of the other inhabitants for that matter, and he missed everything he had before he made the Mirror.

"Saytah understood then that it was impossible to truly appreciate something without experiencing an existence without it. He never truly appreciated the extent of what he had. Saytah's memories plagued him as he remained motionless, helpless, and stuck. He wanted nothing more than to return home to Elirah and Charity, and every part of his being longed to be with them. This certainly was not part of the new Universe he had seen or felt, and he was troubled by the stark difference between the thoughts and feelings in his heart and mind just prior to creating the Mirror and the actual state of his existence after creating the Mirror.

"Saytah, however, had a few thoughts that he could not make go away. He realized that, in all likelihood, Elirah and Charity were still alive, they were still in Heaven. He realized he had always been able to figure out a solution to any problem in Heaven and that he could find a solution to this problem as well. Eventually, he made the decision he would return home, no matter how long he had to work. All of the work in the Universe would be well worth the joy of returning home. Plus, he had made a promise, and he was going to be sure to fulfill that promise. Thus, Saytah set to work to learn about the darkness and how to return someday to be with Elirah and Charity.

"Despite his resolve, this was a very dark and difficult time for Saytah. The Other Side was full of creatures, all constantly attacking each other, and was full of everything dark. While Saytah knew that these things existed, as he was the one dividing the Intelligence Stream and the things on the Other Side were counterparts to what had been created when he divided the Intelligence Stream, he quickly realized how different simple knowledge of a matter was than having actually experienced a matter.

Simply knowing that one could be alone, for example, had not prepared him in any way for the depth and intensity of the pain of loneliness he bore continuously as he remained alone on the Other Side.

"After much time though, Saytah learned how to move in the Other Side. He quickly learned in great detail about the types of beings on the Other Side, all of which were the opposite halves, or counterparts, of all of the Intelligences in Heaven. These beings were opposite in all ways possible, and were constantly fighting with each other. In spite of these beings, he learned how to avoid them and how to cast his light through the darkness of the Other Side.

"Nothing on the Other Side could see his light as nothing there had ever developed senses to detect light, but he could see that his light affected all it came in contact with, and many of the beings, once coming into contact with the light, continued to seek after the light. While his light would shine forth in the darkness and some of the counterparts would attempt to follow it, nothing there could comprehend it.

"After much time and experience—of which volumes alone could be written—Saytah was able to explore and see everything on the Other Side due to the light he carried. I want you to understand that I'm not touching on the smallest portion of what Saytah endured or experienced in the darkness as a being of light. Saytah's experience though exposed him to everything that you, or any other person on Earth, ever experienced. In other words, Saytah was able to fully experience all that existed in the Universe, at least as it related to darkness and the Other Side. His experience of the darkness though helped him to fully understand the light as he was a being of light.

"While his light penetrated the negative spiritual matter of the Mirror, it was reflected back by the positive spiritual matter a few inches from the negative spiritual matter, and so there was still no way for him to return to Heaven. He knew, somehow, he was still connected in some way to those in Heaven, and they were still gaining light through him. Even though he could not make it through the Mirror, everything he perceived and experienced on the Other Side contributed greatly to his understanding of all things on the Heaven side.

"Of course, Saytah's experience on the Other Side was far from ideal. The loneliness was especially hard to deal with, and the negative feelings all around, the constant darkness, and the constant battles with beings from the Other Side made his time there extremely trying. He was always able to win the battles with the beings due to the fact he had light and could see. However, he often wondered why it was taking so long for Elirah and Charity to find him, and he often wondered if his faith was misplaced or if he were truly lost. Yet, despite these worries and the extensive length of existence which had passed, he remained true to his promise to Charity as well as his faith in the feelings he had experienced when creating the Mirror. He refused to let go of faith as it was all he had to sustain him.

"The darkness and evil on the Other Side had seared one piece of information into his heart—the fact that a far better Universe existed, even the one he had felt when creating the Mirror, and he was committed to finding it, as well as finding his way back to Heaven so that he could take everyone in Heaven to the new Universe with him, once he was able to find it. In other words, Saytah stayed true to his faith, his hope, and his belief, and continued working, despite the continual press of the darkness and loneliness.

Ranier was trying to keep up with all of this information, but still didn't fully trust James. "When does my mother get to join us?" he asked suddenly, interrupting James. Ranier did not enjoy being a captive audience to James, and wanted to change the circumstances a little.

"Soon," James replied calmly. After waiting a minute to see if Ranier had any other questions, James asked "Who do you trust Ranier? I know that you don't trust me."

Ranier frowned in anger, upset at the invasive question. "Is that question supposed to make me trust you somehow?" Ranier asked in response.

"No," James replied, "not at all. I just don't think there is a single person you trust besides yourself, especially since you still don't believe everything Elleana has told you."

"And what is wrong with that?" Ranier quickly replied, his frustration growing, "I have sat here and listened to you, what more do you want?"

"You haven't listened to me by choice, Ranier," James responded, "and I just ask that you recognize you don't trust anyone right now, and so you would be equally upset with anyone explaining these things to you. In other words, I am not the cause of your problems, and there is no reason to be upset with me more than anyone else. Try to put your personal feelings aside and listen. It is the only way for you to be healed."

"I don't need you in order to be healed!" Ranier shot back.

"It's true that you don't need me," James said quietly, "but you definitely need the message, and I'm the only one willing and able to deliver the message to you right now."

"That's not true!" Ranier said defiantly, "Elleana can tell me."

James, without waiting for Ranier to say anything else, responded "Elleana can't handle delivering this message to you. The pain you mask with your anger and frustration is too much for her, and she can't bear being with you right now as she is still healing from her pain. She wants nothing more than to be with you, but it has to be at a time when you have let go of enough of your problems to let her feel something positive in your presence. Spirits are extra susceptible to your internal problems, and Elleana is no exception."

"Of course," Ranier thought to himself, forgetting that James could understand his thoughts, "blame it on me. I'm always the problem, and I don't have problems. The rest of the world, including you James, are the ones with the problems!"

James smiled, saying "Ranier, the sooner we can finish, the sooner you can be done with me. Please, I just ask that you put aside your personal feelings against me and listen with an open heart. All of this will be in vain if the necessary points never even get a chance to sink in."

Ranier snorted lightly in disgust while grinding his foot into the ground in anger. He did not want anything more to do with James, but, he did want to be with Elleana again, and since the only way to be there with her and to be done with James was to listen, he guessed that he might as well finish up as quickly as possible. "Fine," Ranier responded steadily, "play your game, I'll listen, and then I expect to see Elleana again."

"It's a deal," James said with a smile, while then proceeding from where he had left off in his explanation of the history of the Universe.

Chapter 7

"**W**HILE SAYTAH WAS ON THE Other Side, Charity and Elirah were working constantly to find a way to get Saytah back" James told Ranier as he continued explaining the history. "Eternity had stretched on longer than they thought possible without Saytah, yet they did not give up their efforts. Most of the other Intelligences had given up on ever getting Saytah back, and they were comfortable and secure now that they no longer had to worry about the darkness from the Other Side. For most, Saytah was now just an ancient story, and the Intelligences lived their lives in purposeless peace and security. The Mirror had truly made Heaven a type of utopia, as it was designed to do. Nothing bad ever happened, and the Intelligences passed each moment in comfort and security, surrounded by light and that which was good.

"Elirah and Charity constantly encouraged the Intelligences to work and learn, but many were not motivated to do so. Due to the feelings of security, many of the Intelligences had given up on ever finding a way to get Saytah back. Some maintained that Saytah still existed, as they claimed it would be impossible for any light to exist if he had been annihilated.

"However, many of the Intelligences didn't think through these things, and the daily concern of many was to ensure the other Intelligences followed the strict laws that held the Mirror in place. Too much movement or too many violations of the law could easily disrupt the forces holding the Mirror in place, and so the Intelligences worked to keep the other Intelligences from violating these laws. This rigid enforcement of the laws made Heaven unpleasant for many, despite its Utopian state, especially since so few understood why the laws existed as they did.

"Despite many of the other Intelligences giving up on finding a way to get Saytah back, Charity and Elirah had experimented with thousands of different ideas in an effort to get Saytah back, but after many attempts still had not found anything successful. They were always limited by the laws then in existence that they were bound to have to follow. Due to these limits, they turned a lot of their attention to the spiritual dimension created before Saytah had made the Mirror. The spiritual dimension gave them hope, and it also gave them necessary breaks from their search.

"They found that if they dedicated all of their time to Saytah, their lives and beings would fall into disarray, and a break from their work was entirely necessary. While they would commit as much time as possible to working to get Saytah back, they had to rest at least one in every seven periods of work. They soon discovered it was not necessary to just sit and let the seventh period pass while doing nothing, but that the seventh period was more restful and rejuvenating when they changed the focus of their efforts and work to helping others.

"As Charity and Elirah had access to the spiritual dimension and possessed spirit bodies, they used the seventh period of rest as a period to work and create spirit bodies for all of the Intelligences in Heaven. While they wanted Saytah back, they found their own light grew brighter and their pain lessened as they shared their advancements and the spirit dimension with the other Intelligences. They worked to bring Intelligences into the beautiful bodies created to house the Intelligences, ranging from plant bodies for the lower forms of Intelligences to animal bodies for the middle range of Intelligences, and bodies in the image of Charity and Elirah for the highest level of Intelligences. Charity and Elirah worked with each Intelligence when it was given a spirit body, and Charity and Elirah treated each Intelligence as their own child, just as they treated Saytah.

"The longer that Charity and Elirah created spirit bodies and produced spirit children, the more they developed affection for each Intelligence housed in each spirit body. They found great happiness in serving the other Intelligences and in teaching them all they knew about the spiritual dimension, as well as all they learned while trying to get to Saytah. Of course, many Intelligences were comfortable in their safety and security and didn't take many opportunities to learn and progress, but those who sought progression were given spirit bodies.

"Prior to the Mirror being created, Saytah had created many beautiful spirit worlds, and the spirits inhabited these worlds as they gained spirit bodies. The spirits found much joy in their ability to progress and learn, and many of the spirits were happy to work to obtain knowledge and learn. Again, many of the Intelligences were comfortable living each day without purpose though, and they continued to do so.

"After much work, Charity decided she needed to rest for an extended period. Her daily focus was so taken up with Saytah and the needs of the other spirits, that she had not had appropriate time to address her own needs. There were still many Intelligences to work with and help, but she needed some time to herself even though she found great joy in being a mother of the spirits.

"She retreated to be alone and to ponder about Saytah, as he was always on her mind and in her heart. 'If only I could communicate with him' she thought in her heart. 'I absolutely believe he still lives, and I absolutely believe we will be together again.' The long march through eternity had not dulled her belief. Rather, it had only strengthened her resolve to connect again. Her desire to see him again had burned brightly inside her through eternity, and it kept her going and working as she exercised faith and sought to obtain that which she could not see.

"'Saytah' she suddenly called out as she often did, in hopes of one day hearing his voice again, 'Saytah, where are you?' Almost immediately after calling his name she thought she heard Saytah's muffled and quiet voice speak directly to her heart. 'Charity' she heard again as Saytah's muffled voice pierced her through to the center, 'Charity'. Charity was too overcome to say anything as Saytah repeated 'Charity' over and over again. Stunned, Charity's eyes darted around her to see where the voice came from.

"After a few moments that seemed to stretch for eternity, she finally gained the ability to speak again. 'Saytah' she screamed in joy as her voice resonated through the area around her, 'Saytah!' Suddenly her being was overcome and she was crying tears of joy. She collapsed from the wave of sheer joy sweeping over her. 'Where are you Saytah?' she was finally able to call out between sobs. 'On the Other Side' she heard in reply."

Ranier was trying hard to not let any emotion escape. He was stuck sitting, listening, with nowhere to go and not much choice in this matter.

He didn't like James, but had an unbreaking fascination with the story. For some reason, any mention of Charity touched him deep inside, and he found himself fighting emotions as he heard of Charity connecting with Saytah again. He stared away from James to try and avoid having James detect that he was touched slightly by Charity and her story to this point.

James could see that Ranier's heart was stirring with emotion. Ranier's faced seemed lost in thought, but James could sense that Ranier was acutely aware of every word he had said for the past little while. Pausing only for a moment to make sure Ranier did not have any questions, James continued with his recounting of Charity and Saytah's reunion.

"Saytah was also overcome with joy. At the same time as Charity had called his name, he had felt to call out to Charity. He had never known anything so sweet as his reunion with Charity, even though he was not yet back with her fully and their reunion only involved the ability to speak again. Being able to speak to her instilled so much hope and joy in him, and he knew that the moment was not too far distant before he would be able to see her again. As he wept with joy, he examined how he could sense her. He realized his belief and his commitment to his promise over this significant stretch of eternity had created a line of communication between him and Charity, a line which transcended all known facts.

"It was then he experienced and knew that faith had the power to create. His faith and devotion, coupled with Elirah and Charity's faith and devotion, had created a line of communication between mother and son. Because of this experience, Charity and Saytah received a witness of their faith, or a confirmation that what they had believed in was true, and they went from simply believing in the promises made to each other to having a firm hope they would be reunited again one day.

"After gaining enough composure to be able to move again, Charity quickly sought out Elirah and had Elirah experience the joy of communication with Saytah as well. Seeing the proof of Charity and Saytah's faith gave Elirah a sure witness that enabled him to reach out in hope—which is a more powerful level of faith as it has a sure witness coupled to the previous belief—and quickly establish his own line of communication with Saytah. There was nothing now that could separate

Elirah, Charity and Saytah from communicating with each other. They always maintained a conversation in their heart as they told each other of all they had experienced. They learned much from each other, and they worked together to find a way to bring Saytah back from the Other Side.

"After significant work, Saytah communicated everything he had learned on the Other Side. Elirah and Charity's hearts broke with Saytah's for the beings on the Other Side, and all yearned to find a way to help them be freed from their dark natures. However, neither could yet find a way to make it through the Mirror, especially since no being was allowed to violate any of the strict laws holding the Mirror in place.

"After much pondering on what she had learned from Saytah, and after pondering on the power of her faith and how her faith had been turned into hope, as well as pondering on the deeper and deeper feelings of affection she had for each of her spirit children, Charity realized that faith and hope were only the foundation for something greater, for something far more powerful, likely for something foundational to the new Universe Saytah spoke of in their communications. She actively worked to understand what this something was and shared her feelings with Elirah and Saytah. Saytah communicated in excitement that this greater something was the feeling He experienced when creating the Mirror, and it was for this key to a new Universe that he had dedicated his life and agreed to live in the Other Side.

"As Charity thought on this greater something, she also thought about how it was that she could actively send feelings to Saytah, almost without even trying now. She had such deep and abiding feelings for him, which were only strengthened through her faith and hope she had in him. She realized there were yet no words to describe what was taking place in her heart, but she recognized it was something grand and glorious and closely followed what Saytah had let her know he had seen and felt when he created the Mirror. In other words, she sensed the workings that made this new Universe Saytah described possible.

"She discussed this often with Elirah and Saytah and all worked to understand the transformation taking place in their hearts. It seemed these grand and glorious feelings were changing their entire beings into something new and better. Eventually, Elirah named the feelings "love," and it became the study of Elirah, Charity, and Saytah to learn how to fully incorporate love into their beings. Saytah recognized that love was what he had beheld when creating the Mirror, and it was for love that he stepped to the Other Side of the Intelligence Stream so long ago. Even that long ago, Saytah exercised faith in the existence of love, and had spent his eternities on the Other Side to understand how to obtain a Universe based in love.

"However, the three struggled to have the final piece of love fit into their hearts. Something always seemed to be missing, no matter how hard they worked together to understand it. It was as if there was not enough room in their hearts to hold all that love required. As Charity pondered on this, she slowly came to the realization that she would have to give up the old parts of herself to be able to fully incorporate love into her being. In other words, she realized she would have to become a new being as her old being did not have the capacity or ability to fit the pieces necessary for pure love to exist inside her. She did not know how to do this however, but she at least knew what had to be done.

"Eventually, Elirah, Charity, and Saytah came to the conclusion that it should be possible to use the power of love to bring Saytah back to Heaven. However, they were not certain yet on how this was to be done. As Charity still puzzled over how to get rid of her old parts to allow her being to be made of love, she came to the realization that she could never do so if she held on to any part of her old being, including the piece connected to her promise with Saytah. She realized the piece holding her back was her own desires and personal requirement she had made for herself that she see Saytah again.

"She realized that her own, personal desires kept her back from achieving a state of pure love as her own desires held her back from letting go of the old and accepting all that love required. She thought how Saytah gave up peace, security and comfort in order to bring love to others. She also thought about all that she had sacrificed as she had worked to find a way to bring Saytah back, but she also realized there was one piece so dear to her that she had not sacrificed or let go of it. She had not let go of her desire to see Saytah again.

"It was her desire to see Saytah again that caused her to hold onto the old pieces of herself, and she could not give these pieces up to make room for love without giving up that desire as well. She was torn as she realized all that the law of love required of her, as it required her entire being to come into line and offer a sacrifice of all that was near and dear to her. In other words, it required a truly broken heart and a contrite spirit.

"At this point, she understood what must be done. She prepared a box to act as a symbol, wrote 'My Own Desires' on it, and buried it deep in the ground. If Saytah was to come back, it would only be on condition that her own personal desires would be let go and sacrificed. Charity accepted the full ramifications of what her newly found knowledge meant, even though Charity could clearly see what would be required to bring Saytah back. Charity could use love to pull him through the Mirror. Charity knew though that she would need Elirah's support since they were bound together by promises to each other.

"As Charity reflected on the ramifications of what she knew, she understood her actions would bring darkness and suffering back to Heaven, but she also knew her actions would bring light to those in darkness. If the Mirror remained in place, the entire dark Universe on the Other Side would forever remain in their fallen and hopeless state, forever suffering while the Intelligences in Heaven sat by idling away their days, not progressing, not learning, and not experiencing any form of true happiness.

"She was truly conflicted as she thought about the beings on the Other Side, and the lack of progression in Heaven, as well as the relative unhappiness that prevailed due to the rigid enforcement of the laws and the inability to progress. 'Intelligence was never meant to sit still' she thought to herself as she reflected on the constant movement of the Intelligence Stream. 'Intelligence has to be progressing or else it will ultimately die. Light can only remain light if it is moving.'

"It was then Charity realized that the Mirror was leading to the slow and painful death of the Intelligences. While their spirit beings would never die and could remain in that state forever, as spiritual matter and its counterpart would never come back together, their Intelligence could not avoid annihilation still. That was why so many Intelligences felt hollow and unfulfilled—because they were slowly dying from an eternity of not progressing. Charity could see that by breaking the Mirror and bringing the darkness and light together, all beings in existence could be taken to a higher plane, to a better existence."

At this point, Ranier, always quick in his thoughts and still struggling form the emotions arising within him, and wanting to throw James off track to mask the fact he was feeling anything, interjected "But on Earth, they teach of Heaven and Hell, and they teach of the Devil and his followers. It appears that she missed something in her calculation of all being taken to a higher plane, as Heaven just appears to be the same place as before, but I've never heard of Hell being considered a higher plane."

"Not so," James replied. "She saw that all beings *could* be taken to a higher plane, if they chose, but she also saw that many beings would choose not to go to a higher plane. Since you brought him up, the Devil and his followers could have gone to the higher plane, but they chose to hold onto the old way of life—of the false utopia of comfort and security—instead of embracing the opportunity to progress and find a higher plane, a better state of existence. Certainly, the knowledge that many would reject the opportunity to progress and find life eternal was saddening to Charity, and it caused her to reflect time and time again on if there was any other way."

Ranier could see James was continuing on without even breaking his train of thought. Ranier was surprised at how well James could handle dealing with him, as most other people would get upset at Ranier's pride and attempts to control the situation. Ranier realized he probably wasn't going to be too successful right now in throwing James off track, so he decided to keep listening, at least until he could figure out another way to try and regain control of the situation.

"As she explained what she had realized with Elirah," James said without regard to Ranier's thoughts, "Elirah restrained her at first. 'The Mirror cannot be broken, commotion will reign and annihilation could ensue' Elirah said at first. 'Yes, that is true,' Charity said, 'but the Mirror is actually killing us anyways as we cannot progress. We both know the Mirror is only a temporary solution for life, and even with the strict laws in place, it has only bought us the time to understand what must really be done.

"'The Mirror will break soon anyways since the relatively few Intelligences who are fighting the decay of their light due to not progressing will eventually rise up in violation of the laws and take actions to remain alive that will shatter the Mirror, and if it is not a controlled break, it will destroy us all. While the Mirror was a necessary part of our life and our existence, it is also becoming the means of our death.' While he didn't like to think of this, Elirah knew it was true.

"After watching Elirah struggle in thought for a time, Charity continued 'You also have to let go of your desires, of your desires to remain with me' she told Elirah.

"'I promised I would always remain with you though' Elirah replied. 'There has to be another way' Elirah said after some silence.

"She smiled weakly. 'I also hope there is another way Elirah, and that is why I have come to you. At a minimum, if this is what is required, we need a plan, a plan of salvation to ensure that all who will may be saved and taken to the new Universe. One thing I know though is that love cannot exist without a sacrifice. And, you can keep that promise to always remain with me' she said with her voice trailing off as she looked into the distance.

"'There is one piece of me that can remain. Here, take this' she said handing him a box. 'It will be all that is left of me soon, as I feel deeply this is the only way.' Elirah carefully opened the box and in it saw Charity's rib, the one closest to her heart, the one that allowed her to transfer Intelligences from the Intelligence realm into the spiritual dimension, or, in other words, the one that allowed her to be a mother.

"'What does this mean?' He gasped.

"Charity looked him squarely in the eyes and said 'It is the only way Elirah. Both of us must let go of ourselves in order to move ahead, to save the Universe from death, in order to get Saytah back. And, in letting go of yourself, you must let go of me. While you will lose substantial pieces of yourself with me gone, you will be able to draw enough from my rib for your Intelligence to continue operating to carry out the plan of salvation.'

"As Charity spoke, Elirah was pierced with a full understanding. He wept openly, embraced Charity, and together they cried. This was surely one of the most tender moments in all of eternity.

"'Charity, I see now, and understand this must be done' he replied. Together they sat and penned the Plan of Salvation—a Plan to bring the entire Universe to a higher plane. They wept openly as they saw all that it entailed, of the sacrifice required of each and every being. They wept as they saw the misery the darkness would bring, and wept when they thought of what would be required of Elirah, Charity, and Saytah.

However, they also knew that at one point all of the suffering related to light and dark would end, that it was the only way to save the Universe from a slow and drawn out death, and that it was the only way to bring light to those trapped in the darkness.

"There were a few parts of the Plan that were the most difficult for Elirah. For the Plan to work, it required one of them to sacrifice themselves to break the Mirror, but also required one of them to remain alive. Both could not live, and both could not die for the Plan to work. Elirah knew he needed to remain alive, but this would require constant sacrifice of him. He knew at some point, he would have to sacrifice Saytah and let him die as well. He also knew in order for all of the Intelligences to gain spirit bodies, especially those Intelligences of darkness, they would need a being to be their mother. He could not bear the thought of being connected to another spirit as he had with Charity, and he searched and searched for another way.

"Charity was confident of what was required. She knew though of how hard it would be to have to connect with another being to allow all Intelligences to gain the chance to progress through obtaining a spirit body, and she readily explained to Elirah over and over why it was necessary. Elirah preferred to simply cease existing with Charity, but he knew that if he did, there was no way to give all of the Intelligences a chance to progress. He knew there was no way to satisfy the law of love, or be just and merciful, by denying any being the opportunity to progress.

"If Charity remained, the Mirror would remain, and the Intelligences on the Other Side of the Mirror would forever be denied an opportunity to get a spirit body as a non-controlled break would destroy everyone. If Charity sacrificed herself to break the Mirror, the Intelligences on the Other Side could only get a spirit body if Elirah connected with, or married as we would say on Earth, another female spirit.

"Compounding the problem though was the fact that, due to the speed at which annihilation would occur after the Mirror broke, one female spirit would not be able to create spirit bodies for the numerous Intelligences in time to give them all a chance to gain a spirit body before the old Universe was annihilated. Because of this, Elirah and Charity knew that Elirah would need to connect with multiple female spirits to be able to give each dark Intelligence an opportunity to have a spirit body and be taken to a higher level of existence. Elirah did not know how this was possible as everything about him had been geared to place all of his affections on Charity.

"For the Plan of Salvation to work, Charity had to fully give of herself by, in essence, dying. Elirah had to fully give of himself through the life he would have to live. He would have to give up everything about himself to be able to connect with multiple spirits to bring spiritual life to the Universe in time, to be able to sacrifice Saytah, and to otherwise be responsible for all that the Plan entailed. This was not easy for him, as his path required an unwavering commitment to do what was right, an unwavering commitment to submit his desires, preferences, and being to the requirements of the Plan, to the requirements of a higher existence.

"Charity and Elirah could see that the Plan would require them to sacrifice everything about themselves, and everything about their relationship. They had to let go of everything dear to them, and they did it for the salvation of the Universe, they did it for each of us. They knew a higher state of existence was possible, but could only be achieved through giving up one's self to reach it. Their hearts also broke because they knew it would require a similar sacrifice from each and every being. All beings would need to be made new to escape the destructive opposition that formed the basis of their current existence, and to be made new, each would have to give up themselves.

"After much preparation, Elirah and Charity finished the Plan of Salvation. They could not bear to share it with Saytah yet, and they also knew that his involvement in the Plan would require his voluntary submission, which would require them to not share it fully until it was disclosed to all of Heaven. Charity and Elirah knew the ideal time for the Mirror to break—a time at which the least amount of destruction would ensue—and they issued a warning to all within the path the darkness would take as it spilled into Heaven through the broken Mirror.

"The warning alerted the Intelligences that darkness would flow through a certain path as the Mirror was set to break. Sadly, many Intelligences ignored this warning and laughed at the thought of the Mirror breaking. A few Intelligences who believed and exercised faith in the warning were able to see many parts of the future for themselves, and they acted to prophesy to the others about what they could see. Despite this, many still refused to believe, even as the time drew nearer.

"As the appointed time approached, Elirah's heart broke as he released his connections to Charity and let go of every desire of his he had ever known. Surely there had never been a heavier day in all of existence. At this point, both Elirah and Charity could fully see all of the ramifications of what was about to take place. They had known this for some time, but at this point everything was crystal clear, and they could see the Plan would ultimately work, despite the opposition that would be launched against it.

"Even with the horrors they could see that would be inflicted by the inhabitants of the Universe on each other, they knew it would all be worth it in the end, and that Saytah would be able to right all wrongs inflicted by the inhabitants on each other. Elirah and Charity embraced again, and then with tears on both of their faces they whispered goodbye. Charity then turned, and traveled to the Mirror.

"The Mirror was held in place by the strict laws governing the forces keeping the spiritual matter together. The laws were made prior to the knowledge of love, and so while every way known at the time of creating the laws had been put in place to stop the laws from being broken, they had not put safeguards in place to prevent the laws from being broken by love exemplified through sacrifice.

"It was the sacrifice of Elirah and Charity that gave birth to all existence, and it would be their sacrifice again that would put the Universe on a new path to a higher existence. At the Beginning, they sacrificed half of themselves and made a Universe, but the Universe was unstable due to the constant attraction between darkness and light, or was unstable because the law of sacrifice had only been partly satisfied. This time though, with the full sacrifice of self involved, they knew the new Universe could be entirely stable, and entirely good as it would be built on a complete sacrifice. They knew sacrifice was the foundation of anything good and lasting.

"At the Mirror, Charity fully let go of all of her own desires, including the desire to see Saytah again and the desire to constantly remain with Elirah, and made her only desire to do that which was right, just, and good. As she did so, she was filled with pure love. Lucifer, a high-ranking spirit and Intelligence, having listened closely to what Elirah and Charity had cautioned about the Mirror breaking, suddenly appeared to attack Charity. Instead of heeding the warning to leave the path of destruction, he decided he had to stop the destruction. Lucifer rushed angrily towards Charity, planning on harming her enough to stop her. He didn't know what she could do to break the Mirror, but he felt justified in stopping her because of the strict laws in Heaven against breaking the Mirror. He rationalized that he was simply enforcing the law.

"Lucifer's actions were a surprise to most people in Heaven, except for those who continually worked to progress. Lucifer had been a 'Son of the Morning', a bright star, so to speak, among the Intelligences. Many in Heaven respected him and looked to him due to the light he carried. While he had a lot of light, he had always rejected faith and only trusted in the things he could see with his own light. Because of this, he had no faith in Elirah's or Charity's plans, and formulated his own plans based on what he could see and perceive with the light he carried at that moment in existence.

"Charity, however, had no fear of Lucifer or the harm he could inflict. She found that when she was filled with true love, she had no fear. She had no fear of death, no fear of losing herself, no fear of harm, and no fear of the future. She was at peace, and knew, absolutely knew, what must be done. She did not have time to complete her work before Lucifer attacked her, making it so he was able to significantly harm her. Even with the serious injury, her love inside did not waiver. With this pure love, and despite Lucifer's attacks to harm her, she was able to reach through the Mirror with love and connect to Saytah. She then reached deep into her heart, down to her very essence, and sent her essence through the Mirror to Saytah.

"At that moment true, pure love was born. Charity had overcome all of the known laws in existence. The Mirror broke and the Universe was rocked by a massive explosion. Even though there was a large explosion affecting the entire Universe, the breaking of the Mirror at this point was necessary as waiting too much longer would have caused the entire Universe to be annihilated if the Mirror broke.

"In the ensuing chaos, Charity's Intelligence was nowhere to be found as her essence had attracted her Intelligence's counterpart to the Mirror at the same time Charity was at the Mirror. Thus, following the breaking of the Mirror, Charity's Intelligence was annihilated, as she had known it would be. Saytah was able to receive Charity's essence, which now glowed brightly with pure love. Charity had managed to give up every part of herself, and in return had satisfied the law of love, which meant her essence was now one of pure love. 'Greater love hath no being than this,' said Elirah with tears in his eyes, 'than she that layeth down her life for those she loves.'"

Chapter 8

RANIER FOUND HIMSELF ALONE AGAIN. Tears were forming in his eyes as he reflected on Charity and the breaking of the Mirror. He had such vivid recollections of the sound of shattering glass, of darkness, and of despair, and his memories made this story seem all the more real.

"Are you okay?" a nurse asked him.

Ranier was quite taken back at the nurse's voice and jumped in surprise.

"I'm sorry," the nurse said, "I thought you knew I was here. We had been talking just a moment ago."

"You're okay" Ranier said as he tried to stop any tears from collecting enough to fall out. He had no recollection of any conversations with this nurse, and did not recall seeing her before. Trying to regain his grounding a little, he asked the nurse "how long have we been talking?"

"About an hour" she said in response, "why?"

"Oh, no reason, just curious" Ranier responded. He was entirely unclear as to how he could have been talking for an hour with no recollection of it. Trying further to understand, he asked the nurse "what exactly is wrong with me?"

The nurse looked at him a little confused. "You were hit by explosions from the bombings and were seriously wounded. Almost everything is wrong with you, and it's a miracle you are alive. Don't you recall everything we just talked about?"

Feeling a little red creep into his face, Ranier said "Well, that is why I'm wondering about the extent of my injuries. I'm wondering if my mind has been affected by any of this."

"Oh, I see," the nurse responded, "but no, your mind is still as sharp as a tack. You don't ever let any of us forget anything, and get frustrated if we're a minute late for any of your meals. No, none of us would say there is anything wrong with your mind. That is the one thing that seems to have escaped any injury or damage from the bombing."

This didn't help Ranier, as he wanted so much to have an explanation for what was taking place. "Are you religious at all?" he asked the nurse.

"You've never been one to feel awkward about much" the nurse said, "but no, I'm not religious at all. Religion is only for those who aren't strong enough to accept the true facts of life."

"That's what I have thought too" Ranier said as the nurse prepared to leave his room, "that's what I have thought too."

Ranier sat reflecting on Charity and the relationship of love and sacrifice. Was it really not possible to possess love without a full sacrifice? He was troubled by these points, as he readily recognized he was entirely unwilling to sacrifice his personal desires, and he was also entirely without love in his life. He didn't like any of this information, and didn't like the thought trying to surface to his consciousness that maybe he was the source of some of his problems.

Suddenly, Ranier saw James by him again.

"It was a bittersweet reunion for Elirah and Saytah" James continued, without even acknowledging that they had been separated for a time.

Ranier was becoming more convinced that something must be wrong with his mind. He seemed to be flipping between worlds in the blink of any eye, yet, he felt so much connected with the story that he knew there was more to this than he could understand right now. Ranier was still amazed at how James never seemed to lose his train of thought as he listened to James continue without a break from when he had last seen him.

"Elirah and Saytah were overjoyed to be together again, but saddened more deeply than could ever be known. However, the entire Universe was in disarray as massive waves of darkness were spilling into Heaven and light was spilling into the Other Side of the Mirror. The entire situation seemed far too overwhelming to deal with, especially since Charity was gone.

"Even though the situation was very paralyzing and seemed to entail more than they could bear, Elirah and Saytah sat together and forced themselves to discuss what pieces remained. Elirah had Charity's rib that allowed for Intelligences to be brought into spirit bodies, and Saytah had Charity's essence, which filled him with pure love. Both discussed the plans they had made to save the Universe from annihilation and to take the Universe to the next level of existence, although Elirah still did not provide Saytah with a complete view of what the Plan of Salvation entailed.

"Of course, all of the Intelligences were shocked and felt at a complete loss with Charity's death. All of the inhabitants adored Charity and the feelings of kindness, affection, and joy they felt around her. It was surely a dark period in the history of the Universe, a time of intense review of self, of the purpose of existence, and of what each being was willing to do to secure an existence. Due to the struggle of the Intelligences to cope with Charity's loss, they decided it best to show respect for her by maintaining a respectful silence about her, as it brought too much emotion to them to discuss having lost her, just as it did when Saytah disappeared. Any discussion of Charity only invoked sadness, as it was too difficult for most any Intelligence to truly understand why she had sacrificed herself.

"However, the inhabitants were also shocked to see that Saytah was still alive. 'He is!' they often said to themselves. Their surprise mainly came because they had not seen him for so long they had accepted their presumption that he must not exist any longer, a presumption long enforced through the silence maintained by most of them on the issue during their time on the Heaven side of the Mirror.

"'Yes,' Saytah would reply when the inhabitants would see him, 'I am,' meaning 'I am still in existence.' Due to the wonder of the fact he was still alive and had survived for so long on the Other Side, he became known as the 'Great I Am.'

"As Saytah reflected on what was to be done, Saytah told Elirah, 'We promised Charity We would never leave her. There has to be a way to get her back. We have to believe that annihilation is not the end of an Intelligence's existence, especially since her essence was not destroyed.' Elirah agreed, and Saytah went to work to create a plan to save Charity and the rest of the Universe from the commotion currently in place. Elirah allowed him to work on the plan on his own as he knew it was necessary for Saytah to come to the realization himself of what was required.

"Even though Elirah had the Plan perfected on paper, for lack of a better term, before the Mirror was broken, Elirah did not fully appreciate or understand the depth of the feelings and sense of loss that would follow the commotion, and he worried about whether he could carry through with all that the Plan required. For Elirah, he had to exercise faith to continue forward from this point, especially with the loss of Charity, since he had experienced significant losses in his existence as well.

"Thinking back on things Charity had said, Saytah remembered her saying that 'Love gives us the opportunity to have an entirely new existence. Everything can be improved and our existence made sure,' she added, 'but there is only one way for this to happen.' Both Elirah and Saytah remembered this, but Saytah did not understand the depth of the sacrifice required to achieve what she meant at the time. Now, he understood she was speaking of sacrificing herself to bring about a greater good in the Universe.

"Saytah could see all Elirah and Charity had already sacrificed, and could see that more sacrifice would still be required. He could also see that Elirah and Charity had spoken of preparing Heaven for the possible encroachment of darkness at some point, and how Elirah had called the few who were willing to listen to begin preparations for such a state of existence. Now, the inhabitants of Heaven were grateful that the few had listened as they had some basic things to work with as they all sought to cope with the reality of annihilation and the darkness in Heaven.

"Of course, even with their intense sense of loss, Elirah and Saytah did not have time to sit and be still. There was much work to do. Lucifer, as one of the more advanced spirit and Intelligence beings, was upset, along with many others, by the breaking of the Mirror and the chaos it had caused. Since his attack on Charity did not work, he further developed a plan of his own on how to restore Heaven to its previous state with the Mirror again in place and forever shut out the possibility of the Mirror being broken again."

At this point, James paused and looked for a minute at Ranier. While Ranier usually didn't mind a few moments to collect his thoughts, Ranier did not appreciate the pause this time. He did not know why, but he had become rather uncomfortable inside at this mention of Lucifer. The feelings associated with Lucifer were not good ones, but they seemed to match the confusion and darkness he had experienced throughout his life. He wasn't sure if he wanted James to continue speaking at this time, but he certainly did not want to admit to James that he was afraid of anything. When James stopped speaking, Ranier remembered he was an open book and was frustrated that he couldn't keep anything to himself.

James ignored Ranier's feelings of frustration and instead responded to a question inside Ranier. "Lucifer is known on Earth as the Devil, or Satan, and is the current leader heading the War against Elirah and Saytah," James said in a matter-of-fact tone. "Lucifer took on the name 'Satan' in order to mimic 'Saytah'. Lucifer always patterns his work on slight variations of truth, and his choice of a name was no different."

Ranier, knowing that this did not explain his feelings, and understanding James could sense his questions anyways, asked "what are these feelings of fear and darkness inside me? Why does this story bring such feelings to me?"

"There are a number of reasons Ranier" James replied in an even tone, "some of which you will not be able to understand for a while yet. But, for now, the main thing to understand about these feelings is that they come due to an internal conflict present in you, the same conflict which is present in all people. You are" James continued steadily, "deciding who to accept as your god. It is impossible not to choose a god to follow. Many people, like you, think they do not believe in a god, but this is simply a lie.

"All of our actions are premised in an internal acceptance of either Elirah or Lucifer as our god, as our entire Universe is on a path leading to one of the two kingdoms, either Heaven or Hell, a better or a lesser existence. Every person will have to choose one or the other because this Universe will cease to exist, and every person will make that decision for themselves. Right now you are struggling to decide if you want eternal life with Elirah, or eternal death with Lucifer."

Ranier help up his hand at this point. "You lose a lot of credibility claiming I have accepted a god to follow, and in claiming we suffer eternal death. There is absolutely no reason why anyone would elect to have eternal death, and so I think it would be appropriate for you to use more truthful characterizations of these matters."

James smiled. "I appreciate your honesty Ranier. Yet, I am being fully honest with you, and I am not mischaracterizing anything. I know that eternal death does not sound like something anyone would choose, yet it is a choice that people repeatedly seek after on a daily basis. One-third of the hosts of Heaven have already elected, with full knowledge, to choose eternal death and follow Lucifer to Hell. Their decision is rooted in the fact that they love their current self more than they love who they could be in the future. The other two-thirds, including you, elected to follow Elirah's plan, and came to the earth as a result.

"Eternal life has a very real cost to it—it requires giving up who you are today to reach your full potential, and it requires passing through sorrow that you can understand the good, light, evil, and dark. When we do nothing in life, we are on the path towards death. There are, no matter how much we do not like it, only two masters to serve, and it is up to us to choose to follow the God of life or the god of death."

James knew that this point still bothered Ranier, but James also knew that most struggled understanding this concept. James had never had to teach someone so much so quickly before, but the instructions to James were clear—Ranier was to be taught the things necessary to understand who Ranier was. The timing was critical, and it was up to James right now to continue to teach. However, he had to find a way to connect so that his teachings were actually accepted.

"Ranier," James asked, "what has made you work to live during your time on Earth? You haven't enjoyed any part of it, so what makes you keep going, especially since death is inevitable?"

Ranier sat for a little time to avoid responding to James. Ranier didn't like how personal the question was, but at the same time some part of him also wanted to know the answer to the question and wanted to hear what he had to say. "Why does it matter?" Ranier finally asked, "nothing I have ever thought has ever mattered before."

"It matters," James replied in an even voice, "because it matters to God. God promised you well before you came to this earth that you would first be given the experiences followed by the understanding necessary to know who you are. It is only in knowing who you are that you can truly make the decisions necessary to obtain eternal life."

"I've never mattered to God, or to anyone else for that matter, except for maybe Elleana" Ranier said in a softer tone.

Ranier was surprised at the sudden and sharp response from James as he heard James say "Ranier!" The tone in James' voice sent a chill through Ranier. "There is one thing I ask of you Ranier—I ask that you at least be honest with yourself. Why in the world would I be sitting here and spending my time with you if I didn't care about you? Why would God let you visit Elleana before your time on Earth was done?

"Just because life has been hard in no way means that you have never mattered. Lest you forget what I told you before, God gave you exactly what you asked for in life, and he has walked every step of your life with you. He knows your pain, he suffered for you, and he has invested great amounts of effort to give you every opportunity necessary to receive a fullness of joy. And deep down inside, yes deep inside, you know this to be true, which is why you have held on to life and still worked every day to stay alive. You believe that you matter, and this belief has sustained you through all of your hardships."

James' tone had softened a little, but Ranier could sense the frustration still in James. "Tell me then," Ranier defensively said in response, "why you care."

"I care," James said immediately, "because" as his voice started to trail off "you are my brother and..." Ranier was surprised at the silence and the change in James. After a minute Ranier could sense James crying. Ranier wondered what was taking place, but he certainly felt something stirring inside him. After a few more minutes of sitting in silence, James continued "we come from the same place Ranier. We have the same origin. We are brothers in every sense of the word.

"When God assigned me to take on this responsibility, I was terrified and felt very inadequate, especially since you were always my superior in every sense of the way. God reassured me this was the only way I would have of showing you I care, even though you cannot remember me or who I was. We all have a lot to learn and experience in life Ranier, but I hope you can recognize that I do care, and I can promise you, there are thousands of others who sincerely care as well."

Ranier, feeling awkward at the rather emotional state of James, asked "But why death James? Even I haven't given up on life and still try to work for something worthwhile. You're telling me that some of the hosts of Heaven followed Lucifer and chose eternal death, and that is a concept I struggle believing. Of course, I haven't decided whether I believe what you are telling me or not, but this seems to be far too much of a claim to make."

"Well," James said with a little of his composure regained, "let me back up for a minute then. Remember, we began our existence as an

Intelligence. Our Intelligence is the driving force behind all we do. It forms the basis of our desires, our thoughts, our identity, and all other aspects of who we are. However, as Intelligence is like light, it can come and go in the flash of a moment unless it is given form and housed in a body.

"After being separated from the Intelligence Stream, the only way for the Intelligences to continue to progress was to be given a form. When the spirit dimension was created, Elirah and Charity took on a spirit body to house their Intelligence in. By giving their Intelligence form, they were able to progress. Each of us gained that spirit form as well and we were all created in the same image, or form, of God.

"The basic law behind the Intelligence Stream is progression. The Stream always moves in an attempt to progress, and even when the light and dark Intelligences were separated from the Intelligence Stream both still moved. Ultimately though, they were attracted back to each other as light could not progress without understanding the dark. Light is always attracted back to dark, just as dark is always attracted back to light. When the two meet however, annihilation occurs, at least annihilation of those Intelligences.

"Light and dark both seek the opposite ends of each other. Light inherently desires to seek, see, and understand, and especially looks towards maximizing potential in the future. Dark inherently desires to maximize feelings in the moment and is not concerned about the future as it has no ability to see that a future may exist. Again though, light and dark have a fatal attraction to each other as both are born of progression, and neither can progress without the other.

"When the Mirror was created, it made it impossible for light to interact with dark. This was necessary for survival and progression then, but the Mirror effectively created a cap on progression as the Intelligences could only progress so far without interacting with and understanding the dark. Elirah and Charity sensed that without progression, the Intelligences would begin regressing and ultimately die from lack of anything meaningful in life.

"However, the Mirror produced a Utopia-like state that many spirits welcomed. They had security and were free from the dark, and they lived their days involved in trivial matters, seeking simply to see or hear some new thing. Most of the spirits became complacent in their utopia and stopped believing that progression was essential to their existence. Progression took work and effort, and the Utopia created by the Mirror pacified many into accepting a false sense of reality. They believed they could live forever in such a state.

"Elirah and Charity saw how the spirits were, in essence, accepting and internalizing principles related to the darkness. Even though the darkness was not physically present, the principles of darkness still reached the spirits. The fatal attraction of light and dark transcended having to be physically present in the same space, and beings of light still sought after and adopted principles of darkness. However, most of the spirits laughed at and scorned those who attempted to point this out. Since the darkness was not physically present, they believed it to be a ridiculous notion that they were embracing the principles of darkness. They felt fine and at ease, and refused to look with an eye of faith to see their true state.

"At this point Elirah and Charity fully recognized that, in the current state of the Universe, nothing could separate light from dark and light could always embrace principles of dark. As light embraced these principles, the light would eventually die, but it would do so in a pain free, euphoric type way so that the spirits never felt it coming, and because they never felt it, they would never believe it was happening.

"As Charity reflected on this and reflected on getting Saytah back, she clearly saw the only way to pull the spirits out of this spiral towards death was to bring the darkness back and allow the spirits to experience real pain. Pain was the only way for each spirit to be able to understand the full effects and end results of their decisions and choices.

"Pain was necessary to see the true state of one's existence. Without pain, it was impossible for these spirits to discern where things really were at in their existence. If Elirah and Charity had not loved us enough to break the Mirror and let us experience pain, we would all have died a slow, pain free death in a utopia of false security."

Ranier interrupted James at this point. "You speak of death, but from what I've heard taught on Earth, the spirit can never die, and Lucifer, or Satan, and his angels will live forever in Hell. Are those teachings wrong, or am I missing something in what you are saying to me?"

James nodded "Yes, it is true that the spirit can never die. The spirit material will always exist and will never be annihilated. Remember, when spirit material was created it was done so under a law that forces the positive and negative material apart. The two sets of material will never touch again, and so the spirit bodies we all have will live. The death I speak of though is the death of the Intelligence.

"When the Intelligence dies, the spirit body it inhabits continues to live since a spirit being will always draw the minimum required for life from the elements around it. However, the individual, Intelligent portion of that spirit can be destroyed, and without that, life is fairly meaningless as it is impossible to progress or really experience much without the individual Intelligence. In other words, the spirit body lives on, but it is without intelligence, passion, desire, individuality, or anything that makes a person unique. It becomes a hollow body, responding to the stimulus around it. It becomes a body to be acted upon, not a body to act.

"God calls this state 'spiritual death'. A spirit is considered dead when it can no longer progress or act on its own. Lucifer and his followers will exist in a place called 'Outer Darkness'. It is named this because there is no light there as their Intelligence portions are completely destroyed and they have no connection to the light from Saytah, they having chosen to sever this connection themselves. When Lucifer and his followers sever their connection to God, they are removing themselves from the light, or positive, spiritual matter.

To continue living, or operating as a body, Lucifer and his followers take on a body of negative, or dark, spiritual matter. Due to this, the only force acting on these spirit beings is the law of attraction, meaning that their spirit bodies are attracted to other spirit bodies. Darkness attracts darkness, and is the driving force with gravity, black holes, and the like. Angels are not subject to the law of gravity as they have no darkness in them, meaning there is nothing for the darkness on Earth to pull them to. This law of attraction, or law drawing darkness to darkness, makes it so that the only thing driving these spirits is the desire to have other spirit bodies join their ranks. They thus work tirelessly to have other spirits commit acts which sever light from them as their only form of gain is to destroy others.

James could sense that Ranier was still quite troubled. James paused for a minute to let Ranier think on these concepts. James remembered well how sickening it was to watch these spirits accept spiritual death.

The War in Heaven started so long ago, yet thinking of the souls who chose death still brought tears to his eyes. Some of his favorite and closest spirits had chosen Lucifer's plan, and there was nothing he was able to do to convince them otherwise. He certainly understood Ranier's feeling on the subject, and knew that an eternity still didn't tend to ease the sickness inside associated with the dear ones who chose death.

After some silence, James knew he had to continue. "The draw, ultimately, Ranier, is that Lucifer promised relief from suffering, pain, and failure. Lucifer promised the Utopia that existed when the Mirror existed. Lucifer's method of saving everyone was to remove anything bad from their existence. Lucifer was modeling his plan after the Utopia-like state that existed with the Mirror.

"The problem, of course, was that the Utopia-like state of the Mirror was not an eternal state. Intelligences were beginning to regress toward death even in that state because they were unable to progress. Light and dark, pleasure and pain, good and evil, all had to exist together to enable progression. This made it so that life hurt, but death brought relief. And, since the relief of a slow, pain free spiritual death was more welcome than the pain of life, many chose to accept death over life.

"Ultimately though, there was one thing which clearly divided those who followed Lucifer and those who followed Saytah." James noticed Rainer's gaze sharpen as James said this. "Faith. Those who had faith followed Elirah and Saytah, while those who refused to have faith followed Lucifer."

"I don't believe that" Rainer said almost immediately. "I have no faith, and yet I supposedly followed Elirah and Saytah."

For the first time in a while, James smiled. "Ranier," James said softly, "you actually have great faith. Faith is how you have come this far. You believe, with great resolve, that there is something good to life, and that you will obtain it. You have persevered through countless hours and days of pain. Even now you still believe there is something better. Sure, you haven't accepted God yet, but this isn't because you don't have faith in God, it is because you haven't been able to understand why God would allow suffering, especially with your precious mother you lost at a young age. You have always believed though that there is a better life, and you have endured tirelessly to reach that better world."

For the first time, James saw tears in Ranier's eyes. James had always admired Ranier, especially for his absolute faith in a better world, a faith never extinguished and always propelling Ranier forward. James felt tears in his own eyes as well, but he continued speaking since his time was short. He knew he should do nothing to allow Ranier to sense that he had seen the tears.

"Faith is required to progress, to live, and to act. Faith gives us power to try since we believe that something good can come from our efforts. We have to have faith to see the good in our future, and we have to have faith to see the bad which can come. In other words, we can only make good decisions when we have faith. Without faith, we do not believe that the things which feel good today will cause problems tomorrow, and without faith we do not believe there is any escape from the pain. Because Lucifer's followers refused to look on their existence with an eye of faith, they would not accept the true ramifications of their actions, and they would not believe that there was any escape from pain except for through death.

"Because of this, Lucifer needed a way to create an existence where faith was not necessary. Lucifer was intelligent enough to see the current course without the Mirror would produce death, but he refused to believe the removal of progression and faith would also cause death. Lucifer's plan was to go back in the past and place mind control in all of the inhabitants of the Universe. The plan for the mind control, he said, was not to regulate individual thought, but to prevent any Intelligence from ever thinking of doing anything that could break the Mirror. Thus, Heaven would return to its previous state, and everyone, he taught, would surely be secure and enjoy the same which they had before."

Chapter 9

J AMES PAUSED WHILE LETTING RANIER think for a time on
these things. Ranier's mind was racing through all of the things James
was saying. Ranier was struggling keeping up with everything, but
he knew it wasn't due to his mind not understanding. He fully realized
he was struggling because his heart did not want to accept it yet.

Ranier sat silently trying to figure out whether he was going to
believe any of this or not. Realizing James could sense what he felt, he
tried to force his thoughts on to something else, and tried to take in his
surroundings. Ranier realized he had not taken any time to understand
where he was at, as he had been too preoccupied with the conversation.
As he focused his thoughts on his surroundings, basic images came into
his mind, even though he knew they did not originate from within his
mind.

The images were hard to discern, but made Ranier sense he was in a
large room surrounded by walls, even though his surroundings seemed
to stretch on forever. The Universe seemed to stretch out before him, but
everything was plain and sterile feeling at the same time. Ranier could
sense he wasn't quite connected enough spiritually to fully understand
or discern his surroundings, and wondered if the disconnect was part of
the reason he was struggling to fully process everything that had been
said.

James watched as Ranier thought for a time. When Ranier appeared
to have returned his thoughts to the conversation, but didn't ask any
questions, James continued discussing Lucifer's plan.

"A main problem with Lucifer's proposed 'mind control', of
course, is that it would ultimately prevent any spirit from thinking
thoughts related to progression, as all progression ultimately led to and
required the breaking of the Mirror. However, this took faith to see,

and since these spirits would not exercise faith, they felt the safety and security they had with the Mirror was the solution, and was the only solution."

"What is so bad about a little mind control though?" Ranier asked. "If it removes suffering from life by allowing the Mirror to remain in place, why is it bad to stop progression that causes pain and suffering?"

James nodded. "It is a question we all must ask ourselves Ranier. The real problem with it all is that it is premised on a lie, one that takes faith though to understand. The lie, simply put, is that we can live free of pain and suffering when we are built on the foundation of destructive opposition. When we remove pain and suffering from life, we remove life itself. Life only exists when there is progression, and progression only exists when there is opposition.

"In our state of existence currently, life can only exist through the opposition of pain and suffering. Lucifer, by seeking to remove pain and suffering and our ability to progress, was removing life itself. His plan was truly a plan of death. If Lucifer was able to recreate the state of the Mirror, all of Lucifer's followers would die a slow death, but they would not feel it, see it, or be aware of it until it was too late as they would lack feelings due to a removal of pain and suffering. The removal of pain and suffering equates to the removal of joy and happiness, and without these feelings, life, or even death itself, cannot be felt.

"Basically," James continued, "Lucifer's great lie is that him and his followers would not die. Lucifer sought to remove suffering and progression from existence, but he was trying to alter a Universe already in existence. Lucifer fully lacked the power to create a new Universe, and the laws of the old Universe would still be in full force and effect and operate even through the Mirror. Thus, while light and dark may not have mixed while the Mirror was in place, Intelligences were still subject to the laws governing life and existence, laws requiring progression and faith to live. In effect, Lucifer's followers were so shortsighted they felt that since they were alive today, they would be alive tomorrow, regardless of the laws underpinning their ability to exist."

Ranier was still troubled by how Lucifer and his followers were so unable to consider the consequences of their actions. He wondered, if God was all-powerful as claimed, why God could not convince them otherwise. It seemed there had to have been more done to save or convince these people. Ranier's mind raced thinking about all he was hearing, yet his heart remained troubled.

James again let Ranier think for some time. James knew the truth did not always bring immediate peace or comfort. Often, it took time for a person to evaluate, test, and have the truth sink in. James remembered how he had sought and longed for another way, a way of peace, ease, and comfort. He too had struggled long and hard to understand what suffering did for life and why Lucifer's plan would ultimately fail. He knew it took time, pondering, and ultimately, faith.

Even though James knew what Ranier was thinking, he waited until Ranier voiced his thoughts. "What did God do to try and convince these people that Lucifer was wrong?" Rainer finally asked.

James smiled at the question, but answered it in a serious tone. "*Everything*" he replied simply. "God tried *everything*." James was quiet for a minute. "Ultimately though, they did not desire to live if they would have to suffer at some point. They did not want to experience any more pain, and so they readily accepted the pain-free existence offered by Lucifer.

"In the way of more detail though," James continued, "Elirah began the work to roll out his plan whereby all of the inhabitants of the Universe, both those on the Other Side and on Heaven's side, could make it to a new existence based in love. Since Elirah, Charity, and Saytah had foreseen the ramifications of the Mirror breaking long before it actually did, they had worked to see the course of action that should be taken to save the Universe from the breaking of the Mirror.

"Together, they had agreed on the Plan of Salvation, as Saytah also, through his own work, had come to the same conclusions as Elirah. The Plan would ultimately bring so much more to the Universe than had ever existed before. Now that pure love was in existence in the Universe, the essence of which was held by Saytah as he held Charity's essence, Elirah and Saytah could perfectly see the details needed to bring about the Plan of Salvation.

"Basically, Elirah and Saytah knew the only way to change the destructive cycle of the Universe was to form an entirely new Universe based on different laws, laws which gave life through different means other than through destruction, pain and suffering. Many thought this to be impossible since life was created by dividing something in existence into a positive and negative form. They refused to understand the importance of Saytah though, since with the creation of Saytah and his abilities, the balance of positive and negative, light and dark, was not 50/50, which is what made life possible in the first place.

"Even now on Earth scientists try to understand why the balance of positive and negative matter is so far tipped to one side. The relative amounts of positive and negative matter are not equal because when a life is created, a portion of the negative, or dark, side of the divided material is consumed. Divisions do happen which do not create life, but the excess positive, or light, matter which exists is an indicator of the level of life in existence in the Universe. One reason evil can never ultimately defeat good is because the darkness is consumed to create life, so when there is life, there is more good, positive matter in existence to accompany life. The only way darkness can be consumed is to have light in existence that isn't subject to annihilation.

"However, Elirah and Saytah were able to see that a complementary type division, instead of a destructive type division, was possible. They knew they could construct a new Universe by dividing material into a complementary form that did not annihilate upon contact with its opposite. Instead, when these two forms came together, they could perpetuate and create more under the right conditions."

James knew this was hard for Ranier to fully follow so he decided to offer some examples to him. "Think of light and dark Ranier. It is impossible for light and dark to be together in the same space. One removes the other. Light and dark are an example of the destructive type division that existed in Heaven as the two are always incompatible with each other, yet are a product of the same material. However, on Earth as we work towards a new existence, Elirah and Saytah also gave us a complementary type division that forms the basis of our life on Earth—they gave us males and females.

"A male and female can exist alongside each other. The presence of the male or female does not destroy the other, and when the male and female come together under the right conditions, new life is made. Thus, light and dark are a remnant of the old Universe, while male and female are at the basis of the new Universe Elirah and Saytah planned to form. The new Universe is patterned and built on the basic foundation of complementary opposition, of male and female, making family the basis for Heaven and the Universe to come.

"Elirah's Plan allowed us to come to a world where we could fully experience the old Universe as well as the new Universe. The destructive type opposition laws are in effect on the earth, as are the complementary type opposition laws. Light and dark constantly attract each other in the world. To help us daily recognize these things, God placed symbols all throughout our existence. For example, think of the 3 primary colors, red, yellow, and blue, which form the basis of every color visible to the human eye.

"With the Mirror in place, all of the light in Heaven appeared yellow, instead of white, as the effects of the darkness on the Other Side still permeated the Mirror, as ultimately its forces, effects, and pulls transcend any object in its way, just as the pull of a magnet can transcend physical barriers. Similarly though, the darkness was always slightly blue, as the effects of the light also made it through the Mirror into the darkness, just as the sky is blue when the darkness of space is tainted by the light of the sun.

"Thus, yellow represents our existence on the Heaven side of the Mirror, while blue represents existence on the Other Side of the Mirror. On Earth, Jesus is often portrayed wearing a blue sash to represent overcoming the darkness, and the fact his light always shown in the darkness, causing it to be blue instead of black."

"What about red then?" Ranier asked. "It is one of the primary colors as well."

"Red," James replied nodding, "represents the new Universe, the one founded in love. Red is symbolic of Saytah's, or Jesus', blood, and how he and Heavenly Father sacrificed his life for us, and how Charity sacrificed her life. Red is symbolic of the laws in place in the new Universe, and Jesus is often depicted as well with a red sash, symbolizing his completion of his great sacrifice and change to the first being made under the laws of the new Universe. Together, red, yellow, and blue combine to create all of the colors we can see on the earth, representing that our existence is a product of the light and dark, or destructive opposition, and of love, or complementary opposition.

"Think about the color green. It is the product of yellow and blue, or light and dark. Green is the color associated with life in the plant kingdom, and is a vivid symbol to our souls that our old life, which still plays into our life on Earth, is a combination of light and dark. Plants have to be nourished from the ground, or Other Side of the Mirror, but also receive nourishment from the sun, or light side of the Mirror. Because they draw life from both sides, their life is reflected in the color green, which is the combination of yellow and blue.

"Green highlights a truth about life on Earth—we are all products of a divided existence, drawing life from the dark and light of existence. As humans, we have impulses generated from the dark, or 'natural' natures inside of us, as well as impulses generated from the eternal potential inside of us. We often struggle understanding who we are due to the dual source of our nature on Earth, but this duality gives us the opportunity to chart our own course and decide for ourselves who we want to be.

"Ultimately, God planned the earth in such a way so as to allow us to experience and see for ourselves which life we preferred. If we chose to embrace life, family, and other principles of goodness, we would qualify to be 'born again' into the new Universe. If we still held firm to the old Universe and the type of person we were there, we would remain as we were and be taken to a similar telestial type kingdom. Ultimately, Elirah's plan allowed us to decide for ourselves as to who and what we wanted to be and what laws we wanted to be governed by."

"Why decide for ourselves though?" Ranier asked. "If God knows everything, why couldn't he just decide for us? I still don't understand why suffering is a part of things."

"The human spirit Ranier is a strong, independent creature. It resists force and compulsion. If you are forced to give something nice to someone, you feel resentful, hateful, and angry. However, if you choose to give something nice to someone, you feel happy, peaceful, and good. Being forced to follow something creates darkness. Agency to choose consequences is the only way we can be happy, and the only way justice can truly exist.

"If God chose life for us, we could blame him for things, including the suffering involved with life. If we choose for ourselves, and are responsible for our own actions, we can blame only ourselves. Remember, due to the old Universe, darkness and suffering brings life. The winter freeze stimulates trees to bear fruit for another summer. A bad year makes you search for happiness for a better year. And a bad life..." James trailed off for a minute, "causes you to search for eternal happiness.

"Without the pain and suffering, none of us would ever be motivated to climb the peaks and do the work necessary for eternal happiness. As it is our will that has to change, we have to do the work as our will is the only thing that is eternally our own. Ultimately, the Universe requires that you be the master of your destiny. God gives you what you need to succeed, but you have to accept it and become something on your own accord."

Even with these explanations, Ranier still struggled feeling life was fair. Others had so much, and he had so little. He lost his precious mother at such a young age. His entire life was one of pain. Others seemed to have so much and suffer so little. If darkness and opposition were really necessary, why didn't others suffer as he did? Why did he need more suffering than others did? He still felt he would never understand all of this.

Chapter 10

A FTER STEWING FOR SOME TIME, Ranier said in a voice laced with some impatience "I am confused about something with agency. I have heard people in the past speaking of agency, but see differing opinions on what it means to have agency. Many people say God can't give them commandments, or a church can't tell them what to do, because they have agency. Others though seem to God gives agency, commandments and law together, or, in other words, he limits agency."

"Yes," James said, "many confuse what agency, freedom, and accountability mean, and don't understand that law is required for agency to exist. Anyone who claims agency means that they cannot be told what to do seriously misunderstands the concept. The word agency, itself, comes from the same root word in Latin as does agent. The Latin root agens/agere means 'to drive, act, or do.' Agents are given power and trust to act for a principal, and they have the ability to carry out acts in the name of the principal. Agency is the bestowal of a trust, power and authority from another.

"On Earth, God gave us all everything, including the ability to breathe. Each of our talents, abilities and strengths come from God. Think about professional athletes. While they had to work hard to develop those talents, they still had the innate ability inside them to reach certain levels of expertise, while many others on Earth, no matter how hard they work, will ever be able to compete at the same level as certain professionals. Each of our abilities is a bestowal of trust by God, coupled with the authority to use those abilities, in a good way. In other words, we are supposed to use them to make the world a better place.

"However, the use of our agency, or trust from God, is accompanied by strict laws. God will not tolerate our misuse of the abilities he gave us, especially when we use them for self-gratification or to harm others. People, like you mentioned, get upset and say God should not tell them what to do because they have agency. They want to be able to be a god unto themselves basically, dictating their choices as well as the results those choices produce. They want to be able to lie to a spouse and yet find fulfillment in the relationship, they want to be able to sleep around with multiple partners and experience deep and abiding peace, or they want to be able to live after all of their carnal natures and experience the immense joy and blessings possessed by God—a being who gave up all of his carnal nature in order to experience such things.

"Certainly 'agency' can be partly defined by our ability to choose, as we choose how to utilize the trust given to us by God, but it is much broader. To fully understand agency, we have to recognize we are agents acting pursuant to the bestowal of trust, power, and ability to impact the lives of others. We must remember that agency is a power to act, yes, but it is really a power, from God, to act, for God, as agents are those bestowed with power from another to act for that other. All agents receive restrictions and instructions on the proper use of the power they receive, or receive 'laws' to govern their use of the powers they received. All use of any power from God is governed by law, just as everything in our existence is governed by law."

"Why is there so much law?" Ranier asked. "It seems the law takes away our true ability to decide, as the decision of what is 'right' is already made for us, and there is no room left for us to chart our own individual course. If there is a law governing everything, then everything would already have the decision made of what should be done."

"You've never been one to be afraid to ask the critical questions Ranier" James said with a laugh. "Well," James said as he glanced around for a quick second while thinking, "I'm sure we will be given the time to answer your question. But, to fully answer it, we have to circle back to the beginning again to understand law and its role in our lives.

"The only way to create something at a higher level of existence, meaning an improved level, is to divide things into opposites and give them an identity. In the beginning, the first division from the Intelligence Stream was light and dark. Light and dark each have an 'identity', or set of laws, establishing light and how it works, along with its opposite. In order for light to exist independent from the Intelligence Stream, it has to have an identity that makes it light. When something is identified, or given criteria or laws establishing its identity, immediately a line, in essence, exists, dividing the light from everything that is not light.

"When things are given an identity, then the thing's opposite has to come into existence as well. When we are given 'life', an identifiable attribute, its opposite, death, also comes into existence, as death now defines or identifies everything that does not have life. Life and death are separated from the Intelligence Stream, just as sweet and bitter, virtue and vice, and health and sickness are separated and divided. All things that form our current existence, except for true Godlike love, were divided from the Intelligence Stream.

"We all enjoy sweet things. In order for the attributes of sweet to exist, there has to be some type of defining law giving sweet an identity, or characteristics, attributes, and expressions which allow us to recognize 'sweet'. Once sweet has an identity or definition, we can experience it, but we can also experience its opposite, as we have to be given the ability to experience whether or not the sweet is there. In order for us to have the ability to detect the sweet, we have to have the ability to detect its absence as well, or to detect bitter. In order for anything to exist, or be identifiable, the thing it is not also has to exist and be made identifiable to us, as we can only have the power and ability to recognize that something is there if we can also recognize that it is not there.

"Consider light for a moment. Our eyes were given to us to discern things of light. They can see light when it is present, but in order for them to see light, they had to be set up to recognize the attributes of light. In order for them to recognize light, they had to be able to recognize when no light was present, or be able to recognize darkness. You cannot have eyes that see only light and never see darkness, as the ability to detect the one thing always includes the ability to detect its absence. Otherwise, we would never be able to discern when it is present or not."

James paused for a moment. "I know this can be hard to follow" he said after a minute of watching Ranier.

"Yes," Ranier agreed, "it will likely take me some time to think about."

"Well," James said with a smile, "it's the same for all of us. We all want to be able to exist without bad things, but 'good' can only exist if its opposite exists, just as with everything else. Something can only come into existence if its opposite also comes into existence, as nothing can be given shape or form without attributes identifying what it is, which means that there are attributes that have to identify what it is not.

"Ultimately," James continued, "it is only through experiencing something and the opposite of something that we truly come to learn and progress. In order for me to truly comprehend sweet, I have to have experienced something bitter. In order for me to experience acceptance, I have to have experienced hate to have a full knowledge and appreciation of what acceptance entails. To truly understand what something is, you also have to understand what it is not.

"Each attribute, thing, or identity in existence has to have laws surrounding it, defining it, and making it what it is. Sweet does not just exist, it had to be created, and to create it, it had to first have rules dictating what it is and—this is important—what it is not. God made all of these things and created everything good, as every good thing comes from God. To define something as good though, the bad, or its opposite, had to be defined as well, otherwise nothing would exist.

"Think about the earth for a minute. The earth operates under the law of gravity. Gravity gives a foundation upon which to operate. It makes things predictable, and the law of gravity is always in operation. People on Earth can readily see, with their limited earthly senses, the benefits of gravity, and people don't complain and claim it takes away their agency. However, gravity makes it hard to fly, jump, or climb, and gravity makes it hurt when we fall. Gravity has killed many people, and yet we don't demand that gravity stop working or that we should be able to dictate our own results when we jump from a high location.

"When it comes to spiritual laws though, the ones we can't readily see with our earthly senses, we immediately scoff and demand that we should be able to dictate our own results. We claim our agency is being taken away when we can't dress the way we want, consume the things we want, or view whatever movies we want. These laws are no different than gravity though. They are always in operation, and are essential to creating attributes of good that allow us to experience joy, peace, and the true beauty life has to offer.

"Like gravity, law is essential to bringing a certain level of functionality to the Universe, which functionality is required for life and freedom to exist. With gravity in place, you have the freedom to walk, run, and travel as you please. You have the freedom to build a home, work, and prosper, all due to gravity keeping you and everything else in a predictable place. Gravity still allows you to work and move, but it provides a basic level of functionality necessary for freedom to exist. Otherwise, we would all just be floating, along with all of the other particles in the Universe.

"For freedom to really exist, foundational laws are necessary. In the world, you have money. If you want a true freedom of trade, you need to have standards in place, standards defining what is a dollar and what is not. When you have standards, the freedom and ability to trade are greatly enhanced.

"Driving is another example. Some people may argue freedom and agency should mean they be allowed to drive on the opposite side of the road or not stop at red lights. However, the basic driving rules in place provide standards whereby we can all be free to travel as we please. We can get in the lanes that are going in the direction we need to be. We can navigate intersections, and we can, ultimately, progress and improve as we are able to function in a far more productive way with the foundational driving laws.

"Some people want to move away from laws though. They want to get rid of restrictions. When this happens, however, it destroys our ability to live and work together. The absence of law devolves to chaos. If there were no rules whatsoever on the roads, the roads would be useless, as they would be so packed with cars trying to go all sorts of directions that nothing would ever get accomplished.

"Ultimately, freedom only exists if the laws in place reflect the proper balance between the extremes of no law and too much law. Besides creating an identity for everything in existence, law has to exist because there is more than one being in existence. As soon as our Universe contained more than one individual being, serious issues existed in how to allow the beings to interact. If the beings were given the power of interaction, they then would be able to hurt or harm another being. Ultimately, as we are all connected through family ties and Intelligence ties to the Intelligence Stream, every one of our actions impacts another being, for good or bad.

"Since we all interact and exist in the same Universe, the law has to govern what happens when we interact in good or bad ways with each other. God allows us to interact, as it is through proper interaction with others we come to truly experience joy, but those interactions have to be governed, just as driving on the road has to be governed. Some laws are like gravity, always acting on us in a way we can't escape, while other laws dictate what we receive as a result of our actions. Either way, the laws are there to create an identity for everything we experience, and without the laws, we have no experience. Oftentimes, we don't believe laws exist because we can't readily see the results with our earthly senses."

"Why aren't we given the ability to sense everything that is happening?" Ranier asked. "It seems we would all make better decisions if we could see what is happening."

"Yes," James replied, "we might make different decisions if we saw everything, and God certainly has not given us all of the senses that exist. We only have five or so of countless senses that exist. However, the purpose of our existence is not just to see things, or hear, taste, touch, or smell things. We are here to determine exactly what we want with our existence. We were born into this state specifically to lack knowledge, as we can only come to know truth when we experience its absence. However, all of us are born with a carnal side and a spiritual side, each of us is given light from Christ, and each of us has a will.

"Ultimately, life and existence require work, progression, and sacrifice, as well as suffering, hardship, and endurance. To achieve anything good, we have to pass through bad. Some beings don't think the good is worth the bad, and they never want to suffer. Internally, ultimately, their unwillingness to suffer means they have no desire to exist. God does not want to force any being to eternally be in a place where it isn't happy or content.

"Because of that, God placed us in an environment where we would act on our ultimate desires. Our lack of knowledge and lack of senses serve to cause us to act based on what we really want with our existence. If we desire an existence free of work and pain, we will choose to consume the things that bring short term pleasure and eventual death and reject the things that bring lasting happiness. The laws and their attendant consequences allow us, ultimately, to choose life or death.

"We will all get what we want and desire out of our existence, and no law stands in the way of that. If we want lasting happiness, we will go down the road to lasting happiness. If we have no desire to traverse the depths of pain and suffering on that road, then we will choose another road, one that suits our desires.

"Our desires—not our knowledge—are the great dictator of our destiny. God promised all of us he would give us the power and ability to traverse any road necessary to accomplish our desires. The power given to us by God is our agency, and we are endowed with the ability to chart our own course based on our own desires. Just as God made the land, the sea, and the air to enable us to travel and move according to our desires, so too he made everything necessary for us to travel our own life based on our own desires.

"Due to the laws necessary for our existence, there are limits on where our desires can take us. A dog, for example, no matter how much it desires it, can never be a human. Dogs were created with certain identifying characteristics. If the dog rejects those characteristics and desires something else, it is rejecting its eternal life. If the dog desires eternal life ultimately, it will seek to appreciate what it is instead of what it is not, and will change its desires accordingly.

"On Earth, there are many people searching for their identity. They do not desire to remain in the state in which they were created, and they seek to obtain another state of existence. They look for identity through surgeries, vulgar expressions, revealing clothing, alternative lifestyles, commandment breaking, or a whole host of other things. Unfortunately, they often do not look for an identity in eternal things, and the identity they create for themselves on the earth will be entirely lost when they die. They can't take a piece of that identity with them, as that identity goes against the eternal identity associated with life."

Ranier had been deep in thought listening to James, but suddenly he could sense a vast stretch of dragons surrounding his location, and he realized the things around him were changing to match the conversation. Nothing seemed fixed about where he was, and he struggled maintaining any sense of location since everything could change in an instant. Gasping a little at the presence of the dragons, Ranier tried to understand what was happening, but the dragons were gone as quickly as they had come. "What was that?" he asked James in surprise.

"The dragons," James steadily replied with no hint of surprise in his voice, "are a prime example of chasing another identity. The dragons were some of the most majestic creatures created. They were very intelligent, and much loved by the other Intelligences. However, the dragons chose to be angry with their identity, and sought to become human. They coveted the attributes humans had, and were not happy with their existence.

"The dragons did everything they could to take on a new identity, one not given them by God, and one not part of their defining characteristics. The more they worked to assume a new identity, the unhappier they became. Eventually, when Lucifer started the War in Heaven you have heard referenced, the dragons joined the fight against God, as they wanted to be the author of their own existence, to write the defining characteristics of who they were. There was simply no way though for the dragons to become human, as doing so would destroy their very essence. The dragons remind us of the importance of reaching to God to understand the purpose and characteristics of our creation, instead of relying on the things we desire to drive our understanding of ourselves.

"For us to understand who we really are and to find our identity, we have to examine the laws in place that define what we are and what we are not. Identity comes through learning to appreciate what we are, as opposed to desiring what we are not. As we strive to take on things that we are not, we are destroying our own life and our eternal life as we can only live under the identity we were created with.

"In other words, to understand our identity, we have to come to understand our roots, the purpose associated with our creation, and draw near to God, the author of our existence. The closer we draw to God, the more we are able to understand about ourselves. The further we remove ourselves from God, the greater the loss of identity within."

Ranier interrupted for a moment. "You know many people, of course, claim that no laws should exist governing them and they should be free to choose to be a man, woman, dog, or tree, as they see fit. Like the dragon, I guess, they are upset at the notion that there are bounds, laws, and commandments set around their identity, their actions, and their desires. Their desire is to exist, but to have no law governing them, as they claim freedom and agency only truly exist if there is no law compelling them to one action or another."

"Yes," James agreed. "The thing they miss though is the contradiction in their desires. They want to live, but they want to live under the terms of their own making. We only live, though, because we were first made.

You could say, to follow a common example from Earth, that they want to be a chicken before being an egg. A chicken can only exist because laws were made to allow it to exist. The laws are absolutely essential for the chicken's existence, and a chicken cannot alter the laws defining its existence without altering its own existence, as chickens, and the rest of us, only exist due to the laws allowing us to exist.

"The dragon could only experience life as it did due to the characteristics and defining laws of its creation, and if it changed any of those to change its identity, it would have lost the thing that made it possible for it to think, act, or feel in the first place. It would have ceased to exist in its quest to become human, as the essence of the dragon was dragon, and to change that essence to human would have meant the dragon essence ceased existing. It is impossible for an essence to be two things at once.

"We receive our ability to think and act due to the laws in place defining our existence, and if we seek to be free of those identifying characteristics that allowed us to think in the first place, we are seeking to be free of life itself, as life can only come through the identity we are given."

Chapter 11

J AMES PAUSED FOR A LITTLE while to get a sense of how well
Ranier was following things. James knew the laws of identity were
not always immediately understandable, and that he probably had
not done the best job in explaining things. James glanced around at their
surroundings to see if anything had come in to view that would signal
anything else needing to be talked about.

God often gave his messengers, like James, the things they needed
to reach the hearts of those they talked with. In the Spirit World, the
environment was also a gift to assist, as it would change based on pieces
or things still needing to be discussed, such as when the dragons came
into view when talking to Ranier earlier.

As the environment would always respond to the person around it,
the general feelings and attitudes of a person could be quickly discerned.
However, sometimes there were questions too fine or specific to trigger
a response from the environment, and so it was always important to
still wait to see if there were any lingering questions. Sensing a general
tranquility to the environment around them, and sensing no questions
from Ranier, James continued the discussion.

"Freedom and agency only exist" he said as he continued in his
teaching tone "because certain foundational laws exist. Foundational
laws are absolutely necessary to be in place before anything can exist,
and those laws have to define what it means to exist and interact. We are
built on foundations of law, and any attempt to redefine our foundation
is an attempt at death. Our power to think, exist, and experience come
only because of the foundational laws upon which we are built, laws that
define thought, existence, and experience.

"Freedom and agency mean we have the power to decide to follow
the laws defining our entire existence and obtain eternal life, or to follow

other paths leading away from our identity, which take us to a place of non-existence, or eternal death. God shows us the way to obtain eternal life, and it is up to us to follow the terms of our existence. We are powerless to create or change the laws of our existence, and we only have power to decide if we accept our defining characteristics, which is the pursuit of life, or if we reject the characteristics, which is the pursuit of death.

"As an example, on Earth our bodies required food, which we had to consume on a fairly consistent basis. It requires work to find and obtain food. If somebody was upset about always being 'forced' to eat food to stay alive, they might try to find alternative solutions, or might pursue a path they think is the ideal way for an existence to operate under. However, if they stop eating, which they have the agency and freedom to do, they will die. If they choose to eat, they can continue to live and enjoy life another day.

"Just as with food, so too does life, especially eternal life, come through obedience to the laws that create our ability to exist. Freedom and agency never meant the ability to write our own laws and define our own existence, as the change to any governing law is a change to our own existence. If we want to exist, we do so under the conditions that caused us to exist. If we reject those conditions, we are ultimately rejecting life itself.

"This is why the scriptures always refer to 'life and death' as being our only two choices ultimately, as our paths in life lead us to one of the two conclusions. Because of this, and going back to your question, laws do not predetermine our destiny. This is so as the law identifying life identifies it as a voluntary choice, meaning we have to choose whether we live or die, in the eternal sense.

"The most interesting thing about life," James continued while reflecting deeply on this subject, "is that life has to be chosen. There are no conditions under which a being can be forced to exist eternally against its will. Ultimately, we have to have our freedom and agency to choose life or death. If this choice was ever taken away from us, we would die spiritually and at the Intelligence level. All of us exist due to our choice to exist. None of us were created against our will. There are many Intelligences that chose to never take the next step to become a spirit. There are many spirits that never took the next step to obtain a physical body, and there are many on Earth who will never take the next step to receive of God's glory.

"Why is that?" Ranier asked. "I'm still confused about a few things, such as death, as I still don't grasp how the Devil functions if he's supposedly 'dead'. I'm also still confused why someone would reject eternal life and choose death instead."

"Yes," James said nodding his head, "to a being who is choosing life, it can be hard to comprehend. We all have, at one time or another, rejected life in some way though. Remember, Saytah had to live on the Other Side of the Mirror to be able to bring life to the Universe. Life takes work, life takes sacrifice, and life takes change. Life also requires that we pass through darkness, that we overcome, that we strive, and that we suffer. Many of us simply decide life isn't worth the work, and we turn instead to the pleasures of the day that allow us to die without feeling what is really happening.

"As to the spirit and its relationship to death, our spirit bodies never do die, as spirit matter will never come in contact with its counterpart, but the life or Intelligence that powers the spirit body can die. The light of Christ, as well as our own Intelligence, power the life in our spirit. Our own Intelligence can only exist with a connection to Christ in it, and when we remove ourselves from his light, we die inside, and leave behind a spirit body that continues functioning only at a basic level. Lucifer and his followers have almost entirely died spiritually. They have removed the light of Christ from themselves, and given themselves wholly to mind control and the powers of darkness.

"Internally, they are dead, or almost entirely dead, but their spirit body lives on, and is used by Lucifer to help accomplish dark works. Currently, they keep their Intelligence somewhat alive by possessing the bodies of people on Earth. They can enter into individuals when those individuals make mistakes and sin, and they feed off of the light of Christ present in those individuals. They are absolutely desperate for people to sin, as it is the only way they can remain alive inside. It's sad to know our sins literally feed them, or allow them the ability to continue their dark works."

"Isn't feeding off of someone else a bad plan for existence though?" Ranier asked. "It seems that one day, there won't be anything left for them."

"It certainly is a bad plan," James nodded in agreement, "and is not an eternal one. The interesting thing about choosing death is that no one chooses death today, but they are okay with it tomorrow, or in the future, but since the future hasn't come yet, most act like it never will. When you live without faith, you live without a belief that the realities of tomorrow will ever arrive.

"The path to death maximizes pleasure along the way, to help stop any feeling of dying. Everything about Satan and his followers makes them leaches. They leach off of the light that exists, and they exploit others for things they need themselves. They have no capacity to produce anything, to sustain life, or to have control of their own existence. They have no power over the law, and—by being at war with God and his laws—are at war with themselves, as they only exist due to God and his laws."

"Is it possible," Ranier asked rather abruptly, "that God made bad laws? It seems to me there should be some other way, some way that doesn't require all of these bad things, some way that would allow for everyone to be saved." Ranier enjoyed challenging James on things and was hoping for some type of anger to show, but he was surprised when James laughed instead.

"We've all asked that question at some point Ranier" James replied. "We all want and desire people to live, and we want to avoid suffering and work. However, God's way is perfect, and is the only way. God is a God of truth, which makes our existence sure, as truth never changes or disappears.

"God has always lived by truth. People often want a God of contradictions. They want God to simply decree we now exist free from opposition even though it is the opposition which allows us to exist. God is all powerful because he lives according to all truth, not because he goes against it and makes some form of a false existence. God is all powerful because he is willing to work and submit to the requirements of life. God is all powerful because he is humble and full of faith, always willing to work and take the next steps to reach the next level of existence. *God is all powerful*," James said with emphasis, "*because he has the power to do all things that can be done*. There is no power in existence to do things that just can't be done."

"I don't fully understand," Ranier said while shaking his head slowly, "you seem to be indicating there are limits on God's power."

"It may seem so at first," James replied, "but it is actually highlighting the limits on our ability to really understand what power is. Consider, for example, a claim often made by people on Earth trying to prove that God does not exist. They often strike at the all-powerful aspect of God, and claim no such thing is possible because God cannot create something too heavy for himself to pick up. They say God's power must be limited, and therefore God must not be all-powerful, because either he cannot create something too heavy for himself to move, or he cannot move something that he created.

"These types of examples though, are examples of contradictions. It is similar to saying that 'God should be all-powerful enough to bless us with life and death at the same moment.' Such things are contradictions, as life and death do not exist at the same moment. They are mutually exclusive, as life is not death, and death is not life. Satan and his followers wanted God to be a God of contradictions and to give them life while on the path of death. They wanted to pick and choose a life of pleasure with a life of health, a life of ease with a life of happiness. Such things though are contradictions, as the two are mutually exclusive.

"No being has the power to maintain a contradiction, as contradictions destroy each other. If God were to contradict himself, he would be destroyed, as are all of us who contradict ourselves, or our most foundational identity. God's all-powerful nature means, and has always meant, that he has access to all power in existence. It does not mean, and has never meant, that he has access to power that does not exist. Power, by nature and identity, implies something that exists, but for power itself to exist, it has to be set with bounds defining abilities that do not exist. If power were everything, it would be nothing, as there would be no bounds to define power and give it form. Therefore, being all-powerful means possessing all power within the bounds of power's identity, or definition."

"It still seems to me though," Ranier said to continue challenging James, "that God created the definition, or identity, of power, and thus should have created different definitions in the first place to avoid these issues. I can understand that once it's set up, things are defined, but I don't understand what compels them to be defined the way they were initially. I guess I'm not seeing why everything had to be set up the way it was. In other words, is God the author, or is something else the author and God simply followed?"

James smiled at this question. "We are certainly reaching the limits of our minds to understand Ranier. You still are subject to linear thinking, where everything has a beginning or an end and moves in a line. However, such thinking is our mortal, or fallen, method of thinking, and is not the eternal way. All of eternity is one great round, or circle. All logic, all reasoning, all life, returns to the same point and builds upon that which has gone before. Everything repeats, but is added unto by the previous round of experiences. It is extremely hard for us to describe the circularity of eternal life to someone still possessing a mortal, linear, mind, but I can try.

"God is the author of everything in existence, but God lives according to truth. Remember, the Intelligence Stream is the light, or product, of truth. All of us in existence are, at our basic level, the product of truth. However, while this next point is hard to comprehend, truth is also the product of the fact that we exist. If only one being were to exist in the Universe, the lone being could define things the way it wanted to and set any manner of laws or definitions, as such would impact only it.

"However, as soon as two beings exist in the Universe, those beings will inevitably interact. Interaction brings with it the power to hurt or help, harm or heal. Thus, as soon as two beings exist, truth is associated with the Universe differently than it was before. Once two beings exist, one could no longer make any laws or definitions it wanted to without impacting the other in some way or another. While the truth associated with the two beings was not created by either being, the fact that a second being came into existence caused different truths to come into play than when only one being existed.

"For each new life that comes into existence, the level of truth adjusts and increases. You could say that life and truth have to balance each other, and so as life is brought into existence the level of truth has to increase to maintain that life. For us as living beings to reach new levels of truth, we have to bring life into existence.

"Prior to creating Saytah, Elirah and Charity considered the full extent of the requirements of bringing beings into existence outside of the Intelligence Stream. They felt if they could create and reach another level of existence, or truth, they should be responsible for setting things up correctly to ensure each being had the necessary conditions in place to allow it to live and progress, as well as to protect it from the choices of other beings who might seek its harm.

"Elirah and Charity planned before they created Saytah. At each level of truth, it is possible to see the requirements of the next level of existence. They could see the requirements of what had to be done to ensure that everyone could exist. They were entirely selfless in their planning, and always looked out for our interests. While they could see certain things, the vision of the next level was only available to the extent of their faith, as they had to first believe that another, higher, level of existence was possible before they could begin to understand what that existence might entail.

"So, to return to your question of whether something controlled God in how he designed the Universe, definitions, identities, and the law, the answer is yes, something did. And what is that something? *It is us.* God could have designed a way to maximize his pleasure and existence by only considering him in the creation of definitions, identity, and law. But the amazing thing, and the reason we worship him, is because he designed everything *for us.* He designed everything to allow us to exist, to progress, and to become like him. At every step of the way, God has gone first and created things to enable us to get to where he is and to enjoy what he has.

"The fact that more than one being is allowed to exist changes the optimal conditions necessary for the Universe. As humans, we are funny beings. We are often upset and feel constrained by the laws and definitions in existence, but we don't understand those are the optimal laws, definitions, and identities that allow us to exist in the first place. Our form, our abilities, the form of other life and its abilities all interact. Changes to our form, or identity, would change the laws governing us.

"There are infinite ways in which God could have designed us, infinite forms we could have been given, but God chose the optimal form and conditions for us and for each level of life. In other words, God balanced all of the competing considerations in creating life to give us the optimal form, identity, and conditions. Any attempt we make to change those forms or identities results, in an eternal sense, in a loss of our potential and what we could have achieved."

"How does God set law and identity? It's probably something I cannot comprehend," Ranier said with some level of energy, "but it is something I do wonder."

James smiled inside at Ranier's question. Ranier never would say thanks or admit that one of his questions had been answered, but he always seemed to express his thanks, or at least his satisfaction with the answer, by asking another question.

"God," James answered, "has unique abilities the rest of us do not have. Saytah, as the combination of Elirah and Charity's Intelligence, has no counterpart. Due to this fact, he can act and cause the Intelligence Stream to divide. He can act, and create and form things, as there is nothing negating his every move, as there is for the rest of us. All of us exist with something else in existence that has the ability to cancel and negate our every act, as we all live as counterparts to something else with equally opposing strengths.

"The reason good always prevails is because, when all is said and done and evil has had its reign and destroyed things, Saytah is always left, as evil cannot touch Saytah. In more of a direct response to your question though, Saytah creates the law and our identity simply by existing. Everything Saytah does becomes law, definition, or identity for us. Saytah cannot move or act without a result flowing from his movement or action. As there is no direct counterpart to negate his actions or movements, the things he does exists for eternity and influences us all.

"Saytah knew of the enormity of the weight on his shoulders to live a perfect life, as everything he does establishes the way that the rest of us have to live by. Saytah, to live a perfect life, followed the directions of Elirah, who planned for everything with Charity before creating Saytah or anything else. Saytah does everything as instructed by Elirah, and Elirah works through Saytah to create, as Saytah is the one with the power and ability to create as he has no counterpart acting on him.

"Thus, in the scriptures we often read of phrases we do not fully comprehend or appreciate. For example, the Book of John discusses the 'Word'. It says 'In the beginning was the Word, and the Word was with God, and the Word was God. The same was in the beginning with God. All things were made by him; and without him was not any thing made that was made. In him was life; and the life was the light of men.'

"On Earth, the reference to the 'Word' is a reference to the Gospel of Christ. This 'Word' is the instruction from Heavenly Father to Jesus, and is how Jesus has always lived his life. Another way to look at it is to say that Jesus' identity is the Gospel, as given by God the Father, as the Gospel, or Word, is the way that best balances all competing considerations of multiple beings existing in the same Universe. As Jesus always chooses to follow the Gospel, or the Word, he becomes the Word.

"Because of this, we are taught that Jesus is 'the way, the truth, and the life: no man cometh unto the Father,' but by him. We have to follow Jesus in everything, as his actions and choices define our existence. To return to your question about being all-powerful, Jesus is all-powerful in that anything he does becomes binding on all of us. However, he does not do things that are wrong, and lives according to the Gospel, or Word from Heavenly Father, as he refuses to exercise his power, or live his life, in a way that would be detrimental to us.

"For Christ, everything he says, does, or touches has power associated with it. Christ can create by the power of his word because there is nothing to negate it. Life and elements even choose to obey his voice, as they recognize that everything Christ speaks is perfect and is optimally balanced to bring about the best for all of existence.

"Because of this, certain things applicable to everyone are revealed to us all through God's prophets, but other things, things that vary among us as individuals, are not revealed through the prophets. Therefore, there is a fair amount not given to the prophets, as individuals need to seek and find what is considered best for them. Ultimately, God's Word carries real power with it, and so God lives a perfect life, to maintain the best situation for us all."

"Why do we all have to experience opposition though, and God doesn't?" Ranier asked. "It seems that Saytah lives above the opposition, and so his life would be quite a bit different than our lives."

James nodded. "Opposition comes in many forms. While Jesus does not have a counterpart truly capable of stopping every one of his actions, his balancing force, or opposition for lack of a better word, is us. All of us are incomplete in some way or another. Our incompleteness causes us to search for companionship. God makes us this way to enable us to experience complementary opposition. We gain far more through our association with others than we would ever gain on our own, and our weaknesses turn into things that bless our eternal existence.

"While most of us seek companionship in marriage, Jesus is married, in a figurative sense, to all of us. He is working endlessly for us, and the scriptures refer to the strength of his connection and commitment to us as a marriage, saying that Jesus is the Bridegroom and the Church is the Bride. While we cannot stop the work of God as we are not true counterparts to God, we can certainly slow the work, bring great evil to the world, and act in all ways that oppose life on Earth and life in the eternities.

"Because of this connection and commitment to us, and despite the opposition we bring to Jesus, Jesus made a way for us to overcome the acts of ourselves and others. He knew we would not live perfect lives and would make choices that did not follow his path perfectly. These choices, he knew, would lead to death for us and death for others, and so he acted to atone for us. He took on everything that man could possibly do to man, and everything that eternal beings could possibly do to eternal beings.

"He descended below all of those things, as it is only through descending below the infinite possibilities of harm that a being can inflict upon another being that he could have the power to correct all of those things. Just as Saytah went to the Other Side of the Mirror to bring life to the Universe, so too he went below all things that beings could do to themselves or each other to have the power to correct anything that takes place.

"As we are, in some limited fashion, a counterpart to Jesus, he lived in a way to negate our effects on the Universe and the destruction we bring to it. He lived in a way to save us all, from the choices of others, and from the choices of ourselves. He atoned by descending below all these things, and brought life through his resurrection. All of this was done to enable us to have a Universe based on all optimal conditions for our existence. His love for us," James said with a pause, and then with a barely audible whisper, "*is entirely immeasurable.*"

Chapter 12

SUDDENLY, RANIER FELT HIMSELF FALLING. Everything seemed to be fading. Darkness was seeping into his body and his mind was blurring. He was quite helpless, but he wasn't scared. It all seemed to be a dream. Thoughts of his past raced in a blinding whirl. Everything was leaving him, even his mother. James had disappeared. Light had disappeared. Everything had disappeared. But he was still falling, falling to extinction. He instinctively knew annihilation was waiting for him.

Ranier pondered on his existence as he fell. While his mind was significantly blurred, he was still aware of the fact he existed. As he thought on what it meant to exist, he couldn't find a satisfactory answer. He only knew pain, suffering, and loneliness. To him, existence meant suffering, and he knew he was done suffering. If life meant suffering, he welcomed death, he welcomed annihilation. That is why, he realized, he wasn't afraid as he was falling. He was welcoming the relief of not existing any longer, and he suddenly understood why others would also choose death over life. It was the only way to avoid pain.

Ranier was unaware of how much time had passed. He realized he was still falling, and was a little disappointed that he hadn't reached annihilation yet. The darkness around him was so thick, it was tangible, it was real. He realized with a start that the darkness wasn't only around him, it was him. Every element of his body was darkness, his hands, feet, body, mind, and heart even, were darkness, and he could only distinguish one piece of himself that wasn't darkness. As he tried to determine what it was that wasn't darkness, he remembered his mother.

He thought about her and the grief she would experience knowing he was forever gone. He weighed that against the grief he knew he would have with existing. He could see there was pain to him if he lived, and pain to others if he died. For him, he felt it was best to stop living, to escape the suffering, and to simply be done. However, his relief would bring pain to others. It troubled him that existences were so intertwined with each other, and that maximizing his own state would negatively impact others.

He continued falling, trying to grasp what gave meaning to existence. There was no meaning in anything for himself, as it all brought pain. He wanted relief from the pain, yet he could sense that his relief would so severely damage his mother. He knew there was something he was missing about all of this, and he was troubled.

The darkness was so real, and he hated everything about it. He also hated everything about life. Except, he realized, he did not hate his mother. Somehow, she gave him a reason to exist. Somehow, she brought meaning to life. Suddenly, as he was falling, he understood something he hadn't before—that meaning in life comes through other people. Thinking only of one's self brought no meaning to life, as it would lead to a place of death due to thinking only of escaping the pain of life. However, thinking of others, and being willing to live for others, brought a sense of meaning and place, and made the pain of life more bearable.

Ranier was beginning to understand that a life committed to other people was a life worth living. As this understanding was growing inside him, his thoughts were disrupted and quickly split as he heard the woman scream "Ranier!" with a voice that penetrated and placed fear to his center. Her voice fully reverberated through him as every part of him was darkness. At the exact same time however, he felt his mother, and, thinking of what made life worth living, reached out to find her, despite the fear present inside from the other woman's voice.

Ranier was suddenly surrounded by light, warmth, and, he realized, love. It was too bright for him to see, and he tried to determine if any part of him was still dark. As he did, he realized he couldn't sense any particular part of him. He couldn't sense his hands or feet, body or head, but he could sense light. The light was an amazing contrast from the dark, and it filled him with hope, purpose, and joy. He was slowly becoming more aware of his surroundings, and although he couldn't see, he felt his mother nearby. He also felt the presence of many others nearby, and he felt they all loved him and cared for him.

He realized after some time that he was back with his mother, back where he had first met her the first time his spirit left his body. Ranier loved this place, and never wanted to leave it again. Some part of him knew though he wasn't here to stay forever, yet. Ranier's thoughts were disconnected and jumped from his experience with the darkness to his experience with the light. Surrounded by darkness, he had no desire to live. Surrounded by light, which was carried by other people who cared for him, he never wanted to stop living. Ranier found himself emotionally torn as he continued thinking on his experiences.

He was jolted back to awareness of his surroundings though as he sensed his mother smile. He could tell she was close by, and his attention focused on her. She was so frail and little, never excelled at much on Earth, and always struggled to get by, but he loved her so much. It was as if all of her weaknesses made him love her that much more because she had tried, and she had loved him and gave everything she had for him. Ranier realized then that he had been blessed to experience the light through his precious mother as a little child, and he had been seeking it ever since.

"Ranier" he heard Elleana say, "I'm so glad to see you again."

Ranier smiled and responded with his thoughts "I'm glad to be with you as well."

After a few moments of both sitting together, Elleana continued "I'm sorry I didn't explain more to you Ranier. I really wanted to, but I struggle having an explanation for everything as I'm still working to understand it myself."

"And I'm sure I'm not the best person to have to explain something to" Ranier said with a smile, "as patience is not one of my virtues."

While Ranier couldn't see, he knew Elleana smiled at that. Ranier then asked, in a slightly more serious tone, "Why do you care about me? I'm as stubborn as a mule, mean, and full of anger. No one else has cared about me, why do you?"

Ranier immediately sensed Elleana was not happy with the question, and he heard her quickly respond "A lot of others have cared about you Ranier. You have just been too hardened to sense their presence, concern, and love for you. But, as to why I love you, it is because I was your mother, I created your body, and with that, I created part of your soul."

Elleana continued "Motherhood is often stated as being next to

Godhood, and it is because it takes you on course where you experience the depths and heights of what life on Earth could offer. God has been down to the depths of what is present in the Universe, but has risen to the top. Mothers sacrifice what they have for their children, and in the process, develop a deep love. Love does not truly exist without sacrifice, and motherhood is the time when a mother passes through the forges of sacrifice."

Ranier sensed Elleana's emotions quivering a little. "I love you Ranier because I sacrificed everything I had for you. And I sacrificed everything I had for you because I created you and had a duty to you. You were mine, and I was obligated to help you. Duty led me to sacrifice, and sacrifice led me to love, just as our Savior's sacrifice for us led him to possess true love for each of us. God created the role of motherhood to involve intense sacrifice on the earth, as through sacrifice we can participate in the ability to become beings of love, just like our Father and Mother."

Elleana paused for a little while to wipe away some tears. "Ultimately, Ranier, love can't be explained in words, it can only be explained by experience. I love you, and that is simply the way it is. Since I sacrificed everything I had for you, I gained an eternal love, one that can never be broken. I have prayed many long hours, days, weeks, and years since my passing that you would be able to know of my love and have a change of heart as it relates to God. There is nothing I want more than for us to be able to live, together, with God again."

Again, Elleana paused to wipe away tears. "God answered part of my prayers by bringing you here and letting you see everything so far. In other words, I asked that you die, temporarily, so we could reach you as it was too hard to do through your physical body which you set to block as much good as possible. God told me though that I had to try and explain things to you, as you wouldn't change for anyone else.

"Due to my own weaknesses and insecurities, I had to work for a long time to feel able to fulfill my role, as I felt wholly unable to perform the task. You are strong willed, intelligent, and outspoken, I am quiet, shy, slow to understand, and weak in many ways. It has taken a lot of faith on my part to finally get you here, but I feel that I have failed already, as James had to step in and help me when I couldn't keep explaining things."

Elleana's tears were falling freely now, but through her tears she said "I'm sorry Ranier. I've given everything I have, but I know it hasn't been enough. Only one thing really matters to me, and that is to be with you eternally with God. But, I fear... I fear I have failed, as I am not smart or wise enough to answer all of your questions, or even," she said with a voice lowered "to convince you that you are loved."

Ranier's heart stung at Elleana's words and he suddenly felt extreme remorse for everything he had done to make Elleana's life hard. Ranier found tears in his own eyes as he searched for words that didn't exist, words that would somehow make everything ok. He knew, deep down inside, that Elleana wasn't looking for words to comfort her, she was looking for him to change, to accept Elleana's love, and to accept God's love. Ranier felt, more than ever, that Elleana loved him, but Ranier still had no way to feel or understand God's love for him.

Ranier, lacking any words to help the situation, reached out and embraced his sobbing mother. His tears fell freely as well as he felt his heart melting under his mother's tears. As he accepted that his mother loved him, he began to recognize a deep and substantial change in his own heart. Her love was erasing his hardness and was bringing light to his life.

After some time of sharing tears together, Ranier finally said to Elleana "Your love has changed my heart more than everything James told me. I don't feel you are a failure. You are everything that matters to me."

Elleana continued to cry "This is the first time I have ever felt light inside you Ranier, since you were a child praying for God to give us food. I watched that light inside you die as we continued to starve, and I did everything I could to keep your light and faith in God alive, even to the point of dying myself as I never wanted that part of you to die. I always felt I failed though as my death extinguished the faith you had inside you and you turned away from God altogether. But, God has let me see light inside you again, and it means everything to me, making it so I didn't die in vain."

Both Ranier and Elleana continued to hold each other as Ranier experienced feelings he had never felt before. These feelings and emotions were all new to him, but they gave him hope and a reason to exist. They were all in stark contrast to the feelings of hopelessness, despair, and loss of will to live that he had experienced in the darkness.

After some time, Ranier's and Elleana's tears both slowed some. Ranier, still holding his precious mother, said "I know we're only a part of the way through this journey. It's probably time for you to finish explaining about God. And, I promise I'll listen better as I would much rather have you share the things of God with me than anyone else."

Elleana didn't yet dare to hope that Ranier would actually listen, so she fought to keep back the sense of hope surging from within her. She had prayed and worked for so long to be able to see light inside Ranier, and she didn't dare lose this moment. She pleaded with Heavenly Father for help, for the ability to know what to say. She felt she always managed to do things wrong, and felt her task of explaining things to Ranier was too much for her to handle. As these fears swept through her mind, she felt the gentle touch of God's Spirit telling her it would be ok. She took a deep breath, trying to put her faith in God and his abilities, and then asked Ranier "What did you last discuss with James?"

Ranier thought for a moment. "We were talking about Lucifer and his proposed plan, agency, and identity. I'm still struggling to fully understand what was taking place though, so I would appreciate hearing it from you. Things seem to make more sense when you are the one explaining."

"What are you trying to understand Ranier?" Elleana asked.

Ranier's eyes narrowed for a moment as he thought. "I don't understand yet the bigger picture. I need a simple way to see things."

"That's lucky for me," Elleana replied with a smile, "because simple is about all I can do."

Ranier enjoyed hearing the humor in Elleana's voice, and smiled in reply.

"I see life this way Ranier. We all existed in the Intelligence Stream. Elirah and Charity combined and each gave half of themselves to create something new, something which had never existed individually—Saytah. As Saytah was the product of two Intelligences, he had no counterpart as dark counterparts would never combine and give of themselves to create something new. Because Saytah had no counterpart, anything he did would not be immediately destroyed by opposition. He could build, act, and create things. He could divide the Intelligence Stream, and began by separating light and dark from the Intelligence

Stream. He became the Creator, and acted under the direction of Elirah, as all things had to be created by Saytah, but Elirah had the plan and knowledge in place on what to create.

"As things progressed, Saytah divided spiritual matter from the Intelligence Stream, separating it into a positive and negative state. Light and dark, to exist, had to be separated in a way that made them attracted to each other, while spiritual matter could be separated in a way that repelled the spiritual positive and negative counterparts away from each other so that they would never come in contact with each other again. Thus, spirit matter creates an 'eternal' state, since it will never cross with its counterpart.

"In that state, God created a Mirror for us to keep light and dark separated so that we would have a chance to grow and develop. It was necessary for us to have a period of time in which we were protected from the dark. However, after a certain point, the Mirror would do more harm than good, and our Heavenly Parents knew it was time to break the Mirror.

"Saytah had created the Mirror with him on the Other Side. Most people in Heaven believed Saytah was gone, but our Heavenly Parents knew he had to still be alive, and they worked for so long to communicate with him. Once they did communicate, Charity learned of the existence of love, and learned it took sacrifice to follow the law of love. She knew it was time for Heaven to move from its old state of the Mirror protecting from cyclical destruction to one founded in love. She knew that existence was built on sacrifice.

"Charity sent her essence through the Mirror to Saytah. In doing so, she sacrificed her existence at that point. Charity gave her essence to Saytah, an essence forged in the realm of sacrifice, and Saytah was able to have her essence to use to begin the foundation of a new universe."

Ranier cut in at this point and asked "Was there any other way to create things from the beginning? Why was darkness a necessary part of things? I'm still struggling to understand why God created any darkness, and why he didn't just begin the Universe as one founded in love. Why all of the suffering to get to that point?"

"Well," Elleana said as she gathered her thoughts, "life had to start somewhere. The law of love is a grand law requiring a lot of understanding, development, and progression to satisfy. Just as an infant cannot walk, talk, or build magnificent buildings, so too a being has to progress to a point where it is capable of satisfying the demands of love.

"Essentially, the Universe had to begin at its most basic, or infant, points, and beings had to progress through the steps required to satisfy higher laws and truths that existed. Once satisfied, beings that follow the truths can build worlds without end founded upon the laws of love, as the proper foundations have been put into place by Saytah. The first foundation to establish was life along with its corollary death, and before we can build further upon this foundation, we first have to decide the extent to which we accept our foundation of life."

Elleana stopped for a moment to think before continuing. "The point we all have to reach is to understand it is only through opposition we truly progress, or truly live. In the state of the Mirror, we were able to grow some, but we were not progressing. Elirah and Charity continued progressing because they were actively working to establish communication with Saytah and get him back. In other words, they were working against opposing forces to find a way to overcome things. Those in Heaven that helped them also progressed further than the others, but many lost faith in Saytah's continued existence and stopped working.

"Think of things on Earth for a little bit Ranier. Kites fly high in the face of opposition. It is the opposition that carries them higher. Planes push against the air, engines burn fuel to produce energy. You push against the ground to jump, to walk, to climb. Gravity pulls you to the earth, but gives you a foundation in which you can climb mountain peaks, step by step. If it were not for the pull of gravity, you would never be able to work or live as successfully as you did. Gravity has consequences, such as falling and getting hurt, but it also brings the ability to live and work.

"Essentially, there can be no force to propel something up if there is no force dragging something down. Our existence has to progress through stages, starting with the very basic forces of opposition. Just as a mansion is not built starting with the roof, so too a universe and existence are not built beginning with love. Love is the crowning piece to our existence, and we had to reach it by building a universe piece by piece, line upon line, precept upon precept, just as a mansion is built starting with a foundation, then raised brick by brick from the foundation.

"To say it again Rainer, opposition brings life. We can only exist with opposition, as our existence in the form as we know it is dependent upon a division, or separation, of Intelligence into counterparts, a positive and negative form, or light and dark. Opposition is the foundation of our existence, as something can only exist if there is something else that is not it. Identity and opposition are directly related, and both are required for life."

Ranier interrupted at this point, "So, if opposition is the foundation, what hope do I ever have of being free of the dark and being free of the pain? From what I know, God promises that those things will be removed."

Elleana smiled warmly. "Yes, Ranier, God does promise that those things will be removed. Since he has worked to fully satisfy all of the laws in existence, including the law of love, he is able to take us to a new level. While opposition is always necessary, it does not always have to be destructive or dark. Opposition can be complementary and build upon each other, and the law of love changes opposition from a destructive state to a complementary state."

Elleana could sense Ranier was still struggling with these concepts, so she quickly added "I have been working to understand this for a while too. I think it will help if I continue with the history of Heaven." Ranier, deep in thought, nodded his head in agreement.

"When the Mirror broke, the loss of Charity was overwhelming for Saytah and Elirah. While it was wonderful for Saytah to be back, it was heartbreaking to have lost Charity. Elirah and Charity had prepared a plan prior to the Mirror breaking on how to deal with and overcome the effects of the break. Saytah, upon receiving Charity's essence, an essence now of pure love, knew it was possible to bring Charity back along with the rest of the plan. This knowledge created hope which gave Elirah and Saytah the strength necessary to continue working.

"Meanwhile, the inhabitants of the Universe were grappling with how to deal with the waves of darkness and other negative matter rushing in to Heaven. Many planets had been separated in the wake of the breaking of the Mirror, families and friends were separated, and their communication channels were broken and destroyed. Slowly, the inhabitants organized into various groups and did what they could to survive, similar to how nations were created on Earth. They each made their own rules and chartered their own courses.

"However, the few who had listened to Elirah prior to the Mirror breaking were actively working to reestablish communication and travel and provide other necessities. Slowly, they were reaching out and establishing contact with each group, and they often found beings completely isolated from everyone else. At this point, many joined in the efforts to reach out and find every inhabitant as each who had been rescued felt a strong duty to reach out and continue rescuing others. It did not seem right to be found in the darkness and not reach out and continue searching for the others who were surely stuck in the darkness as well. With the darkness present, individuals felt the great call to be part of a rescue mission, a mission to bring people back from the things that bring death."

Chapter 13

ELLEANA TOOK A MOMENT TO collect her thoughts and try to calm down. It was hard for her to teach Ranier, and it was hard for her to understand all of these things herself. When she did hard things, she often became anxious, especially when she cared so much about the outcome of what she was doing. She knew Ranier could probably tell how anxious she was, but she tried to calm down and focus on what she had been asked to do. She had to try and trust this would all work out somehow, even in spite of her weaknesses.

Elleana thought back to her childhood. She often dreamed of being a hero or superstar. She had always been a quiet child, reserved, and never had many friends. Her parents were often too busy to pay any attention to her, especially because she stayed quiet and didn't demand much attention. Since no one ever paid her any attention, she found herself feeling alone, worthless, and not loved.

Her path through life had been one of loneliness. She remembered holding Ranier as a baby, overwhelmed by the joy she finally felt having someone to call her own. She remembered the pain of watching him grow and become independent, especially as she sensed him begin to pull away from her. She remembered the tears as he grew too embarrassed to hold her hand in public. But she especially remembered being entirely powerless to provide for him then, and giving everything she had in an attempt to keep him alive.

Elleana knew she was terrified. Everything inside her told her she would fail again, just as she had failed at everything else she had tried. She was certain this was her last and only chance though, and it took all of the faith she could muster to keep moving forward through the paralysis of fear that she would lose him again, the one person she couldn't bear to live without. As the fear intensified, she remembered

James telling her to think instead on the light of Christ, and focus on his love for her. Grasping desperately to do so, she worked hard to shift her focus to the light of Christ, silently begging for help to continue. She needed the power to escape the constant failures of her past.

After a few minutes with her eyes closed, and without explaining the pause to Ranier, she picked up where she had left off once she was sure she wouldn't cry again. "There were many problems for the inhabitants though, and one problem in particular loomed for everyone on Heaven's side" she said. "Namely, in addition to the darkness coming from the Other Side, multitudes of strange beings were coming over as well, the dark counterparts to the light in existence.

"These dark beings were all hideous to behold, were violent, and produced great fear among the inhabitants of Heaven. The dark Intelligences had been able to work with dark spiritual matter to increase their ability to act. Many inhabitants received serious wounds and damage from the beings from the Other Side, and it became critical for the inhabitants to retreat to areas still untouched by the darkness while they tried to find ways to cope with these beings of darkness.

"Elirah and Saytah directed the rescue missions and imparted knowledge of how to deal with the darkness and the beings from the Other Side. Saytah had learned everything there was to know about these beings during his time on the Other Side, and his full knowledge of the Other Side was critical to Heaven's survival at this point. Saytah's ability to spread light through the darkness on the Other Side enabled him to see and learn everything, and he knew more than the dark beings did, as no being of darkness ever comprehended or could see the light.

"At length, all of the inhabitants of Heaven had been found through the rescue efforts of those who heeded God's command, and communication and travel channels had been opened through the darkness to all of the locations where light remained. At this point, Elirah called a council for all of Heaven to attend. It was, and always will be, the Great Council in Heaven.

"There, Elirah presented that he had a plan, a Plan of Salvation, to save the inhabitants of the Universe from the impending destruction amongst them, the destruction due to the combination of the darkness and light slowly self-annihilating. Before giving further details, however, he stated it would be essential to have one worthy to carry out the plan.

"Immediately, Lucifer volunteered himself. 'I can carry out the Plan of Salvation,' he stated. 'I have devised the perfect system of mind control and we can travel back to before the Mirror broke and place this system in every inhabitants' mind. It won't force you to think anything,' he continued, 'it will only prevent you from thinking thoughts that could lead to the destruction of the Mirror, or the destruction of your fellow beings.'

"Lucifer's plan was well received. It seemed that giving up the freedom to think destructive thoughts was such a little thing to give up in order to bring about safety and security for all. The mind control could be injected into a being and would only affect those who thought thoughts that could lead to the destruction of the Mirror. In other words, it would only affect those who could be guilty of bringing chaos to the Universe again, and all others could enjoy their security and tranquility away from the darkness.

"'Anyone who refuses to receive the mind control,' Lucifer continued, 'is obviously not concerned for your welfare or wellbeing. How could any being ever profess to care about you if they are not willing to do what is in the best interest of all and submit to the common good?' Smiling slyly, Lucifer looked straight at Elirah and continued 'How could any being profess to 'love' when 'love' brings such destruction and despair? We've already lost Charity, how many more of you do we have to lose before you see that there is no other way?'

"The applause was thunderous. Most of the inhabitants agreed with Lucifer, as they wanted to survive, and they wanted to be secure in their existence. They liked the thought that any being who professed to love another would act to ensure the security of all. After the applause quieted down, Saytah began to speak. 'Here am I, send me,' he said softly to Elirah, 'I will offer myself up to save all beings, and I will do so in a way that leaves the freedom of the mind, heart, and individual intact, and that brings everyone to a far better state of existence.' Elirah smiled warmly as each inhabitant strained to hear and understand the meaning of Saytah's words.

"After a few moments, Saytah continued 'listen to Elirah and the details of his plan. Again, I will offer myself up as a sacrifice to bring about the plan, and I will do so that you all may live and partake of a fullness of joy, if you so choose.'

"With the inhabitants of Heaven listening closely, curious about Saytah's sacrifice, Elirah then presented the details of his plan. Saytah, he said with confidence and firmness, could create a universe governed by the laws of love, a universe where opposition would not destroy or annihilate, but one where opposition would perpetuate creation and progression. This universe, if created upon the laws of love, would be based on a form of 'complementary opposition,' instead of a form of self-destructive opposition like that currently in existence.

"To be able to create this new Universe, it would be necessary to create a place subject to all of the laws then in existence, but in a manner that would not automatically self-destruct. This place would be subject to all of the conditions of light and dark, and would be called 'Earth'—a place whereupon all inhabitants of the Universe, no matter their level of Intelligence, and no matter whether they were light or dark, could be sent to dwell.

"Earth would be governed by all of the laws that had ever been in existence in the Universe. Saytah would be sent to live in such a way that he perfectly followed each law. By following each law, he would never become subject to the demands, or consequences, of the laws. This would make him free from all constraints of the entire known Universe, and his mission would be to perfectly satisfy even the demands of the law of love, which requires a selfless sacrifice.

"Eventually, to fully satisfy the demands of love, he would offer himself up as a sacrifice for all beings. This sacrifice would require his annihilation to become free from the laws of destructive opposition currently pulling on and having a tie and claim to his parts. Elirah would have to be the one to literally sacrifice Saytah, as it was impossible for Saytah to be annihilated otherwise. Elirah would have to sever the connection where Elirah's and Charity's Intelligence halves had joined together to create Saytah. Once severed, the two pieces could be annihilated as the two pieces, individually, had counterparts."

Elleana paused for a moment, letting things sink in for Ranier. "If you remember, Ranier," she said after a minute, "the story of Abraham and Isaac in the Bible. Most people, including you, are extremely troubled that God commanded Abraham to sacrifice Isaac, but we're taught that the command was in similitude of the sacrifice of Jesus Christ. God was teaching us all about the depths of the pain and emotion he was to experience with the sacrifice of Saytah, and it was a way to teach Abraham and Isaac as well as a way for us to understand."

Ranier broke in at this point "So God had to sacrifice Jesus? I thought he died on the cross."

"Yes," Elleana replied with a nod, "Jesus died while on the cross, but the cross did not kill him. Jesus was immortal and not subject to death or annihilation. That is why Elirah had to sever Saytah's two halves, so that he would lose his protection. Only Elirah could sever it, and that is why it was considered a sacrifice, and that is why the whole law of Moses, with all of its sacrifices, pointed to the great and last sacrifice."

Ranier, after thinking for a moment, said "They don't seem to teach it this way on Earth."

"Yes," Elleana agreed, most fail to see the symbolism in what took place. Lucifer tries very hard to distort our view of God and see him as an unjust being that doesn't love, as that is how Lucifer has portrayed him since the Mirror broke. However, we have to always remember the depth of the love they have for us, and remember all they have done and will still do.

"The purpose of the annihilation of Saytah's Intelligence was for him, as part of satisfying the law of love, to descend below all things and reach the very essence of existence. Due to his ties to us through the light present in each of us, Saytah would be able to take all of our dark parts with him, and have those annihilated and reborn as well. Thus, Saytah would use this time as a means to suffer the pains of the rebirth process for us, if we chose to accept him.

"Once annihilated, Elirah would use his own essence of love, forged through his sacrifices of allowing Charity to be destroyed, his sacrifices associated with living and giving up everything he cared about, and through sacrificing his Only Begotten Son, to create a beacon for Saytah's essence to follow.

"Elirah and Saytah were certain that although an Intelligence could be annihilated, a being's essence never truly stopped existing, and Saytah planned to have his essence follow the beacon created by Elirah. Since Elirah and Saytah knew Charity's essence had survived the destruction of the Mirror, Elirah and Saytah had faith that Charity's essence, and all essences, if refined to be made of pure love, could never be destroyed.

"Saytah's path from annihilation back to Elirah would create a portal to a new Universe where all things could be created under the laws of love and where nothing could be destroyed again. The power of love is so great, Elirah told those at the Great Council, that Saytah would be able to live again. As Saytah would be the last being annihilated, he would bring an end to annihilation, and would bring the beginning of a brand-new state of existence, just as he began our current state of existence. Due to this, Elirah affectionately referred to Saytah as the 'Beginning and the End.'

"At this point, the beings in the Universe fell into much disagreement amongst themselves and the Great Council was adjourned for a short time while the inhabitants considered what they had heard. 'Elirah's plan is impossible' many would say. 'A being cannot return from being annihilated,' others said. 'There is no way for Elirah to have enough strength to actually sever Saytah's Intelligence being, especially since Saytah is all he really has left of Charity,' they continued.

"Yet, every being in the Universe had felt something stir within their hearts as Elirah and Saytah spoke. When the Great Council resumed, Elirah pointed out their feelings and indicated they all were feeling the beginning of love, and it was something that would grow greater and grander the closer they got to it.

"Elirah and Saytah then made a promise to all of the Universe, promising that their plan would work and all could be saved. Sensing he was losing ground, Lucifer also swore with an oath he would do everything necessary to make his plan work. 'There is only one thing we really need,' Lucifer offered, again smiling slyly, 'as Elirah is so into offering up sacrifices to satisfy this so-called 'law of love,' then he should offer himself up as the first to receive the mind control. Once Elirah has mind control in him, the rest of Heaven will follow suit before too long.'

"Lucifer then demanded that Elirah submit himself to Lucifer and provide access to his mind and heart. In other words, Lucifer demanded that Elirah provide his power and glory so that it could be taken and used to bring mind control to the rest of the Universe. Elirah, of course, refused such a request, and said it would deny all inhabitants the opportunity of ever reaching a far better state of existence and would ultimately lead to the death of the Universe as such mind control would stop all further progression, and life cannot exist without progression.

"'Love' Elirah countered back, 'does not require one sacrifice himself foolishly for any cause, it requires a sacrifice for a cause that will make things better for all involved, and your plan will not bring any more good to this Universe. In fact, it will ultimately bring despair and destruction as your plan cannot succeed in bettering our existence.'

"Due to Elirah's rejection of Lucifer's demands to impose mind control, and due to the oath he made to bring his plan into existence, Lucifer then devised plans to use force to impose mind control in all in existence. In Lucifer's mind, the end goal of saving all justified the means of force, since many were too hard-headed to see the relevance of his plan and the benevolence of his heart. When Lucifer decided it was appropriate and necessary to use force to bring about his plan, darkness found its way into his heart. Thus was the beginning of the War in Heaven, which still rages on the earth to this day.

"The War has affected us all, and will continue to affect us all. There have been many tragedies as a result of this War, and many have been lost." Elleana paused, waiting for a response from Ranier while Ranier reflected on what he had heard.

At length, Ranier finally asked "But why? Why is a war necessary? War is so ugly, why couldn't we all just decide on the best way and go with that?"

Elleana nodded in understanding. "Many have asked the same question Ranier. The answer boils down to one simple word—faith. Those who chose to believe and chose to exercise faith could feel the truth of what Elirah and Saytah had spoken. Due to their faith, they knew, or at a minimum hoped, that there was a better way. Those who supported Lucifer chose to have no faith and to have no hope. They simply wanted security and to return to their old way of life—a life with no problems, but a life with no progress either."

"But," Ranier interjected, "I don't see how a being desiring comfort and security would turn into a being at war with the other inhabitants."

Elleana nodded again, "Yes, it is a contradiction and hard to see at first. However, all of Lucifer's ways are contradictory. Remember that Lucifer's plan involved mind control, and since his plan required all in existence to accept mind control, the free spirit of just one in existence, or even the essence of others not then in recognizable existence, such as Charity, would defeat his plan. Lucifer and those who followed him missed one critical aspect of the Intelligence Stream—it always moves.

"In other words, the foundation of our existence is based in always progressing, and thus it is impossible to fully restrain an individual. Lucifer, though, had so much faith in his mind control and the power of the mind, he was convinced his plan would work and would forever restrain our progression. This path, though, would cause our ultimate destruction as progression is what brings life to the universe."

"The ultimate point of all of this," Elleana continued after pausing for a minute, "is that there would always be a being who chose to try and progress as it would eventually become a matter of life and death if no progression took place. Many beings, such as Elirah and Saytah fully recognized and understood this, and thus refused to submit to Lucifer's proposed plan.

"Lucifer, though, placing more faith in his own self and understanding, felt it was the only way. Then, as he placed so much faith in his plan and accepted that it was, in his mind, 'necessary,' 'right,' 'essential,' 'loving,' and the like to save the Intelligences made of light from the darkness, he then accepted that he was compelled to find any way possible to bring his plan to pass. That meant, for his plan, he had to use force to insert mind control since others would not volunteer to submit to his destructive plan.

"This made force and compulsion exist at the foundation of Lucifer's plan as he allowed the end—his goal of safety and security—to justify the means, or the use of force. When others elected to follow him, they fully submitted themselves to mind control, and thus became agents of Lucifer, under his power and control, to go forth and use force and compulsion to implement mind control in the other inhabitants. There are many contradictions in all of this, of course, but the main contradiction is that life cannot be forced. It has to be chosen."

Elleana could sense this was still hard for Ranier to fully understand, and she sympathized with him. All of the inhabitants of the Universe who chose Elirah's plan had wondered at how those who followed Lucifer could turn into the destructive and violent beings that they did, and it took some time understanding the principles at play and the ultimate end of the path and principles that they elected to live by. Few who followed Lucifer believed they would become what they are now, but accepting and committing to certain principles inevitably leads one to the end produced by those principles, just as those who followed Lucifer all were led to the end of force and violence.

After letting Ranier think for a time, Elleana suggested she continue explaining the history as it would help Ranier further understand these matters. Ranier thought for a few moments, and continued to reflect on his own heart and the principles he had chosen to live by. At this point, he wanted to know himself and who he was, but wasn't certain where his path in life was leading him. He thought that Elleana was likely leading him to this point though, so he nodded affirmatively. Elleana smiled, and continued recounting the events at the Great Council in Heaven.

"While darkness was entering Lucifer's heart, the Great Council continued. Elirah was now speaking. 'All of you who follow Saytah will receive an immortal physical body and all but a few will ultimately be taken to the new Universe. In the new Universe, there will be divisions of glory, or kingdoms, where you will dwell based on how close you can come to satisfying the law of love. In the highest, or Celestial, kingdom, all who enter will need their very essences changed to be one of pure love.

"'In other words, they must take on the essence of Charity. They will need to be 'reborn' and fully give up their old being. This will be the only way for them to exist and progress in the universe founded in love. Others who develop essences with good attributes but who fail to develop charity will reside in the middle, or Terrestrial, kingdom. Those who choose to keep their carnal, or darker, natures will reside in the lowest, or Telestial, kingdom.'

"The darkness in Lucifer's heart grew quickly though as Lucifer embraced his plans. 'I will exalt myself above Elirah' he swore, 'as I will make sure this chaos can never be caused again.' Lucifer quickly set to work to gather recruits to aid his cause. 'Finding recruits is far too easy' he thought to himself with a smile, 'as all I have to do is place a doubt in the mind of someone to get them to stop believing in Elirah's plan. Since Elirah's plan requires so much, it is far too complex for any being to fully understand all of the details.'

"Lucifer found much success in raising doubts and producing feelings in others that drove them away from Elirah and Saytah. In a short amount of time, he had secured many of the hosts of Heaven. In order to follow Lucifer and accept the mind control required of his plan, each being had to sever its connection to the light of Saytah, which connection came when they were split from the Intelligence Stream.

Ranier could sense this part was not easy for Elleana. He wondered about this process and what it would entail, and why Elleana seemed to struggle here. Elleana, sensing his thoughts, solemnly said "We lost a lot of loved ones then Ranier. Nearly everyone dear to me followed Lucifer, and it left me quite broken and alone. I felt as if there were many pieces of me that died then. God promised me though he would give me someone who I could love and never have to leave."

Ranier was puzzled by that, as his father had never remained part of the picture. "Who did God promise you?" he asked inquisitively.

Elleana smiled weakly, "He promised me you."

"Me!?" Ranier replied in surprise. "I'm a horrible choice for that. I can't be counted on for much of anything at all. Now you are really making me doubt even more the supposed wisdom of God."

Elleana was not pleased with this response, and Rainer could sense her displeasure. "Don't ever demean God by demeaning yourself Ranier" she said sharply. "What that really means is that you entirely fail to see who you really are, and" she continued with a weaker, sadder voice, "you entirely fail to see everything you mean to me."

Chapter 14

RANIER COULD SENSE THE TEARS falling from Elleana's eyes, and he was stung by Elleana's words. Ranier's mind raced as he thought about how his view of himself projected itself into his view of everything else in the world. He certainly didn't know what he meant to Elleana, especially since she had been gone from his life for so long. But he was deeply troubled, troubled by how a negative view of his own self might cause him to see everything in a false light.

He had never thought on these things before, but he suddenly realized how his negative view of himself and of life in general might project itself into creating a false light for everything else he experienced. He was ashamed at how lightly he had treated what Elleana was saying, and especially how he kept hurting her.

As his regret for what he had said set in, he seemed to be moving away from Elleana. The only words that would come out of Ranier's mouth were "I'm sorry." He heard himself say this a few times, but he felt himself moving farther away. As he tried to understand what was happening, he realized guilt was starting to set in. This was a new feeling for him as he had never allowed himself to feel guilty for anything before and had kept his heart as stone.

He had always valued his emotional strength and refused to ever question anything he had done, always believing it was right, somehow. However, Elleana's tears cut through to his center, and he was stung by all he had done throughout his life. He felt as if his guilt were encircling him, pushing him further away from Elleana.

Most of his being wanted to hide from Elleana in shame. Somehow, her tears over the fact that he couldn't recognize her love for him were too much for him to handle. Yet, even as his being tried to find a place to hide, a part of him also longed to reach out to Elleana. To tell her sorry in a way she would understand that he truly was sorry—and ultimately, though he didn't dare allow this to surface, to accept her love for him. Something inside him longed so badly to be loved, but it went against everything he had built, every defense, every strength, and every piece of himself was built to resist feeling loved, as it also prevented him from feeling hurt.

However, as he found himself torn by these emotions, he realized that the pain had made it into his heart. Despite his years of hardening through his rough life, he had not prepared himself to see his mother cry as she said "you entirely fail to see everything you mean to me." Due to the fact that so many feelings had been repressed for so long, he found that waves of emotion were surging through his heart. Despite this, he also recognized the impossible task of changing everything he had built. Everything inside told him to fight feeling loved as it would only bring pain later.

He remembered the pain of seeing his mother frozen and dead. He remembered shutting out all feeling after that. He could see every decision he had made to reject anything good and to maintain his impenetrable heart. He could see he had survived by shutting out all good as he wanted to avoid all pain since he felt the pain of his mother's death as a child was too much for him to ever experience again.

But now, he was with his mother, and he was hurting her. The person he had become to deal with her loss made it impossible to be with her again. He had refused to believe he would see her again, as he had felt that such a hope would only bring a deeper pain if it turned out not to be true. He could see how his lack of faith drove out all light and hope, and welcomed in the darkness, just as Lucifer's lack of faith had welcomed in the darkness. At this time, he could poignantly sense the extent of the darkness through his being, and he found himself losing hope that he could ever change and be the person his mother thought she loved.

As his mind continued its struggle between emotions, he found himself wishing he could go back to that child crying by his dead mother and do everything over again. He longed for a second chance, but the pain and the guilt continued to increase, and he found himself feeling alone, desolate, and burning inside. There was so much he had done wrong, and so much he needed to fix. He found himself at a point where he wanted to disappear forever to make things better, or where all he wanted was a second chance. He felt himself tearing at the pull of emotions, with most of his being pushing to disappear forever, but a small part of him crying for a second chance.

As he thought about the options, he could see the pain on his mother's face if he were to disappear forever. Deciding he had hurt her enough already, he knew she did not want him to disappear forever. Somehow, he knew that he needed a second chance, and that if given the chance, he could do things right. Suddenly, he heard himself say "I need a second chance." Again, he cried desperately "I need a second chance."

Suddenly, an image of Jesus on the cross flashed through his mind. Ranier did not remember ever praying, but somehow knew he needed to pray now. "Dear God" he cried "forgive me. I'm a lost soul, and I need help. I need a second chance. My poor mother. Please. Help." As Ranier spoke, he felt arms reaching toward him, and his heart was suddenly touched by a hand. The feelings in his heart changed instantly, and he found himself crying. Somehow, he knew he had been forgiven, and he knew he had his second chance. All of this came to him in an instant. He didn't know how he knew it, but there was no doubt about it.

Ranier suddenly started with surprise when he heard Elleana say "It's ok Ranier. I'm still here." Ranier realized he had not gone anywhere, even though he had felt so far away. Ranier was puzzled as he had felt that he had disappeared for an extended length of time. "I'm sorry" he said again to Elleana, and then "Please give me another chance."

"Of course I will Ranier" Elleana replied simply. "I love you too much to give up on you."

Elleana's words swept through Ranier's being and Ranier felt something that he had never felt before. He felt loved, loved by Elleana, and loved by . . . , by . . . , he realized he wasn't quite sure where the other feelings of love were coming from, but they felt good. Ranier again found himself torn as part of him wanted to soak up every minute of the feelings, while the other part of him was terrified about losing the feeling and being hurt again.

Elleana reached out to Ranier, touched by something that had just sunk in for her. "Without faith, Ranier, you will always fear loss. With faith, you can have an assurance you will one day forever be with those you love. You have to exercise faith to enjoy the good there is in our existence. Through faith, I can always be with you. Through faith, we can always be with God. Through faith, we can always keep good in our hearts. You just have to choose to believe."

Ranier knew she was right, but it felt too simple, and he struggled trusting. He felt he had been hurt so many times before that he knew he couldn't just trust again. "Just start with a desire to trust, Ranier" Elleana said encouragingly. "God knows where you are at, and he doesn't ask you to trust everything right now, he just asks that you start, and the place to start is with a desire to believe. That desire opens a place for a seed of faith to be planted. If you carefully protect that desire, your faith will grow and blossom. I'm in the process of having my faith grow. It isn't perfect yet," Elleana smiled weakly, "but it is growing. I'm changing every day. God gives us time, and we develop line upon line, one step at a time."

Ranier still struggled daring to believe. All of this was so new to him, and his guard was down. But, he couldn't deny the light and hope that had infused into his soul as he felt touched and forgiven as he cried for a second chance. His mind was whirling, and Elleana let him take his time to think.

For Elleana, she found herself not daring to believe what she was witnessing in Ranier. She had prayed for so long for Ranier. Daily it had broken her heart to see him suffer so much, and she had missed him so much when she left the earth. She had pleaded with God and begged daily in prayers for a chance to reach him.

During her life on Earth, she had given everything she had for him, and it broke her heart to have to leave him as a child. She loved Ranier so much, as he was the only thing good that had ever happened to her. She had lost most everything throughout her life, and it continued to break her heart to feel she was losing Ranier too. Life on Earth had taught her one thing—nothing else matters except for family.

Elleana had left Earth with nothing, and had taken nothing with her into the next life. She reflected, as she often did, on how she had always been alone on Earth. Ranier was the light of her life since he conveyed love for her when he was a child. Elleana remembered all of the embraces, all of the tears, all of the long nights where she held him telling him it would be okay, especially as she tried to keep him warm during the long nights of winter.

Elleana also remembered the innocent laughter, the things Ranier would say to try and make her happy, the sticks and other scraps he would bring her as "food" that he had found. As a child, Ranier had always wanted to make her life better. Ranier had always wanted to make her happy, and Ranier had always turned to her in his times of distress or need.

Elleana's mind whirled through all of her memories, and she tried to contain her emotions. She barely dared to hope for anything good now that Ranier was with her for a time. Earth had hardened Ranier so much. Life there had beat any of the little light inside Ranier to near nothingness. Ranier was hollow, full of darkness, and hardened. Elleana had pleaded numerous times for God's help. She didn't want to lose Ranier, and it caused her so much pain to see Ranier's life continue on in such pain and suffering. Nearly everything that could go wrong had gone wrong in his life, while nearly nothing had gone right for him.

Yet, God had promised Elleana in the pre-mortal life that he would give her someone to be with, someone she could cherish. Now that she was in the Spirit World, she remembered this promise. However, it was extremely hard for her to exercise faith or hope in this promise, as she struggled to believe it would ever be fulfilled, until now, of course.

After years and years of praying and pleading, she could suddenly see a sliver of possibility as to how God's promise from years ago might be fulfilled. If this didn't work though and Ranier continued on the path towards darkness, she would be totally and entirely crushed. Because of that, she tried to fight back the feelings of hope that kept pushing their way into her heart. The fear of failure made it very hard for her to want to believe, as she didn't want to suffer the loss of hope.

Elleana knew there were a number of reasons that made this so hard for her. The first and main reason is that she still had never seen God since her life on Earth began. She had faint memories of him from the pre-mortal life, but those were mainly associated with the promise she had received.

After leaving Earth, she still had not seen him or been visited by him. Instead, missionaries, like James, would come and teach her about him. She struggled to understand why he would not visit, even though she had been told she was not ready yet. Despite not fully understanding, she was trying to believe in God.

For Elleana though, she had a much deeper struggle than her one with her belief in God. More than struggling to believe in God, Elleana struggled believing—in herself. James and others had consistently taught her that a belief in God meant a belief in herself, or her power to accomplish things. They had taught her that if God was all-powerful, it meant she could accomplish everything she needed to as God could give her the power to do anything truly necessary for her life.

She told them repeatedly she had always failed at everything she tried, and would often cry thinking of her repeated failures. She had no faith in her ability to accomplish anything, and she would plead repeatedly for God to have mercy and change things in her life. From her perspective, nothing had changed, and this circled back to why she struggled to believe in God. She simply did not feel loved.

Tears came to her eyes as she thought about the loneliness, the repeated failures, and the feelings of rejection associated with the night-after-night pleadings and requests to God. Despite her full efforts in prayer, she had felt nothing, seen nothing, and received no relief. This was compounded by leaving Ranier at such a young age, as she felt she entirely failed as a mother as well. If only she had been able to learn enough to hold down a job, things could have been so different for them.

James had listened patiently, Elleana remembered, as Elleana had told all of these things to him. She was explaining why she struggled believing in God, and ultimately, why she couldn't believe in herself. In other words, she had been telling James why he was wrong, why the things he was sharing as a missionary weren't true. In essence, she was saying they were not true because the things he talked about were just not part of her life.

That day talking to James though had softened Elleana's heart. After listening to all of the reasons why she felt God didn't love her, why she couldn't believe in God, or herself, and why she felt entirely alone, James responded with one simple statement. "You felt that way about all of those things that happened Elleana" he had said firmly, "because *you* never truly opened *your* heart to what God had to give you."

Elleana remembered staring at him in disbelief and at first was angry he was blaming her. "Did you not hear me?!" Elleana remembered nearly screaming at him, "I plead daily and got nothing. There was nothing else I could have done!"

James had again waited patiently until Elleana had calmed down a little. "You did plead daily Elleana," he agreed, "but ultimately you were pleading for what you felt would solve the problems in your life. Deep down inside, you did not want what God had to give you. You wanted *your* solutions, not his. The darkness and loneliness are always a sign that we want something other than what God has to give us. Maybe we want a bit of scripture to be different, a bit of history to be different, or a piece of our future to be different. Maybe we want a warm house instead of another night on the street, maybe we want to feel okay in our sins, maybe we want money instead of poverty.

"To find God, we have to open ourselves up to what he has prepared for us. God has prepared the riches of eternity for us, and any of us, at least in the pre-mortal life, were willing to go to Earth to sleep cold on the streets in exchange for the riches of eternity. When we could see what God had prepared for us, life on Earth was an easy decision—meaning it was easy to decide to go through trials and struggles to obtain eternal life.

"However," James had continued, "once we were on Earth we were immediately blinded by what Earth had to offer. Earth offered physical riches, Earth offered acceptance in sin, Earth offered ways to gratify our pride, our lusts, and our passions." Elleana vividly remembered how James' eyes had narrowed at this point as he looked at her. "Earth," James continued, "offered a way for us to enjoy our time destroying our future, it offered the pleasures of today in exchange for the life of tomorrow.

"When you were pleading to God, Elleana, you were pleading for the things of the earth instead of the things of eternity. You wanted short-term relief, God wanted long-term healing and prosperity. As you didn't want that, you kept rejecting what God had to give, and you remained alone and in darkness as you kept rejecting the things he had for you."

Elleana remembered the tears that fell as he had talked with her. Ruby had been there too, and had kindly put her arm around Elleana and held her as she cried. Elleana could feel the truth of what he had said. On Earth, Elleana wanted a house, warmth, friends, a job, all of the things that others had. She wanted to give Ranier the riches of the world, and she wanted God to let her have all of those things to give to Ranier. In the midst of her suffering, she certainly was not interested in the things of eternity.

"I don't understand though," Elleana had said to James, "why did so many people get to experience the riches of Earth? If those are not the things of eternity, why did they get them? In other words, why couldn't I be blessed even a little? A small job would have helped me provide for Ranier, and would have helped to keep him from becoming so hard inside."

James smiled. "Elleana, you have the same heart you left Earth with. You do not see the harm that the things of Earth can bring. You look at those as a blessing, yet they are more of a curse. When you are surrounded with peace and security, you feel you have no need for God, and you trust in your own strength. When you have no suffering, you never reach out for the things of eternity. Suffering causes us to reach down deep inside to discover the true meaning of things, to discover the true meaning of life, or of eternity. Suffering is the catalyst that helps us see past the things of today into the possibilities of tomorrow."

Elleana remembered the sting associated with the truth that rang through his words. She knew, better than anyone, how much she had longed for the things of Earth. She had been surrounded by people who laughed, drove cars, traveled, vacationed, ate whatever they wanted, and who had people to visit and be with. They had jobs, they looked important, they dressed nice, and all of them had a house. Her prayers to God were always that he would give her the things that they had. She based God's love for her in how much of Earth's things she had in comparison to others.

Elleana's mind continued to race through the things James and Ruby had taught her. "Elleana," Ruby had said gently, "the reason the riches of life are not necessarily a blessing is because we did not go to Earth to learn to accumulate things, we went to learn to *let go* of things. God knew all of us were attached, in some way or another, to the things of our first existence. He knew none of those things would last forever, especially after the breaking of the Mirror. He prepared a better place for us, a place far superior to the things we had. Yet, since we could not see it, we struggled believing it existed, or that the work was worth it."

Elleana always felt peace in Ruby's presence, and that moment had been no different. James was good at saying things as they were, but Ruby had a gift to help the message be received with a feeling of kindness and softness to it. Elleana admired Ruby, and found herself wanting to be like her. Elleana remembered Ruby's look of seriousness as Ruby had looked her directly in the eyes while saying "There is great power attached to what God has to give us, and we cannot receive those things until we have *let go* of every pull and tendency of darkness inside of us.

"In other words, we have to *let go* of our pride, our passions, our lusts, our desires for the things that fade away and die, and, in the end, we have to *let go* of our being. In other words, we have to *let go* of who we are, and accept who God wants us to be. Our test is in whether we love the things that will disappear and die more than we love what God has in store for us, and it is a test that the rich, or any that made it to Earth and saw riches, often fail."

Chapter 15

E LLEANA STILL SHIVERED AS SHE thought of Ruby's emphasis
on the phrase "*let go.*" Every time Ruby said "*let go*" something
resonated deeply within Elleana. Elleana certainly had never
judged her success in life on what she was able to happily give up, or let
go of. She had always felt like a failure for the things she did not have.

"Our things" Ruby continued "tie us down and hold us back from
what God has for us. We have to be willing to walk away from everything
the earth or our pre-mortal life offered us. Otherwise, we will never be
prepared to receive the things of God. The test for each of us is ultimately
the same—to let go—whether of the earthly riches we have, or of the
desires we have for the earthly riches we don't have. Charity let go of
everything, and so must we."

Elleana had spent much time pondering and reflecting on what she
had been taught. She had decided James and Ruby were teaching her
truth. Since then she had worked on letting go, on trying to accept what
God had for her. Letting go, she knew, was the hardest thing for each
person to do, but it was the same thing asked of each person. All people,
she knew, would have to give up things they loved and placed great value
on, such as family members, talents, abilities, identifying characteristics
or traits, wealth, etc. All people had to learn to let go of the old to be able
to embrace the new.

Elleana looked at Ranier and again tried to fight back the hope
swelling up inside her. She couldn't handle feeling broken again, she
couldn't handle losing something so precious to her. James and Ruby
had assured her all would be well since God had promised it would be.
Elleana spent years without understanding how God's promise would be
fulfilled, especially as she watched Ranier become more hardened and
suffer through more things each day. Yet, as she sat with Ranier now,

she couldn't believe the promise was beginning to come true so soon. Ranier's heart had undergone a massive transformation in so short a time that she found it hard to believe this wasn't all a cruel dream.

James and Ruby had assured her that God's promise would be fulfilled. But, they also told her she had an important role to play, and it was up to her to reach Ranier during this short time as she was the only person Ranier would truly open up to. The enormity of this task overwhelmed her, and she had plead in prayer for another way.

James and Ruby had reminded her she was falling back to her ways on Earth, where she didn't want to accept God's way but wanted her own way. They assured her God would give her what she needed when she needed it, and reminded her that belief in God meant belief in her ability to do things through God's power. Plus, they had told her, by being a key person in Ranier's change, she would forever be able to enjoy the blessings of being a part of the change that took place.

Elleana realized Ranier had been watching her. She was surprised she had become so absorbed in her own thoughts that she had lost track of what they had been talking about. She stared blankly for a few moments, trying her best to recall their last conversation. Nothing came to her mind though, and she remained silent. Ranier also remained silent as he gazed intently. Neither one spoke. There was something that seemed to be telling both of them to listen, but neither seemed able to understand what it was they were listening to.

After some time, Elleana heard, ever so faintly, the sound of a woman screaming "Ranier!" Her eyes darted about as she tried to locate the source of the sound, but she knew she wouldn't find it. She looked at Ranier and could see he was very troubled. The sound seemed to be coming from inside him.

"What is that?" Elleana finally asked. Ranier's head snapped up at the sound of her voice.

"I was going to ask you," Ranier said with fear in his voice. "I can't escape her, and she is always screaming my name. Every time I hear her voice I am surrounded by darkness. I don't know who she is, or why she wants me. And, I certainly don't understand why God lets me be tormented by her."

Elleana shivered. She didn't want her hopes about Ranier's potential for change to be crushed, but the woman's voice was quite unnerving.

Elleana knew she shouldn't be able to hear the woman's voice so well, and that Ranier shouldn't either. The fact he could hear it deeply troubled her. It meant the darkness was even stronger inside him than she had realized.

"What are you thinking?" Ranier asked. "You seem to know who she is."

"Yes," Elleana replied solemnly, "I once knew her." Elleana was not ready yet for this conversation, and fear began to rise inside her as she felt she would say something wrong and lose Rainer forever.

"Who is she?" Ranier asked.

"You shouldn't be able to hear her" Elleana replied softly. "You shouldn't be able to hear her."

"Why not?" Ranier asked as he tried to understand the effect the voice had on Elleana.

Elleana tried to regain control of herself. She fought desperately to keep the fear out of her and to trust in what she had been told. "When will I know he is ready?" she remembered asking James. "When he asks" James had replied. Elleana knew she had to believe what she had been told, as James had been sent to her bringing instructions from God himself. She certainly didn't feel it was the right time though, and felt Ranier had so much more that needed to change inside before he knew about the woman, as it would tell him who he really was. Acting in fear, she tried to find a way to stay away from the subject of the identity of the woman.

After an uncomfortable pause, Elleana finally replied "Because of the veil Ranier. You shouldn't hear her because of the veil."

"The veil?" Ranier asked with a confused tone in his voice. "What is that?" Ranier could see that something on this subject had hit deep inside Elleana.

"We hadn't reached that part of our history yet Ranier, but the veil is what causes us to forget everything when we come to Earth. In the creation story told in the scriptures, there is a point where it discusses a firmament being placed in the Heavens. That firmament divides the 'waters from the waters', or the Heavens from the Heavens, and is similar in purpose to the Mirror."

"Didn't the Mirror break though?" Ranier asked.

"Yes, Ranier, it did. But that brings us to another important point.

Our existence on Earth repeats many of the conditions and situations as we had in the pre-mortal life. The Book of Ecclesiastes in the Bible says it the best:

The thing that hath been, it is that which shall be; and that which is done is that which shall be done: and there is no new thing under the sun.

"During the Great Council in Heaven, Lucifer and his followers saw they could not persuade all of the Hosts of Heaven to follow them. Since Lucifer knew his plan only had a chance of working if all of the Intelligences in Heaven submitted to it, Lucifer and his followers realized their existence depended on forcing everyone else to accept Lucifer's plan. Because of that, they felt they were morally justified in implementing force, and so they gathered together and drew up plans whereby they would force all to come under the mind control.

"Those who followed God were not interested in the mind control, and wanted to protect their individual freedom to pursue their chosen course of salvation. Thus, a literal war commenced, a war that was fought over the right to control one's thoughts and minds. Lucifer and his followers were not trying to kill anyone, but they were trying to forcefully place the mind control in the other Intelligences."

Ranier was quite fascinated as he listened, and found himself wishing Elleana would tell the story a little faster. She kept pausing for the right words, and he could tell she was unsure of herself. "You're doing fine." Ranier reassured her. "Don't stress too much, I'm very interested by this all. I still want to know about the veil though" he said with a smile.

Elleana appreciated hearing something kind from Ranier. She knew she had to keep going with the history or else she would fall into too much internal fear and doubt in her own abilities to be able to continue. "The War was a very sad and dark time Ranier. Almost all of the people I used to love and trust joined Lucifer, and I found myself attacked constantly as they tried to force mind control in me. My spirit was damaged extensively, and I came to Earth still carrying many of the scars of the war.

"I was a frail child, prone to sickness and depression, as my spirit was not in good health. Losing people so close to you and having them attack you in the most deprived of ways alters a person significantly, and it takes serious time to heal. While God can and will heal everything, there is a time during which we use the pain we carry to help us find God, as it serves as a gauge of sorts to help us know how close we are."

Ranier stayed silent as tears fell down Elleana's cheeks. Elleana smiled weakly at Ranier. "I don't want to lose you Ranier. You are the only person from my pre-mortal life or Earth that I have the hope of being with eternally. That's why . . . that's why . . ." Elleana's voice was breaking, "that's why this is so hard for me. If I lose you, I will blame myself."

Ranier responded immediately "you can't blame yourself for my actions. I am my own person, and I am the one responsible for how I act."

"Yes," Elleana said through a weak smile, "we are ultimately responsible, but we all also impact and influence each other, and it does no good to deny the influence we all have on each other." Realizing she would again receive a protest from Ranier, she quickly added "But I will do my best to avoid blaming myself. I just wanted you to understand why this is so hard for me. Revisiting my past can still hurt sometimes, but I don't fear it for myself. I simply fear it as I don't know what impact it will have on you, and I don't want to lose you."

Ranier had never found himself at a loss for words so many times. On Earth, he always knew what to say, but he never had experiences like this either. All that came to his mind was to say "I won't leave you Mom. I promise. This has done more for me right now than anything else that has ever happened to me. You can keep going, and I won't leave you."

Elleana knew Ranier did not fully understand what he was talking about, as he did not understand what it really entailed to stay with her forever. She did appreciate his confidence though, and she knew he would take his promise seriously. "Ok Ranier." Putting her hand on his, she continued "you promised me. You have a long road ahead still, but don't ever forget that promise. I want you and me to be family forever."

"I certainly will remember" Ranier replied confidently.

Continuing on Elleana said "The Book of Revelation in the Bible describes parts of the War as seen by John. To get to the point from Ecclesiastes, Lucifer was very advanced in the use of time and timelines. Just like all rivers run to the ocean, timelines can be directed to bring all events to the same place. John describes a dragon casting water out of his mouth to destroy the woman John saw, and John describes the Earth swallowing the waters to protect the woman. Those waters John saw were timelines. Lucifer had gathered all timelines together, that, when run into one, would lead to us losing the War. He had released these timelines, or waters, specifically to stop Charity from ever being brought back and from stopping anyone from following in her path.

"The Earth, however, saw it could alter things—alter things, just as all things are altered for the better in our existence—through sacrifice. The Earth possesses a form of Intelligence, and as it was then in the creation process, it had a place in it for the placement of timelines directing certain events that would take place on it. All planets created have a place for timelines, and they receive their timelines when they are assigned their mission.

"While the Earth had not yet specifically received its mission, it reached out to sacrifice itself and absorbed the timelines released by Lucifer. These timelines were all timelines which had played out pre-mortally, and were all timelines that ended in something bad. Since these timelines filled the Earth, they made it so the dark parts of our pre-mortal life would repeat on the Earth."

Ranier suddenly remembered a certain fear related to repeating, or events repeating. A part of him already knew that everything would repeat for him, and that knowledge filled him with dread of the future. Thoughts flashed back to when he was dying in the war on Earth, to the thoughts he didn't understand of everything repeating.

"Yes," Elleana said softly, "it isn't easy to know what your future holds. Lucifer was convinced that since we all had suffered through so much in relation to the Mirror breaking and the War in Heaven, we would lose hope knowing what our future had in store for us as most of us wouldn't want to relive the pain and heartache.

"God also knew that knowledge of our future, especially one full of suffering and heartache, would be more than most of us could bear. So, to remedy the situation, God took the timelines and reorganized them. While the timelines would all play out on Earth and cause events to repeat, he reorganized them to cause the timelines to run together in ways that Lucifer did not anticipate.

"For example, Lucifer put in the timelines associated with the bad resulting from the Mirror breaking. To have those be effective though, there had to be a Mirror, or something like a Mirror. God used the firmament described in the scriptures to divide the waters from the waters, or the timelines from the timelines, in such a way that they could not all interact with each other all at once, just like the Mirror divided the light from the darkness.

"The firmament was a unique type of creation made in seven layers, with each successive layer being more porous, for lack of a better word, than the layer over it. The firmament created a block in our memory and operates as a veil over our minds, as it doesn't let us reach into our past to remember things from before this earth. It also operates to cause us to forget many things on the earth, as no one can perfectly remember everything from their childhood.

"The veil, or condition of forgetfulness, was a blessing from God, as it allowed us to face our future with hope and confidence. Forgetting our past made our future unknown to us, and the state of forgetfulness would ultimately cause humankind to reach for a result better than that achieved in the past. When we can't remember our failures in the past, we will try one more time. When we remember all of our failures though, we are extremely unlikely to even try again.

"There was a lot that went wrong for all of us in the pre-mortal life, especially in relation to loved ones we lost in the War. Lucifer was convinced he could capitalize on all of the bad which had occurred and convince us there was no hope for something better. God blessed us though with the firmament, or veil, and the forgetfulness it caused was a foundation for our faith in a better today and a better tomorrow. While many people view our lack of memory as proof that God doesn't exist, it is actually a tender mercy from him that gives us a significant advantage in escaping our past and gaining a greater and better existence."

Elleana paused to collect her thoughts for a minute, and then remembered the point she was trying to reach. "As I said about the firmament, it existed in seven layers. As the earth progresses in existence, each layer is removed. John, in the Book of Revelation, described each layer as a 'seal' on a book. At some point, each seal, or layer, is opened, or removed, from the firmament. The outermost seal on the firmament, or the first seal, was super fine and kept most evil, and the corresponding good, away from the earth. God was giving people a time in which to not be subject to the full powers of evil, and Lucifer was limited in the tools he could employ. The limits on evil also placed limits on good though.

"However, as each seal was opened, each layer became less fine, or more porous, allowing more powers of evil and good through to the earth. Slowly, as seal after seal was opened, the powers of evil and good increased significantly. The seventh, or final, seal only kept back a few of the worst evil powers possible to exist. But, it also kept back some of the greatest good powers that could exist.

"Once the seventh seal is opened, all powers of good and evil will exist on the earth at the same time, and it will be a period known as the 'fulness of times.' It is the 'fulness of times' because all timelines will be in operation with each other, without any firmament between them, and because all powers of good and evil will be present. In addition, knowledge of our past, future, and present will rain down from Heaven. It will be a time in which all things will become known, except for, maybe, things about our own self, as that knowledge will never come through to us until we are in a place where it won't destroy us."

"What do you mean by 'destroy us'?" Ranier asked. "I don't understand how knowledge will destroy anything."

"Well," Elleana said as she thought for a minute, "we are ultimately beings based on an Intelligence. Intelligence can be destroyed when its two counterparts come back together. So, if we gain knowledge, or light, but have darkness inside of us, the Intelligence inside of us can be annihilated. Since God wants us to live, he keeps back certain light and knowledge while we have certain darkness inside of us, as he doesn't want to destroy the Intelligence inside of us. Instead, he asks us to replace the darkness with goodness, and then we will have the ability to have the light and knowledge associated with our own identity. Until the darkness is gone though, we cannot have the light, or else we self-annihilate."

Elleana continued thinking for a moment, and then said "The firmament, or veil, exists in two places. It covers the earth and keeps certain timelines away, at least for a certain period. This is the firmament, or veil, that is removed in layers as the seals are undone. However, a firmament, or veil, also exists inside us, to keep our dark and light parts from coming in contact with each other, which ultimately keeps us from knowledge of ourselves and allows us to live in a fallen world without self-annihilating."

"Why do we have dark and light parts inside of us?" Rainer asked. "It seems strange that God would give us those."

"Yes, we have a unique situation on the earth. When Adam and Eve were created, they were in a body full of light, and only light. All of their parts were light, and their physical body was made of a single-stranded DNA of light. When they partook of the fruit of the tree, the fruit contained a single-stranded DNA chain of darkness. As dark and light always attract, these two DNA strands combined, causing an intense feeling of euphoria, which made the fruit feel delicious to the taste since feelings were produced from the foundational level inside of Adam and Eve.

"As a result of eating the forbidden fruit, Adam and Eve gained a double-stranded DNA, or a physical body that housed parts made of light and dark. The firmament, or veil, runs down the middle of the DNA strand, and is essential to our existence. Without it, the two DNA strands would cause us to self-annihilate. This veil acts a lot like the Mirror, and keeps us from seeing half of who we really are. We often wonder how people are so blind to the way they act, and it is because of the veil inside of us. We can act one way, but believe we did it for a good reason, when we really can't see that it was our dark DNA motivating us to act. Or, we can only see bad in ourselves, and entirely miss the good and potential that exists there.

"God allowed for this state of existence to occur so we could ultimately decide who and what we really wanted to be. God's plan is to take us to a new existence, one founded in love, where we can enjoy everything that God has, including his power and knowledge. Before he can trust us with his power and knowledge, however, we have to be tested to see if we will succumb to the evil pulls and tendencies which exist.

"For example, one of God's greatest powers is the creation of life, as one of his defining characteristics is creation itself. God creates, and he makes wonderful things. However, he does not do so arbitrarily, or for his own self-interests. The power to create has an intense pull to use the power to gratify self-interests, but it can never be used in this way or else life itself will begin a spiral down to non-existence.

"The interests of the life being created have to be considered before your own interests, and your own interests always have to be subordinated to the interests of the life just made. All of God's creations have some level of life to them, even the earth, and God does not create something until he is acting for the right reasons, as opposed to any selfish reasons of self-gratification.

"Because of this, God gave us a limited power to create life while on the earth. We had to experience a portion of the pulls of creative power to see if we could develop our character into something that would not give in to the pulls and lusts of self-gratification. If we successfully developed self-control, we would qualify to receive more creative power in the next life. If we were overcome by the self-gratification aspect of creation, we would lose all creative power in the next life.

"In life on Earth, our creative power is experienced through sexuality. Lucifer has convinced the world to focus solely on the self-gratification aspect of sexuality. Movies, songs, and books are replete with sexuality. Women daily dress as sexual objects, feeling that the measure of their self-worth is found in being sexually pleasing. People refuse to have children, yet engage in sexual activity constantly. People consume sexuality on a daily basis, and unfortunately do so in an entirely selfish manner.

"One of God's most serious commandments relates to the law of chastity, which essentially states that sexual relations can only exist between a man and a woman, appropriately married and committed to each other and to raising children. This is a serious commandment as obedience to this commandment has more effect on our state in the next life than almost any other commandment, save probably the commandment not to kill.

"Both of the most serious commandments relate to life and our selfish interactions with the power to create and take life. Abortion is almost always the selfish taking of a life. Breaking the law of chastity is always a selfish exercise of the creative powers entrusted to us. Many fail to see why the law of chastity or the command to not abort a life is so essential, but it is precisely because the proper exercise of these powers is fundamental to eternal existence. No being can possess these powers in an eternal existence if they wield them in any type of selfish manner on Earth, without properly repenting, as they will carry these same selfish tendencies with them into the next world."

Chapter 16

E LLEANA PAUSED, KNOWING THIS WAS a sensitive subject for Ranier. He was deep in thought, but she could tell he was troubled, likely by many of the tendencies and pulls he experienced on a daily basis. She also knew it was important for him to fully understand these things though, especially as it related to past tendencies he had possessed and recent tendencies inside of him, and so she prayed for help as she continued.

Ranier was thinking back to his time on Earth. His mind was full of all of the times he had engaged in sexual activity, and he reflected on the motivating force behind those interactions. He thought of the many people he had used and abused, all in an effort to satisfy his lusts, and his lusts alone. Faces of the people he had used were appearing in his mind, faces he had worked hard to suppress and forget. For his second time now, guilt was entering his heart as he thought on his vicious cycle of selfishness and the pain he had left others in its wake.

"In your current situation, Ranier," he heard Elleana break in and say, "many in the world are promoting the 'rights' of people to engage in sexual conduct, including the rights of homosexuals to marry, and you find yourself supporting them as well, mostly due to recent similar feelings arising inside of you. They are having great success, but are upset by those who maintain that it is immoral and contrary to God's will that sexuality be limited to that between a man and a woman, properly married. They say that, if God loved everyone, he would love those who are attracted to those of their same sex or who are sexually active and not married, and would provide a place in Heaven for them to be with their partners eternally. They demand the same treatment as that given to a married man and woman, and expect God to do the same.

"However, they miss two important principles. The first is that *any* exercise of the sexual powers outside of the marriage relationship of a man and woman is based in desires for self-gratification. This means any exercise of the sexual powers outside the marriage relationship of a man and a woman feeds the dark parts inside of a person, and gives counterparts and other darkness more access and control. Of course, a man can abuse his wife and use her for self-gratification, or vice versa, but that is also very wrong and leads to the same consequences as sexual relationships outside of marriage, including the loss of such powers in the next life.

"However, a man and woman, *acting properly* in marriage, will bear, or be willing to bear, children, will ultimately put the interests of the other first, and will remain with each other to take care of the children of their union. Staying united as a married couple, and staying true to each other and to the children who come, helps beats selfishness out of the couple, and promotes their ability to act in a non-selfish manner as they learn about all of the responsibility the creative power entails. Proper exercise of sexuality is always conditioned on willingly accepting the responsibilities associated with creating life.

"Everyone one of us are directly the result of the union of a male and female. We all have a father and a mother, and there is no way for us to understand our true identity unless we are raised by our father and mother, or raised in a situation as closely situated as possible, such as with an adoptive couple. God did not give us our creative powers solely for our own existence. He gave us creative powers to see if we could utilize powers to create life in appropriate ways, as we would have to be able to restrain our desires to promote ourselves if we want to have the power to create, like God, in the next life.

"To use our creative powers correctly, we need to use them in situations solely where the children can know their parents. Every one of us needs the ability to know and interact with our parents. We cannot deny the source of our creation and expect to get anywhere. While you don't like to think about it Rainer, you had a father. I was desperate to feel or be loved, and I turned to the ways of the world for finding love.

"Your father said he loved me, he said I was everything to him, and he used me to gratify his own pleasures. I gave in because I was seeking to gratify my pleasures of feeling loved and wanted. You came into existence through our selfish actions, and your father immediately left me when he found out I was pregnant. He had no interest in being responsible for the consequences of his choices.

"Prior to him leaving, he demanded that I have an abortion. This would have compounded the level of selfishness associated with my actions. Luckily for me though, I was too timid to have an abortion, and you came into my life." Elleana smiled for a moment. "God has a way of taking things we do wrong, and still allowing them to turn into something good for us. You mean so much to me, and I feel you are God's way of telling me that everything will be worth it in the end. God is taking my mistakes and turning them into great things. Of course, I understand that my mistakes contributed directly to a bad situation for you" Elleana said as her voice trailed off for a minute.

Elleana was afraid to say what she knew she needed to say, but she closed her eyes to help drum up the courage. After another few moments, she said carefully "I know you struggle with this knowledge as you hate your father, but you have to realize and accept that he is your father. Until you understand him, you will not be able to understand yourself, just as you will remain unable to understand life until you understand God."

At this point, Elleana took a deep breath. She was amazed at how she had been able to say all of these things without breaking down. In the past, any thoughts of this situation had caused her to weep, especially as the evils associated with Ranier's father acting purely on his lusts ran through her mind. She had quickly learned that sexuality and love were very different, and while sexuality could be an expression of love, it could also be an expression of some of the darkest evils in existence. These evils had been a part of her life once, ones she had voluntarily accepted as the only way to find happiness. Her heart yearned for all of the people still looking for love and acceptance through gratifying lusts, as she knew of the heartache and sorrow that was sure to result at some point for them.

Elleana looked at Ranier again, and found Rainer looking steadily at her. He was trying to avoid expressing any emotion to her at this point, especially on these topics due to the guilt setting in and the various pulls he had experienced related to all types of sexuality. However, he knew there was something he needed to understand to get past the guilt, and wanting to get off of the subject of his father, he asked in a steady, firm voice masking his underlying emotions "You had said there were two reasons why homosexuality is forbidden by God, and you talked about the self-gratification side of things and the effect it has on us. Is there another reason, or was the second reason wrapped up in your explanation somewhere?"

Elleana could sense that Ranier asked this question trying to move on past the uncomfortable nature of where she had paused. Something in Ranier wanted to know and understand, while part of him fought against knowing. "There is another reason, yes, which I haven't gotten to yet. To understand it you have to understand more about the nature of our existence here.

"We are, as you recall, built with dark and light DNA, or dark and light parts. Our dark DNA gives us drives towards the darkness, and is sometimes referred to as our 'natural man' tendencies. Darkness and light, virtue and vice, good and evil, are a division and separation of Intelligence matter. The level of division possible depends on the progression of Saytah, as he is the only one who can divide Intelligence since he has no counterpart to counteract what he does.

"In the beginning and up to his atonement, Christ made things through dividing based on the light and dark type divisions, meaning that the two divided parts, if they met their counterparts, would annihilate and return to the Intelligence state they were in. This caused a circle of life and death, where death would bring new life, as certain Intelligences had to be brought back together to keep life going for others. Of course, this was not an ideal existence, but it is one which trained us well in searching for something better.

"This earth gave us the chance to exist with the opposition inside of us, something we could not do in Heaven. Our double-stranded DNA gave a place for us and our counterpart, or a being who followed Lucifer if both counterparts chose to follow God, to reside in us. Both are trying to gain control of our mortal body, and it is our soul who decides who ends up with control. An old Indian tale states that we have two wolves inside of us, with both fighting for control of us. A young Indian child once asked how we know which one wins, to which a wise old Indian replied 'It depends on which one you feed.'

"Immorality, or sexual conduct outside of a marriage between a man and a woman, feeds the dark wolf inside of us, or our counterpart or being who followed Lucifer that exists as part of us as a result of our DNA. The being seeking to control our dark DNA has no place with God, and by allowing our counterpart or other being to gain control of our soul, we are losing our opportunity to be with God. Counterparts can gain access to just one part of us, or to multiple parts of us. As they do, we begin to struggle with our identity, as the counterpart pulls us in competing ways from our other parts. Counterparts cause us to feel the opposite of what we really are.

"Sometimes people are born with DNA that allows a counterpart to have control of certain parts, other times people, through feeding the darkness inside, build up enough darkness that the counterpart gains access and control. For many who are transgender on the earth, they are trying to deal with the effects of having a counterpart gain access to their gender identity part. When a counterpart gains access to this part, it becomes exceptionally hard to understand one's gender identity, as counterparts are always the opposite sex of us. The same thing happens in all aspects of identity though, and identity becomes lost as counterparts gain more and more access.

"Besides improper sexual conduct, there are many other things that feed our dark DNA as well. God gave a commandment on the earth known as the 'Word of Wisdom', and it contains restrictions on the consumption of certain substances. For example, it states that one should not drink alcohol, tea, and coffee, as these items contain substances which literally feed the dark DNA inside of us. The Word of Wisdom also states we should eat meat sparingly, as meat also feeds the dark DNA inside, but is necessary to bring some portions of the light DNA in animals to us as well. Because it helps and harms at the same time, we are instructed to consume it sparingly.

"Besides food, our dark DNA can be fed through what we view and listen to each day. Lucifer convinces people to dress immodestly, as viewing or dressing immodestly feeds the dark DNA of the viewer and the person dressing that way. Our dark DNA is fed extensively by viewing human skin, and so Lucifer encourages people to remove all of their hair on their body. Hair was a natural covering given to us by God to help balance out the dark and light DNA, but many work to remove all hair and show as much skin as possible in the way they dress.

"As the dark DNA is fed through seeing skin, Lucifer promotes immodesty and a focus and obsession with obtaining a body type that feeds the dark DNA inside. Pornography is a feast for the dark DNA, and dramatically increases the power of the dark DNA inside, even to the rewiring of brain circuits to follow darkness rather than the light that was originally wired in. Certain types of music, with their dark beats, tempos, and lyrics, also feed the dark DNA.

"You had asked earlier, Ranier, about false assumptions you carried. Many false assumptions, including those that significantly affect our view of the world, stem from a misunderstanding of the light and dark inside. We often assume we are good when we are bad, or bad when we are good, as we all struggle reconciling the competing things inside of us that arise from the dark and light DNA. Our views of ourselves are projected onto our view of the world and existence, and it is natural for us to assume we are good.

"Often, our understanding of the world is premised on the assumption that we are good. When we make the assumption that we are good though when we have bad parts of us, it warps our view of existence as our judgment is impaired by the bad inside we accept or view as good. Ultimately, humility is the only way to see ourselves clearly, as humility is seeing ourselves as God does—as a being with eternal potential, but one with dark parts, or weaknesses, inside that must be overcome, as well as light parts inside.

"Due to our divided nature here on Earth, Christ atoned for us and our sins. Christ's atonement in our behalf, or Christ's satisfying the demands of the law of love, enabled him to have the power to create a new universe founded in love. The division of Intelligence that takes place pursuant to the law of love is one of a complementary, as opposed to destructive, type division. This means that opposition in our new existence is complementary and builds when counterparts come together, instead of destroying when counterparts come together. Males and females are an example of this type of complementary opposition, and their union produces further life without destroying anything in existence. Therefore, for us to become like God and exist in a universe built on the laws of love, we have to learn to exist in complementary roles.

"The one and only way to disrupt this type of existence, since the complementary opposites do not destroy, is to stack the same things with each other. Think of magnets. When the same poles are put together, they repel. It is similar with complementary opposites. When two of the same things are put together and joined, they create a rift in the foundation as their two similar states do not join together.

"The fabric, or foundation, of the new existence in the new Universe is built through the unions of complementary opposites, but is destroyed through the unions of things that are the same. Lucifer desperately wants to destroy the new Universe, and his way of achieving this is to join male with male, and female with female, by causing an individual's counterpart to gain access and control. This type of union resulting from homosexual activity disrupts the foundation of our new Universe, and is the only type of thing containing the potential to cause rifts in the foundation of the new Heaven itself.

"Because of this, God zealously safeguards human exercise of sexuality. God has strict commands related to sexuality and how we are supposed to act on these powers. These commands are strict because the misuse of these powers has such serious repercussions on Earth and in eternity. We must allow our counterpart of light to gain control of us, and it is only through denying our natural passions that arise as a result of the dark DNA inside of us.

"Because of the physical body, any access a counterpart gains feels as if it is part of us. Males can be entirely attracted to males and feel their attraction is who they are, and these feelings of identity can be just as real as other temporal feelings a person experiences. For example, a person may define themselves as athletic, artistically talented, or intellectually gifted, not recognizing that these are temporal gifts given for a moment. Others may define themselves as ugly, broken, or with no self-worth. All of these people, whether defining themselves as good or bad, focus on the things of the temporal and project this into eternity, assuming that who they are today is who they will be forever. Our path is to understand the temporal, or physical, condition is not reflective of our eternal nature or potential, and work to let go of everything that is not in line with our eternal selves.

"One of the greatest gifts we can give to our children is to live God's law of chastity. When we live this law, we significantly promote the control of the good, or light, DNA inside of us. When we have children, we pass on the same measure of light DNA to our children, whether such light was obtained through living the law of chastity, the Word of Wisdom, or by following any other commands of God.

"Conversely, when we act on our lusts and consume pornography, entertain other lustful thoughts or actions, or otherwise feed the dark DNA inside, we significantly promote the control of the bad, or dark, DNA inside of us. And, when we have children, we will similarly pass on the same measure of dark DNA inside of us to our children. God speaks in scripture about our sins cursing our children to the third and fourth generation when he speaks of this effect, as our DNA will carry through to at least three or four generations."

Knowing this next part would not necessarily help Ranier at the moment, but knowing he needed to know in order to work things out in the long run, Elleana continued "Your father, Ranier, was almost fully controlled by his dark DNA. He acted in accordance with all it encouraged him to do—swearing, drinking, violence, and plenty of sexual immorality. You were born with the full measure of his dark DNA already operative inside you. However," Elleana said knowing full well where this would go, "you cannot hate him for it. You just have to know that is the point your life started at."

Elleana could sense the swell of emotions within Ranier. She knew very well of Ranier's past and how he had likely broken almost every command related to the law of chastity. She knew he wasn't proud of the things he had done and the pain he had caused others along the way. She had watched him, daily, and had been heartbroken, pleading to God to help Ranier see the light and follow it.

She knew there was no light or lasting anything in breaking the law of chastity, only temporary gratification to cover the pain and darkness inside. It was heartbreaking for any of the spirits in the Spirit World to witness the immense flood of immorality on Earth, as they were acutely aware of the full effects it had. It was as if the world was voluntarily on a self-medicated slide to eternal death itself, and it was sickening to watch.

Elleana's thoughts were broken by Ranier as he expressed his frustration. "How is it fair? Why am I born with such a disadvantage? God, if he does exist, doesn't deal justly with us. One of the things that made me decide God didn't love me or exist is that if he did, he wouldn't allow me to be born in grinding poverty, the son of a worthless father who doesn't even want his own son, while allowing others to be born into exceptional riches, comfort and security. Still others are disabled and never even get to experience many of the things we do. Where is the love in that?"

Elleana reached out and placed her hand on top of Ranier's, just to have him quickly pull away in anger. Elleana silently plead for help. She had been afraid of being tasked with explaining things to Ranier as she would be heartbroken to lose him, and these things often required a lifetime for people to understand. As she asked in her heart for help, she remembered the promise she had been given. It was a simple promise, and not at all unique to her. It was simply "those whom I call, I qualify."

God, through James as a messenger, had told her she was called to be Ranier's mother. She knew of the pains of parents worldwide who felt inadequate to raise a child, yet she knew each of them were called by God, and could be fully qualified for each child if they turned to God. She knew she had to have the same faith, that despite her weaknesses and timid nature, she would somehow be qualified by God to reach Ranier.

"The love in that, Ranier," Elleana suddenly found herself saying, "is that God doesn't treat you like everyone else precisely because you aren't everyone else. We are all individual, and God's love is deep and infinite enough to chart the perfect path precisely for you. You don't need earthly riches to find the riches of eternity, you don't need DNA full of light to find God, and you don't need an earth surrounded by friends and family to find your place in eternity.

"God knows you, perfectly, and perfectly loves you. His love always balances the needs of today with the reality of eternity, and he provides you with the things you need to live on Earth but still obtain the riches of eternity. Earth is such a short measure of our true existence, and it is much too short to give us all the same things.

"Remember Ranier," Elleana said as she found herself wiping a tear from her eye and wasn't sure why she was crying, "love can't, by definition, treat us all the same as we are not the same. If we are truly loved, we have to be treated in a way that recognizes and respects our individuality. There are certainly principles that apply to us all as certain things are universal, such as God's commandments. However, there is also a part of us that is truly unique.

"You could say we are part universal and part individual. The individual portion of us is what makes us of infinite worth, as our individual portion only exists in us, and it will never be replicated again. Our individual portion is of such worth that God spent eternity working out the perfect plan for just you. Your path is different than anyone else's path, but in the end, it takes you through the things you need in order to experience the things of God in eternity."

Chapter 17

ELLEANA SUDDENLY REALIZED WHY SHE was crying as she spoke. She realized the things she had just told Ranier were things she had long tried to understand herself. She had agonized for so long as she watched so many others on Earth possess the things she longed to have for herself. She wondered often why God didn't love her as much as others, and even though she had discussed this with James and Ruby earlier, it wasn't until now, until explaining things to Ranier, that she finally had the knowledge sink into her heart.

The fact that she was treated differently was proof God did love her. God had perfectly designed her path to enable her to fully enjoy and experience the riches of eternity. While her path was not designed to fully enjoy the things of the earth, it did not need to be as her time on the earth was over, and she had eternity to live now. God always had eternity in mind, as his love was great enough to focus on the most important part of her existence by leading her on an earthly path that allowed her to obtain the wonders of eternity.

As Elleana pondered on these things, she suddenly felt her heart melt as God's love touched her. Elleana remembered a void, a pain, a darkness, in her heart for so long, and she had yearned to feel or experience God's love, or someone's love even, for her. She had plead repeatedly for someone to love her, and it is why she had given in so readily to the men who came into her life. Each man though only compounded the darkness and disappointment inside of her.

When Ranier came, she remembered basking in the opportunity to hold him. He meant everything to her. She had often wondered why God took her away from him when he was only seven, but she could suddenly see that God did so in mercy to her as the dark DNA inside Ranier would take full effect at age eight. Age eight was known as the age of accountability, as it was the age at which the full pulls of the light and dark DNA would set in.

Prior to this time, the full effects of both strands of DNA were not in complete operation, and a child was not fully functioning under the direction of the child's soul. At age eight however, the soul was given the ability to fully direct the body, but this also meant that the full effects of both strands of DNA would be in effect.

For Ranier, age eight meant that he would experience some significant changes. His dark DNA would lead him to stop turning to her and would have caused him to treat her just as poorly as the other men, and it would have broken her heart. Instead though, she could see that God separated them in mercy to enable Ranier to always maintain a portion of love for her despite the depth of the darkness in him, and she always retained fully happy memories with him. This pocket of love, she could suddenly see, was the light that had kept the darkness from fully overcoming Ranier. If she had remained though, the love for her would have fully disappeared, and Ranier would have been a being of complete darkness.

Elleana wept as she understood these things. While it had been so hard to be separated, she could see God providing a perfect way for both her and Ranier. Her heart was full of gratitude as she reflected on the depth of sacrifice and experience necessary to reach her eternity of riches, her eternity with God in his new Kingdom. But, she also realized she was well along the path, things would work out, and truly, one day, God would wipe all tears from her eyes as she would be able to see the importance and relevance of every hardship she had experienced.

Elleana's short moment of realization and gratitude was abruptly interrupted by Ranier as he said with sharpness "I'm certain I could have used a few things I never received on Earth. I could have used a real dad, not some deadbeat, some more money, and less pain." Elleana immediately sensed that the feelings she had were not being shared by Ranier, and she remembered they were still on their own individual paths.

"Yes, there are many things we are certain we can use," Elleana replied, trying hard to control her emotions as she wiped her tears away. "But those things are often based in satisfying our dark DNA. There are many things that will make our dark DNA feel good, but God will often withhold some of those from us, as such feelings are temporary and fleeting and lead us down the wrong path.

"In the scriptures, there is the story of Esau, who sold his birthright, or his future potential, for one meal. The effects of his one meal provided satisfaction for a time, but fully vanished in a few hours, and Esau was left right where he was before, but without any of his future birthright potential to ever receive. Our dark DNA always entices us to trade our eternity for a few minutes of satisfaction today, and when we don't get the satisfaction today, we feel angry, upset, or unloved because we see others who are wallowing in the satisfaction of the moment."

"So you're telling me it is my dark DNA that makes me want a dad?" Ranier asked rather coldly. "I thought family meant something to God, and I don't see how wanting a dad is a bad thing. All of the other kids had dads, but not me."

"Certainly," Elleana replied cautiously, "not all of our yearnings are from our dark DNA. Our light DNA also entices us to work and long for good things, such as a father. You have to remember though," Elleana paused to get the courage to continue, "you have a father" she said softly. "The yearnings of our light DNA entice us to give up the things of our dark DNA in order to achieve them. Your light DNA causes you to seek and long for a father. Since you have a father, it is ultimately encouraging you to take the steps necessary to forgive him and accept him as your father. In other words, it is encouraging you to let go of the darkness inside."

"He has done nothing to merit any forgiveness!" Ranier nearly yelled in frustration. Through clenched teeth he continued "I have hated him ever since I can remember. I hated every boy I saw with a dad, and I hated how he was never a part of my life. That man has no place in my life!" Elleana always withdrew significantly with anger, as it was a hard emotion for her to deal with in others. She tried though to control her voice and not shut down in the face of Ranier's emotions.

"Ranier, you have to realize . . ." Elleana was trying to steady her voice, "you have to realize that your hatred of your father translates into hatred of yourself." Elleana cringed as she sensed a new flood of anger rush through Ranier, a flood that was directed at her. "Please Ranier," she nearly cried, "give me a chance to explain." As her voice shook heavily, she said "I don't do well with anger, and never have, please, please, let me explain."

Ranier shook his head. Any reference to his father had always angered him, and he was too upset to continue talking at this time. "I need some time to calm down," he said in a voice close to yelling, "I need to get away from here for a little while."

"I don't know if that will help much," Elleana replied in a broken voice, "but you can certainly go and see for yourself" as she motioned to the outdoors. "However, I am certain you will not like what you find out there."

Ranier didn't pause to think about what she had said and took off walking. He had found his vision would come and go intermittently now, but he could see at this moment. As he began walking, his thoughts and emotions continued to churn as he thought about his father. Nothing, in his mind, could even justify any forgiveness for his father, and the thought of it filled him with exceptional rage. If there was one person that should have been there in his life, it was his father.

Ranier walked without any sense of direction, time, or purpose. He passed countless buildings and countless trees and other plants. He had no way to find his way back to Elleana, but he didn't care about that right now. He knew he couldn't stay if Elleana insisted on talking about his father, especially if she even suggested again about forgiving him, or suggested again that hatred of his father was hatred of himself.

As Ranier continued walking, his emotions began to gradually calm a little, and he started paying attention to where he was at. As he began looking around, he found himself annoyed with his surroundings. Everywhere he looked he saw families. While everyone appeared about the same age, he could tell that parents were with their children. The resemblance was impossible to deny, and something clearly indicated fathers, mothers, children, brothers, and sisters.

Everyone appeared to be in families, and there were groups all over. Most paid no attention to him, but he was extremely bothered by the fact that everything appeared family based. His father, or his lack of one, had left a serious void in his life, and he had decided he could make do without family for the rest of his existence. While he had longed for a dad, he had longed for a good one, not the one he had, and he wasn't about to do anything to accept his father again.

Suddenly, Ranier stopped walking. He sensed something different about the small group of three ahead. This group was intently focused on him, and he could sense serious animosity coming from two of them. One in the group projected feelings of kindness though, and that one broke ranks with the other two in the group and began walking towards Ranier. As Ranier looked at the man's face, he stepped back in shock as he saw a reflection of himself in the other man. To Ranier, it was as if he were looking at a mirror image of himself, at least in facial features, although the man was taller and more muscular looking than Ranier.

Ranier found himself unable to move and unable to take his eyes off of the man. As the man approached, he spread his arms wide and said with excitement in his voice "Dad! I have waited so long to meet you!"

As Ranier heard this, he felt a shock wave rip through him, rocking him from head to toe. He nearly crumpled to the ground. By this time, the man had reached him and embraced him. While Ranier never allowed others to touch him, he was too shocked at this time to resist and found himself just trying to regain control of his senses.

After a little time, the man said "It's okay Dad. I have forgiven you. It took me a long time, but I have forgiven you. I just want us to be able to start things on the right foot." Ranier's mind was still reeling. He had no idea who this man was or why he was calling him 'Dad'.

"Who are you?" Ranier was finally able to sputter out as the man released his grip on Ranier. "Who are you?"

The man smiled a kind smile in return, "I am your first son."

"You must be mistaking me for someone else," Ranier said in a low voice while knowing that it wasn't true due to the way the man looked.

The man smiled again, "Yes, I was told you didn't know about any of us. Don't worry though, I understand, and I have forgiven you."

"Us?!" Ranier gasped in surprise, "Us?"

"Yes," the man said pointing to the two others he had left, "the three of us and the two others still on Earth."

Ranier was just beginning to grasp what was happening, but everything was still significantly blurred. "I have five children?" he finally asked at length.

"Yes, you have five children," the man said, and then continuing cautiously "five children who never knew their father."

"But, but, but . . ." Ranier was at a loss for words. "How could I not know?"

"Our mothers couldn't find you to tell you. You would come and go so suddenly, they had no way of letting you know."

Ranier finally sat down, as the emotions were too much for him to handle. He knew very well of his past and of how he had treated everyone whom had come into his life. People were simply tools for him to use to get what he wanted, although he could see now he never really found what he wanted. He had always wondered why no one ever cared for him, but he was starting to see that he never really cared for anyone either. Ranier was without words, and felt sick to his stomach.

The guilt and shame inside Ranier was growing. Most of all, he felt absolutely sickened by the fact that he had followed in his father's footsteps. He thought of all the nights he had cursed his father for not being there for him, for all of the boys he cursed for having fathers, and for all of the times he cursed God for letting him be born without a father. He had never once even paused to think he might possibly have children of his own, children who, like him, never knew their father. Ranier's heart completely sank as he realized he had entirely become everything he hated. He had become his father.

Ranier found himself crying and unable to look up. He was too ashamed. The man, Ranier realized, was waiting patiently beside him, but Ranier couldn't bring himself to face his own son, a son who looked just like him. Eventually, Ranier realized that the man's hand was on his shoulder. The man's touch was kind, but it hurt Ranier so readily. Ranier felt he didn't deserve kindness from a son that he had abandoned, he felt he deserved hate just like he hated his father.

The kindness in his son's touch penetrated deep into Ranier, making him want to escape into a place away from all kindness, away from all light, away from existence. Thinking of how it must have been for his children was too much, and he had no way to explain anything to them. He simply knew, absolutely knew, that what he had done was wrong.

At length, he finally heard the man speak. "It's alright Dad. It really is. I'm okay, and I just want to let us start from here. God helped me to let go of my past, and he can help us both."

Ranier finally looked at the man. He still couldn't believe the kindness he felt, and his mind and heart were still whirling from everything.

"God gives us all second chances" the man said with a smile, "and he is certainly giving you yours."

"What is your name?" Ranier finally managed to say through a broken voice.

"Ranier" the man said simply and calmly.

"What?!" Ranier asked, "you're named Ranier?"

"Yes," Ranier, the son, replied.

"Why would you have my name?"

"Mother never stopped loving you Dad. You meant so much to her. She prayed daily for your return. She wanted to always remember you, and she wanted me to know something about you, so she named me after you. She wanted me to always have a reason to think about and be proud of my heritage. Mom often told me that even though you weren't with us in person, a part of you had stayed inside of me. She always spoke highly of you, and said I was her gift from you."

"However," Ranier's son continued, "I hated you, and I hated my name. It broke my heart that you weren't around, so I refused to let people call me Ranier. I became known as Junior, and I lived a life of trouble. I was shot and killed in a gang fight when I was 22. Mom was absolutely heartbroken to lose me too. Things were certainly tough for Mom, and I never helped one bit."

"Where is she now?" Ranier asked weakly.

"Now?" Junior asked, a little surprised. Then, seeing that Ranier was serious, he said softly "She's looking for you Ranier. She saw you on the street one day, recognized you, and is trying to get back into your life somehow as something inside her feels strongly you will change one day and see her for who she really is. She even found a way to join the military in her older age to try and stay close to you. She knows you have been hurt, and feels it is an answer to her prayers to have an opportunity to try and be with you again. However, she's pleading with God to keep you alive. Remember, she's been praying daily for your return, and it would mean the world to her to have you back, but it will absolutely crush her if she loses you again."

Ranier was entirely at a loss. The pain, confusion, guilt, and flood of other negative emotions was so intense that he felt himself withdrawing to try and handle things. He still couldn't bring himself to believe he had a son, or had children, or that someone loved him enough to pray for his return daily, or to name a child after him. He was drawn back to his thoughts while he was falling in the darkness, where he saw how intertwined his existence was with other people.

As he thought on his impact in the lives of others, it made him sick inside to think of those he had hurt or left behind. He could not comprehend how anyone could love him, especially Junior or Junior's mother. As his thoughts slowly spiraled downward into despair, he remembered falling and how crying to God for a second chance had suddenly brought him back to Elleana, with a very welcome relief from the darkness.

He wasn't sure if he wanted to be saved this time though. Right now, the thought of becoming extinct resonated fully through him. He was sure he couldn't bear the shame of looking his children, or their mothers, in the face. He had left them for no good reason, and had continued on his path of selfishness in life.

He had been searching for something good in his life, but had walked away from it when it was presented to him. Now, he felt he fully deserved to be banished and never seen by anyone again, and he was sure his pain would be too great if he had to face things again. He kept his eyes closed, hoping that everything around him would disappear.

At length, Junior said softly "I don't mean to intrude Dad, but you have to remember that your feelings speak as loud as words here."

Ranier cringed, both at the thought Junior was still there and at the thought Junior knew what he was feeling. There seemed to be no escape for him.

"If I may," Junior said quietly, "offer something that may help."

Ranier remained silent for a time, but recognizing that everything inside him still spoke, he nodded approval with the ever so slight nod of his head.

"Love was an extremely hard thing for me to accept too, Dad." Ranier sensed deep emotion in Junior's voice. "You had left me, and my life was extremely hard. I felt that God had left me, and I was surrounded by people full of darkness and hate. Somehow, Mom remained strong throughout it all and loved me, but I rejected her love."

"You see," Junior continued, "love can hurt. Another's true love for us hurts when we hold onto the dark parts of ourselves. Love always brings light with it, and it penetrates to even our dark parts of ourselves.

The light always destroys the dark, and so it can hurt if we are choosing to hold on to the darkness inside. We often get used to the darkness and return there because we fear the light. We fear the light because our dark parts recognize they cannot exist there, and they fill us with fear to stop us from accepting the love someone offers. Those parts know that if we accept or feel love, they will cease to exist, and so they build walls to keep love, and light, out.

"It's a self-protection measure. When we love our dark parts more, we keep true love—the love from others—out. We run from other people, especially those who might make us recognize the love they have for us. You had built walls inside you to keep love out from every person on Earth. However, you had not built them for Elleana, since you lost her at such a young age. Your lack of faith in God and the next life caused you to keep one point of access to your heart, which is why Elleana was asked to talk to you. The information she brings isn't as important as the love she carries for you, as it is her love that ultimately begins reaching into the depths of your soul."

"How do you know about Elleana?" Ranier asked.

"For one, she's my grandmother" Junior said with a smile. "But, I've been watching you both this entire time. I've been working on forgiving you and getting past the fact that you left. I had years of emotion to unravel and let go of, and so God placed me in a way that I could observe you and the things you carried. Grandpa sat teaching me, just like Elleana was teaching you, and explaining your weaknesses, fears, and other things you had been through on Earth.

"Upon understanding, my anger and hate washed away, and it turned to compassion and forgiveness. I hold nothing against you, Dad, and I truly love you as well. Forgiveness is the most amazing thing I have ever experienced, and one of the most precious opportunities and gifts we have been given from God. All of our darkness can melt away in a moment, and we can be full of God's light."

Chapter 18

RANIER SAT IN SILENCE, his emotions continuing to whirl. He despised the idea of being watched, but he appreciated that his son was able to get past his feelings of hate and anger. Ranier realized that one day he would have to thank . . . , wait! "Who did you say taught you while watching me?!" Ranier suddenly exploded.

"Grandpa" Junior calmly replied.

"My dad?!" Ranier asked with poison laced throughout his voice.

"Yes" Junior calmly replied again, "your dad."

"He has no business being anywhere near me!" Ranier nearly screamed. Ranier could not stand even the thought that his dad still had anything to do with him. He wanted nothing to do with his dad, and wished that the worst possible thing, even though he didn't know what that was, would happen to him.

Junior stayed silent for a minute while Ranier collected himself a little. "Dad, you are acting like a little kid. Elleana may be afraid to say it, but I'm not. You need to grow up and recognize that life is about family, and not only about you. Grandpa is a good man now. He has changed. He was killed in a car accident as he was running from Elleana. He had run away in fear, he had asked her to get an abortion because he was afraid of the responsibility of fatherhood. As he was driving aimlessly one night, he was killed by a drunk driver. The man was drunk because he had just lost his young wife to cancer.

"Upon entering the Spirit World," Junior continued, "Grandpa immediately realized the poor decisions he had made, and so he assumed the post of caring for you and Elleana. He worked day in and day out to try and give you something good in life. He helped clear the path for you both. Your life would have been so much harder if it weren't for him," Junior said as he clearly spoke each word. "Grandpa has cried daily ever since coming to himself, and cried to God daily that he be given the chance to make things right."

Anticipating Ranier's next question, Junior continued "Grandpa hasn't shown himself to you or Elleana yet because he knows neither of you is ready yet. Elleana was so broken, and so frail, that it has taken her time to recover from what Earth handed her. Grandpa knows he can't see her until she has support from you. He also knows he can't see you until you let go of the hate inside. I've sat with him as he has wept watching you, and I know the depth of the remorse he feels. Despite this, he has not stopped working for you or her, and constantly arranges everything he can for you, down even to making it possible for mother to work in the military to be able to follow you."

"Why!" Ranier exclaimed as tears entered his eyes. "Why do I have to endure this? I can't deal with all of this. My entire world is turning upside down, and I have no idea what or who to believe." After a minute of silence, Ranier yelled "Are you watching me right now? Do you enjoy what you see?"

Junior, calmly as ever, replied "No, he's not. He's away helping arrange things for Elleana at the moment. He knew you wouldn't appreciate him watching our conversation, so he left, to show respect for you."

"Why can't I just never see him again?" Ranier asked icily.

"Because he's family," came the simple reply from Junior.

"He gave me DNA, that's it. That doesn't entitle him to torment me forever" Ranier retorted.

Junior smiled. "No, that's not 'it', Ranier. Science can only detect a transmission of DNA, but family brings a whole lot more with it. You can never escape your heritage Ranier, never, unless you choose to go and live with Lucifer, at which point you give up everything good about yourself as you give up yourself to be there."

Ranier was looking at Junior coldly. "If we're into honesty, I'll be honest. I don't like you."

"I know" Junior said while laughing softly, "I know. You hate everything about me that reminds me of you."

Ranier knew that was true, and he fought having a smile creep over his lips.

"But, that only serves to highlight the point Ranier. I am an extension of you. You are an extension of Grandpa and Elleana, who are extensions of their parents. While each of us have an individual portion that makes us truly unique, we also have a family portion to our being. There are many aspects to the dual nature of our beings, from our light and dark in our DNA to our individual and family parts.

"Our family parts are collections and extensions of every person who came before us. They passed DNA to us, but they also passed different spiritual parts to us. If we cut a person in our ancestry out, we lose the part of them that they contributed to us. If we cut our entire heritage out, we lose all parts of us that are made of family, and we would, effectively, cease to exist. Just like our dark parts try to convince us that they are good and worth having, our individual part, though remotely small, convinces us that it is everything to who we are and that we can do without our family parts.

"There is, of course, a natural tension, or opposition, between our individual and family parts. The individual interests must bend to the family interests, while the family interests must bend and recognize and respect the individual nature of each family member. The opposition is a righteous, or complementary type, opposition, one that propels us forward and brings life. We can only live due to the contributions of each family member who has gone before, and cutting even just one out will disrupt the chain of life.

"Family members," Junior continued, "help each other by carrying certain loads for each other. Our bodies, physical and spiritual, are divided into many parts, such as the heart and mind. Our spirit bodies were created by God, and we are all spiritually brothers and sisters. Life itself comes from our tie back to God. However, our spirit bodies can be filled with darkness or light, based on the Intelligence inside of us. Do you remember," Junior asked, "when Elleana spoke of one-third of the hosts of Heaven following Lucifer?" Ranier nodded. "Some of these were Intelligences of darkness, while others were Intelligences of light. Same for the two-thirds who followed God. There were some based in darkness, and some based in light."

"While our spirit body is created by God, our individual spiritual parts can be based in darkness or light, just as our physical parts can be. The spirit body fully reflects the Intelligence inside, and so a spirit body's parts may become dark when the Intelligence itself is dark inside. For the Intelligences of darkness, their path was surely a rough one indeed as they had so much to overcome to change who they were at their core. They all recognized the value of the light, and wanted to move past their existence based in darkness. God promised them the ability to be reborn, and to be a being made fully of light.

"However, the portion of the two-thirds of Heaven who were Intelligences of light felt moved with compassion for the dark Intelligences, and all sought to help in some way to make the journey easier for the Intelligences of darkness. Many beings of light offered at least some part of him or herself to place in a being of darkness, and in a small way, undertook to be a 'Savior on Mount Zion' as spoken of in the scriptures.

"In the book of Jacob, Jacob describes the Lord's vineyard and how the Lord grafted wild and tame branches together in an attempt to spread good fruit among wild trees. This so-called 'grafting' applies at many levels, from the extent of certain people in certain nations down to the individual level. This concept of 'grafting' applies in our families extensively. One of the ways our families were arranged on this earth was by the people who volunteered to give the dark counterparts parts of their light being."

Seeing that Ranier was mostly confused, Junior clarified by saying "Imagine a counterpart of darkness in a spirit body. All of its parts would reflect darkness, and its parts would drive it to act on the pulls and demands of darkness. Contrast that with a being of light, whose spiritual parts would reflect light. The situation seemed lopsided to most everyone, and so one spirit would volunteer, say, to give his heart of light to a being of darkness, and receive, in return, the dark heart from the being of darkness.

"Our spiritual parts are fully interchangeable, or 'graft-able'. Due to this, God arranged for families where dark parts and parts of light would be interspersed throughout us. These were tied, of course, to our DNA, but were arranged by God to help balance the level of light and dark inside us all.

"Most importantly, due to the chain and relationship family creates, our ancestors, or descendants, can carry parts of darkness for us, or give us parts of their light. All of us are attempting to overcome the dark parts by changing them to become parts of light, and if we accomplish our goal, we can return the parts we changed to light to the Intelligence counterpart of darkness. Our work of perfecting ourselves, in other words, contributes directly to perfecting the entire family chain, as parts of us are parts of our ancestors and descendants, carried in a great work of love as the darkness we carry is quite often carried for someone else."

Pausing for a moment to feel where Ranier was at, Junior sensed that he could go on. "Think of life on Earth Ranier. This entire grafting is played out before our eyes, in the physical world. Due to the veil, we would forget these things and lose track of who we really are. We would forget that our dark parts did not define us or limit us. To help us remember this battle of light and dark, God gave us all different skin colors. White and black help us remember that we are beings of light and dark, while brown skin, like the majority of the world has, reminds us of the grafting, or mixing of light and dark, which exists inside of us all."

"So black people are the counterparts of darkness?" Ranier asked.

"No, oh no" Junior exclaimed. "Skin color helps us remember something about our premortal past. Plenty of beings of light are born with black skin. Many such beings volunteered for the black skin, as they wanted to better be able to understand and have compassion for the counterparts of darkness. Unfortunately, people use their eyes to judge a person, but the color of a person's skin generally has nothing to do with what is inside."

"Is there ever a time when skin color tells us anything about a person?" Ranier asked. "If the skin color doesn't match what is inside, what is the point of it?"

"The point," Junior said patiently, "is to help us recognize that we are one family. It may sound counterintuitive at first, but it is to help us overcome a deeply rooted part of ourselves that originated in the pre-mortal life. In our pre-mortal life, the Intelligences of light despised the Intelligences of darkness. Most of the Intelligences of darkness always acted on their dark nature, and they would take every opportunity to destroy, hurt, and otherwise terrorize Intelligences of light. Saytah learned how to deal with them all during his long stay on the Other Side, and he ultimately gained compassion for them and the ability to truly love them, despite their dark nature.

"When the Mirror broke, the Intelligences of light were suddenly with the Intelligences of darkness, and the mixing of the two caused many problems. Most Intelligences of light developed deep animosity for Intelligences of darkness, something we would likely recognize in the racism that exists on the earth. Due to this animosity, many Intelligences of light were not happy in the least bit when Saytah revealed that he planned to save every Intelligence of darkness who would come to him. Various prophets have expressed the great mercy of God in denying none who come unto him, as this is a mercy many Intelligences of light were not willing to extend themselves.

"Due to the animosity that arose in the Intelligences of light," Junior continued, "we had to have a way on the earth to overcome such animosity. Due to the veil placed over our memory, it would be necessary for our physical body to see differences in color. This would draw these issues from our pre-mortal state to our consciousness, and would allow us to recognize and work to change the deep animosity we held towards Intelligences of darkness. Ultimately, the different skin colors help us recognize that we are all alike unto God, and he provides a way for all that come unto him, regardless of race, gender, or dark or light Intelligence.

"Again though," Junior said as he was wrapping up his thought, "the color of skin does not mean anything about what is inside. Actually," he said after thinking for a minute, "mixing what is inside throughout all skin colors helps us recognize and get past our animosity faster. When we encounter good people of any skin color, our animosity that may exist is lessened. The more good, or light, we see in people of other skin colors, the faster we can overcome the animosity that pre-mortally arose in many of us."

Ranier was interested by these thoughts, but he still didn't feel he understood everything Junior was talking about. "You still didn't answer my question," Ranier stated after a minute of Junior being lost in thought.

"What question?" Junior asked.

"The one about whether there is any skin color that always indicates a certain type of Intelligence inside."

"Sorry," Junior said, "I got a little lost in the other things I was saying. I don't know the full history on this as I haven't made the effort yet to learn about all of the groups who have lived on Earth, but I know of two groups who always had certain Intelligences inside of them. One such group was called the 'Lamanites', and existed on the American Continent from sometime after 600 BC or so. At that time, those who were led by their 'evil nature', or Intelligence of darkness, were given a darker skin to help the Intelligences of light recognize and not intermarry with those carrying the evil nature.

"As Intelligences of light were trying to gain strength and increase the amount of good DNA they could pass on to posterity, God often made commandments against intermarriages with other groups to help preserve a good DNA and spiritual line that could ultimately carry through to most on the earth now. Rules against intermarriage were especially important in the earlier times, when it was necessary to establish a good, or strong light DNA strand that could continue through the end of the earth. Once the DNA strands were strong enough, rules against intermarriage were no longer necessary. Abraham received the promises associated with the good DNA and spiritual line flowing through his posterity, but this promise also meant that, for a time, his posterity had to follow strict commands on who they could marry.

"Going back to the Lamanites though," Junior continued, "they existed at a time when it was still important for Intelligences of light to not mix DNA with Intelligences of darkness, and so their skin color served as a way to indicate the level of control of their evil nature inside them. There were times when portions of the Lamanites would follow God and reject their evil nature, and when they did, their skin color often followed the level of light Intelligence that they had accepted. Currently, on the earth, no person's skin color changes with the level of light and dark inside them, which means that skin color, at this time in the earth's existence, is not tied to the level of dark or light Intelligence inside of a person."

After thinking for a moment, Junior continued "One other group I know of though is the Jews. Jews with a pure bloodline are all 'children of the light', or God's 'chosen'. The 'chosen' in this context doesn't mean preferred or better than another, but it means, instead, that they were 'selected' to be in a body that was not grafted in with parts from other Intelligences of darkness. This, ultimately, would mean more hardship and suffering for these people, as they would be hated by all who had a graft of darkness in them as darkness hates the light, and would also be tempted and blinded in ways different from others.

"When we are grafted with different parts, we quickly experience the pulls of light and dark and can more easily recognize and see what is good and what is bad, and we can recognize we lack knowledge and understanding as there are dark parts, internally, we don't understand. When our whole Intelligence is light, however, this creates a situation where the being may be easily persuaded to believe it understands, or sees, everything, even though it doesn't due to its physical limitations.

"Intelligences of light, in other words, walk by their own light as they feel they can see so much. They, in scripture language, kindle their own fire. Isaiah states 'Behold all ye that kindle fire, that compass yourselves about with sparks, walk in the light of your fire and in the sparks which ye have kindled. This shall ye have of mine hand—ye shall lie down in sorrow.'

"The sorrow comes as the light has a strong attraction to the darkness, and the light portions of ourselves will often embrace principles of darkness due to the force of the ever-pulling attraction between light and dark. The light cannot recognize the darkness though, because it has nothing internally to compare it to, and so a being lacking grafts of darkness has a much harder time recognizing and accepting that it is operating on principles of darkness as it has no internal gauge to measure it by.

"Any reader of the Bible can see this play out. The Jews were Intelligences of light, but they became entirely confident that they were right and followed the 'law'. They despised Jesus when he came, and the children of light, sadly, were the only group of people blinded enough by their own light to crucify their Savior. Any other group, with any level of darkness grafted in, would have recognized their Savior, as the darkness in a being greatly aids in its ability to discern.

"Ultimately, because the Jews then did not have darkness from within, their periods of interacting with light and dark comes from without. Sadly, the Jews, or Intelligences of light with no grafting, were some of the most abused and persecuted groups of people, and generations of persecution and suffering is helping to shape the Intelligences of light to be able to recognize and get rid of the principles of darkness accepted by their ancestors during the Savior's ministry on the earth. There had to be a group of people who helped train parts of light to recognize when principles of darkness were operating and when the light itself blinded a being from the truth, and the Jews were those 'chosen' to help bring this part of understanding to all of our light parts."

"How is that fair?" Ranier asked. "I still don't think the God you and Elleana speak of is a fair God, and I'm still not sure I want to believe in him." Ranier could sense Junior smiling, and he glanced at Junior slightly angry that Junior would find his question funny.

"Honestly Ranier," Junior said, fully perceiving Ranier's anger, "that is an extremely lame excuse to not believe in God." Ranier felt the anger rising through his body, but Junior kept going. "Do you really believe that you are all-knowing enough to understand the individual nature of each person, to understand the full balance of light and dark given to a person, to understand how mercy and justice have different demands on different people based on the level of light and dark in them?

"Do you really believe you can see enough to tell God he isn't fair? You have been listening to Elleana, me, and probably others for a while now. You've been told all kinds of things you never knew or had never even considered. These all have opened your mind to new possibilities. Somehow though you still are smug enough in your own understanding and vision to believe you see everything that takes place from beginning to end, to believe you can see enough to make a judgment call as to what is fair!"

Ranier was surprised and taken back by Junior's response, but Junior wasn't done. "I'm not perfect Ranier and I have a temper just like you. One thing I can't stand, just like you can't stand, is when people make judgment calls without knowing all of the facts. God is giving you so much right now Ranier! Can you not see that?! Only a few people ever get to visit the Spirit World and return to Earth! Why is it 'fair' you are here and others are not?! Why is it 'fair' you were born to Elleana, one of the most loving and forgiving people? Why is it 'fair' you get all of these experiences and all of this knowledge while I went my entire time on Earth without it, or without even a father for that matter?!

"And how, might I ask, are you able to determine what is 'fair' when you fail to consider the entire picture, from your existence as an Intelligence all the way through eternity? Instead of saying something isn't fair, you should instead ask what you don't understand about the situation! You have no clue who you even are Ranier, and your reference to things not being 'fair' highlights how blind you are to everything God is doing for you and for others.

"When you and others talk about 'fair' most of you are referring to 'equality', or suggesting that to be just, each being needs to be treated equal. I'll tell you something about 'equality' though," Junior said as he pronounced the word with disgust, "people view others with different things and assume God must not love them, just because they don't have everything that someone else does. Yet, these people are all entirely blind to what they do have. They have things no one else has, and yet they feel unloved because they don't have everything they want.

"It's entirely wrong to judge God's love for you based on what someone else receives, as you have such limited understanding of them or you. Additionally, the fact that we all have different things is proof of God's love for us as an individual. God gives us what we need, and we all need different things because we are all different. Can you imagine if you needed something, but God had to say 'sorry, can't give that to you because no one else has been given it?!' Justice, fairness, and love is not found in disregarding individual needs and giving everyone the same thing. Rather, it's found in a one-on-one ministry, where you get what you need. Difference, not equality, shows true love Ranier."

Junior was pacing now and Ranier could sense Junior's frustration. Normally, Ranier would have responded to Junior's anger with more anger, but this time, Ranier was silent. Junior's words were certainly true. He couldn't see what God was doing in his life or in the lives of others. His judgment of what was 'fair' was always based on what he could see and comprehend, and it never included the big picture, from start to finish, from pre-mortal life all the way through to eternity. Ranier was beginning to see how his lack of faith in a bigger picture contributed to his lack of ability to see God in his life.

When he only believed in existence as being what took place on Earth, his perception of life, God, and many other things was significantly limited. Now that he was in the Spirit World, his perception of life, God, and other things was expanding significantly. Ranier sensed the truth to Junior's words, and decided to do something he had never done before.

Chapter 19

"I'M SORRY" RANIER SAID. "I was wrong in saying that."
Junior immediately stopped pacing and stared for a minute.
"I'm sorry too," Junior replied, "I shouldn't have spoken that way."

"No," Ranier said, "I needed it. It's good to have someone speak to me direct like that. Somethings," Ranier said with a slight smile, "only a family member could get away with saying." Junior laughed and nodded his head in agreement.

After a minute of sitting while their tensions eased, Ranier, still unwilling to fully face the fact he had a son and other children, tried to change the subject rather than continue thinking about how he had failed them.

"One thing I don't understand yet," Ranier said while trying to shift the focus away from family things, "is the difference in treatment between Lucifer and his followers and those who came to Earth. From what I gathered before, and I could have misunderstood, Lucifer and his followers only received one chance, and when they did not follow God, they were forever banished from Heaven. Yet, God seems to give me chance after chance, and even a little bit ago I asked for a second chance and was given that. I honestly struggle understanding why all of those who followed Lucifer will never receive a second chance."

"Well," Junior said, "that is a valid concern, but it assumes some things that aren't true and highlights a misunderstanding of other things. Your statement, for example, seems premised on the fact that Lucifer's followers did not receive a second chance. They did though Ranier. They received countless chances to follow God.

"Most people fail to grasp the length and duration of the War in Heaven. When the Mirror broke, there was a significantly extended period of confusion and chaos as the Heaven Side and the Other Side of the Mirror mixed together. God took the time to gather everyone out of the darkness. After the significant time of gathering, the great Council in Heaven was held. All of Heaven, and all of the Other Side, was in attendance. The light and dark Intelligences weren't in the same space, but both participated in the Council. There, Elirah explained his Plan of Salvation, and his plan to take us all to a better world. Lucifer explained his plan to bring security to our existence.

"When Lucifer and his plan were rejected, they resorted to force to carry out Lucifer's plan. The War in Heaven though did not take place like a typical battle you see on Earth, with one side shooting at the other side. The War in Heaven was a war based largely in ideology, faith, and hope. Spirits contended with each other, with neighbors, friends, and those we would call their family. They debated principles of good and evil, principles associated with each plan, and whether it was ultimately possible for Saytah to sacrifice himself to satisfy the law of love and create a new universe founded in love.

"This War, or debate, raged for an extremely long period in our pre-mortal existence. God wanted nothing more than to have all of the Intelligences accept his plan and be saved, and God did everything possible to give every spirit and Intelligence every piece of knowledge necessary to understand what they were doing. Each spirit and Intelligence who followed Lucifer did so under full knowledge of the ramifications of their choices.

"We get second chances in this life when we are not acting under full knowledge of what the consequences of our choices are. God keeps things veiled from us so we can experience the bad associated with certain choices without forever condemning ourselves. This is a merciful act that helps us decide we don't want certain bad things in our life. Our time on the earth is given to us to repent and change and accept the truth. Even though they were before this earth, Lucifer and his followers were given so many chances Ranier, and all powers of persuasion possible were used to convince them to accept life."

Sensing that Ranier still struggled understanding why so many people would follow Lucifer and his plan, Junior continued "spirits followed Lucifer, ultimately, because they didn't want to work to exist. Life requires work, life requires effort, life requires change, life requires faith, life requires family. These beings wanted an existence without work, they wanted to be provided for without providing for themselves. They believed they could live without working, without expending effort, that their life was a 'right' that should be supported by others. They believed they could exist without exercising faith. Lucifer promised them a safe and secure place, free of effort, free of conscientious thought, and free of pain. They believed the Universe would always provide. It was, to them, an ideal worth fighting for, and so they put their faith in Lucifer's plan."

"Doesn't fighting contradict what they were seeking for?" Ranier asked. "If they wanted security, freedom from pain and work, etc., it seems that fighting was the opposite of that. Why would they work so hard to never have to work again?"

"It is a conflicting thing," Junior agreed, "but all of Lucifer's plan conflicted. It had no foundation. God's plan would work because it was based on the foundation of Christ, the Creator of all things. Lucifer's plan though was based on nothing other than selfish ideals, and it was a plan with a lot of circular reasoning.

"Ultimately, the beings believed that because they existed, their existence could now take an existence independent of the source from whence they came. Many of us experience the same thoughts and tendencies. We quickly become blinded to how we came to be, to those who came before, and we assume we have no need of them. However, it is never possible to cut ourselves off from the source from whence we came, as it is the source that brings life. In essence, at the heart of Lucifer's plan, each being felt they could become the source of their own existence. They viewed life from the lens of their own existence, and felt their independent existence could always be sustained in whatever manner they so chose.

"The violence and work involved with Lucifer's plan came because Lucifer's plan involved submitting to mind control, so once the spirits submitted irrevocably to Lucifer's mind control, they became his subjects to act. As it is anytime that one follows Lucifer, you never get what you were promised. His followers were promised freedom from pain and work, but they fully adopted a path of pain and work. They enlisted to fight to force everyone to accept their plan, as they knew Lucifer's plan would not work and they would cease existing if even one person didn't join in Lucifer's plan.

"There were many more problems, of course, with Lucifer's plan. The Universe doesn't just produce or provide, it takes effort and work to create the items necessary for life. Additionally, Intelligence requires progression in order to remain alive. Remember, the Intelligence Stream always moves. If it ever stopped, life would cease. Life is found in progression, and the two cannot be separated. That is why God is a God of eternal progression, as he is the God of life.

"Progression though requires work and effort, and ultimately, faith, and those who followed Lucifer did not want a life based on principles of progression, work, and faith. So, they chose a course to death, a course that would free them from effort, conscientious thought, faith and other required uses of their Intelligence. To them, the cost of living was too high as they never wanted to have to suffer. It was sad to see so many reject life itself. We lost so many, including some of the magnificent animals."

"Animals?" Ranier said with surprise, but then he remembered the dragons James had mentioned.

"Yes," Junior said surprised that Ranier was surprised, "even animals followed Lucifer."

"Wait," Ranier said with hesitation as he thought about the dragons, "animals have the ability to choose?"

"Yes, Ranier, animals are Intelligences as well, each at a different level of Intelligence, and each below the level of human Intelligence. However, each animal also had to choose what it wanted, and we lost a lot of the animal creations in the War. People still often remember glimpses of some of the animals that followed Lucifer, including the dragon, and these animals are often passed down in tradition or folklore."

Junior could see Ranier's brow furrow as Ranier was thinking hard on this concept. He let Ranier think in silence for a minute. Finally, Ranier said "I don't recall hearing about how animals fit into everything on Earth. Why would God create vicious animals? Why would he create mosquitos, spiders, snakes, and other creatures that bring so much fear to people?"

"The animal kingdom is a fascinating one," Junior said as he nodded in agreement with Ranier's question, "that most makes sense when considered from the perspective of beings of light and darkness. For every Intelligence of light that was a lower Intelligence, there was an

Intelligence of darkness. Many of these Intelligences of darkness, even though part of the Other Side, were attracted to the light. These beings all caused fear to reign among the Intelligences of light. They were dark, scary, and vicious, and couldn't be trusted due to their dark nature. However, at a base level, they had a desire to become a being of light, and God prepared a way for them to do so.

"The way was to bring them all to Earth, both the animals from Heaven and the animals from the Other Side. Animals such as the shark and snake are from the Other Side. Insects show the wisdom of God. On Earth the insects are small and can be dealt with by humans. Many insects are from the Other Side, and all caused a lot of terror as they were quite large pre-mortally.

"At the Council, nearly all questioned how it would be possible to live with the life forms from the Other Side. God smiled, and indicated that while each being needed a chance to come to the earth, there was no requirement as to what size they had to be on the earth relative to what size they had been pre-mortally. In other words, many of the large, vicious life forms pre-mortally, such as spiders, were reduced to a small size, one that allowed for humans and spiders to live together. People retain deep fears of them though, as they have memories deep inside of large spiders attacking or injuring them or those close to them after the Mirror broke.

"Ultimately, the circle of life on the earth was accomplished through a carefully balanced graft of light and dark natures in the animal kingdom. Animals of light, such as the lion, were grafted with parts of darkness, which caused them to consume and kill other animals. Once the Savior comes again though, animals and insects will have worked enough to overcome all of the dark parts inside them, and each will receive parts of light, the new light from the new Universe. The parts of light will bring peace in the animal and insect kingdoms."

"What about dinosaurs?" Ranier asked suddenly, as he had always had a fascination with them since being a child. "Did they ever live on the earth, or live at all?"

"Yes to both questions" Junior said. "There weren't many dinosaurs though that followed God's plan. Most followed Lucifer. Generally, entire sets of animals either followed one or the other plan. However, dinosaurs split, with a few following God. Those that did were given bodies in their usual size here on the earth since they would not have enough of them to make it until the humans were formed on the earth.

"As animals were created before humans on the earth, dinosaurs lived and died before humans were ever placed on the earth. Humans and dinosaurs, in their normal size, were incompatible on the earth, which is why we never co-existed. God promised them though that people would still get to know about them, and it is one reason that their bones have been preserved.

"Once all of the dinosaurs that had followed God received bodies though, none of them could have any more posterity, and they died off, just as other animals who have become extinct. Animals are promised they will last long enough on the earth to allow for each spirit that followed God to have an opportunity to come here, and extinction only follows a species once all of the spirits associated with that animal type have made it to the earth."

"So how old is the earth?" Ranier asked. "Scientists say it is millions of years old."

"I honestly don't know the exact age of the earth Ranier. But I do know it is old, from our perspective. When God formed the earth, he spoke of different days of creation. Each day was based on the rotation of the pre-mortal planet that God resided on at the time. That planet rotated extremely slow, and a day to God on that planet translated into many millions of earth years. Currently, God lives on a planet near Kolob, and that planet has a rotation time of 1,000 earth years.

"So, the earth's creation took roughly seven days, and the earth's existence will be roughly seven days. But, after God's day of rest that he took from the creation process, he moved to a new planet Kolob, and the length of the days changed dramatically. Because of this, we know that the earth will have about seven thousand years of existence from the time Adam and Eve left the Garden of Eden, as it will exist for seven of God's current days, but we cannot compare the days from that time to the days of creation itself, as they were measured according to very different measures."

Ranier suddenly looked about as he realized he had become absorbed in the conversation and unaware of his surroundings. He had forgotten about the two women Junior had been with earlier, but he somehow realized they were watching him. Junior had said these were his daughters, and he was caught with guilt rising up in him again. He had always thought he knew everything and was quite convinced of his intellectual abilities. However, he was realizing now how far off he was in his assessment of himself, as he didn't even know that he had children. This time in the Spirit World had certainly opened his eyes to many things, and he could sense his time would eventually be done here. He wanted desperately to make things right with his children here before he left though.

Ranier looked at Junior, and again did something he had never done before. He suddenly hugged Junior. "Thank you," he said as he embraced him, "thank you for forgiving me. I don't know how to make it up to you."

"It's okay Dad," Junior said as he embraced Ranier back, "let's just be a family."

"How though?" Ranier asked. "They still hate me" he said as he nodded towards his two daughters in the distance.

"And you still hate your Dad" Junior responded. "All of it has to go for us to be a family."

While Ranier didn't want to believe it, a part of Ranier knew what Junior said was true. Yet, he had no idea how to forgive. He had never forgiven anyone before, and until now, he had assumed that no one had ever forgiven him. Ranier thought about all of those he had left, hurt, or used. He wondered what they thought of him, and he especially thought of those he had left who had carried his children. It still was so foreign for him to realize he had children, and he absolutely hated that he had done to them what his father had done to him. But, he was amazed at Junior's acceptance of him. Junior's forgiveness and acceptance of him made him think that maybe forgiveness was possible. Maybe it was possible to start over again.

"Will they talk to me?" Ranier asked Junior, nodding his head towards the two women a way off.

"Probably" Junior said matter-of-factly, "but don't expect anything kind from them. They haven't left yet though, which is probably a sign they are at least expecting something from you right now. They went through a lot on Earth Ranier, and not having you present caused a lot of heartache for them."

Ranier slowly nodded his head in understanding, and started walking towards his two daughters, entirely unsure of how to even begin.

Chapter 20

AS RANIER DREW CLOSE TO his daughters, he was amazed at how beautiful they were. He realized he found them beautiful since they carried many of the attributes of Elleana. As he recognized Elleana's influence on them, the level of turmoil inside him increased significantly. He could also see himself in his daughters, and it took his heart to the breaking point as he reflected on how much he hated his father for doing the same thing he had done. Ranier finally reached them, but found himself fully unable to say anything. He felt he could barely stand as his emotions continued to whirl inside of him.

Suddenly, Ranier found himself crying, something that would have never happened before. The tears fell steadily as he tried to see through them, but it also gave him an excuse to look at the ground as he couldn't bring himself to look his daughters in the eye. Ranier felt that the emotions racing through him were telling a story, a story of his past, of his knowledge, or lack of it, a story of who he longed to be. He didn't want to be his father. He didn't want to abandon his children. He just didn't know.

There was, however, a dark part he tried to keep repressed, a part about what would have happened had he known he had made someone pregnant. As he stood in front of his daughters, the darkness inside told him another story, a story of how he hated children, a story of how he would have left even if he knew, a story of how he would have mistreated his children's mothers.

Ranier was appalled at the depth of the darkness and the emotions it produced. The awfulness of the darkness caused his tears to slow as he tried to understand the emotions going through him. As he focused on what the darkness was causing him to feel, he suddenly heard the woman scream "Ranier!" He gasped and jumped in shock while looking up, scared that his daughters had left, scared that he wouldn't be able to make things right. Surprisingly, his two daughters were still there.

Ranier tried to calm down enough to speak. He still didn't know what to say but he knew he had to say something. As he tried to regain control, he suddenly sensed a mix of hate and pity, but somehow it felt different from his own emotions. Suddenly, he understood that he was feeling his daughters' emotions, and the mix of darkness and light inside them. A part of them wanted to talk to him, but a part of them hated him. Their emotions were entirely open to him, and he could see how the mix of their emotions also left them unable to move or to talk to him.

Ranier remembered that spirits were an open book. Up to this point, he had not been able to sense other spirits much, but they could always sense his thoughts and emotions. He wasn't sure why he could suddenly sense his daughters' emotions and thoughts, but he could, and as he did, he realized they could fully sense his as well. While none of them had said a word, they all were speaking to each other, fully sharing every heartache, every pain, every broken dream, the hate, the anger, and the longing. The longing for something better. The longing that the bad childhood could be made better. The longing for a place to call home, for people to call family, for things to exist in a non-broken state.

As the emotions of the three continued to course through each of them, Ranier could sense that the dark emotions were losing their hold. Somehow, the light emotions were becoming more prevalent as the emotions related to a desire for family were taking over the other emotions. Ranier realized that his dreams ever since being a small child were to take away the suffering of children like him, for him to have a mother, a father, sisters and brothers. He had watched other children and always hated that he was so different, that he lacked anything about being a family. He realized that his hatred of his situation caused him to hate other children, as he didn't feel it was fair that other children would get would he had wanted for so long.

Something struck deeply in Ranier as the three stood, unable to speak. Ranier sensed and understood that a part of him, and a part of his daughters, had never grown up, had never matured, and had never developed. Rather, it had regressed until it was almost non-existent, like a small embryo. The lack of presence of a father for the three had caused regression of this part, instead of progression. Ranier didn't understand what part it was, but could suddenly see that the presence of a child's parents was absolutely necessary for this part to develop and grow, as it was only their presence that could touch and influence this part. Ranier realized then how incomplete he was, and how incomplete his daughters were, since they all had never known their fathers.

As Ranier looked at his daughters, he saw so much of himself in them, even though most of the pieces of him had been repressed by his daughters. He wasn't sure how, but he was beginning to suddenly understand different things. He realized that the part inside of him, the part that hadn't developed, was a part from the new Universe founded by Christ, the new Universe founded in love. The part was a small portion of the light, or Intelligence, of Christ, shared with each person. The part existed with Christ as the Father, but was contributed to and grown by those with Christ-like tendencies, and was most contributed to and affected by a child's family.

Each physical parent contributed a copy of their light of Christ to their children, and each physical parent had direct access to that part of light, to act in a way that helped it to grow, or to act in a way that diminished it. Ranier could see how the part of the light of Christ was a full combination of all of the light from ancestors before, all the way back to Adam himself.

The part was unobtrusive, gentle, quiet and calm. It did not shout and was hard to sense. It was hard to recognize its influence, unless one acted to help the part grow and develop. Ranier could sense that a knowledge of ancestors and family could help the part grow and develop, as knowledge of each ancestor would cause that ancestor's contribution to be able to be sensed, felt, and acted upon in the individual.

Ranier saw that life was about more than an individual, that life was about more than himself. Life came through the family. Ranier had no family on Earth, and he was nearly dead spiritually. His light was almost non-existent. That part of the light of Christ was nearly gone, but it still had something left to it.

As he pondered on what would keep that part of light alive, understanding poured into his mind. He suddenly saw a beautiful building, white, with spires pointing towards Heaven. He remembered seeing similar buildings on Earth and hearing them referred to as "temples". He suddenly saw himself inside this temple, in a beautiful room of simple decoration. There were chairs in the room, surrounding an altar which came a few feet up into the air. The walls on either side had two mirrors set exactly opposite each other, with the mirrors reflecting the contents of the room back and forth, seemingly forever.

Ranier then saw people dressed in white enter and kneel down across from each other at the altar. He saw them "sealed" to each other by a man glowing with light and authority. As he saw this, he suddenly saw the ancestors and posterity of the couple "sealed" together, and saw the light of Christ, the light in that part he sensed, grow. He sensed that the "sealing" he had witnessed forever embedded the couple's contribution to the part with the light of Christ in each ancestor and each individual of their posterity. The sealing caused a ripple back and forth in that couple's line, a ripple that reflected through eternity, just as the mirrors in the room reflected everything in the room forward and backward forever.

Ranier was in awe at the images in his mind. As he continued seeing, he saw that nothing could overcome the contribution of light from the couple to the part he was now sensing existed. Ranier saw that two of his ancestors had been "sealed" together, ancestors from long ago, even as far back as Adam. This "sealing" had caused their contribution to his part to always remain alive, and that contribution was keeping the family part from totally regressing to a point of non-existence.

Ranier could now see others, children who were born into families sealed together, even with generations of ancestors sealed together. The family parts inside them were vibrant and strong, with each ancestor's contribution directly continuing to influence the individual. Even with the vibrancy and strength of these parts, developed and nurtured by parents and ancestors, individuals would still make bad choices as the level of darkness inside was also quite significant. Those with highly developed good parts tended to have high levels of grafting of darkness in them as well, and many still struggled understanding and separating the two.

However, Ranier could see the only thing that would ultimately reduce the light from the couple was the couple's own actions. If the couple chose to act on evil, the light diminished throughout their ancestors and posterity. If the couple chose to remain virtuous and good, the light stayed strong and vibrant, and Ranier watched as countless children and descendants eventually overcame the darkness inside due to the strength and vibrancy of the light inside. In other words, he saw how the good actions of a parent helped fill a child or descendant's being with light.

Ranier stood in awe at the beautiful simplicity of it all, and the beauty of the family throughout all ages. He saw countless people who cared and loved an individual. Each ancestor had DNA and a contribution to the part with the light of Christ in it in each of their descendants. Everyone was tied to someone else. Everyone was a brother or sister, a son of Adam or a daughter of Eve, and ultimately a child of God. Everyone had a place in God's family, and everyone had a place in a smaller family.

Ranier realized he had always wanted to have what he—in reality—always had. He had wanted a place where he was home, where others cared about him, where he had a place with others who wanted him to be there. Ranier could see the thousands of his ancestors who provided just that. He could see how family was a natural part of a person, an integral part. Every person was an individual, but every person had a part inside them—Ranier understood now—that was a family part as well. No person was meant or designed to be alone, and everyone had a part that made them want to be part of something greater than just themselves.

Ranier could see how the longing for family stemmed from two sources—from the collective nature of Intelligence all existing in one great whole in the Intelligence stream and from the contribution of each ancestor to every individual. Ranier could see how Lucifer played on this natural longing to be part of something more than one's self. Lucifer would mock, taunt, and tease to make an individual feel excluded.

Everyone, in one way or another, would act to try and find acceptance with something more than themselves. The fear of being left alone drove many people to act in ways contrary to their light inside, and Lucifer would keep people in his grasp by mocking them and making them feel they would not fit in with others, ultimately driving many people to immorality, drugs, long hours at work, or other places that had negative effects on an individual.

Of course, there was no true acceptance in what Lucifer set up. It was all an illusion, and acting against the light inside to try and fit in would just make one feel sad, depressed, and hollow inside. Ranier could see the depression that ravaged people as they sought for acceptance in the wrong places. True light, and true development to the family part in an individual, only came through the family, through service, through acting on the principles of light itself.

As Ranier began to understand the role of family in existence itself, he saw that the family enabled eternal progression, or eternal life. Life only came through a circle of individuals tied together and lifting each other up. Christ, even, was the Father of everyone as he enabled their creation on Earth, but he also became the Son by being born on Earth. His daughter, Mary, became his Mother. Thus, he was the Father and the Son. All of humanity, Ranier saw, also had to be a father and son, or mother and daughter, in order for life to exist. All helped and contributed to each other.

Ranier saw how Christ, as Saytah, had created a physical body for Elirah, or Heavenly Father. Everybody created required another being to put the Intelligence and spirit inside of it. There was no way for a being to create its own body, or to put itself inside of a body. Because of that, Saytah, due to his power to create and divide elements, had first created a spiritual body for Elirah and Charity, who then, in turn, created a spiritual body for Saytah.

Thus, Saytah was the "Father and the Son" in this sense also, just as Elirah was also the "Father and the Son". Ranier could see that individuals were powerless to give themselves life, and that all life was predicated upon the existence of others who could serve and help each other. The circle of life gave everyone an opportunity to help and be helped. In other words, it enabled service and sacrifice, and service and sacrifice enabled life.

Again, the beauty and simplicity of it left Ranier struck with amazement. He looked at his daughters, and saw the beauty they possessed, a beauty that came from the contributions of countless people who went before. While everyone was an individual, they were also a part of a great whole, a beautiful tapestry stretching through eternity.

Ranier could see that no part of the human family could be left out. Everyone had to be sealed to their immediate family to produce an intricate web of connectivity. The sealing brought life, and kept each part of a person alive. Ranier continued to understand and see that the sealing also tied everyone, ultimately, to Christ. The sealing tie to

Christ was essential to pull everyone to the new Universe. As Ranier watched, he saw the heavens being destroyed as the darkness and light fully mixed together after the last seal of protection was removed from the firmament. He watched in horror as the waves of annihilation swept through the Universe he knew.

He realized as he watched that the waves of annihilation traveled faster than light itself and that those on the earth would never see the annihilation coming. He saw as well that annihilation took place in stages, with different levels of darkness reaching the earth at different times. The earth would begin to break down, with an increase in earthquakes, fires, and pollutions. People would also begin to break down, as their parts were slowly destroyed.

Eventually, Ranier saw that the earth and heavens were both destroyed, but that God had provided a way for everyone to be sealed through vicarious work in the temples to their family. This great welding link provided a way for Christ to pull each individual from the destroyed Universe to the new Universe founded in love. If everyone had not been sealed together and an individual left on the earth, the waves of annihilation would have rippled through the parts of everyone tied to the person left. In other words, it was essential for all that everyone be sealed, so that there was no way for the annihilation to overtake those in existence.

Ranier realized his daughters were feeling and seeing the same things. They could see that Ranier was an integral part of their existence, one they could not escape from. They all stood in silence as they absorbed the things they were seeing. As they stood, Ranier could readily discern the hatred they had for him. Usually, Ranier would get angry himself when he sensed another's hate, but not this time.

This time he realized he felt something new. He felt compassion for them. He understood what it was like to hate a father. He understood what it was like to be abandoned, and he now could sense that their hatred of him caused a hatred of themselves, just as Ranier's hatred of his father caused a hatred of himself. Somehow, Ranier could sense that due to the integral parts of family inside each person, it was impossible to hate a family member without hating a part of one's self.

"I'm sorry" Ranier suddenly heard himself say. "I'm so sorry." Ranier's daughters looked away at the sound of his voice, but they didn't move.

Ranier could sense the complex range of emotions running through each as they tried to decide what they should do. He found himself continuing "You have no reason to talk to me. I understand I did not do my part, not in the least. I was, and still am probably, a very bad person, thinking only of myself. I hurt both of you, and I don't have any way to ever give back to you what I should have done from the start.

"However," Ranier found himself continuing, "I'm trying to change. I want to be a different person. There is a lot I didn't understand before, and a lot I still don't understand. I know I don't deserve a second chance from you, but I will do everything in my power to be who I am supposed to be to you if given a second chance."

Ranier knew his words weren't necessary right now. The three of them could fully understand each other's feelings, and there was nothing hidden between them. He only spoke as it was what he was used to doing. As he stood in the silence surrounding the three, he was amazed at the new range of feelings he felt in his heart. Never before had he felt anything closely resembling compassion, concern, or even love, but as he felt everything his daughters felt these new emotions continued to grow inside of him.

Chapter 21

R ANIER WAS BEING SHOWN THINGS AGAIN. Images and understanding whirled through his mind as the compassionate feelings grew inside of him. He could sense that the feelings were the result of light inside of him, and that the light brought understanding with it. The light felt so different than anything he had ever experienced. His being had been full of darkness for so long that the light brought amazing healing and relief, even though it was only a small sliver of light entering his heart.

As he focused on the understanding the light brought, he understood that family was an integral part of existence, and an integral part of conveying light. Everyone, it seemed, could have compassion or concern for one's self. Seeing a part of him in his daughters, and seeing that parts of many individuals made up one individual, instantly made it easier for compassion to exist, as he began to see that others were simply an extension of himself, and that he was an extension of them.

Ranier remembered what Elleana had said about how a hatred of his father translated into a hatred of himself. He could see now how this was true, as he was an extension of his father, and due to the interconnectivity between them both, hating his father made him hate all of the parts his father had passed along to him.

As Ranier reflected on this, he could see that the hatred of any other person translated into a hatred of one's self, as all people were connected in some way or another. Ranier could see that while many people may not recognize their hatred of themselves, it was a feeling that lingered inside them as they harbored hate for others, and a feeling that made them act in cruel and unkind ways as they sought to blame others for the way they felt inside.

Ultimately, Ranier was beginning to sense that his hatred of others, and himself, translated into a hatred of God. For one, Ranier could see how all were connected to God. But, Ranier could also see that hatred immediately made a person's mind think that something was wrong with the person hated. It was impossible to hate without having thoughts affected to see something as being wrong. When a person hates another, that person sees the person he hates as being a mistake, which ultimately means, to the person's mind, that God made a mistake.

It saddened Ranier to see how blinding hatred was inside of people. Feelings of hate literally shut out reality for the person who possessed the hate, as the hate made the person blind to what is right and caused them to only see what was wrong. Ranier could recognize it would be impossible for him to have real faith in God unless he let go of his hate.

As Ranier reflected on this, he also realized that hatred and faith operated similarly, at least with respect to God. Just as hatred of one's self or others ultimately spilled over into feelings about God, so too did faith in one's self spill over and effect the level of faith possible in God. When a person was willing to believe they were capable of doing a task, even if it was with God's help, that belief, or faith, in themselves, translated directly into faith in God. However, if a person lacked faith in themselves, it really meant they lacked faith in the ability of God to give them the power or ability necessary to accomplish the task at hand, which meant, in turn, they lacked faith in the omnipotence of God.

Reflecting on hatred and faith, Ranier could see that the family was designed to help with both. Living with people meant becoming very familiar with their weaknesses and hypocrisies, and it was often hard to love those who are the closest, but it was hard not to as well because they were family. The family, Ranier could see, provided the perfect environment to help teach about hate, learn that love is better, and also learn that many things are possible through exercising faith, accepting help, and working together.

Ranier could see that the family was ordained of God. He didn't fully understand what that meant, but he felt it. He could see the family made it possible for light to exist inside each person, the family gave life to each person, and the family was forever part of a person, regardless of whether their parents were a part of their life or not. Learning to accept and love one's family was a prerequisite to loving and accepting one's self. Ranier could not have a full measure of light inside himself until his family had the same measure of light.

As Ranier thought on the things he was sensing, he could see the destructive nature of divorce, of single parent families, of parents forsaking their responsibilities to their children. Even when divorced, parents were still tied together through their children. He saw how divorce did little to fix things for most people, as it made their ability to have a full measure of light harder. He could see many good people who had been divorced, but integral parts of them had gone out, parts that were necessary to be complete. He saw the extinguishment of light in the children as parents were divorced or separated, and his heart began to break. He knew he had suffered under the loss of light from not having a father, and he knew his daughters had as well.

On the other hand, faces from Ranier's past were going through his mind. He saw families who had stuck together, even through extremely dark times. He saw children he envied while growing up, children whose parents had remained together, who spent time with them, who nurtured the light inside them. As he saw them this time, he didn't feel envy or hate as he did when a child. Instead, he saw the beauty that a family created. Father, mother, brother, sister, all tied together, created the most beautiful and intricate work he had ever beheld. As he focused on the beauty these people possessed, he suddenly realized that he was looking at their souls.

Ranier also realized he was feeling another new emotion—hope. He realized that such a relationship was still possible for him. He could have what he had always longed for, provided he could bring himself to forgive his father, and provided he could be given a chance to work to make things right for his daughters. It wasn't God keeping him from having what he always wanted, it was himself. As Ranier stood before his daughters, he could see that experiencing their feelings towards him was helping to begin to wash away the long-accrued feelings of hate and bitterness for his own father.

"Ranier." A man's voice, quiet and soft, cut through Ranier. Ranier was extremely surprised as he had not sensed the presence of another man besides Junior who had been watching from nearby, and he jumped with an audible gasp at hearing his name. He had not yet seen the man who had spoken, but something inside him fully knew the man. Now, a cascade of emotions rose in Ranier, just as it had in his daughters. Ranier did not have the power to turn and look, but stood with his eyes locked on the ground as his body shook from the emotions now coursing through him.

All of the light, compassion, and goodness Ranier had felt quickly disappeared. The darkness inside of him was so strong, so overpowering. He realized though that his response to this situation would set how his daughters would respond to him, and he struggled intently to remain in control of his being. He managed to look up quickly to see his daughters gazing fixedly at him, still entirely silent. Maybe it was best, he thought, to handle the situation like they did, remaining silent and not moving.

The few moments of silence following hearing his name seemed like an eternity to Ranier. He was fighting the urge to turn and say horrible things, to run and not look back, to give the man a piece of the hatred he had carried for so long. Ranier was starting to feel desperate. He could sense he was beginning to lose control, and that the darkness present inside him for so long was beginning to take over, just as it always had before. Ranier would have fully given in to such darkness before, but this time he fought it only because he wanted to preserve a possibility of reconciliation with his daughters, and if he gave in now, he was sure it would all be over.

As Ranier stood being ripped apart by the emotions fighting to overtake him, he suddenly felt a hand on his shoulder. Junior was standing by his side, looking intently at him.

"You can do it." Junior said encouragingly. "Just let go of the hatred inside."

Ranier realized that Junior's words were directed at him and his daughters. As the hate built inside of Ranier, so too the hate was building again inside his daughters.

"I don't know how to let go" Ranier tried to say, but was only able to produce an inaudible whisper.

Junior, not needing to hear to understand, kindly replied "You give it to Christ. He takes the darkness for us. Ask him for the help you need."

At this point, Ranier was stuck in a dilemma. He had always promised himself of all the things he would say and do if he ever met his father. He had also always promised himself he would never pray to God again. Both of those promises had become strong resolutions inside of him.

He realized he might have broken the one already about praying to God when he cried out for the second chance, but the resolve hadn't been so strong when he was facing destruction. Now though, the darkness inside was filling him and telling him to follow his previous resolves.

The feelings were overwhelming strong and were pushing him to do something he knew he would regret. He was racing to find a solution, some way to gain control and push back against the darkness inside. He glanced up again, to see his daughters still gazing intently at him. This time, they didn't look away. Ranier's eyes connected with one of his daughters, and he could see the darkness in her as well, the darkness that came as a result of Ranier's absence. Ranier knew the same darkness was present in him and that she was seeing it as well.

Ranier had lived with the darkness for so long, it was all he knew. The light he had tasted for a moment as he spoke to his daughters had felt so amazing, but the feelings he now had stood in stark contrast to the feelings of light he had just previous to hearing his name. Ranier could sense he was at a crossroads—he had to decide if he was going to embrace the darkness that had been present for so long, or if he was going to embrace the light he had just felt.

Ranier had lived with darkness for as long as he could remember, it was what he knew, it was where he felt comfortable, but it also was everything he hated about himself and life. Ranier's mind was coursing with images running through it, images of broken lives, of loneliness, of pain, of suffering, the abuse he had suffered from those who cared for him on and off as a child, of everything the darkness brought with it. At the same time, images associated with the compassion, concern, love, and hope he had just felt were going through him as well.

Suddenly, Ranier made a decision. He was going to pursue the light and would pursue it at all costs. Ranier had lived a life of darkness, and there was nothing worthwhile in any of it. It only produced loneliness and despair, but Ranier wanted the beauty he saw present in the family relationship. He wanted his daughters to accept him, to be a part of his life, and for him to be a part of their life. As Ranier made this decision, he immediately found himself praying to God for help. His prayer was simple "Please help." Then, he found himself, for the first time, intentionally adding, "Please help, O God."

As he prayed he found no sudden, readily discernible change.

However, he could sense that something was different inside himself. Something had changed, even though he could not tell what it was. Continuing to wait for a minute, the power of the darkness was easing. He was gaining control again of himself. Even though the darkness was still there, its power over him continued to weaken.

At length, he finally turned to face his father behind him. Ranier was entirely taken by surprise at the sight of his father. Tears were falling down his father's face, even though the tears were not what surprised Ranier the most. His father was a small man, with hair far lighter than Ranier's. At first glance, Ranier could see little resemblance between him and his father. Ranier wondered how they were related, even though a part of him still knew for certain it was his father.

As Ranier thought more on what little he appeared to share with his father, Ranier realized that the similarities they might have were entirely foreign to him as he had tried hard in his life to reject everything he possibly could associated with his father. Even though Ranier had never met his father on Earth, Ranier had always despised small, weaker looking men. Ranier himself had tried to be strong and never convey any weakness. Ranier could see that everything he had tried to develop and be was in an attempt to reject every part of his father inside him. While Ranier hadn't consciously known what his father was like, parts of him certainly had, and his hatred of his father had led him to hate and reject those parts of himself.

Ranier knew his daughters behind him were realizing the same things. They too hadn't seen the resemblance they had to Ranier as they had tried to reject that part of themselves. Ranier could see there was no way though to reject the parts of him given to him by his father, just as his daughters could not ultimately reject the parts of Ranier they had received. Attempting to do so produced a division internally, one which brought darkness and depression.

Nobody had spoken yet. Tears were still falling down Ranier's father's face, and his father did not appear to be in control of his emotions yet. Ranier glanced back at his daughters, who were still watching while trying not to register any emotions on their faces. Ranier could sense though that their hatred of him had ebbed a little. Ranier knew the internal emotions of him and his daughters were an open book to each other, and so even though their pride kept them from outright registering their emotions on their faces, they were still able to fully know the feelings of each other.

Even though Ranier had prayed for help, he still wasn't willing to be the one to speak first, and he wondered how long his father would wait before speaking. At length, his father finally said through many tears "I'm sorry . . . I'm so sorry. I . . . I tried to come back, but . . . but, I shouldn't . . . I shouldn't have left . . . in the first place." Ranier could see it was all his father could do to get his words out. His father was certainly a simple man, and Ranier, still struggling with his own emotions inside, still tried to understand how he and his father were related.

Ranier was entirely at a loss of what to do. His pride of being able to handle any situation was again dealt a blow, as this situation also felt entirely out of his reach. Junior was still standing to the side, watching. Ranier's two daughters, still not open to establishing a relationship with him, were behind him. His father was present, the man he had hated for his entire life. The hatred still coursed strong throughout his body, but he knew he couldn't act on it if he wanted any chance to salvage things with his daughters.

Everyone, apparently, was in the same predicament, as nobody spoke, nobody moved, and nobody knew what to do. For some reason, Ranier knew that everyone was waiting for him to say something. For some reason, each person considered Ranier the unspoken leader of this little group. Ranier didn't appreciate recognizing that each person there considered him to be a leader of sorts, and he found frustration increasing inside.

Finally, as Ranier's frustrations reached a breaking point, he found himself losing control slightly and blurting out "Why?!" As soon as he said this, he knew nothing more was necessary, as all of them could discern his internal feelings and knew he had grown extremely frustrated at the recognition of leadership in him.

Junior, grateful to have a point to finally say something, and registering no awkward feelings with Ranier's question itself, responded matter-of-factly "It's because you were born to be a leader Ranier."

"I don't know what you mean" Ranier replied back.

"That's because you don't want to know Ranier. You, like all of us, have run from something you feared. Your father," Junior said nodding towards Ranier's father, "ran because he was scared of fatherhood. They," he said nodding towards Ranier's daughters, "ran, and still are running, from their fears, including of you. You," Junior said nodding at Ranier, "are running from who you were foreordained to be. You fear what God gave you to do, and you have spent your life running from it."

Ranier still did not understand what Junior was saying, but Ranier could feel that the words were true. Even though Ranier could feel the truth of the words, he seriously struggled with Junior's words, as Ranier liked to feel he had never run from anything in his life. Ranier had purposely undertaken to face every conscious fear he had, to be strong, and to never let another person or thing get the best of him. There was nothing Ranier consciously knew of what he was running from.

"Most of us," Junior continued, "have no conscious knowledge of the things we run from. We all have fears, traceable to events or situations from our pre-mortal past that we have never quite recovered from. You have a great fear of leadership, and the one thing you have consistently refused in life is to be a leader. You have never wanted or allowed another person to rely on you, because you fear the weight of the responsibility associated with leadership."

Not knowing what else to say, but feeling his pride continuing to be wounded, Ranier responded "But why? Why would I fear that if I don't fear anything else?"

"There are many reasons, Ranier," Junior said, "but two main ones are that you are built on a core of solitude and that you lost many people as you led them in the War in Heaven pre-mortally."

Despite his experiences in the Spirit World so far, all of this was still so foreign to Ranier. "What do you mean by 'core'?" he asked, trying hard to keep a conversation going to reduce the awkwardness of the situation.

"As Intelligences," Junior replied, "we are all a division of light or darkness, or a division of the truth that makes up the Intelligence Stream. Each sliver of truth that is divided from the Intelligence Stream forms the core of that particular Intelligence. Something resonates deeply inside each of us, as it resonates with us to our core, or our base Intelligence. The base Intelligence is entirely unique to each one of us, and does not exist in exactly the same form in any other being in existence.

"Solitude is a general description that could be used to describe others as well, but you have a specific version of solitude that no one else has. Your language just doesn't have enough words to describe the specifics of your core, and so, for simplicity's sake, we just use the general description you would understand.

"However," Junior continued, "while each of us is defined by our core, there are things which are directly in opposition to who we are inside, or who we are at the core. For you, leadership, including people looking to and relying on you, is directly opposite a state to your particular form of solitude. Your form of solitude includes solitude from any duty or responsibility to others, and so to lead, you would have to get past the very core, or essence, of who you are."

"Why would I ever want to get past the very essence of who I am?" Ranier asked with sincere puzzlement. "People claim God loves all of us, and if he doesn't love me as I am, why would I be interested in being with him?"

Junior smiled while shaking his head. He was often amazed at how smart, yet how ignorant, Ranier could be at the same time. "God does love you Ranier, even with your core of solitude. Due to that love, he wants to take you to the best state of existence possible. He knows there is far more for you than solitude will ever bring. He loves you enough to not force you to abandon who you are, but if voluntarily choose to do so, he can make so much more of your life.

"God is a God of love. This means, Ranier, that God's core, or very essence, is love. Our purpose on Earth is to get to the point where we can exchange our core of solitude, or whatever it may be for each of us, for a core of love. We are here to become a new creature, a new being, a new person, precisely because God does love us and has provided a much better way.

"We never lose our individuality by taking on a core of love, as love embraces all of the good associated with our original core, and we will always have the ability to maintain those good parts associated with our unique personality. But, we will also gain the ability to add so much more to our personality, to our nature, and to our existence.

"To help us reach a place where we can exchange our core, God takes us to a place completely opposite of who we are at the core. God gave us all missions to perform as well as duties here on this earth. Ultimately, the tasks that lay in store for us take us to a point where the only way possible to move forward is to offer our old self to God, and ask him to help us have a better self. This is known as offering a 'broken heart and contrite spirit', or offering our core to him, recognizing that it is impossible for us to go forward relying upon the limited nature of our own core. When we offer up our core to him, he can then fill us with a core of love, a core that empowers us to accomplish any task we were asked to accomplish."

Chapter 22

J UNIOR COULD SENSE THAT THE fact he was saying something was helping everyone present to ease their tensions. Not wanting things to return to an awkward state again with those present, he decided to keep talking. "Many people criticize God for not understanding these things, for not understanding that they should be able to remain as they were as Intelligences. They argue that they are good, perfect, or complete as they are. They argue that no one should ever tell them that they could be better, or that it is bad for them to act a certain way. This same lack of understanding leads many people to also criticize God harshly while reviewing the Old Testament. They do not understand the Law of Moses, nor why it was so harsh and so focused on sacrifice. All of it though was tied to helping us give up our cores and become like God."

Junior realized as he spoke that maybe everyone didn't even know what the Law of Moses meant, or maybe these things didn't matter to them. He looked around at each person present. Ranier kept his eyes focused on the ground, trying hard to not be overcome by the hate and anger inside him. Ranier's father looked terrified, and Ranier's daughters looked angry. Junior could certainly understand their anger as he thought about their time on Earth.

They were abused, he knew, although they refused to speak of much of it. He knew far more than they had ever shared, as he had been tasked with helping them recover. For them, life had been extremely difficult, just like it had for Ranier. They had no one to love or care for them, and they found themselves bouncing around from abuser to abuser as they desperately sought for a place to feel accepted, a place to feel loved. On Earth, they never found what they wanted, they never found the peace and happiness that comes from a good family relationship. They knew that everything would have been different if Ranier had done his part, but then, they also knew that if Ranier had done his part, he would have stayed with the first woman he had a child with and they never would have been born as they were.

To them, God was unfair, unjust, and cruel. Their situation felt like a no-win situation, cursed regardless of what choices they made, cursed by the choices of other people. Junior wanted nothing more than to be able to help his family get past the pain. He had felt the joy of forgiveness, and knew they could as well. First though, he had to stop this situation from blowing up. He glanced around again, trying to gauge where everyone was at. Nobody knew what to say or do, and none of them focused much on him. He knew that talking was the only way to get the darkness out and more light in, so he continued, praying that he would be able to reach each one of them.

"Pre-mortally," he said cautiously, breaking the silence again, "we all had to be given a time and place in which to come to the earth." He knew this was an extremely sensitive subject for Ranier's daughters, and he found the fear inside him made it difficult to speak well. He didn't want to set them off, and wasn't sure why he was going down this path right now. It was the only thing that would come to his mind though, and he knew he had to say something. Unable to find anything else, he continued, trying to mask his uncertainty.

"There are countless factors God considered in making these placement decisions for each of us, but one of the main factors related to our core." He suddenly realized he might be able to address the placement issue through the Law of Moses he had awkwardly mentioned earlier, so he jumped back to that. "Those who were born in the time of the Law of Moses recognized the limitations associated with their cores. Most of them had cores that caused them to reject the things of God and quickly pursue after any evil that came across their path. These people recognized this pre-mortally, and so, fearing they would not make it to the better place with God in a world full of evil, they asked God for specific help to be placed in an environment where they were constantly reminded of everything they needed to do.

"The Law of Moses served a number of purposes. One, it allowed for the strict laws pre-mortally associated with the Mirror prior to its breaking to have a place on the earth." Sensing that Ranier and his daughters weren't fully following his disjointed discussion, Junior went back a little. "Remember that everything pre-mortally has to repeat on the earth. The earth swallowed up the pre-mortal timelines, as seen by John in the Book of Revelations, in an attempt to help save the future. Those timelines all operate here, and each of the pre-mortal events will repeat in some way or another. Prior to Christ's coming, the firmament in Heaven had to have certain pieces remain in place to create the necessary situation for his time on the earth.

"The only way the firmament could remain in place long enough was to have some strict laws in place governing behavior, so that enough people on the earth would do enough good to maintain a certain balance. God led many of those who were part of the 'House of Israel', or those subject to the Laws of Moses, to many various locations all around the earth, in order to help keep the firmament strong enough to keep the necessary pieces intact. This is known in the scriptures as the 'scattering of Israel'.

"Due to the need for the firmament to be strong though, it had to be rather thick, which also resulted in a thicker veil as the veil corresponds with the thickness of the firmament. The thick veil made it even harder for people to see and discern spiritual things on their own, which in turn made them more reliant on a strict set of laws to help guide them.

"The righteousness of these groups of the House of Israel around the earth, as they followed the strict law of Moses, helped keep the necessary pieces of the firmament intact long enough for Christ to be born and fulfill his mission, which righteousness was only achieved due to the strictness of the law and the constant reminders it provided. The Law of Moses provided constant reminders as it served as a physical representation of the spiritual consequences of certain actions. Adulterers were stoned to death, as adultery literally kills the soul and Intelligence inside a person, and the physical consequence served as a constant reminder to these people to nourish spiritual things.

"The harsh physical consequences served as an act of mercy to those people, as their cores required a constant reminder and physical witness of the consequences of evil, especially since the veil was so thick at the time due to the strength of the firmament in place. The people with cores so blind to spiritual consequences asked God to be born during this time, as it was the only way they would be able to see enough to take the steps necessary to progress to a better state of existence.

"The Law of Moses also reiterated, constantly, the need for sacrifice. Animals were sacrificed to help highlight two things—the sacrifice of Christ to save us all, and the sacrifice each of us must offer up, that of our core, or of a broken heart and contrite spirit."

Ranier, still trying desperately to find a way to not be overcome by anger at the presence of his father, and to maintain a chance with his daughters, interrupted at this point and voiced a concern he felt he sensed in himself and in his daughters. He hoped that if he spoke for them, it would bring them one step closer, even though there were many more steps necessary, to reconciliation. "Why is sacrifice required?" he asked. "Why can't there be an easier way? Why does everything have to be so hard?" Upon asking the questions, Ranier could sense the questions resonated deep within his daughters, and he was glad he was able to speak for them for a short moment.

"The answer is simple, really," Junior replied, trying hard to keep his fear under control, his fear of losing this moment with his family members together. "It is," he said as he strained to keep his voice consistent and calm, "because our entire existence is premised on sacrifice. The greatest philosophers, professors, thinkers, and others have long debated how we came to exist. They all seem to recognize there had to have been some moment of causation, some moment when the known Universe changed from a state of simply sitting to a state of active expansion. They entirely miss what that moment was though—it was the moment Elirah and Charity sacrificed half of themselves to make Saytah. In other words, sacrifice was the great catalyst that all of our existence outside of the Intelligence Stream is based on. The greatest thinkers miss the simplest things, that our entire existence came as a result of sacrifice.

"Sacrifice builds. Sacrifice creates a sustainable future," Junior said as he regained some confidence. "Sacrifice creates an existence of goodness. And, ultimately, sacrifice satisfies the law of love, enabling us to gain a core of love, just as God did. The secret to existence is to lose one's life, to lose one's identity, and to lose one's self. As our existence is entirely built on sacrifice, all things we do have to include sacrifice as the way to continue living.

"As we give up the imperfect things, we build a more perfect existence, a more perfect self, and a more perfect way to live. Every time we sacrifice, we contribute to building a better Universe. Sacrifice is only hard when we focus on today, rather than on tomorrow and the remainder of our existence. The moment we exist in is such a small part of our eternal existence. If sacrifice feels hard, it is because we have focused too much on the moment and not enough on the big picture of our existence."

Sensing this had satisfied their concern for a moment as they tried to process what he had said, but not wanting them to have time to process enough to raise questions that others weren't ready for yet, Junior tried hard not to lose his train of thought and keep talking. "Your core is one reason you fear leadership Ranier, but the other is because of the War in Heaven. During the War, pre-mortally, you were given the assignment to lead a group of individuals in the fight against Lucifer. You worked hard, but ultimately, you lost all of those you were leading. They all ended up joining Lucifer's side in the end. Just like you lost everyone you cared about on Earth, so too you lost everyone you cared about pre-mortally."

Junior suddenly realized he probably should have stopped before switching to the War in Heaven and Ranier's leadership. Junior realized Ranier would have no way yet to remember the War or what had happened to those he had led, and he sensed that the topic was not received well by Ranier. Not knowing what else to say to make the situation any better, and fearing he had ruined things, Junior fell silent, joining in the awkwardness of his grandfather and sisters.

Ranier's mind was racing. For some reason, the things Junior had said about sacrifice, his core, and the War had sunk especially deep inside him. Ranier had no reason to believe anything Junior had said, other than that the words resonated through every part of him. Somehow, the words rang as true as they struck a certain chord deep in his heart, and Ranier could sense that something was changing inside him.

The changes were washing over him making him feel powerless to stand or otherwise function. Ranier was trying to understand what about Junior's words had struck him in this way, but he couldn't pinpoint what it had been. Something inferred in everything said was resonating through him, but he couldn't consciously pin it down. Cores, sacrifice, and a War. "What was it?" Ranier thought to himself, "What is going on?"

At length, Ranier's father spoke "You're starting to understand who you really are Ranier" he said with caution in his voice, "at least pieces of you are catching on."

Due to the strength of the feelings inside, Ranier was unable to process anger at this time, and so his father's words did not produce the angry response inside of him that he predicted would have normally come. Suddenly realizing something, Ranier asked "Am I the only one in the dark here? Do you all know who I am?" Ranier saw his father and Junior smile at his choice of words as they nodded in the affirmative. Turning his head to his daughters, Ranier saw they were still quite serious, but they nodded in the affirmative as well, the first response he had received from them.

"Why do you all get to know who I am but I don't?" Ranier asked.

"We know who you are," Ranier's father said hesitantly, "because it is part of our healing and forgiveness process."

"What!?" Ranier asked, feeling the anger rise inside at the thought of his father seeking healing and forgiveness as a result of something that Ranier had done. "You left me!" Ranier said angrily.

Before Ranier could say anything else, Ranier's father firmly interjected "just like you left them." Ranier immediately stopped the rest of what he had to say to his father, as Ranier had forgotten, momentarily, his daughters still watching behind him.

To Ranier's father, he had waited a long time for this moment, and had tried hard to prepare for it. He knew he would meet Ranier one day, and he had asked God, daily during his stay in the Spirit World, to make it happen in a way that would allow him to actually talk to Ranier, to explain a thing or two. Ranier's father hadn't known how things would transpire, but God, through his Spirit, had told him he would certainly meet Ranier in a manner that would allow him to say more than a thing or two.

Ranier's father took a short moment to express gratitude to God for arranging such a perfect situation. Ranier had to stay somewhat workable because of his two daughters. Ranier's father recognized he shouldn't be so surprised, but he was always amazed at the wisdom of God. Ranier's father couldn't have asked for a better situation himself for his first face-to-face meeting with Ranier.

Of course, Ranier's father thought, he had been with Ranier for years, almost all of his life. He had served as one of his guardian angels, to the limited extent he could as he was still waiting for all of his saving ordinances to be performed by those on the earth. Ranier's father had walked almost daily with Ranier, talked to him wishing Ranier could hear him, and prayed for him. He wanted so badly to make things right, and it broke his heart to see the hatred Ranier carried towards him throughout Ranier's life. But, Ranier's father fully understood where the hatred came from, as he had not been there in Ranier's life.

Knowing that the reminder about Ranier's daughters being present would keep Ranier somewhat in line for a few minutes, Ranier's father answered Ranier's question. "We all need healing Ranier, healing from the things we did wrong, and healing from the things others did wrong to us. The harm I caused you has also caused me great harm, as it is impossible to injure another person without injuring yourself, and the closer someone is to you by family ties, the more severe the harm you suffer when you injure them. We are all connected, especially as family, and family bears the load of what others suffer, or what others do well with.

"When you were conceived, Ranier, I gave a part of myself to you. While the part was small physically, it carried with it much spiritually and at the Intelligence level. When Elirah and Charity divided themselves to form Saytah, they remained connected as Intelligences. When something was originally one, and becomes two, the pieces remain connected at the Intelligence and spiritual level. A feeling of completeness, or wholeness, can only be achieved as family, together, because parts of you are present in each person, and this takes place forwards and backwards throughout the generations. Every descendant is affected by the creation of a new person, as their parts get passed on to the new person, and they immediately are connected to that person.

"These connections though cause us to feel, or for most, to be affected by, the burdens and happiness of those we are connected to. As Saytah divided us all from the Intelligence Stream, a connection was made to each of us. As Elirah gave us spiritual bodies, a connection was made to each of us. Saytah and Elirah have no veil on them, and all of our sufferings pass through to them unfiltered. They sorrow with us, they cry with us, and they laugh with us, just as I have sorrowed with you, laughed with you, and cried with you.

"God tells us in the scriptures that 'Inasmuch as ye have done it unto one of the least of these my brethren, ye have done it unto me.' This is so because every time we help another person and relieve a little suffering, we are relieving the suffering that is flowing through to God. It is impossible to lift another without those same things flowing through to God.

"I have walked daily with you Ranier. I have been working to change my heart, to change the effects of the wrongs I committed and that caused you to suffer. The only way for me to fully get there though is to understand you. To understand your weaknesses, fears, and insecurities. To understand how the darkness and light is dispersed throughout you. The more understanding I have, coupled with the more I try to serve you, the better able I am to experience love. Misunderstanding, or lacking a full knowledge, often produces hate, anger, and strife. Knowledge and understanding help bring healing, love, and peace."

"Why then do we speak of faith so much? If we need knowledge, why aren't we given the knowledge we need for healing?" Ranier asked in an attempt to shift his father's constant gaze, in an attempt to let some of his frustration out. The question didn't faze Ranier's father though, and he kept looking consistently at Ranier.

"Faith is the means by which we gain knowledge and understanding Ranier. Knowledge, information, and facts float around on the earth. Some of it resonates with you, some of it does not. Knowledge has no effect on any person until that person first believes it is possible. Belief is required to open the mind and heart to receive knowledge, and once the mind and heart is opened through faith, true learning can take place. Knowledge does nothing if it is not received, and it can never be received until one believes it is first possible. Faith has to precede everything, as faith opens us up to be able to receive.

"God greatly desires to teach all of us everything he knows. God pours down knowledge constantly, and we miss almost all of it, as we have shut our hearts and minds to the truth. Due to the dual nature of our beings here on Earth, knowledge has to permeate both our mind and heart before we will make any changes in our actions. You have learned a lot while you are here, but you still haven't had most of it sink into your heart. Because of that, you will have no permanent change from any of this until you open your heart to it, and the only way to do that is to first believe, to exercise faith that this is all possible.

"Many of us work for years to try to have faith. We feel it is something complicated, something that takes years of work and effort. We struggle to get answers, to talk with God, to learn. We feel we have faith because we pray, or go to church, or read the scriptures, maybe even for many years. For many, nothing they recognize as being from God comes throughout this time, and they lose their faith. The continue to suffer and receive no healing, just as you have.

"You used to pray Ranier, but I never came back, Elleana never got better, and you were left alone. The reason your prayers were wholly ineffective is because you prayed, seeking for things you desired—rather than seeking for what God had for you. You were being the author of your own salvation and telling God what you needed, seeking desperately to have him give you the things you wanted. You felt that was faith, simply because you asked.

"Most of the world is the same. They may pray once or twice, or for years, go to church, or read the scriptures. At some point, they give up, saying it isn't for them, God doesn't speak with them, or God must not exist. *However, the thing they miss is that they never truly opened their hearts to God.*" Ranier's father placed great emphasis on this line. "There is no faith in seeking for something you want, that you see will help you, or that you think will be good for you. Faith is letting go of what you want, of what you see, of what you feel you know, and asking for God to give you what you truly need.

"Faith is trusting that God knows more than you, and that the things you desperately are asking for may not be what you need at the time. Faith is recognizing you don't see everything, but you desire to see all that God sees. If you ever want to see all God sees, you have to let go of what you see and understand. Faith, ultimately, is a belief in the omnipotence of God coupled with a sincere willingness to act on anything he tells you.

"You can only learn, and heal, if you open your heart and mind to possibilities Ranier. Many of us demand answers from God, but the answers that come just bounce off of us because our desires and our wants shut out entire universes of possibilities, or because we just aren't willing to put in the work the answer directs. We may pray for healing, not understanding that the trial facing us is what brings the healing. We may pray for help to eat that day, not understanding that another day without food brings us closer to the riches of eternity.

"So, while we should always ask God for things we think we need, true faith is admitting that we don't see it all, and asking him to give us what we really need, as opposed to what we think we need. Knowledge comes as quickly as we're willing to believe with a sincere willingness to accept, healing comes as we can believe and act willingly, and our lives change drastically as we're willing to put more trust in what God sees than in what we see." Ranier's father stopped at this point, realizing he may have been too direct and forceful, and may have lost an opportunity he had prayed for so long to have. His eyes closed in despondency as his heart let out a desperate prayer for help.

Chapter 23

EVERYONE WAS SILENT FOR A MINUTE. Ranier's father finally opened his eyes and looked around again. The anger or frustration he expected was not there. For some reason, everyone was looking at him, expecting him to continue. He wasn't sure how, but grasped that his fears were unfounded. Ranier and his daughters hadn't recoiled, but were intently listening. Racing to think back to what he had been talking about, he realized he still hadn't fully answered Ranier's original question about why they knew so much about Ranier, and so he decided to circle back to where he had begun.

"All of this is just to say that each of us has been learning about you Ranier. We learn about you and who you are. As we do so, we are better able to open our hearts to God and his ways, and to start to believe it might be possible for you to one day be a part of our lives. Knowledge alone can help someone decide to believe, but belief is always necessary first to receive more knowledge, as everything is built upon faith and the belief that God sees what we don't."

"So why don't I get to know about myself?" Ranier asked with some anger still in his voice, the anger his father had feared would be present. "You all get to know all about me, so why don't I?"

"The same reason that we still don't know everything about ourselves" Ranier's father replied cautiously. "It's far easier to see things about someone else than it is to see things about one's self. The veil present in each of us, keeping our light and dark parts separate, prevents us from seeing ourselves. We can only truly see who we are inside once we exercise faith in what God sees. We have to see ourselves from his perspective to truly see ourselves if we still have any darkness left inside of us, and that takes faith. It takes faith to see our potential. It takes faith to see the good inside. It takes faith, even, to see we are loved . . ." His voice trailed off at this point, breaking with emotion.

After regaining his composure some, Ranier's father continued, "Since it is easier to see others and their actions, we can often start learning about ourselves as we learn about others. The more we reach out to and serve others, especially family, the more we come to understand them, and the more we understand them, the more we can understand ourselves. I have been doing everything I could for you, since the day I died, and have tried walking in your shoes. Since I am still working to overcome all of the darkness inside me, you are helping me to better understand myself, as we are a part of each other."

Ranier didn't like thinking that his father was a part of him. He still had no place for acceptance, but he wanted so badly to have his daughters accept him. He found himself wondering if his father and him shared the same feelings, desperately wanting to connect with a child who hated them. Ranier wanted so much to connect with his daughters. As he thought about the situation he was in, a thought suddenly flashed through his mind "You can teach your daughters how to accept you by accepting your father."

Ranier did not know where the thought came from, but he knew it wasn't his own. Due to the repulsive nature to him of accepting his father, he almost outright rejected the thought. He was torn as he did not want to accept the things his father had said about faith and missing answers due to a lack of willingness, but he realized he lacked willingness to change, which meant, ultimately, that he lacked faith.

As he reflected on his life, the truth of what his father said grew in him slowly. He recognized he had not been willing to change his life. He had always demanded that God make things his way, that God provide the things he felt he wanted. Whenever someone suggested that he change, he scoffed at them and put them down for even daring to suggest that he wasn't good enough as he was at the time. Standing in the middle of his father, who he hated, and his daughters, who he had just learned he had and who hated him, he realized he was not enough on his own, and that change would certainly be necessary to resolve many of his problems in life.

As Ranier continued to think, his mind was opened to see countless individuals praying for God to give them something. Each individual wanted something to change about their own life. Maybe it was depression, lack of money, suffering, sickness, family issues, loneliness, or something else, but each was asking God to change the people and situations around them. They were asking God for a miracle, and felt they were exercising faith, simply because they asked.

However, these countless people all were lacking one important thing—they were not looking to change anything about themselves. They wanted to continue on in the same path, but have that path produce different results. Ranier saw how backwards this type of thinking was, as individual situations are often determined by the path they are on. If people want different situations to exist in their life, Ranier saw how critical it was that they change the path they are on. In other words, Ranier saw readily how prayers shouldn't focus on changing the situations on the path individuals are on, but rather, should focus on how individuals can change themselves to adjust to a new path to be on. In other words, an individual's prayer should focus on the things they could change within themselves to make their situations different.

Thinking on these things, Ranier could somehow see he had never truly prayed in faith, as he had never prayed with a willingness to change anything about himself. Ranier could see, in his mind's eye, countless paths stretching out before every person. Thoughts, desires, actions, and words all lead people down different paths, and each path had its own reality, or consequences, associated with it. No path was free of external suffering, but he could see there was one straight path, free of internal darkness and full of peace. Very few people took this path, as very few people were willing to admit they were wrong in their thoughts, desires, words, or actions. Only the people who looked to God in every thought and sought to follow all of God's commandments remained on this straight path.

Ranier saw that God provided commandments to direct and help individuals know what is required to stay on the path. Only those with a sincere willingness and humility to trust that God knows more than they do were able to remain on the path. Everyone else was pulled from the path due to some form of pride or selfishness, as they were more interested in what they saw and felt as opposed to what God had in store for them, or they trusted more in their ability to understand than in what God had told them.

Ranier saw that the straight path was the only one to be free of negative consequences, in the eternal sense. All of the other paths lead to unpleasant places, and it was often in those unpleasant places that people would start to pray to God, begging, essentially, that God make the path of their choices free from the consequences and darkness associated with their path. God, however, would not support someone in the wrong path, and would always answer their prayers with how to change themselves to correct their course and return to the path of happiness.

Ranier saw that the straight path lead to the new Universe created by Jesus Christ. Existence in the new Universe required changing the very essence of a person's current self. While many loved themselves and did not want to give up the core pieces of who they were, Ranier saw that everyone had to change and accept that there was something better. Everyone had to be born again, and the straight path was the way towards losing one's old self to gain a new self, one capable of attaining and enjoying the marvelous things in the new Universe.

All of this brought Ranier to a decision point. He could fully see his options were to change himself and let go of the hate, anger, and darkness which had defined him for so long, or to continue on in a path of no return, a path leading to nowhere. His life had been miserable for as long as he could remember, and nothing he did ever changed that as a constant hollowness remained inside of him despite his earthly successes. Ranier could see that God had wonderful things prepared, and that it was up to Ranier himself to change—to let go of his pride and accept that he had been wrong—in order to accept and receive the things that God had for him.

Ranier could now see that the things he had really, but not consciously, desired and prayed or pursued an entire life for could be found in one act—the act of forgiveness. But he also knew that everything he had consciously worked and strived for would be lost in the same act, as his existence had been built around harboring grudges, creating distance, and furthering hate and anger. Ranier was at a place where he had to choose to hold on to his old self, or become someone new.

Things were becoming less clear to Ranier. His internal conflict seemed to literally be ripping him apart and severing connections inside him. Parts of him sought desperately to remain, and were clenching with full force to pull him back to selfishness and the darkness he knew so well. Ranier searched to understand what part of him was pushing for him to accept the path of forgiveness, but he couldn't find it. Everything inside him seemed overwhelmingly dark, and nearly everything inside him seemed to pull him back to his old ways.

Ranier started to feel a little desperation as he felt himself losing ground to the darkness inside. He was certain he would forever regret staying who he was, but he placed so much value on his own identity that he was struggling to let go. All of this was happening much too quickly, and he felt he lacked the strength to make the right decision.

Falling to his knees from the depth of the conflict within, he searched for anything, anything that might be a part of light inside him. His thoughts, mind, and heart only grew darker though, as all of the light seemed to be gone. "Why is there no light?" he thought through grimaced teeth. "Why am I consigned to fail? I've never lived free of the darkness inside. I've never been able to escape it. What am I missing in understanding who I am?"

As he thought these things, and as the darkness continued to grow, he suddenly saw the woman's face and heard her voice pierce through the depths of him as she screamed "Ranier!" The vision Ranier had witnessed of the Intelligence Stream, the beginning of creation, and the creation of the Mirror flashed through his mind. Ranier knew he had seen these things from this woman's point of view, but he remembered first seeing her as she split off from the Intelligence Stream as a being of light, and he remembered searching for himself but being unable to find himself. Ranier now realized that during this time he had only seen the light side of the creation, and had not witnessed the dark side. James had told him he would understand everything about himself in one word, and the realization of that one word hit him like a ton of bricks broadsiding him and causing him to start to pass out as Ranier finally understood—*counterpart.*

He was the screaming woman's dark counterpart. And, he realized, she was his counterpart of light, a counterpart that had followed Lucifer.

Ranier realized why darkness had always followed him in life and why it pierced him to such a deep level. He was one of the beings of darkness who had chosen God's plan, one of the beings who had decided the life God had to offer was worth giving up every part of himself to receive. He realized his life was a reflection of his past, but that it did not have to be a reflection of his future, as God was offering him the opportunity to be an entirely new person.

The conflict was reaching a breaking point inside of him, and he could sense he was nearly entirely unconscious. As he understood he needed to let go of everything in order to gain everything God offered, he made the decision he wanted nothing to do with the darkness anymore. At that instant, before he fully lost consciousness, he prayed to God and asked that he be forgiven, and that Christ accept his offering of his own self.

Chapter 24

RANIER CAME TO IN THE same place he had passed out, although he was unsure how long he had been unconscious. This time everything seemed far different than it did before he passed out though. He could fully see and sense the world around him. New sensations and understandings were washing over him as he realized he had new senses beyond his normal five senses.

Elleana was holding his head in her lap, crying. "I'm so sorry," she said repeatedly, "I'm sorry I couldn't tell you that you were the dark counterpart."

Ranier was still too overwhelmed to speak, so he simply squeezed his mother's hand. Looking around, Ranier saw his father still in the same place, his daughters, and Junior, all still standing, watching. None of them had moved, but Ranier could sense that so much had changed inside each one of them.

Ranier could now sense the terror and depth of emotion emanating from his father, and Ranier felt sympathy for him. Ranier realized, somehow, this was the first time his father had been allowed to see Elleana in person since he died, making his father entirely at a loss of how to handle things. He could sense as well that Elleana was at a loss, and was only there due to her deep concern for Ranier. Elleana had always given everything she had for Ranier, and the sincerity of her love touched him deeply as he was able to feel and experience these things with his new senses.

For Elleana, she was brimming with joy and terror at the same time. God had promised her she would never lose Ranier, and to see the change occur so quickly in him amazed her beyond belief and filled her with great joy at watching God's promise unfold. She finally felt she would never have to be alone in the eternities, and seeing Ranier change brought a peace and wonder to her existence which transcended anything she had experienced before. The pain and years of loneliness were washing away, and the joy present was too much to describe. She had never tasted anything so beautiful, and her heart sung at the wonders racing through and cascading over her.

James and Ruby had taught her that her future was accessible through faith. They had taught her that if she had faith in God's promises, the peace, joy, and hope she felt now could be a part of her life before Ranier actually changed. For Elleana, this meant she would have to let go of her fears and the things she saw in Ranier with her own eyes, and it was too hard for her to do as she relied too heavily on her own senses and embraced too readily her own fears. For some reason though, she knew what James and Ruby had taught was true, and that her lack of faith kept her during her time in the Spirit World from experiencing these blessings promised by God.

Even with the sheer breadth of joy currently inside her, she had the same amount of terror inside her as well due to the fact that she was in the same location as Ranier's father. She had not seen him since he left her, heartbroken and alone on the earth, and she did not feel she had the strength or ability to interact with him again. She felt as if her being was slowly ripping apart, and she struggled knowing how to handle the situation. The only thing she could think of was to try and relish the good of the moment with Ranier, and to work to let go of the fear and awkwardness associated with being by Ranier's father.

For Ranier, everything inside him seemed to tingle with sensation. There was so much to take in, and he was entirely at a loss of how to process it all. He had a significantly heightened sense of everyone's feelings, and could feel the happiness, terror, and other emotions running through his various family members present. Not wanting to have the moment become too awkward for everyone though and lose this opportunity with his daughters, he tried to stand up. As he did, a hand reached down to help pull him up. Ranier looked up and recognized James standing next to him. Somehow, even with the additional senses, Ranier had not sensed the presence of James. Ranier took his hand as he stood, and saw James smiling broadly.

"You did it Ranier" James said excitedly, "you let go of your old self." Ranier suddenly sensed the brotherhood between the two. "I too began as a dark counterpart" James said with more enthusiasm than Ranier had yet experienced with James, "and I too accepted God and gave up my old existence. All of us rejoice every time another counterpart lets go of the darkness and accepts the better way given by God. Christ has truly provided a way for all of us."

Ranier smiled. The feelings of peace and joy inside him were something entirely new to him. He could sense he was a new person. Ranier looked at his father, and ran and gave him a hug, picking him up off the ground as Ranier laughed with excitement. Those long years of darkness, loneliness, and anger no longer mattered. The light inside replaced it all, healed it all, and brought intense understanding.

"It's okay Dad" Ranier assured his father, "I can let go of the past to accept the future. We will have plenty of time to sort things out, and plenty of time to be together." Ranier's father remained speechless, too much in shock to be able to register anything to say. However, the sheer joy emanating from his heart was palpable, as he too had prayed for years that one day he would be able to have a second chance with his son.

Ranier put his father down and turned to the rest of his family still waiting there. "I'm a new man" he said with a smile "God has shown me a better way, and I will do what I can to correct the things I did wrong." Reaching out to Elleana, Ranier said, "This is Dad. He left due to the darkness inside, but he too is a different person. You can trust him now."

Elleana was crying, as was Ranier's father, and both looked as helpless as little children who have no idea what to say. Ranier knew Elleana had years of emotions and heartache to work through, but also sensed that his experience of change would give Elleana the strength to enable her to be able to let go as necessary to sort through things with his father. Ranier, smiling at his mother, said in good humor "I had to sit and listen to you explain things. Now it's your turn to sit and listen to Dad explain his side of things."

Elleana didn't budge, too entrapped by fear to face Ranier's father again. The long years of hurt and loneliness had beat her down, and she struggled knowing what to do, as her pride, anger, and frustration demanded that she leave and never speak with Ranier's father. However, the light inside her that came from watching Ranier change compelled her to stay as it whispered of the ability to change, to be healed, and to fully *let go* of the past to embrace a better future. She knew, deep down, that her future was up to her, and that this was God's way of bringing her face-to-face with everything she had to get past in order to embrace life and the ways of God.

She had prepared by listening over and over again to James and Ruby, but she always fell back to fear. Knowing she did not want to have her past remain a part of her, she cried out to God in her mind for help, for strength, for the ability to do now what she needed to do. As she did, she felt a hand gently push her, and gasped as she realized Ranier was gently leading her to his father.

Trembling, she closed her eyes and tried to keep her emotions in check, but they overflowed as readily as a river in a torrent of rain. She cringed as she knew she was an open book, open to the fact she had never stopped loving Ranier's father. She desperately wanted to hide those feelings, to keep him from knowing how much it had hurt for all of these years, but they were swept out along with everything else, open for anyone to read.

"It's okay Mom" Ranier said, breaking through the waves of emotion inside her. "Dad has the same feelings inside him. All he wants is to make things right, to be the person you always knew he could be, and to be there for you. Dad isn't going to leave this time. It's okay to trust, to have faith, and to give others a second chance. You gave me far more chances than I deserved, and it's time you give Dad his second chance."

Elleana was in tears, and could sense no other option at this point. She nodded weakly as she perceived the flood of emotions coming from Ranier's father, as she perceived he was in much of the same state as her. She stayed silent as Ranier led her and his father to a location a little way away from the rest, sitting them both down across from each other. Ranier knew neither would say anything for quite some time, but that they would be able to begin to sort through things by feeling the emotions of the others, just as he had done with his daughters. Something inside Ranier told him Elleana would need some time, but that she would eventually be able to let go of her past.

Ranier glanced around at the location, and was amazed at the goodness of God. They were in a place surrounded by beautiful nature. Elleana loved nature, as it was the only place she felt peace on Earth. A small stream trickled by, providing the perfect amount of beautiful, calming sound. Elleana's favorite tree, the Crabapple tree, was next to them, in full blossom, with waves of beautiful grass sweeping around the other majestic trees present. It was a glorious sight to behold, and he was just now taking the time to notice it all.

"I'll be back Mother" Ranier promised. Elleana, still full of tears, nodded weakly again, too worked up to say anything else. "When I come back Dad, we'll take more time together then" Ranier said as he looked at his father. His father also nodded weakly, still too in shock at Ranier's quick change and the presence of Elleana. As Ranier walked away, he smiled at Elleana and his father sitting frozen by their fears and hopes, but knowing the hopes would overpower the fears, and they would start talking at some point.

Turning to look at his daughters, Ranier knew both were still not ready to accept him as their father, but that their hearts certainly had been softened to the idea. Ranier knew they too needed time, but that this experience had been a critical one for them to witness as they watched him let go of his past and forgive his father. Ranier knew they might need time to let the fears, anger, and hurt melt away, and to experience the pulls of hope before they could change as he had done. He felt himself brimming with faith and hope that it was also possible for them to change, and he rejoiced at the beauty of Christ's atonement for them all.

When Ranier reached them, he said in a controlled tone "I will do everything I can to make things right, and will work for the remainder of my existence to correct everything I did wrong. Please give me a chance," he said as tears entered his eyes, "please give me a chance. I will leave you alone now, but will forever try to stay connected as you will allow."

Sensing no response yet from his daughters, and sensing they were still uncomfortable talking to him, Ranier turned to leave, and Junior and James joined him. Ranier's daughters, both of whom had remained silent throughout this whole time, stared at him as they had since he came. They were very hurt by everything they had been through, and found it difficult to talk to Ranier as he, or his absence, had been the source of so much that had gone wrong in their lives. However, as Ranier started to walk away, one of his daughters felt a slight "thank you" slip out, not through her words, but through a connection in their minds, a connection she didn't realize she had with him.

Ranier, pausing for a slight moment as he walked away, responded through the same connection "I have done nothing, but accept what God has prepared for me by letting go of myself and my past. I hope that you too will accept what God has prepared for you. I will forever try to make things right. There is a better way."

Ranier knew both of his daughters had heard his thoughts, and so he continued to walk away, guessing that they still needed more time.

"Wait" he heard as he was almost too far to see them anymore. He stopped at this, unsure of whether to turn around or not. "Can I come with you?" he heard one of his daughters ask, the same that had said 'thank you' earlier. At this, Ranier turned and saw one of his daughters coming towards him, while the other stayed. The one remaining made clear she wasn't ready to talk about anything, but that she was okay if the other came along. Ranier smiled at them both, and responded to both of their thoughts, saying he would try to be available when the one was ready, and welcoming the other to come with him. The joy in him was indescribable as he tried to grasp that he was going to be able to speak with one of his daughters.

Chapter 25

RANIER WAITED WHILE HIS DAUGHTER walked to reach them. Junior and James waited as well. Ranier wasn't sure what would be best, whether to ask Junior and James to leave or whether to have them stay. Ranier didn't have to wonder long as his daughter answered the question when she came and stood next to Junior, rather than Ranier. Ranier hadn't noticed Ruby approaching, but saw her now as she came and gave his daughter a hug, and then stood beside James.

Ranier glanced around. He saw a lake a little way in the distance, fed, in part, by the small stream he had seen earlier. The lake was a beautiful blue, almost glowing with light, and surrounded by short hills covered with trees. The sky glowed beautiful shades of red and yellow as the light danced across the sky, and he was taken in with the pristine beauty of it all. He hadn't paid much attention to things before, and he was realizing he probably had missed out on a lot of the wonders of this world he was in.

Ranier looked back at the small group. They were all waiting, looking at him, so Ranier motioned his head towards the lake and started walking that way. He walked until he found a smooth grassy spot. He had planned on sitting down there, but realized it may be too awkward still for his daughter to sit as well, so he remained standing, with his mind racing trying to decide how to start a conversation.

As he thought on what to say, he looked at his daughter again, realizing the beauty of her spirit. He could also tell, somehow, that people on Earth hadn't seen the beauty of her spirit. It had been hidden under layer after layer of abuse from her mother, who had become addicted to drugs and alcohol in Ranier's absence. It was hidden further due to the men who came into and left her mother's life, and from the others she associated with on Earth, the kids who would torment and tease her, the boys who would use her, and the other people who refused to help her, saying that she should get a job or otherwise take care of herself.

It was as if Ranier was seeing his daughter's life play out before him. He watched her time on Earth as she desperately tried to find self-worth, value, and appreciation. She even tried attending various churches, but never looked the type to fit in very well. There was little happiness in her life, mainly darkness, interspersed only with the occasional burst of a false hope that the new boy expressing interest in her would actually love her. His heart broke as he saw the similarity to Elleana, to a beautiful soul searching so much for acceptance and love.

As he stood there, he realized he didn't have to begin the conversation. She had done so, and was sharing with him her life story. He found tears running down his cheek as he watched her beat down spiritually, mentally, emotionally, and physically. She dropped out of school and went out on her own, unable to stand the pain of associating with her abusive mother, and unable to stay around the other teenagers who bullied and tormented her as they did. She had prayed extensively for help, for her father to come back, for anything, but her life continued in a downward spiral, with her feeling powerless to change it.

Eventually, she ended up with some extremely bad men who only wanted one thing from her—her body. Even then, they quickly grew tired of her, telling her she wasn't beautiful enough to ever be loved, and their abuse drove her to a point of utter despair and loneliness. She had no one to turn to, no one to call for help, and no one who had ever loved her. She cried for days straight at that point, laying frozen in a state that only complete despair and abandonment can bring. The men grew extremely upset with her for not responding to them, and one of the men, in a drunken state of rage, killed her.

When she arrived in Yuli, the Spirit World they were currently in, she was terrified of everyone and everything. Ruby had been there to greet her, and had held her for days as she cried. The loss was exceptionally intense for her, the pain too much for her to bear alone, and the years of loneliness were etched into her soul.

The tears were flowing freely for Ranier. He looked at his daughter, amazed to see her courage in sharing everything she had shared. He knew it must not be easy to open up her heart as she had, especially to him since she still had carried such anger towards him for so long. Certainly, certainly, he must not break the trust she had extended to him. Ranier prayed silently in his mind, pleading for help to not mess up right now, to know what to say or do.

Ruby also found herself in tears. Ruby's life had been very different, where she had been born to good parents, in good circumstances, with a good upbringing. She was able to learn of Christ and accept him into her life. There had been some hard times, but her life had been one mostly full of light, happiness, and many blessings from God. When she prayed, she had found her answers, and readily followed the inspiration she would often receive.

Ruby had been asked to work specifically with Ranier's family. She had often wondered how it would be possible to do, especially since she came from such a different background and had not walked in their shoes. Ruby felt exceptionally inadequate for the assignment, and had tried her best, often feeling that she was failing badly since so little had changed in any of Ranier's family. Elleana had shown the most progress of anyone, but even then, the progress had been remarkably slow since Elleana struggled trusting so much. Ranier's daughters had almost no progress, and Junior had worked mostly with James, connecting better with him than Ruby.

For Ruby, she had felt herself struggling to trust in God and his assignment to her at this time, as she did not see how she was making any difference. The only thing she had been able to do effectively was listen to all of them. There were a few times she had been able to teach or explain some things, but those felt few and far between. The rest of the time she simply held them as they cried from the pain or loneliness they carried and listened when they were finally able to talk about things.

As she stood here watching though, she could suddenly see the role she had played. When she had listened, over and over and over again, to their pains and frustrations, they had all developed the ability to share their pain without it breaking them. Due to this, Elleana had been able to share with Ranier and work with him, and would now be able to also share things with Ranier's father to be able to start to heal there. Ranier's daughter was also able to share her story with Ranier due to the long hours Ruby had spent with her, just listening.

Ruby now realized her call had been to listen. She wasn't called to heal them, as she had assumed, she had been called to help them learn to talk and share. It was only as they shared their pains, heartaches, and deepest longings with the person who had hurt them so much that they could be healed. Ruby's role was to build them enough, through listening, to enable them to share, and she could now see how essential it was to their healing. She felt peace wash over her as she realized that perhaps she hadn't failed, that maybe God did have a reason to ask her to help Ranier's family. She said a silent prayer of thanks to God, and committed again, as she had in the past, to do whatever God asked of her. It was the least she could do, she felt, to show gratitude for the goodness she had received from others throughout her life.

Ranier was still trying to process everything his daughter had shared. No one had yet said a word, but his daughter had shared everything directly to his mind, and probably, he realized, the others were able to see these things as well. Now though the mood and tone of what was being shared was shifting dramatically to a scene of light. Ranier was confused for a short moment as to what was taking place, until he realized he was witnessing his daughter's life that never came to be—the life she would have had if he had done his part.

Ranier saw himself, caring and providing for his daughter. He saw the light inside her grow from the love and attention from him as a father. He saw her confidence blossom, and her true inward beauty radiate through her eyes and smile. He saw her life lead to good places, good relationships, and good results, and he saw the happiness that could have been—if he had done his part.

The radical difference in the actual events in his daughter's life and the events that could have been if he had done his part was astounding to him. He had never realized the power he carried, the power of one person, a parent, to so radically affect the life of another. As his daughter continued sharing, he saw that not only did it affect his daughter, but it affected generations to come. His choices and actions rippled throughout eternity, destroying the hopes and dreams of many generations to come, bringing darkness to so many who should have had light.

Ranier knew his daughter wasn't showing him these things to be mean. She was showing him to teach him just how important he was to her and her life. A father could make all the difference in the life of his daughter, and he hadn't made the difference he was capable of making. The pain of it stung him deeply, and he found himself sobbing for a while.

Eventually, he looked up at his daughter and saw her eyes were full of tears too. From what he could see, her anger and hate were being turned into sadness, into a longing for that which never was, into a pain expressing itself in tears instead of a hardened heart.

"I'm so sorry" Ranier said through muffled sobs. "I'm so sorry." At this point his daughter broke down completely, and Ranier reached out and embraced her. In what may have been one of the most tender hugs in all of eternity, Ranier and his daughter held each other, sobbing at the overwhelming feeling of light brought about by the forgiveness and acceptance each had for the other.

Junior, James, and Ruby were also overcome by the intense emotion. None of them had believed that so much change was possible so quickly, and their eyes were moist as well as they witnessed years of darkness washed away in a moment of forgiveness, a moment that would forever remain a part of their souls.

Ranier had no idea how much time had passed. The relief and hope he felt as he held his daughter brought so much joy to his heart. Embarrassed at needing to ask, but knowing he needed to know, he finally ventured, as he held his daughter close, "What did your mother name you?"

"Jess" she replied softly, pausing silently for a moment. "What would you have named me?" she then quietly asked Ranier after gathering the courage to finally ask a question she had wondered her entire life, a question which had mattered more to her than most anything else.

The tears stung Ranier again as he thought of all he had missed. He hadn't even been able to participate in naming any of his children. He didn't know what he would have named her then, but he did know what he would have named her now. "I would like to have named you Charity" he said, "as I've never encountered anyone with such a pure and beautiful heart as you have."

Jess cried as she heard this, feeling the sincerity and genuineness in Ranier's words. Her prayers from her childhood, from her teenage years, and from her entire short life were all being answered at this moment. She had a father now, she had acceptance, and she had love.

While her prayers hadn't been answered when she wanted them to be, she recognized now that they were indeed answered.

Jess thought on all she had been taught while in Yuli. She had remained angry at God, upset that things had been so bad on Earth, and upset that she couldn't have things her way. While watching Ranier struggle through his change and forgiveness, she had realized something though. Her prayers had demanded, in essence, that God require somebody to change. As she witnessed Ranier let go of himself, and now as she also forgave and let go, she understood that these changes had to come from within, and she understood that God provided ways to accomplish these things. However, each change takes time, and cannot happen instantly, even with the most insistent demands to God.

At length, the tears slowed, and Jess and Ranier sat down by the lake, inviting the others to join them. They both still glowed with the light of forgiveness, a light directly from Jesus Christ. Neither had ever thought it possible for things to be made right, but they now understood that with the infinite power of Jesus Christ, all things could be made right, even their own lives.

Chapter 26

R ANIER AND JESS HAD BEEN talking with James, Ruby and Junior for some time now, as they all shared their experiences of letting go of themselves and accepting God. For each, it had been a very different process. Ranier's and Jess's were compacted into a short timeframe, while James had taken a long time to change and let go of a piece of himself at a time until he had let go of everything. James explained that many people were like himself, in that they could only give up a piece at a time rather than everything at once, but that God worked with everyone in the way that was best for them. For Junior and Ruby, they were able to see the good in letting go, and were able to let go and move on from their old selves at a pace faster than James had been able to.

As they talked, Ranier remembered more and more about his past, including from before the earth. Ranier had asked God for a hard life, precisely so he would learn to despise darkness. Ranier knew he needed a constant reminder from life itself that he did not want to continue on the path of darkness. Since Ranier was a dark counterpart initially, darkness permeated everything about himself and his life. But, something in Ranier sought for the light, and had always carried Ranier forward.

For Jess, she was actually a counterpart of light, but had taken on many dark parts to carry for others she dearly loved. She accepted the bad that would come in her life so that others she loved wouldn't have to experience it. She had given up her place in a fully functional family so that another person she loved would be able to go there. As Ranier heard more of Jess's story, he thought more how accurate it was to want to have named her Charity. He couldn't imagine going through what she did for another person.

Realizing he still didn't fully understand the change process, Ranier asked James and Ruby "How was I able to make the decision to change? What in me gave me the power or desire to overcome my dark nature?"

"Your will" James said in simple response.

Ranier thought for a minute, but still didn't understand.

Ruby added to what James said with a longer explanation. "Each of us is given a will, Ranier. Our will is entirely unique to each of us, and has no counterpart. It has no counterpart because it was created by the selfless sacrifice of Jesus Christ. When he divided the light from the darkness, he gave each light and dark Intelligence a portion of himself. In other words, Jesus Christ took a sliver of his light and gave each of us a piece. He combined this piece with our own Intelligence, and this combination produced, as it did when Elirah and Charity combined themselves, something that has no counterpart as evil will never give of itself. Christ's sacrifice of himself enabled each of us to have something without a counterpart.

"The light of Christ inside you gives you your will, Ranier. As it is unique and has no counterpart, it has the power to create, to change situations, to change individuals. Only those who choose to exercise their will will ever be able to be like God. We go through bad situations and reach points of desperation as God is allowing us to use our will, or utilize our connection to God to create, improve, and change things for the better. The only way to know how to exercise our will properly is to look to God, as he knows all things, and we can gain great fulfillment by aligning our will with God's will. In this way we can create, grow, and progress, and find true meaning to our life.

"God asks us for our will. This enables us to sacrifice something, to contribute to a Universe of life, and to contribute to our own life as sacrifice builds so much for us. We all need the humility to give our will to him, as our will forms the basis of our existence. When we hold on to our own will, we forever remain stuck with the dark parts inside of us, and we never reach a better state of existence, just as Charity, by holding on to her own desires, would have been forever unable to see Saytah again.

"Many of us, unfortunately, love the darkness inside more than the potential for light, and we don't let go of our own will. While the darkness inside you was powerful, resonating down through your core, it had no power to overcome your will as darkness cannot destroy that which has no counterpart. Your will makes you unique and similar with everyone at the same time, as there are no two wills that are the same, but all wills possess the same properties to enable a person to exercise their own agency."

"I have seen so many people who have entirely lost their will though" Jess replied. "Most of those I associated with on earth were addicted to powerful drugs, pornography, and the like, and it as if they have no will at all anymore."

"Yes," James agreed, joining the conversation, "addictions are powerful things. Ranier, do you remember Seth, the man you met with your mother?" Ranier nodded. "Jess met him too, shortly after she came to Yuli. You got to meet him to see the power of the will inside of us all. Seth was addicted to most everything bad. He was born in a poor situation and lacked any type of love or guidance in his life. At a young age he was subjected to many different abuses, similar to Jess, things that no person should have done to them.

"Seth, though, exercised his will. Typically, wills do not break everything all at once, they are strengthened line upon line, precept upon precept. They grow in strength and power. However, no matter the depth of junk or darkness piled on them, they can never be darkened. Seth, just like the rest of us need to, accessed his will through calling on Jesus Christ, as our will is a direct product of the light of Christ. Our will is accessed through faith in Jesus Christ and the power he has to heal, to take things away from us, and to cleanse us.

"I myself am a direct beneficiary of Jesus Christ and his atonement. When I finally turned from my dark ways, I gained the power to grow line upon line, precept upon precept, and to be reborn as a new person. Turning my will over to Christ was the best decision I have ever made."

Ranier could see that James had been moved to tears, and Ranier could sense feelings he had never felt before arising within his heart as well. Ranier was still trying to process everything, but he certainly was taking on a different view of God. He had always viewed God as an arbitrary being, establishing arbitrary laws and rules, but had never considered how much God had done to even make life possible. Life, he was beginning to see, required a balance of competing demands, and God had structured things to enable life to exist for all. In particular,

Ranier had never fully understood God's work to make life—a good life—possible for all.

Ruby, giving James time to regain his composure, and sensing Ranier's thoughts, said "Yes, we only exist due to a Being who was willing to sacrifice and forego optimizing His condition. As soon as two beings exist, any selfish tendencies result in the promotion of the one over the putting down of the other. God, though, did not want to put us down. Rather, he knew that for all of us, by tempering our selfish natures, we could gain far more together than we could alone. So, while we submit to some things that seem to be restrictions at the moment, they bring far greater results to our existence. We work to achieve the best life by submitting our will to his, as his will is what made it possible for us to even exist at all.

"Ultimately, God knows the most ideal conditions for our existence are in establishing unity, one where each individual voluntarily unifies with others. In marriage, we are happy when husband and wife are on the same page, with the same goals and pursuits. In life, we are happy in a society with the same goals and pursuits, one where we help each other out. The Celestial Kingdom, God's highest kingdom that we can go to from this earth, is a Kingdom where all live together in unity. His Celestial law is one of unity, where we overcome selfishness, where we love, and where we serve others. This means, of course, that we are loved, served, and ultimately, that we have a place of everlasting meaning. Thus, it is through denying ourselves that we find life, as life comes through others, never through ourselves."

Jess had heard these things before, but they had never sunk in to the same depth as they were now. It was as if the truths were permeating her entire being, washing over her, and becoming an actual part of her. She found it impossible to keep the tears back, tears of gratitude, joy, and life itself. She was finally experiencing what it meant to live, and it had taken until this time, a time when she accepted her father.

Junior was beyond grateful for this entire situation. It was all he could do to restrain himself from jumping and yelling in excitement as he watched his family start to piece back together. While his life hadn't been perfect, it hadn't been as bad as some of the others in his family, and he had been able to learn and embrace a lot of the truths he had been taught.

Joining the conversation as a way to channel his excitement, he said, talking quickly, "Our entire existence is built on this principle that life comes through another, and it has to be this way since our life came through Jesus, and everything he does establishes the pattern, or law, for our existence. We can only exist because of Jesus, because he gave of himself to give us life. Life, then, comes through others, just as it came to us through our various mothers at birth.

"Jesus is the only being who has the power to give life because he is the only being with the power to overcome opposition. Every action we take that produces or contributes something to our existence is only capable of lasting if we first draw on his power. The only things that can last are the things that are undertaken drawing on his power, or acting in his name, as he is the only being without a counterpart."

Everyone smiled at the fast pace and excitement in Junior. The joy he felt at the moment was palpable, and Jess found his enthusiasm contagious. Reaching her hand down into the cool waters of the lake, Jess sent a splash of water straight towards Junior. As the water hit him, Junior looked up, surprised at first, but quickly racing to join in the water fight as he saw the laughter on Jess's face. Junior had never seen her laugh yet, and wasn't going to miss this moment for anything.

Water was splashing in every direction now, and the laughter permeated the air. Ruby had backed away as she never much enjoyed getting wet, but she also sensed something else. She scanned her surroundings, trying to grasp what it was she was feeling, and finally recognized the presence of an individual in a bunch of trees close by. She went the short distance to the trees, to find Ranier's other daughter, watching in sadness as the group laughed together in the water.

Ruby could see the tears in the daughter's eyes. Ruby quietly knelt down by her, and embraced her tenderly. The tears fell freely for the daughter, and at length she asked "Why? Why am I such a reject? Why does no one love me? Why can't I just be normal like everyone else? I hate myself" she said in disgust.

Ruby held her more tightly. Thoughts raced through Ruby's mind as she tried to think of what to say. She hadn't been allowed to work with this daughter yet, and was unsure of her background. The daughter was good as well about keeping her feelings in, and Ruby had a hard time reading or sensing what was driving the feelings.

Ruby could only think to say "People do love you. Those people out there love you. God loves you."

"Then why would he make me this way?!" the daughter quickly interjected in anger. "I'm a loser, never capable of anything, never beautiful to anyone, and never able to do anything right. This," she said pointing to the group still laughing as they threw water at each other, "is the story of my life. Others have good things, and I sit on the sidelines, unable to join in."

As she spoke, Ruby was picking up bits and pieces of her life as they escaped out from behind all of her walls and protections inside. This daughter had been adopted by a wealthier family, but had never been fully accepted by them and always treated by the other children born naturally to the couple as an outsider. From her view, she was always a second-class citizen in the home, and never had the gifts or talents necessary to match her adoptive siblings' talents. They could sing, dance, play music, get good grades and the like and she could do nothing they could. She sensed her adoptive parents were disappointed in her for her lack of talent, and so she tried her best to stay quiet and out of the way while her siblings possessed the limelight and received the attention from her parents.

Ruby could sense that the daughter's heart was breaking now as she sat again, watching, just as she had for her time on earth. At length, Ruby whispered encouragingly as she continued to hold her, "The light of Christ is shared with us all to enable us to overcome opposition. His light is never subject to extinction, annihilation, or any other form of extinguishment as there is no counterpart that can act to negate it. We are taught that everything we have comes from him—even our power to act comes from him. God has given you a beautiful power to act, and you just need to find what it is and act on it. If you rely on your own power, this power can be negated by the opposition we face, but if you accept God's power to you, you can do beautiful things.

"Ultimately," Ruby continued, "Jesus gives us each access to his power in the things that he gives us in this life. Our ability to create, our ability to act, our ability to think, to learn, and progress, all come from him. It is his light that powers all of us, and nothing we do is accomplished without drawing, ultimately, on his light, or, in other words, on truth. While God doesn't give us all of his power at once, he gives us pieces as we learn and grow. You just never got to see what power you were given," Ruby said encouragingly, "but if we focus on what you do have, instead of what you don't, we can start to embrace and accept more light and truth."

The group had now calmed down with the water fight, and had noticed Ruby was not with them anymore. James had watched as Ruby had gone into the trees, and could sense from Ruby that they shouldn't come over right now. James told the group Ruby would rejoin them shortly, and invited them to sit down, but this time a little further away from the water. James could sense Ruby indicating he needed to keep the group together a little longer, so he tried to continue the previous conversation.

"You can see the joy that comes through meaningful interactions" he said in reference to the water fight. "Meaningful interactions with others bring life, and our interactions bring life to others. While we do not give life in every way that Jesus does, every person is endowed with some form of power to pass something on to others. Mothers can give temporary physical life to their children, friends can help bring needed encouragement and support to continue living, and loved ones bring more meaning to our life. We can enhance life for others, and others can enhance life for us. We are powerless, though, in an eternal sense, to work solely for ourselves and make our own existence better, as all life comes through or is enhanced by others.

"While we cannot build our own life by working for ourselves, we can make another's existence better. As we serve others, we enhance their existence. Ultimately, we will be served one day, and our existence will be enhanced as well. While God has power over our existence, we have power over the existence of others, and the highest state of existence possible only comes as we help each other get to that level. God helps us, and we help others."

"How does God get to a new level though if no one helps him?" Ranier asked. "If life only comes through another, who gives life to God and helps him progress?"

"The simple answer," James said, "is that Elirah and Saytah give life to each other. Saytah refers to himself as the 'Father and the Son,' but Elirah may also be referred to as the 'Father and the Son', as Saytah is what his Father is. This goes back to the circularity of eternity. Elirah and Charity gave life, as an Intelligence, to Saytah as their 'Only Begotten'. Saytah, in turn, divided the Intelligence Stream and created spiritual bodies that could be inhabited by Elirah and Charity's Intelligences. Saytah could make these for them, but he could not make one for himself, as all life always has to come through another. Life always has been, and always will be, a gift and sacrifice from another.

"Because of this, Elirah and Charity, after receiving a spirit body made by Saytah, then made a spirit body for Saytah, as well as the rest of us. Thus, Saytah was the 'Father' of Elirah and Charity's spirit bodies as he created the bodies, but they, in turn, created his spirit body. Elirah and Saytah always circle and take turns bringing life at the next stage of existence to each other. Saytah creates the conditions, allows Elirah to enter into those conditions, and then Elirah in turn gives the next stage of life in those conditions to Saytah."

Jess, breaking in at this point, asked "But what about Charity? How does all of this work without her?"

James nodded. "Right now, of course, we are in a somewhat stalled stage of progression as Charity's Intelligence does not exist" he said. "However, as part of the Plan, Jesus will bring her back to life when the situation and conditions are right and appropriate. When she returns, our existence will have many things restored to it which are currently missing, such as the powers and priesthoods unique to women that do not exist without Heavenly Mother. God promises that all things will be restored, and this promise includes one to bring Charity back from her annihilated state.

"Until that moment though, we have to be patient and learn the things we need to in this state. As is the case with all opposition, this state of lacking the best of everything will ultimately bring us to an even more enhanced state of existence. Thus, while we suffer without our Heavenly Mother, we are given even more opportunity to reach out to those who are suffering and struggling, and to help all of us improve our existence. Ultimately, we do need male and female to eternally progress, and so Charity's return will be an essential part of our continued progression."

"I have never fully understood the differences between male and female," Ranier said as he reflected on what James had said about Charity. The conversation went silent at this point as Ranier thought on the thing that troubled him, as he was unable to fully understand what he was feeling inside. James and the others waited for a few minutes while Ranier explored his thoughts.

As they sat, Ranier looked around, realizing, suddenly, that his surroundings seemed to have changed. Everything felt so natural to him that he hadn't noticed a change. Looking to understand where he was, Ranier sensed the others still present, but also sensed they were at a crossroads of sorts, a location where something intersected. The entire place felt hollow and without any bounds, and he could see nothing that suggested any end to the place. He realized that part of his inability to understand what he felt with Charity and males and females was due to the feelings associated with where he was at. As he continued trying to understand, he sensed movement, as if upon water, and he realized he was not located on solid ground.

Perplexed, he turned to James and asked "Where are we? What is this place?"

James, in his typical calm fashion, replied "by the Intelligence Stream, in a place just after it gets divided by Saytah."

"Why are we here?" Ranier asked.

James remained silent, but focused his gaze behind Ranier. Ranier turned, and gasped slightly as he saw a finger reach out and touch what appeared as water moving toward him. He watched in fascination as light and dark separated at the point of touch.

As he continued to watch, he realized there was something else present, the something that created the crossroads-like feeling. He realized he could see a finger from each hand, one touching the Intelligence Stream, while one touched something else, something he couldn't see, but could sense. The two seemed to exist in the same space, but didn't seem to connect in anyway until touched by the fingers of, he presumed, God.

There was nothing spectacular looking about the sight, but he could sense something stirring within his heart. He knew he was witnessing something sacred, and as he continued watching he understood he was witnessing the formation of life, the taking of something that had existed and giving it form, substance, and movement. As he watched, he saw Intelligences and watched as they received a spirit body. Each Intelligence, he could tell, was housed in a male or female spirit body.

"How does God decide if we will be male or female?" Ranier suddenly asked.

"That is all based on who we are" James replied. "Each of us is individual, and different from everyone else. Here, you are witnessing the Intelligence Stream and the new Universe at the point where they intersect. All things that exist intersect at some point or another, and here, at this place, destructive opposition reacts with the complementary opposition. The identity of each piece divided from the Intelligence Stream is driven by the interaction of these two forces of opposition, and all receive their identity as male or female depending on the attributes that define them and give them life."

"But the new Universe hasn't always existed," said Ranier.

"Yes," James agreed, "it has not, if you look at it from a linear perspective where time controls progression."

"Then how did all of the Intelligences prior to the new Universe receive their identity as male or female?"

"That," James replied, "came as a result of the same principles at work. When parts were divided from the Intelligence Stream, the unique parts they had would react with complementary opposition to give an identity of male or female. Even though the Universe founded on complementary opposition was not in place yet, the defining characteristics of male and female were in existence, as complementary opposition is a truth which has always existed, and so the spirit bodies and physical bodies we received were in line with these defining characteristics."

"What, exactly, are those 'defining' characteristics of male and female?" Ranier asked.

James smiled. "Welcome to the 'mystery' of God, Ranier."

"What do you mean?" Ranier asked, confused.

"In the scriptures," James said in response, "there are many mysteries spoken of. However, in the tenth chapter of the Book of Revelation, John says that 'the mystery of God should be finished.' Prior to this particular mystery being finished, John speaks of an Angel who is 'clothed with a cloud: and a rainbow was upon his head, and his face was as it were the sun, and his feet as pillars of fire.'

"Each of these items are symbolic, in some way, of gender and male and female. The cloud represents all that we do not know about gender, the rainbow symbolizes the world's quest to understand gender, the sun representing gender as a source of life, with the pillars of fire representing gender as a foundation that provides movement and ability to our existence.

"Essentially, Ranier, there are many things we just do not know. While we each have a gender and each are born as males or females, we cannot see or understand everything represented as being covered by the cloud on the Angel. In other words, the pieces that truly define man and woman have been entirely hid from us."

"Why would God hide something though?" Ranier asked, still confused about the reference to the mystery of God.

"It has to do with achieving the best future for us all" James replied. "The power that controls the future is the power of knowledge, and God is working to bring about the best future possible, which means he controls the knowledge we have. For example, if I decided to go hiking and I started down a path to reach a lake, my future would involve me walking on that path if I didn't know any reason to avoid the path. However, if a hiker came running down the trail shouting about an angry bear ahead, the knowledge I just received would cause my future to change. Without the knowledge of the bear, I would have walked down a path towards an angry bear. With the knowledge though, I change my path, and my future then changes as well.

"God has promised us a future free of destructive opposition. To get us to that point, he has to carefully control the amount of knowledge we have, often keeping us ignorant of certain things so that we take the paths which will bring us the most growth and development, as knowledge will often cause us to choose a path that is not the best for us. Sometimes, even though there are bears on a certain path, God will help us past the bears to get to our final destination. If we knew of the bears though, we would likely avoid the path altogether, and entirely miss the benefit of the final destination.

"Because of our own weaknesses and inability to trust, God cannot tell us everything, as we will avoid paths that bring pain. It takes extreme faith to have knowledge, and most of us do not have the faith necessary to walk the paths we are supposed to walk knowing everything that those paths hold.

"A further advantage of ignorance is that our ignorance translates into ignorance for Lucifer as well. He only knows things he learned before the War began and things we as humans know now, and so God's best kept weapons in the battle for our souls are the things we do not know—as Lucifer has no way to prepare a defense against something he does not understand or comprehend.

"So, coming back to gender and what truly defines us, we do not know what either fully means. There are pieces we can see, yes, but there are things we do not see or understand. This 'mystery' spoken of by John is the mystery of gender, of males and females, and of what truly defines us. It has been kept hidden all of these years, especially as it relates to women, as women are carrying something that enables the War to be won, and the truths they carry are hidden from us to keep us on the correct path towards an optimal future, and to keep Lucifer in the dark.

"Lucifer, of course, recognizes that women present a big unknown to him. Because of that, he has worked tirelessly to keep them subjected to men, objectified, used, and abused, hoping to destroy their role in God's plan. As women have gained freedoms previously not available to them in the world, Lucifer has turned his attack into one focused on making them feel their only self-worth is found in their ability to be sexually pleasing to men, and to be free of children—the product of sexuality. This is accomplished through immodesty, pornography, abortion, and an obsession with appearing beautiful."

Jess nodded as she listened. She knew well of Lucifer's attack on women, she herself being a victim in nearly every way possible while on the earth. She had always wondered why the imbalance seemed so great between men and women on the earth, and was listening intently to what James was saying.

"In society, many are becoming upset that women are still treated differently than men, including in churches, where women are still denied the ability to be ordained to the Priesthood. It takes faith to navigate the unknowns, and these last days before the Angel comes, or the knowledge is revealed, will take great faith indeed."

"Is there nothing we know though about men and women though?" Ranier asked. "It seems that after all of this time, we would know a little something at least."

"On Earth," James said in reply, "people know very little honestly. However, there are a few points to know. One is that the Priesthood of God, existing in his Church, is gender based and its functionality, while stemming from Christ, is tied to specific parts found in males. The Priesthood complement though, which provides the complementary powers, is also gender based, and its functionality is tied to specific parts found in females. Since the head of this complementary Priesthood, Charity, does not currently exist though, the complementary Priesthood is not functional, and will not be until Charity is brought back.

"Due to this loss, for life to continue, women had to be given another function that complemented the Priesthood. The Priesthood provides, at a basic level, a portal, for lack of a better word, that enables certain of the powers of Heaven to operate on the earth. The Priesthood portals can operate in parts found in the man. However, the Priesthood is not operational without the Holy Ghost, the third member of the Godhead.

"The Holy Ghost is not found in any of the accounts of the pre-mortal world, as the Holy Ghost, looking at things from a linear perspective again, did not exist pre-mortally. When Christ atoned for us and his Intelligence was annihilated, he could only be brought back in the new Universe if he first divided himself, just as Heavenly Father and Heavenly Mother had done, in order to create something that had not existed before. Each stage of existence can only be reached by creating something that has not existed before, and that can only be accomplished through sacrifice.

"When Saytah's two parts were severed by Elirah and the two pieces annihilated, each was made new in the new Universe. In other words, there was a male and a female part that were restored in the new Universe, and, prior to joining back together in the resurrection of Saytah, they divided again, just as they had when Saytah was first created. Out of that division and subsequent union of the divided parts came a resurrected Saytah and the Holy Ghost, a being also one with Elirah and Saytah.

"The Holy Ghost was created and left in a spirit body, so that it could enter into the hearts of humans and prompt and persuade us to follow the right path, confirming that the new Universe fully exists and instilling hope into our souls. Saytah was resurrected and given an immortal physical body, enabling him to move ahead and create our places in the new Universe, worlds without end."

"Didn't the Holy Ghost exist on Earth before Christ was born though?" Jess asked. "I was taught about how prophets and others before Christ responded to the Holy Ghost."

"Yes," James replied, "it did. The Intelligence Stream is a fascinating thing, just as creation itself is. With the law of opposition in place, counterparts always have to be created. If there was to be something that exists now and in the future, its past also had to be created. The past is the counterpart to the future. God teaches us that 'all things are present' before his eyes. This is so as every day created requires another day of past created. While this is extremely hard for our limited minds to comprehend with our forced linear thinking, all creation stems from its meridian point, not from its 'beginning' point. Since there will always be another tomorrow, there will always be another yesterday as well."

Sensing that things were still confusing, James tried again. "Think of numbers. They are perhaps the easiest way to understand the concept. '0' on a number line is the meridian point where creation occurs. If you add one to the number line, or add a tomorrow, then you also add a negative one to the number line. For every positive number you add, a negative number is added as well, and things extend from the meridian point into eternity, into something with no beginning and no end.

"So, for the Holy Ghost, even though it was not created until Christ reached the new Universe, it is able to extend throughout and touch all of creation, except for the meridian point itself. Christ came to Earth in the Meridian of Time, and when Christ was on Earth the Holy Ghost was not fully operational, as it was too close to the meridian point. The apostles had to wait for the Day of Pentecost for the Holy Ghost to come, as they had to wait for the meridian point to finish and the point '1' on the number line to begin. Just as the Holy Ghost could access point '1', or the first day after the meridian, so too could it access point negative '1', or the past from before the meridian point."

Jess shook her head. "This is all too much for me. I've always had a simple mind."

"It's too much for all of us, honestly" James replied with a smile. "Our mortal minds comprehend so little, that it takes faith to open our minds to the possibility before we can start to understand it. Once our minds are opened with faith, God will add understanding though, line upon line, precept upon precept.

"To go back to gender, though, with our original discussion, since the Holy Ghost is a product of the new Universe, it also needs a portal, like the Priesthood, from which to operate on the earth. The Holy Ghost needs the Priesthood to function on the earth, and the Priesthood needs the Holy Ghost to function. Pieces of women that define the female gender were given the portals necessary for the Holy Ghost to function and operate on the earth.

"In other words, women carry the portals necessary to enable the Holy Ghost to function on this earth. God teaches that righteous women are an exceptional power on the earth, and that women working together in unity can accomplish amazing things. This is so because the Holy Ghost comes to earth through them, and the Holy Ghost has more power than anything else to change the hearts of humanity by conveying God's love to all.

"Currently, while men have the portals of the Priesthood tied to them, women have the portals of the Holy Ghost tied to them, and the Priesthood and Holy Ghost cannot operate without each other, just as the man and woman cannot operate without the other. One is not more or less important than the other. During periods of the most oppression of women, such as during the Dark Ages, the Holy Ghost is the least operational as its operational abilities are tied to the level of freedom of women. This also makes it, though, so that the world advances exceptionally fast as women are freed from oppression, due to the power of the Holy Ghost being increased to inspire the hearts and minds of those on the earth."

Jess realized she had never thought about what women were given, she had always focused on what they did not have. The world she lived in was always full of anger and frustration towards men, and taught her to only focus on what was not hers. Hearing James talk made her realize she would have to think through these things more to be able to understand God and the things she had been through on the earth.

"Look again at the Intelligence Stream" James said with some emphasis.

Ranier and Jess looked again, and this time saw the Intelligence Stream completely connected to the new Universe. While Ranier knew he did not begin to understand it, the new Universe was glorious and beyond his ability to describe. He could see that the new Universe overlaid and touched all of the old Universe, making it so that the power of Christ's Atonement and the Holy Ghost could touch and affect all on the earth, even those on the earth prior to the Atonement taking place.

Ranier's mind was being opened and he could somehow see and understand that Jesus was born in the Meridian of Time. This Meridian was a point at which everything connected, the 'cross', so to speak, of all existence. In this place where everything aligned, Jesus could carry out his mission and take its effects to all of existence, the past and the present, the old and the new.

The only limit was that in the Meridian of Time itself, or the place where everything connected, the things that happened in the Meridian could not be fully operational, as that is the only place where time could dictate an order to things. In other words, he could see that the power of the Holy Ghost could not be fully operational on the earth while Christ was there, since that time was the only time in existence where the Holy Ghost had to be created first in order to operate.

Junior understood what Ranier was feeling, and chimed in. "God's purpose is to bring about the immortality and eternal life of each of us, in a state free from destructive opposition and powered instead by complementary opposition. He provided a way that all of us can follow and achieve, and he has individual details worked out for each of us, including for Heavenly Mother who gave her life to bring life to us all, just as Jesus did. His way is designed for the weakest of us, yet capable of refining even the strongest among us. Ultimately, Jesus forges through the hardest of everything and creates a path, and we are only required to walk that path with his help. One day, all of these mysteries will be made known to us, including all of the pieces inside each man and woman, but until then, we walk the path by faith."

Chapter 27

....

STILL STANDING AT THE CROSSROADS of the Intelligence Stream and the new Universe, Ranier continued staring for some time, deep in thought. He was comforted that Jess stood there as well, also deep in thought. It meant so much to him to have some time with his children. "With all of this though," Ranier finally said, slowly, while still thinking, "I still do not understand why we have to be given freedom and agency. I know we started talking about that a while ago, but I do not yet fully grasp why they have to exist."

Jess nodded her head as well. "I know God won't just change somebody as that change has to come from within them, but I also struggle understanding agency, as it brings so much darkness and pain to our existence. At least it did to mine" she said softly, not wanting to make eye contact with Ranier.

"Sorry about that," James replied, "there is so much to talk about, and it is rare I get to share so much at once, so I don't have a lot of practice sharing all of these things. I guess I got a little sidetracked with some other important points.

"But, to your questions, the simple answer is that no Intelligence or light can exist without freedom or agency to act. If we want life, we have to closely guard the basic unit of life inside of us, which is our Intelligence. The reason that life depends on freedom and agency is because freedom and agency are a major part of the definition, or identity, of the concept of life.

"With the law of identity, when God created the concept of life, he had to divide things that were 'alive' from things that were not 'alive', otherwise life would be an unintelligible concept. Part of the identity, or definition of life, is something that thinks and acts, or functions, on its own. Consider a rock. A rock can be moved, shaped, molded, or otherwise utilized. However, people recognize a rock is not alive as the rock lacks the ability to think and act, or function, on its own. It is entirely dependent on another living thing to make it function.

"The ability to think and act on our own only exists through freedom and agency. Something is alive and capable of acting only if it has the agency and ability to act on its own. If agency or freedom is removed from an individual, the individual loses life, as the individual loses the ability to think and act on his or her own. While a physical or spiritual body can continue for a time with the removal of freedom and agency, the Intelligence dies, and a lifelessness follows to the rest of the bodies that exist for that Intelligence.

"Freedom, in other words, is an integral part of life. A being with freedom and agency is alive as it has the power to think, act, respond, and process its own decisions. This ability is life. If this ability is taken away entirely, a being becomes a robot, or drone, which simply responds as it is told to respond. While robots can talk, walk, work, and do other things, they are not 'alive' and do not possess life because they are not free from the programming and instructions they have. They have no power to go against their foundational programming.

"Living beings, on the other hand, have the full ability to choose the ways of death as they are not subject to programming like a robot. Life's essence requires that a being choose to live. Life cannot be forced, as life is not a compulsory matter. God has told us that the Heavens withdraw themselves when another exercises control, dominion, or compulsion upon another person. This is so because life and choice go hand in hand. Nothing can truly be alive if it cannot choose, each day, to pursue a path of life or a path of death. If I undertake to force a person to do something, I am taking away some measure of that person's life, in an eternal sense. In the world, you may not see the negative results if you look only at the physical body, but force, even there, destroys the soul.

"Ultimately, freedom and agency allow us to experience the greatest depths of human existence—true love. Not the romantic type of love, but love which endures and gives meaning to life. True love comes from God, the type of love that endures all things, the type of love that helps us overcome all things, the type of love that forever gives us a place to call home.

"Returning to the point of when more than one being would be created in the Universe, if two beings existed, they would have the power to interact. That power to interact could be used to harm or help the other being. Love is, by identity, a free will choice of another being to act in a selfless way for your benefit. If a robot acted for us, or gave its life for us, in accordance with its programming, we would never feel love from that robot, as love can only be felt when coupled with a free will offering from another being.

"Love means something to our existence because it means that something with free will and the agency to choose, chose to sacrifice something it wanted for us. Love means something because a being with free will chose not to harm us. Love, ultimately, is meaningful, because it means that a being with free will places more importance on our existence than it places on its own existence. When we feel everything that choice entails—the choice of a being feeling we are more important than the being itself—we feel love.

"Love, like life, is always critically tied to choice and agency. If we take away agency or freedom, we take away life and love. In other words, if we take away suffering and death, we also take away life and love. Suffering exists in the world precisely because love exists. Love can only mean something if a being makes a choice, a free will choice, to exercise its power of interaction in a way that recognizes your importance, rather than in a way that minimizes your importance.

"So, while I'm getting off on a little tangent from the original question, the fact suffering exists in the world is proof of the existence of a God who loves us. Why does God allow us to suffer? It is so we can experience the depths, beauty, and joys of being loved, of being in the presence of a being who voluntarily chooses to not harm, but instead chooses to recognize our great worth. If we had no ability to harm another, then we could never feel the true depths of love as we would never experience the choice of an individual to voluntarily choose to treat us right and recognize our inherent worth.

"As is the case with all opposition, the power and ability to love comes from the same power and ability to harm and cause suffering, just as the ability to choose life comes from the same ability to choose death. Just as the eye is a tool to discern light and darkness, so too is human interaction the tool to experience love, as it is also the tool to experience suffering at the hands of others. Again, the choice of a being to interact with you in a positive way, instead of that being interacting in a selfish way that hurts you, is what enables love.

James could sense he was talking too quickly, especially for Jess who hadn't been a part of all of these conversations, and tried to slow down a little. Taking a few moments to help slow down his pace, he said "Lucifer's plan was to remove agency. He wanted to ensure that the Mirror could never be broken, and he wanted to place mind control in everyone to stop certain thoughts from ever being thought or acted upon. As Jesus created all things under the direction of Heavenly Father, they both knew that *any* degree of force or compulsion outside of the laws giving life would lead to the loss of life. *Any* degree of individual force upon the soul of another individual, if maintained, is like a poison to the soul, and it slowly kills off the being it is in force upon. Removing agency, or removing law and consequences and requiring everyone to go to the same place, was removing life itself, for everyone.

"Lucifer and his followers did not believe this though. Instead, they believed that annihilation, suffering, pain, darkness, etc. were the cause of the loss of life. They looked at the big, obvious things that brought death, and made a plan to avoid those. The plan Lucifer made though, ignored the little things, the foundational things upon which all existence is predicated.

"Ultimately, as is the case with gender, no being can see everything it is built upon. Our eyes and senses open us up to the world around us, but not to what is inside our own self. We have to rely, in faith, on our Creator to know everything that is inside each of us, to know what is required to sustain life. Only God knows everything that is required for life, as only God created life.

"Those who followed Lucifer placed more faith in their ability to see and reason than they did in their Creator though. Their beliefs about the mind control and the force they wanted to impose to maintain a utopia-like state were based on their own observations and experiences, or on their belief in how good Lucifer's plan sounded. 'Yes,' they thought and reasoned, 'life should be free from pain and suffering, from failure, from darkness,' and ultimately, they reasoned, 'I should be free from my own consequences of my decisions.'

"In other words, they wanted two opposite things to exist at the same time. They wanted to redefine what life meant, but they lacked all ability to see or understand what types of implications that would bring. They just believed that if they wanted it, it must be possible. They twisted every definition in existence to support their interpretation. 'No being who truly 'loves' you would allow you to suffer,' Lucifer would say. This type of reasoning though negated the true meaning of love, as love is only meaningful if the power to harm is present. If the power to harm is taken away, so too is the power to feel love.

"Ultimately, one-third of the hosts of Heaven followed Lucifer. While this one-third is a lot of people, it is a testament, ultimately, to the power of free will as two-thirds still elected to follow God's plan, or the plan for life. Under strict laws of opposition, only half would have been expected to follow the path of life.

"However, a significant portion of beings from the Other Side of the Mirror, the dark side of the Mirror, such as you and me, exercised their free will to reject everything about their nature and pursue a path of light. Their desires to be like God and obtain what he had overrode their dark natures, and they followed God. Since many beings of light chose to follow Lucifer, there was a significant number of beings of darkness who chose to follow God.

"Life is a great power, but love is even stronger. The thing that enticed so many beings of darkness to choose the path of light was the love of Charity and the love and light of Saytah. They recognized the power and desirability of such a life, and God prepared a way for them to be saved, to be reborn, and to experience the depths of joy that exist with love. Jesus came and died not only for the beings of light, but for the beings of darkness as well."

Ranier interrupted James. "Why is it fair that only beings of darkness have to overcome their identity and give up themselves? It seems beings of light have it a lot easier."

"Yes," James said with a little laugh, "I obviously have failed to include everything I need to. I have spoken of overcoming dark natures as that relates to you and me. However, all beings have to go through the same process and give up their core. Beings of light have incomplete cores, and light, in the old Universe sense, is attracted to the dark. Thus, whether a person is a being of light or dark from the beginning, they both have to give up their core to be made new.

"Due to a lack of words in your language, the old light and the new light—the light that is part of the new Universe—use the same word. So, while you are seeking for light to fill your being, you are seeking for the light associated with love and complementary opposition, as opposed to the light associated with the Intelligences when they were initially created.

"All of us have counterparts Ranier. For almost every being who followed Lucifer, its counterpart chose to follow God. Thus, some part of nearly every being will exist eternally. There are a very few situations though where both the counterpart of light and dark chose to follow Lucifer, and where no part of that being will be saved. For the few that exist, they are especially sad situations. Lucifer is one of those. Lucifer was a being of light who rejected life and love, and his counterpart did as well. Due to this, Lucifer gained a title of 'Perdition', meaning, in the language of Heaven, 'all is lost.'

"On Earth, we are told about 'Sons of Perdition,' or beings who live in such a way that they remove themselves from God's plan and turn to live with Lucifer and his followers forever. These Sons of Perdition are beings where both counterparts elect to follow Lucifer. For counterparts who initially chose to follow God and come to the earth, the only way for them to become a Son of Perdition is to voluntarily choose to remove the light of Christ from inside them while they reside on the earth. God protects us from our own stupidity and shortsightedness in life, and so the light of Christ is kept safe deep within our soul where we cannot accidentally or inadvertently sever the connection.

"In order to reach the light of Christ inside of us, we have to obtain a very high level along the path towards the new light. We have to have lived according to truth and light and obtained an absolute knowledge and testimony of God through the Holy Ghost. After having received this knowledge and access to the light of Christ inside, a Son of Perdition would then have to sever all access to this light of Christ in order to be with Lucifer. This is referred to as committing the unpardonable sin, or denying or blaspheming the Holy Ghost.

"The act of committing the unpardonable sin is always accompanied by cold-blooded murder, as inflicting death on another is the only way to bring eternal death to one's self. Just as life comes through another, so too does death, ultimately, come through another's death, and so a being choosing to follow Lucifer and become a Son of Perdition will always choose to murder in cold-blood. This is how Cain became a Son of Perdition. He reached a point where he did not want to live eternally, and he rejected the light of Christ inside and brought death to himself by murdering his brother Able in cold-blood.

"The sin is unpardonable because a being voluntarily, and with full knowledge, severs the connection to Christ. In other words, the being fully exercises its free will to die, in an eternal sense, and God will not force any being to live, as force and life do not ever go together. In order for eternal life to exist, there has to be a way for a being to choose eternal death, and the fact that a counterpart can choose to follow its other counterpart and be a Son of Perdition is proof of the eternal nature of life.

"Fortunately, the number of counterparts who both choose eternal death is very limited indeed, and the majority of at least one of the two counterparts for each being chose life. The War in Heaven that you heard referenced earlier when you first arrived in Yuli, was a War that arose as Lucifer and his followers tried to carry out their plan. The War began as Lucifer and his followers started to try and forcefully implant mind control in other beings. They knew that if even one being did not submit, it would throw off their entire plans.

"Thus, in the beginning, Lucifer and his followers began fighting in an attempt to create the conditions they believed were necessary to sustain life. A part of them, based in light or its attraction to light, desperately wanted to live, and so they became exceptionally aggressive with force in trying to force mind control into others. For those following God though, they wanted desperately to save the beings following Lucifer, and so they responded by trying to convince and persuade the beings to reject the ways of Lucifer."

Ranier suddenly noticed that, somehow, they were all back close to the lake. The Intelligence Stream was nowhere to be seen, and he still wasn't used to how quickly the environment could change. While James was still talking, Ranier sensed something else. Looking around, he noticed a grouping of trees and felt there were people there watching. He didn't know how many, but he knew, somehow, that even though he wanted to know who they were, he should ignore them for the moment and continue listening while he still had time here.

Chapter 28

"WHY DO YOU THINK YOU CHOSE, pre-mortally, to come to the earth?" Ruby asked Ranier's daughter. Ruby could tell she was still very distraught, but still couldn't fully understand why this situation was so distressing. Her question was just an attempt to keep Ranier's daughter talking, and it was all that would come to her mind.

"I came," the daughter said through grimaced teeth while choking back tears, "in hopes of finding someone who loved me as I am. It was an entirely wasted effort though," she said in barely audible tones. "It was all for naught."

Ruby could tell that something inside the daughter had broken at an exceptionally deep level. "What could possibly be keeping her functioning?" Ruby thought to herself. "This just doesn't make sense" she thought as she reviewed the strength of the walls in the daughter and how much she was able to keep away from Ruby. "No one so broken should have such strength left."

*　*　*

Junior felt uncomfortable as he sat listening to James. He could tell James was uneasy for some reason, and Junior was trying to figure out why. James would trip over his words as he spoke, and Junior knew someone must be communicating with his mind directly. Junior looked around for Ruby, and sensed her presence a little way off in a group of trees. Once he realized she was there, he tried to tune his mind into what was taking place. Based on the worry coming from Ruby's mind, he suddenly understood that Ruby was with his half-sister.

Junior thought about his attempts to reach her. Jess was the only one able to remain near her for long, as she shut everyone else out. Her walls ran deep, as deep as the pain she felt inside. It was a tough situation, one that he didn't know how to deal with. For some reason, he could sense this was a critical time, but didn't know why.

As James continued to struggle keeping his thoughts together, Junior decided it would be best if he gave him a break. "The War in Heaven was an interesting war," Junior said to Ranier and Jess, jumping into the conversation. James nodded gratefully at Junior as Junior continued speaking.

"The War was one where beings following God would submit themselves to great persecution and suffering at the hands of those following Lucifer as they wanted to convince them to turn back and come to God. The beings following God knew that force could never bring life, and they tried everything in their power to persuade Lucifer's followers otherwise. Thus, for a being following God, the main 'weapon', for lack of a better word, used was the weapon of speech and example, the weapon of choosing not to harm, or of turning the other cheek.

"Lucifer and his followers, on the other hand, were aggressive, forceful, and full of hate for those that, they felt, opposed their way of 'life'. They wanted to construct an 'alternative' way to life, and they had to demand that everyone come with them in order for their way to work, under the terms they wanted to construct themselves. Of course, their way could not work, as it ran counter to life itself, but under their belief system all had to come with them.

"The War became exceptionally brutal and ugly and many beings suffered intensely while trying to convince others to not follow Lucifer. Lucifer and his followers began seeking to incite those following God to return the anger and the hate, to return the pain and suffering inflicted, as doing so brought darkness into an individual that Lucifer and his followers could then try to capitalize on as they pursued their course of force.

"The weapons of good and life were testimony, example, patience, and love. Many people imagine war as being one where good fights and destroys many 'bad' people, but this was not how the good side fought in the War. The fight for those following God was a fight to keep as many people as possible from following Lucifer. The War in Heaven was not a war to kill and destroy individuals, it was an all-out fight to instill hope, faith, and a desire to live in those professing to follow Lucifer, in hopes of keeping them in existence. It was, in other words, a War of love, of long-suffering, of patience, of courage to speak truth, and of attempts to persuade the free will of each being that life was worth the work involved.

"While one-third still chose to follow Lucifer, the War was quite successful for those fighting for the side of light and life as the number following Lucifer was reduced from one-half to one-third. In other words, through the efforts of those who wanted light and life, many of those who initially chose to follow Lucifer changed and followed God. Ultimately though, Lucifer and his followers reached a point where they, fully aware of the entire ramifications of their actions, entirely severed their connection to the light of Christ. For those in Heaven, it was akin to a mass suicide, and was one of the saddest days in existence. We all lost many people we loved dearly" Junior said as his voice trailed into a whisper, his mind on his half-sister. He knew she hadn't followed Lucifer then, but she seemed so close to losing everything now, and he didn't know how to reach her.

After a few moments, Junior fixed his gaze on Ranier, and said with directness in his voice, "the War in Heaven rages on the earth today. Lucifer is still trying to destroy, to control minds, to implement force. Once Lucifer and his followers severed their connection to the light of Christ, they became exceptionally bent on destruction. Since they had no light in them, darkness filled them. Darkness collects darkness, just like a black hole collects matter. As the darkness continues to collect, it causes an eternal spiral downward. After all that could be done for Lucifer and his followers, they had to be cast out to preserve the safety of those who remained in Heaven. They were cast out to the earth."

* * *

Ruby had sat silent in the trees, but was paying attention through her mind to what was being said as no thoughts were coming to her. She suddenly realized that the walls inside Ranier's daughter blocked Ruby's access to her feelings as well as Lucifer's access. Ruby understood now that the walls built inside were walls of apathy, of not caring either way, of a neutral feeling. Ranier's daughter had grown apathetic about existence as it was her only means to cope with her destroyed hope.

Ruby watched as Ranier's daughter still had tears trickle down her cheek. "She cares about something still" she thought. "What is it though?" Ruby decided she may never know if she never asked, so she ventured cautiously and said "What do you still care about? What other things matter to you in addition to being appreciated for who you are?"

"I want to live" she responded quietly, "and I've always, always yearned for my father. While I had an adoptive father, he didn't accept me for who I was, and I figured that since my own father made me the way I was, maybe, just maybe, he would accept me . . ." she lowered her eyes as her voice trailed off, " . . . because he made me."

Ruby had tears come to her eyes as she saw the pure innocence of this woman. Ruby could now see that Ranier's absence had been a blessing, in that Ranier would not have accepted her during his time so far on the earth. This would have crushed her, and left her without any hope to sustain her flickering desire to live. However, having Ranier absent from her life when he was controlled by the darkness kept the light alive in this daughter enough to carry her forward, despite losing her other hopes. Certainly, things would have been great for this daughter if Ranier had done as he should have while on the earth, but God, in his wisdom, kept an important piece of this daughter alive, thereby keeping her alive as well.

Ruby gave Ranier's daughter another long hug. "Your father is here now" she said. "But it looks like you don't want to talk to him."

Ranier's daughter nodded her head in agreement. "I can't. If he doesn't accept me, I'll be crushed. Everyone else has rejected me. Even though he has changed a lot, I have been rejected by many good people, people who still failed to see me, and I'm not in a position where I can take that risk. I have to wait to see how his time on earth goes and how he treats the simple and untalented, the not beautiful, and the lonely. I only have once chance left in me, and I can't open myself up for that chance to be destroyed without losing all of me."

* * *

James had appreciated Junior jumping into the conversation with Rainer so that he could focus on communicating with Ruby through their minds. He had been able to follow and understand what was going on and what the problem was now, and knew that Ruby would be able to convey what he discussed with Ranier and Jess. James knew what needed to be said for the other daughter's sake, and so he waited for a pause in the conversation lead by Junior.

When there was a moment to break in, James took it and continued the conversation with Ranier's other daughter in mind. "While Lucifer and his followers were cast to the earth, their outlook is bleak indeed. God formed an entirely new Universe, one based in complementary opposition, that he is taking us all to. There is one path only to get there, and it is the path Jesus walked to get there. Lucifer and his followers, however, will have no place there. When they severed their connection to the light of Christ, they knowingly severed their connection to being pulled through to the new Universe. All of us have to be connected to Christ through his light and by sealing ordinances to be pulled through to the new Universe. All of us, at one point in our creation, had this connection and this light, because Christ cares about saving each one of us" he said with emphasis.

"Due to the destruction of the Mirror, the Universe is self-destructing as matter and its counterpart is meeting up again. You cannot see it happening, as the light from any destruction that occurs is destroyed as well. All of the light you see in the sky is from many years ago, and is not representative of the current state of the Universe. God placed the earth, after its fall, in the second to last location to be destroyed in the Universe. Prior to its fall from Adam and Eve partaking of the fruit, the earth was in a location and state in the light spirit matter, where annihilation of the spirit matter would never take place. Thus, the earth would remain forever there if Adam and Eve had never partaken of the fruit, but we would have never come to be.

"For Lucifer and his followers, they will still be on the earth once it is annihilated, and everything will become a void of nothingness. The nothingness produces a sense of burning for a spirit body, as spirit matter was made to exist in conjunction with something else, and its separation from everything causes it to react to the loss. Spirit matter never stops experiencing the sensation. Thus, the scriptures refer to eternal burnings and lakes of fire and brimstone to describe the state of those who remain in Hell. Hell, or Outer Darkness, as it is more appropriately called, is a state of nothing. It is a void. No being has the power to create anything besides the Savior, and so any person in Outer Darkness will forever remain in this state of burning as they are powerless to create or modify their situation there.

"Jesus will come to Earth before it is fully annihilated. Prior to this time, annihilation waves will begin hitting Earth, and different things will begin to be annihilated. The first annihilation waves always hit things we cannot see, but that are foundational to our mortal, fallen existence. As annihilation waves hit Earth, its climate will begin to slowly spiral out of control. Earthquakes will occur across the earth. The sea will heave itself beyond its bounds. Many fires and calamities will result.

"Not just the earth will be impacted though. Individuals and other life, such as animals, will also be impacted. Some that are extremely connected to their foundation will start to die quickly, like the honey bee, while others, like humans, will start to spiral downward slowly. Individuals will begin to be annihilated part by part. Mental illness and emotional instability will continue to climb. People will feel broken, they will feel darkness inside, hearts—meaning courage, hope, and will—will fail, and people will wonder where God is.

"Foundational things like natural affection, decency, and the ability to see reality will all be subject to annihilation. Emotional and mental parts, unseen to the world, will be annihilated. Cancer will continue to climb, as it is an outgrowth of the annihilation taking place inside of us. We will not all annihilate at the same rate or speed, as we all have different parts and pieces inside, but we will all begin to break down in one way or another."

"Why does God let us live through such a slow process of death?" Jess asked. "It sounds like a horrible time to be alive."

"There are many reasons, of course," James said while looking into the distance, "but ultimately it is because God loves us. God's heart breaks at all of the suffering which takes place. He weeps, just as he did when Jesus suffered and died for us, but he knows the quality of our eternal life will be established based on our ability to endure and overcome the darkness, or our ability to let go of who we are." James tried hard to communicate these things clearly to Ruby, as he hoped Ranier's daughter would be able to understand these concepts. "There is so much to gain through suffering while on this earth, or so much to gain from letting go of our old existence, that God exercises eternal restraint to not pick us up and move us from the heartache as he knows what is coming. Remember, it is through letting go that we obtain the new and the better, and often suffering is necessary to convince us to let go.

"Additionally," James continued, "there is, for lack of a better phrase you would understand, a serious time crunch involved in all of this. The waves of annihilation were set in motion when the Mirror broke. With the exception of Elirah, who already passed his mortal experience on another planet, every being who wants to be taken to the new Universe must pass through this earth or others like unto it. This earth is the last fallen planet not annihilated though, and so we have to remain here until we have allowed every remaining soul to touch the earth and gain a physical body.

"Elirah was the first being to receive a physical body, and he went to a world where he, like Adam, partook of the fruit of the Tree of Knowledge of Good and Evil. He did so under the direction of Saytah, and did so at a time and in a way that would not produce a fall for the rest of the Universe.

"Elirah lived in a fallen, mortal body. His purpose was to ensure that the mortal conditions we would be subject to would not completely overpower us, but would allow the right choices to be obtainable and possible. Elirah was not willing to send us through an experience he had not lived himself. While he knew, based on his ability to see and comprehend, that the conditions would be appropriate, he still lived them before asking any of us to live them. Once he finished what he was supposed to do on that planet, he partook of the fruit of the Tree of Life, an exceptionally bitter fruit, and regained an immortal body.

"Elirah's immortality could come as a result of the Tree of Life, as he lived his life perfectly in his fallen state. Adam and Eve and the rest of us could not partake of the fruit of the Tree of Life to gain eternal life though. This was so because when Lucifer was cast to the earth, he integrated a piece of mind control into the forbidden fruit. Thus, Adam and Eve were commanded not to partake of the fruit, as it had been tainted by Lucifer. The mind control placed in the fruit would become a permanent part of the fruit and a body that partook of the fruit, and it could not be removed without bringing death to the person. When

Adam and Eve partook of the fruit with the mind control piece, mind control became a permanent part of their existence.

"The mind control piece placed limits on human logic and reasoning. It forced all reasoning into a linear fashion, making it impossible to reason and fully understand the eternal ways of God, as all creation and existence is circular, not linear. Additionally, it made it so that a physical body would gain power over a soul when sins were committed, and it would gain this power through addiction. Linear logic and addiction were the results of the mind control piece placed in the fruit. Due to this, Adam and Eve could not partake of the fruit of the Tree of Life as these pieces would forever remain in them if they did. Thus, they had to die to have these parts destroyed. Lucifer was convinced they would live though, as he was certain God would not allow them to die, since 'life' was such an important part of the Plan, and since they would be able to partake of the fruit of the Tree of Life and live forever, just as Elirah had done.

"When Adam and Eve were driven out of the garden and not allowed to partake of the fruit of the Tree of Life, Lucifer's plan was foiled and he had to come up with a backup plan to reach everyone as his physical mind control would be lost when an individual died. Thus, it became necessary for him to seek to move the mind control from the physical body into the soul, the piece of us that never dies, by having us embrace sin enough to have it transcend the physical and become part of our soul.

"Due to this, Lucifer strives to tempt us in every way possible, even if to only have us start to accept sin as the norm. He wants us to make mistakes, to be tainted at a spiritual level, so that the mind control will move from our physical body into our spiritual body. As we are fallen and all make mistakes, we needed a way to be cleansed from our mistakes, or we would forever be subject to the mind control placed in the fruit.

"Thus, Jesus atoned and died for us, so that we could be cleansed and resurrected. When Jesus atoned for us, he took on himself all of our old Universe dark and light parts. Due to the light of Christ inside of us, he was able to pull all of our parts to him, and he took them upon himself as he was annihilated, effectively removing our sins, darkness, and problems from us. For us, we can partake of his Atonement and free ourselves from all of the bad by giving ourselves to him and letting him carry these pieces of us with him to annihilation. However, for the atonement to be truly effective, we have to give up the old parts of ourselves, or let them suffer a 'spiritual death', so that the mind control will die with them.

"When we give ourselves to him and allow the pieces of ourselves to be annihilated with him, we then can receive of the new parts that come along with his Resurrection in the new Universe. Christ passed through the process of annihilation, or death, and rebirth for us, and he is our path to the new Universe. The way is by giving up the tainted parts of ourselves to receive the new parts wrought in the atonement of Christ. We simply do not have to do it alone, and there is no reason for us to not partake of his love and sacrifice for us by receiving the new parts he has for us."

James realized there was an important point to make, one that Ranier's daughter needed to understand. "Ultimately though," James continued carefully, "our suffering on the earth as it spirals out of control will do something exceptional for us. It will cause us to realize we are powerless to secure or control our own existence. All of us, ever since first being separated from the Intelligence Stream, tend to ignore the facts of our creation and believe we are in control. This underlying belief keeps us from ultimately finding God and from finding the source of our life. Once we realize we are wrong, that we cannot secure or control our own existence, it will drive us to look for something solid that we can turn to.

"At first, most people will look to the government of the country they reside in. For those who don't believe in God, the government is where they will first put their trust. It is the only thing they can see that has the power to correct things. As is the case with all human vision though, governments are not all-seeing enough to prepare for hardly anything that is coming. No government can change people's hearts, and no government will be able to fix what is happening to the earth, yet people will try.

"As their level of desperation increases, the laws will become more rigid and strict and many freedoms will be lost. As freedoms are lost and morality decays and annihilation continues, societies will become more and more unstable, until they too fall apart. At that point, people will have nothing left to turn to but God, their Creator.

"God doesn't desire to make people suffer. He desires to bless us, and he has blessed the earth in this time with more riches and wonders than have existed in the sum of the rest of the earth's existence. Yet, these riches take people away from God, because they promote the lie that we are in control of our own existence and security. When people can turn to their riches or knowledge for help, they will ignore God. When they ignore God, they continue to die inside, as they have to turn to the source of their creation to continue to receive the nourishment they need to fully enjoy eternal life.

"Due to this, things will be taken away from us, piece by piece, until we are willing to admit that we do not have the ability to secure our own existence, until we are truly willing to turn and look to God. God does not do this out of self-aggrandizement, he does it simply because he is the life. He wants to give us life, and when our riches, our governments, and our prosperity are keeping us away from life, when they are slowly killing us inside by keeping us from the source of life, God will take those things away as they have become the instruments of death.

"On Earth, we kick and scream when we lose our things. We wonder how a God who loves could possibly allow people to be poor, to be hungry from day-to-day, to be without talent or beauty, or to have sicknesses. These things are there precisely because they bring life by pointing us to the source of life. They help us cut through the lie that we have the power to control our own existence. Lucifer and his followers all believed they could establish a Universe different from the one God created. Lucifer was even bold enough to demand God's power to go and make his version of a Universe, one where no one suffered, no one failed, and one where no one could ever do anything wrong.

"Lucifer would only see himself. Lucifer did not do what he did out of the goodness of his heart for others, he did it to aggrandize and promote himself. When Lucifer only saw himself, his view of truth and reality was significantly distorted. Pride is the term we use when we see only ourselves. Humility is the term we use to describe those who are able to see the big picture and their actual place in the great circle of life, or in God's eternal round.

"There were countless reasons why Lucifer's plan could never work, yet it was appealing, because it offered something for nothing. It promised life without consequences, in other words, it promised life without law, and that is just an impossibility. Law is a foundation of life, as life is a free will exercise of choosing between something that is and is not, and the only way that something is or is not is through a law that establishes boundaries and identity.

"Suffering, therefore, is to help us get past ourselves. As part of gaining an identity, a body that has shape, form, and boundaries, we tend to see only ourselves in the picture. We have to get past seeing just us though, and that usually requires we lose things we care about. We fight so much to keep ourselves aggrandized that we have to be driven to a place where we will see we are powerless. As we are slowly taken through a prolonged annihilation, we will begin to see our life is out of our control. Drugs, government, and science will have little in the way of help. We will slowly begin to return to our God as we realize we have to let go and place ourselves in his hands."

Junior broke in at this point. "People often talk about hitting rock bottom" he added. "This is an interesting phrase, as it suggests we can only fall so far, or that we fell to our foundation. Jesus is referred to as 'the Rock', as he is our foundation, and we can never fall further than our foundation. While it hurts us a lot to be reduced to nothing more than our foundation as we lose things that we have set importance on, God is giving us an opportunity to see that we are powerless to do anything on our own. When we are reduced to our foundation, if we turn to God, who is our foundation, we can still build and become something wonderful. We have to learn though that nothing we do ever lasts, and we have to build our life with Christ as our foundation, or else the things we build and do in life will be repeatedly reduced to the rock bottom in our lives.

"Lucifer and his followers end up in Outer Darkness, or the void left when everything in this Universe is annihilated. The scriptures discuss the Heaven and Earth passing away, and this is referencing this process. Jesus, of course, returns to the earth prior to it being completely destroyed, but a lot of things are destroyed prior to his Coming.

"When Jesus comes, the earth will be taken to another location—to a Terrestrial state that existed in the old Universe—as it is the last place that will be annihilated. This state will be protected from annihilation for a period of approximately one thousand years, as it still has a firmament surrounding it, a firmament that evil will not be able to get through until the end of the thousand-year period. Those capable of receiving a Terrestrial type body will also be taken with the earth.

"The scriptures refer to stars falling from the sky, and, while there are many things referenced in this symbolism, two meanings are that the stars fall from the sky as they are annihilated and their light stops reaching the earth, as well as because the earth is moved to a new location, a location without stars in a protected Terrestrial state. This place is where the pre-mortal existence began, and where God dwelt. It was the most protected by intricate firmaments that kept out darkness and evil, and will be the last state left when everything else is annihilated."

"Yes," James said when Junior finished talking. "In that state, which is still in the old Universe, people will work actively to perform necessary ordinances for those who lived on Earth but never had their ordinances performed. These ordinances are necessary for them to be able to be changed to enter the new Universe, and include ordinances such as baptism and sealing to their parents and spouse. Everybody has to be baptized by immersion to be able to have their old selves 'buried', or let go, in order to receive a new body built on complementary, as opposed to destructive, type opposition. Everybody has to be sealed, or connected, to their family, which will enable them to be connected to Christ and pulled through to the new Universe.

"This work has to be performed in the old Universe, where the spirits of those who died without receiving these ordinances must wait until they receive them. Without them, they would be unable to make it to the new Universe, and so it is absolutely critical that these ordinances be performed for every individual who ever came to the earth. Once these ordinances are complete, the firmament surrounding the Terrestrial state will finally be annihilated, and Lucifer and his hosts will be standing ready to make their last attempt at implementing their mind control before everyone is pulled through to the new Universe.

"As Lucifer and his followers will have experienced the burning sensation of Outer Darkness for the thousand-year period, the ability to interact with other matter again will bring them a welcome relief, and they will aggressively pursue a course to try and possess the physical bodies of those still on the earth. Lucifer and his followers will know that the Terrestrial state of the earth is the last location in the old

Universe that still has matter present, and they will know it will be their last chance to try to attack and overtake God to obtain his power.

"They will do everything they can to prevent us from being taken to the new Universe, everything, that is, except change. Everything they want will only bring death, and they will continue to refuse to change, having fully embraced the path to death. They will continue to believe their lies, and will believe that if they get mind control into each of us, including God, they will then be able to create a Universe built on lies.

"Due to this, they will wage an exceptionally aggressive war as they will be similar to a cornered animal that knows it is about to die. This battle is known as the battle of Gog and Magog, or light and dark, positive and negative counterparts, good and evil, etc. This battle is an outgrowth of opposition in all things. If it were just up to us to fight, we would be annihilated by our counterparts. However, with the blessings and protections obtained through Jesus and his ordinances, as well as the new life gained through our rebirth, or baptism, we are able to work to forever sever every being from their counterparts without being annihilated.

"Every individual is tied, to some extent, to their counterpart. Lucifer and his followers capitalize on this connection to try and enter the bodies of everyone in existence. The last battle of Gog and Magog will be a battle to forever cut these connections, and allow each individual to exist without being connected to their counterpart. This battle will involve the Sword of Justice, as it is only the Sword of Justice that has the power to cut the connections and finally give each being the consequences, or results, of their decisions and actions. This Sword will be wielded by those in God's army, and will cut through and sever these counterpart connections.

"It will be an exceptionally hard battle, and quite draining emotionally. The War in Heaven that began so long ago was hard, but it deferred use of the Sword of Justice until every being was entirely left without excuse for the Sword to be used. God gave Lucifer and his followers every chance to stop what they were doing, but they only continued in their ways, and continued to insist they receive life on their path to death. As they desired death, and always undertook actions that caused death, in the end, they receive death as they are severed from their connections to us, or their connection to life."

Chapter 29

J AMES KNEW IT WOULD BE hard for Ranier to internalize everything associated with the course of events. James knew too it would be even harder for Ranier's other daughter to understand or accept these things right now. He could tell Ruby was selectively passing this conversation along to Ranier's daughter, in a way that wouldn't hurt her too much. James was always grateful for Ruby and her ability to be delicate with people, as it was a skill he was still working on.

James thought on how it was hard for anyone to think through and understand the role of justice in existence, and how choices today lead to different eternal destinations. James looked across the lake and admired the sheer beauty of creation, a beauty that caused a sense of wonder to arise in his heart every time he saw it. He had always loved the outdoors, and it was because it surrounded him with the amazing beauty and wonder of God.

James could sense though that Ranier and Jess were still thinking on some questions they had in their minds. Jess had been mostly silent during this time, appearing to be trying most to get used to the fact that her father was with her now. James knew Jess wouldn't hear too much of what was said at this time, as she would be sorting through her own emotions. James could also sense that Ranier's other daughter needed to see something from Ranier, something before Ranier returned to Earth. Knowing there wasn't much time left before Ranier would return to his body on Earth, James continued his explanation to Ranier, hoping to find the piece that Ranier's daughter needed.

"Nothing that is still a part of the destructive type opposition can exist in the new Universe. The new Universe is meant to remove the destruction from our existence. God refers to the destructive type opposition as 'unclean'. This is a simple, yet powerful, way for us to understand and comprehend that the new Universe is different and based on different principles than this life. 'No unclean thing can dwell with God,' means, no being with destructive type opposition still a part of them can dwell with God.

"When we sin, or go against God's laws, we are choosing a path towards death, a path that embraces, or feeds, the dark side of the opposition. When we act on these things, we make the destructive type opposition a part of us, and we have to remove that before we can dwell with God. We can remove these 'impurities' through repentance. Jesus atoned for us and made a way for us to have the impurities removed through his power as he took on all of our impurities and had them burned as part of the annihilation, or death, process when he died for us. If we accept Jesus and his atonement, we can be made clean, or 'reborn' to the complementary type opposition and qualify to exist in the new Universe.

"If we do not accept Jesus, then, when we die, we go to live with Lucifer and his followers for a time in the state of annihilation present in Outer Darkness, or Hell. In this state, all of our destructive type opposition is slowly burned out of us as it is annihilated. The scriptures refer to this process as 'eternal burning', 'fire and brimstone', etc. It is not a pleasant way, but there are only two ways to have the impurities removed, either through accepting Jesus and repenting, allowing him to take our impurities on himself, or through having them annihilated out of us in a state of annihilation and burning in Outer Darkness.

"While we haven't discussed it much, Jesus' Atonement is the grand key to our being reborn. Jesus' Atonement helps us to repent, meaning that we become free from the demands of the laws we broke, and free from the darkness we made a part of our being. When we are free from these demands and the darkness inside, we are able to be made new. Jesus' Atonement is the key to all of our changes, all of our progression, and all of our happiness.

"Due to the laws associated with our existence, pieces of us die each time we go against the laws that define our existence and our identity. If God removed the consequences associated with breaking these laws, he would be removing our identity and our existence, as both come due to the division of what is our identity and what is not our identity. Because the removal of consequences would translate into the removal of law, which would then remove life and identity itself, Jesus came to Earth to suffer for all of our sins and to bear the consequences of the law, or the consequences of our existence and doing things that go against our true identity.

"While Jesus made the conditions that defined us and created our identity and existence, he was willing to suffer and make part of his annihilation process a part where he took on our dark parts and annihilated them as well. As our parts are fully interchangeable, we can literally give our dark parts to Jesus by accepting the parts he has for us—parts we gain through humility, faith, charity, etc. This makes it possible for us to have a second chance, to have eternal life, and to be changed to a new state of existence.

"Due to this, Jesus died on the Cross for us. The Cross is deeply symbolic, as it symbolizes the place where the old Universe and the new Universe meet. Just as with the Cross, there is only one point where the two Universes connect, and that is through Jesus. Jesus is the connecting point between the two Universes, and thus is the only means of salvation. All of us must follow Jesus. The Cross reminds us of the central point where the two Universes meet, of our death in this Universe, and our rebirth in the new Universe.

"By dying and atoning for us, Jesus was able to perfectly satisfy two competing demands—the demands of justice and the demands of mercy. Justice means the law must be carried out to preserve existence and identity for all of us. Mercy means the withholding of punishment, the granting of a second, or another, chance. Jesus' Atonement is the foundation for our existence, both in this Universe and the next, as it keeps the laws giving us our identity and existence intact, and it gives us the ability to try again, to become new, and to overcome our mistakes.

"Each of us who came to this earth chose eternal life in the premortal world. We all made the decision that no matter how much we suffered, we wanted to live in the new Universe. Therefore, whether we accept Jesus or burn for a time in Outer Darkness, we will have the impurities removed so we can make it to the new Universe.

"Prior to a spirit being sent to Outer Darkness, they will have the opportunity to listen and accept Jesus and all that he did for them. This is why people like me serve as missionaries to those in the Spirit World, as we are teaching everyone that they can avoid Outer Darkness by turning to Jesus. If they choose not to, they will be left as the old earth is destroyed by annihilation and will not be taken to the Millennial state along with the restored earth.

"Right now you are in the Spirit World Ranier. This Spirit World is on the earth, but will not be moved with the earth. Only those who have accepted Jesus will be moved to the Terrestrial type state in the Millennium. The others who refused to accept him will experience the void of Outer Darkness, or the void of annihilation.

"Once the destructive type opposition is entirely burned out of them, they will be lifted up by God as they will be able to enter into the new Universe at that point and receive a place in one of the three Kingdoms there. For some, this will be a short process as they will not have a lot to burn out, but for others, who committed much evil, they will be there for the duration of the Millennium until the annihilation process of their dark parts is complete.

"Lucifer and his followers will try to hold these individuals in Outer Darkness as a type of ransom. They know God promised each individual who came to the earth, except for those who intentionally chose to become a Son of Perdition, that they would be taken to the new Universe. For the beings who chose to be purified through Outer Darkness instead of through Jesus, they will have to be reached and reclaimed as part of the final battle of Gog and Magog. All of the prisoners of Lucifer will have to go free, but Lucifer will fight tooth and nail to keep them. However, God will not leave any of us behind, and so the battle will be fought.

"At the end of the battle of Gog and Magog, every person will have been taken to the new Universe. To be taken there, each person must be resurrected, and part of the battle of Gog and Magog will be to allow for the resurrection of those who chose to have their bad parts annihilated in Outer Darkness. Lucifer and his followers will try to latch on to these people and follow them through with the resurrection to the new Universe as well, but the door to the new Universe will be forever closed on them.

"It will be an amazing sight to witness how all of the hosts of Lucifer are kept out while every individual who came to the earth, except for the Sons of Perdition, are pulled through. This accomplishment will be entirely dependent upon the sealing and other temple ordinances connecting families to each other and to Christ. The Sons of Perdition though, as part of God's promise, are resurrected and receive an immortal physical body before the door is forever closed, but they are not pulled through.

"Once the door to the new Universe is closed, those who followed Lucifer will be without any connection to God or us, and will remain in a state of nothingness. They will only have their spiritual bodies, but will lack their Intelligence. Those who are Sons of Perdition will have a slightly higher capacity than the other spirits who followed Lucifer, due to the additional material they have with their immortal physical body, but all of them will exist in a void, with no ability to act or to be acted upon. They sought for an existence with no law, and they received an existence with no law, or, an existence with nothing."

Ranier was silent. He was amazed how much he did not understand about his own existence. When he realized earlier that he was a dark counterpart trying to be good, he understood why darkness followed him and was present so deeply throughout his being. The understanding reached as deep as the darkness inside him. He could see that he had asked God for a hard life, one that would constantly remind him of the consequences of following the darkness, of following who he started as when he was just an Intelligence. He had wanted his life to be hard, he realized, to remind him to work hard and pursue the things of light, to help him let go of the things of darkness that ran so deeply through him.

He understood too that his counterpart, a being of light, had followed Lucifer, and that she sought desperately to get to him, screaming his name whenever she knew she could instill fear in him, as fear always gave counterparts more access to an individual. She was constantly working to get to him, and he could see that all beings had a connection to their counterpart, one that Lucifer used to tempt and try to persuade them to follow the deep feelings associated with things of darkness.

He could see that, due to the depth of these feelings, whether emanating from DNA, counterparts, or actual darkness inside, an individual was much more than these parts. He could see how he should not be defined by his past as a dark counterpart or by his counterpart who chose to follow Lucifer, but by his potential, his potential as a being who could be reborn, his potential to become like God. Somehow, he understood far more than he had been told, and he knew it was his time to return to the earth, to return to his body there. He longed to stay as there were still so many questions he had, but he knew his stay was ending.

As these realizations hit him, he glanced back up at the trees where he had noticed people before. Somehow, he suddenly knew that his other daughter was there, with Ruby. His mind was opened to see his daughter as God saw her, as a being of infinite worth, worth living and dying for. Ranier was taken back by the magnitude of what he saw, and he gasped at the understanding flowing into him. The others looked at him, curious. He responded with a glance to Jess and a glance to the trees, "I have the most amazing children a person could ever ask for."

Ruby watched as Ranier's daughter heard this. It appeared to Ruby that many walls inside her shattered, and a flood of emotions came racing out, emotions long buried and kept from others. Ranier's daughter was sobbing, as a piece of her knew and understood what Ranier said was true. He had truly seen her infinite worth, and truly understood her intrinsic value. Her prayers had now been answered as well, and while it would take some time to sort through the internal process of cleaning out the remaining walls and rebuilding a healthy framework, Ranier's daughter was well on her way. Ruby's heart was touched at the mercy and wonder of God's power, and she said a silent prayer of thanks for being allowed to see such beauty, the pure beauty of a soul experiencing true love for its first time.

James smiled too at what Ranier had said. He knew, without even communicating with Ruby, that Ranier's daughter had what she needed for now. Ranier had to stay long enough for the daughter to understand that Ranier truly saw her worth. Now that she understood this, he knew Ranier would be leaving and returning to Earth. "Before you go Ranier, you should know you were given all of this information for a reason. You are expected to fight in the War in Heaven."

"How do I do that?" Ranier asked, still trying to process everything he had been told, and still wondering if he would be able to talk to his other daughter or not.

"By sharing God's principles with others, and teaching them what they must do to be able to accept Jesus and make it to the new Universe." James replied. "The War is fought through words, actions, and thoughts. It is a unique war that is waged, one where Lucifer wants the highest number of casualties possible, and where God's side is willing to suffer extensively to help recover souls. Lucifer fights with force, violence, and other harmful things, while God fights with patience, brotherly kindness, humility, and love. On God's side, we endure the suffering imposed by Lucifer's side, so that we can help point and bring souls to Christ, to the new Universe. In this War, we are willing to suffer extensively in hopes of bringing another soul to Christ, as we are fighting to save, not to destroy.

"As the new Universe is new, we have to use faith to get there as we have never been there or seen it, as it is impossible to see or experience it without first being reborn, down to the Intelligence level, to a new state of existence. To be pulled through to the new Universe, we need our family and the sealing ordinances found in God's Church, and to fully live and enjoy all of the wonders that life has to offer, we need the freedom to do so, as freedom brings the ability to love, and being able to truly love is an essential part of being reborn, as complementary opposition and love are inseparably tied together.

"Additionally, you should find your family still alive. They will be the most important people for you to connect with. You are responsible for them, and it will be up to you to teach them, to connect with them, and to be a father to them. Ultimately, you will need to find God's Church on the earth and receive of the necessary ordinances of salvation, such as baptism to complete your rebirth, as not all parts of you can be made new without the ordinance of baptism. You will also need the endowment, which we have not discussed yet, to enable you to have the knowledge and ability to pass through into the new Universe in the Battle of Gog and Magog, and the sealing ordinances, to connect you to Elleana and your children, as well as your father, for these ordinances to have effect in your family.

"Ultimately, Ranier, you cannot be given an experience like this without the attendant responsibility to teach others what you know. Anyone who experiences something of this nature is called to share Christ with others. God will not reveal these things to people who are not ready to return and dedicate their life to teaching others, and so many remain in the dark as they are too afraid of what others think to bear testimony or share these things with others. You are now called to teach Ranier, and to spend the rest of your life doing so."

"How I am supposed to do all of that? What am I supposed to focus on?" Ranier asked. He felt overwhelmed with this all. "There is so much, and so much I'm sure I still don't understand. I don't even know the name of God's Church on Earth" he said trying desperately to gain a little more time in the Spirit World.

"Yes," James replied, "there is still so much more, this is only a very small piece. You will be able to keep learning," James said with a smile. "As to finding God's Church, it will not be hard, as there is only one main Church on the earth that bears Jesus' name and teaches principles associated with everything we discussed, and only one with his name that offers ordinances to seal families together for eternity. When viewing the big picture, God's Church is not hard to find or separate out from the others, as the others even refuse to believe that we ever had a pre-mortal life.

"Ultimately though, once you have found your family and God's Church, you should focus, Ranier, on teaching people some of the basic principles, on teaching them about the importance of faith, family, and freedom. Faith gives us the ability and power to work for good things that we can't yet see or experience, family gives us meaning, support and a place in life, and freedom gives us an existence and opportunity to work and build based off of laws based on truth. All of this circles into a necessary truth that we must know, the truth that all of humanity runs from and that causes them to not understand who they are, that we are all counterparts and a mixture of light and dark, good and evil, and we are both inherently good and inherently evil at the same time, with the need to leave behind all that we do not want to be and fully embrace our eternal potential.

"These things teach them, ultimately, about Jesus, and it is him that must be a part of everything, as it is only through him that we have life, power, opportunity, hope, or anything lasting. Our faith, our family, and our freedom are important tools or items necessary for us to repent, to let go of ourselves, to embrace our potential, and ultimately, to enjoy the things and ways of God, or the things and ways of life itself."

Chapter 30

"RANIER. RANIER. RANIER." Ranier heard a woman calling his name and felt a hand shaking him. He winced as he remembered his counterpart screaming his name, but he realized this voice was different. This voice had a level of kindness and mildness to it. He tried to open his eyes, but he felt so tired. His world was spinning, or maybe it was only his mind, or something else even. He wasn't sure, and he was too disconnected to understand what was happening. He tried to move his head to see better, and as he did so pain shot through him. Gasping from the pain, he realized he was back in his body. He had forgotten just how much pain his body had been in, and had been too preoccupied with other things to fully appreciate his absence from the pain.

As the woman continued to call his name, he found that the pain was making him more aware of his surroundings, and he found himself slowly coming to. There was so much he didn't want to face in this life, and wished he could have moved on to the Spirit World rather than coming back. After some time though, he finally was able to open his eyes. He looked around and realized he was in the hospital still.

Ranier could see he was connected to all types of machines and instruments. He couldn't even see most of his body since he was so covered with tubes and other items. He didn't recognize the room, but felt he must be under some type of close watch due to the room's solemn environment. All of this was so different than the lake he had just been at, and he shook his head still at how quickly things could change for him.

As Ranier gained more awareness of his surroundings, he looked for something to remind him of where he had just been. His mind felt foggy and he was worried that maybe it was all a dream, maybe he hadn't experienced the good he felt he had. He could tell he was already losing pieces of the details of the experiences he just had, and raced to find something to make it more concrete in his mind.

He looked around the room, noticing the sterile, slightly tanned, white color on the walls. There were no pictures on the walls except for a picture of a lake surrounded by trees. He stared at the picture, questioning himself even more now, as the picture was a nearly perfect rendering of the lake he had just been at. "Did I dream this all up?" he thought to himself. "Did I really go there? If I did, had this artist been there too, or did I just imagine that based on my surroundings here?"

"You have been through a lot Ranier" he heard the nurse say. "The doctors had to work hard to keep you alive, and you were in a medically induced coma for some time. Because of that, your body needs to get moving again, and it is time for you to get up and start moving around. Your physical therapy starts today. After a few months, we expect you to be able to regain full movement and use of your body, so if you work with us, we'll get you there."

Ranier could tell that the woman was a little timid as she tried to talk to him and seemed to be choosing her words carefully. He found himself smiling inside thinking how she must have been warned about his angry personality so that she was trying hard to not upset him. She was in for a surprise, he thought, since he was going to work to be a different person now.

Still trying to fully come to, and not responding yet, Ranier realized he felt different inside. He felt hope for the first time in his life. Even though he had a long road to recovery ahead, and pain was coursing through his body, he didn't feel angry or discouraged. He was ready to work and accept all that he needed in order to be made whole, to be made new, to embrace the ways of eternal life. He realized he never had the chance to say goodbye to his mother, son, and daughters, but he also realized he didn't need to. They would be with him as part of this journey, and his return to Earth was not a goodbye, but the beginning of an adventure together.

The hope inside told him something certain—that it wasn't just a dream or his imagination. This hope was tangible, it was real, and it came from a place far beyond the earth itself. This hope produced light, it produced purpose, and it was something Ranier had never had before while on the earth. The hope was a sure testament to him that he did experience what he did.

With a start, he suddenly remembered he still had two daughters on the earth, as well as women he had left when they were pregnant with his children. As his senses were coming back to him, he remembered his instruction to teach about Jesus and the necessity of faith, family, and freedom, as well as to find God's Church and his family. He could sense that his most critical mission would be to reach his own family and repair everything that had gone wrong there. He felt so inadequate for it all, and wondered how he could possibly make things right.

As he worried about how he might find or connect with his daughters, he suddenly felt an embrace from the Spirit World. He instantly knew it was Elleana. While nothing had been spoken by her, he felt her reassurance that all would work out if he would just trust in God, as God always prepared a way for him to accomplish the things he was commanded to do.

As his eyes turned to the nurse speaking to him, he saw that she was a young nurse. She was waiting, timidly still, for him to respond about his physical therapy, and her timidness reminded him of Elleana. Suddenly, he found himself asking her, "You remind me of someone. Who are your parents?"

Surprised by the abrupt question, the lady paused awkwardly and then answered, timidly and with some deep pain that he could somehow sense "My mother disappeared when I was younger, and I never knew my father. He left my mother when she was pregnant. I bounced around in foster care for some time, and am just trying to do my best right now to get by. I have worked hard to get through some schooling, and just started here a few weeks ago. Why do you ask that question?" she said. "Is it obvious that I struggle with life or something?"

Ranier smiled kindly at her. "We all struggle, just look at me. And I ask . . ." Ranier said as his voice trailed off, trying to say the right thing, "I ask because I too lost my parents. And," he continued after a minute, "I lost my children as well, and need to find them again." The nurse looked at him, puzzled, and asked "How did you 'lose' your children?"

"Because I was a bad person, and made some serious mistakes in how I treated people." Ranier said in response. "But I am different now, and need to make things right."

The nurse stared at him for a minute, then said "Well, hopefully you can find your kids." Then, after pausing for a minute, said softly "I wish you the best with that, as I sure wish my dad would do the same and make things right."

Ranier smiled again, this time at God's amazing power and mercy, and replied, "Well, we just might have a lot to talk about."

Afterword

T HIS BOOK IS FICTIONAL, and the stories told of our pre-moral existence are simply that—stories. The purpose of this book is not to try to reveal any new facts about God or Heaven, as facts about God and Heaven come through a properly ordained prophet, as exists in the Church of Jesus Christ of Latter-Day Saints. The purpose, rather, is to highlight how the things that have been revealed to us by God's prophets today could fit into a bigger story.

God, I am certain, could write hundreds of thousands of different stories with entirely different scenarios, but all of which would highlight the truth of certain principles foundational to our existence and all giving a way for our entire existence to make sense. The point of this book is that God has an explanation for everything. If there are things we do not understand about life, God's Gospel, or anything else, we can exercise faith and seek to understand a story that teaches us about God and his ways. We can do this because there really is a story, a true story, yet to be revealed to us about all things in our existence.

One of the highlights of this story is the importance of faith. Faith is essential to progressing, improving, and learning, and we have to accept that fact before we can find answers to our deepest questions. We have to exercise faith in God and let go of the things we see, hear, and understand.

Ultimately, many people do not take the time or effort to find their answers to their questions. They see something that conflicts, and simply walk away from God. They experience pain or suffering, and assume that God must not love them or even exist. They do not take the time though to find God amidst the suffering, doubt, and questions, and just walk away from the best thing they could find in this life.

I wrote this book because I know that God lives, and I want to share that reality. I am a member of the Church of Jesus Christ of Latter-Day Saints, which Church is led by living prophets who teach true principles, and many principles associated with the teachings of this Church were presented in this book. This Church contains the ordinances necessary to seal families together, and the ordinances necessary to be made new. Even though the story herein is just a story, the principles it discusses are true. God created us. We are his children. He has a plan for us to be able to obtain a far better existence than the one we have here. This earth is but a stepping stone into eternity, and it is up to us to embrace the ways of eternal life.

Regardless of who we are or our circumstances, Christ atoned for us, died for us, and lives for us. All of us, and I repeat, *all*, of us, have to change to be like God as none of us are in a state that meets his. Changing who we are now into something better brings life, happiness, and joy, as such things are found in progression and improvement. All of us have different trials, paths, and experiences, but this highlights the love and devotion of God in giving us each a one-on-one ministry by providing a life tailored to our individual needs and progression. True love is found in providing a unique situation for the one.

Please take the time to talk with God, to ask him questions, and to find answers. God may tell you a story to teach you a principle, he may tell you truth directly, or he may wait until you have changed something inside. Whatever he does, he does out of recognition for you and who you are, and you can trust that God knows and sees far more than you do. If your expectations of God have not been met, consider that maybe you need to change your expectations and understanding, rather than simply assuming that God does not exist.

We did not come from nowhere, and did not come here by chance. We came from an eternal family, our life has purpose, and God has provided us with the ordinances, knowledge, and truths necessary to change, to find him, and to make it to a far better state of existence. This I know, and I hope you will take the time to know as well.

The Author

Austin writes various fiction books about pre-Earth events, as well as articles about other topics. This is the first novel in a planned collection of stories, and complements a short-story series in the works. The War in Heaven short story and novel series will explore possibilities that help define and explain our own existence. The first short story has already been published online, and is called Heaven's Orphans.

Austin is married with six children. He works as an attorney by day at Hepworth Law, LLC, a father at home, and an author in the early mornings.

You can find more of Austin J. Hepworth's works online.
Like Faith. Family. Freedom. on Facebook:
https://www.facebook.com/offaithfamilyandfreedom/

Visit the Website:
http://www.offaithfamilyandfreedom.com/the-war-in-heaven-novel.html